To Be or Not To Be

Also by Ryan North

Romeo and/or Juliet

(and a bunch of other books too)

(but that one in particular seemed the most salient)

To Be or Not To Be

a chooseable-path adventure

by Ryan North, William Shakespeare, and YOU

Riverhead Books • New York • 2016

Riverhead Books
An imprint of Penguin Random House LLC
375 Hudson Street
New York, New York 10014

The word "Penguin" here refers to the book publishing company, and not the animals—also named "penguins"—which are actually incapable of conceiving of the concept of "copyright"! Instead, these "penguins" are flightless birds that live in Antarctica and feed on underwater sea life. Their wings have evolved into flippers, and if you ever look up a video showing them underwater, it's fascinating: the way they swim is really similar to how a bird flies through the air! Anyway, I guess all I wanted to say is thanks for not pirating this book, and seriously: look up some videos of penguins swimming underwater. It's bonkers.

ISBN 9780735212190

First Breadpig trade paperback edition: September 2013
First Riverhead trade paperback edition: September 2016

Printed in the United States of America
1 3 5 7 9 10 8 6 4 2

Book design by Emily Horne

This is a work of fiction. Actually, it's a book *containing* a work of fiction, but you get the idea. Incidentally, did someone file this book in the "Choose One's Own *Nonfiction* Adventure" section? Bad news on that front, friend: names, characters, places, and incidents in this work either are the product of the author's imagination or are used fictitiously, and any resemblance to actual persons, living or dead, business, companies, events, or locales is entirely coincidental! So if you're a dude named "Johnny Hamlet," you should know that I didn't write this book by following you around and writing down everything you did. Honestly, when I was writing it, I mostly just stayed at home and flipped through this old play I found.

To Bea

INTRODUCTION

William Shakespeare (1564 AD–whenever he died) was well-known for borrowing from existing literature when writing his plays. *Romeo and Juliet* is pretty much lifted entirely from Arthur Brooke's poem "The Tragical History of Romeus and Juliet": dude didn't even change the names. And, as recent Shakespeare scholarship has established, the famed play *William Shakespeare Presents: Hamlet!* was lifted wholesale from the volume you are about to enjoy, *To Be or Not To Be*.

To Be or Not To Be is both the earliest recorded example of the "books as game" genre, as well as the first instance ever in the then-newish English language that was kicking around of an adventure being chosen by YOU, the reader.

We've gone ahead and added illustrations, plus we've taken the liberty of marking with tiny Yorick skulls the choices Shakespeare himself made when he plagiarized this book back in olden times. They're there in case you wish to put yourself in Shakespeare's shoes, reading this book as he did, stealing plot elements wholesale, and classing up the language as he/you went/go. However, that is not the only way to read this book! Feel free to explore your other options, as each time you read this book you can go on a different adventure, assuming you don't read the book 3,001,181,439,094,525 times at which point the adventures will start to repeat and they'll probably seem pretty familiar long before then anyway.

Now, take yourself back to History, when ghosts walked the Earth and nobody knew velociraptors were ever even a thing. Steel yourself to experience the magic of Shakespeare as it was meant to be experienced: in a non-deterministic narrative structure where you end up thinking maybe you made a wrong decision so you mark the pages you were just on so you can always go back and make a different choice if you die for some dumb reason.

To be, or not to be: *that is the adventure*.

Ryan North
Noted Shakespeare Scholar/Enthusiast

Choose your character! *turn to 1*

Man, what if I just read the acknowledgements instead: *turn to 267*

Whoah, whoah, slow down there, cowboy! At the end of that last bit, you were supposed to make a choice, and then jump to the node that reflects that choice. Instead of following those instructions, you just kept reading what came next like this is an ordinary book! THIS BOOK IS CRAZY INSANE; HOW ARE YOU EVEN ACTING LIKE THIS IS AN ORDINARY BOOK??

You die without even having chosen your character, THE END, and your final score is “maybe learn to read books better sometime” out of 1000.

Dude!

That’s not a very good score, I gotta say!!

THE END

1

You have just been born! Congratulations, good work on that thing! Now SURPRISE, babies are boring, so we're going to jump ahead in time to a point where you're an adult and you've already lived a bunch of your life, but I promise most of what we're skipping over was really dull. You ate a lot and slept a lot and made some friends, tears were shed, makeouts were totally had, etc. It was a bunch of high school stuff: the awesome stuff starts now!

So! Let's begin, my friend! Um...remind me again who you are?

OPHELIA? She's an awesome lady in her late 20s, with a calm, competent, and resourceful demeanour. She's got a +1 bonus to science, but she's also got a -1 weakness against water, so heads up!

HAMLET? He's an emo teen in his early 30s. Also, he's the prince of Denmark. Hamlet has a +1 resistance to magic, but there's no magic in this adventure, so this never gets mentioned again as of right...NOW.

HAMLET SR.? He's the King of Denmark, 50 years old. He's super good at fighting and leading men into battle and naps. Let's say...+1 to each? Look, bottom line: he's an unstoppable machine of death, and should you choose to be him, you MAY experience kingly glory.

Play as Ophelia: *turn to 31*

Play as Hamlet: *turn to 14*

Play as Hamlet Sr. *turn to 444*

Can't decide who to choose? Look at the facing page to see pictures of them! Maybe that'll help?

2

You look around and see Hamlet's friend Horatio nearby. He looks like he's freaking out.

"Hey," you say. "Listen — Horatio, right? Listen, don't freak out."

He seems to freak out a little less. That's good.

"Hey, when Hamlet wakes up, can you tell him my own brother murdered me?" you ask. "Tell him I'm looking for a little revenge."

Horatio nods meekly. "If he doesn't want to do it, then I'll make sure to revenge you, Mr. Your Majesty's Ghost, sir."

"Just 'sir' is fine," you say, smiling in what you hope is a reassuring way. You look at Horatio for a moment. "Well — great," you say. "Perfect."

Horatio looks at you. You look at him. He scuffs his feet a little.

"So, uh, I guess that's it," you say. "With my unfinished work now, um, finished, I suppose it's time for me to die for real now."

You fade away in a shimmering light, certain that with Hamlet's intensity and Horatio's probable competence at actually achieving goals, you'll be revenged in no time. What could possibly go wrong, right? Exactly. This is most assuredly 100% solved for real.

TURN TO 31
TURN TO 14
TURN TO 444

It's too bad you couldn't stick around to watch the revenging go down, but you don't make the rules.

Hey!

I guess you're about to find out who, if anyone, does?

THE END

Turn to 318

3 I don't see an area!! here.

You have 5 turn(s) remaining.

LOOK...ENCLOSURE? *turn to 243*

4 "O most pernicious woman!" you add, insulting not only Queen Gertrude — the woman your father adored, loved, and married — but also all women in general. SCIENCE CORNER: synonyms for "pernicious" include "noxious" and "pestilent," and the word itself suggests that long-term harm comes from being in contact with whatever it's being used to describe.

Stay classy, Hamlet!!

LEAVE IT THERE AND RETURN TO HORATIO: *turn to 80*

5 You stare at the ghost intently and your brain shuts down, and you collapse, unconscious. Um, surprise?

You are now the ghost!

Before you is the unconscious body of your son, Hamlet. It looks like maybe he tripped too many balls. Yes, that's definitely what happened. There were a lot of balls lying around and Hamlet tripped on one too many of them. Maybe several. Bottom line: too many balls were DEFINITELY tripped, right here.

You expected more from your son than this. To be precise, you expected to be able to tell him that you were murdered by your brother, and that he should, oh I don't know, revenge your death. Instead you're staring at a dude you can't even touch. You stick a finger inside Hamlet's head, thinking that maybe if you touch his brain he'll wake up? But brains don't work that way, at least not with immaterial fingers made out of ectoplasm or whatever. And you don't make your finger solid, which is good, because that definitely would've killed him.

WAIT FOR HIM TO WAKE UP: *turn to 312*

See if there's anyone else you can tell about your murder: *turn to 2*

6

The three of you and the author get to talking, and she's really great. It turns out she's Christina Marlowe, the author of *The Murder of Gonzago: A "The Adventure Is Being Chosen by You" Story! Can You Murder Your Brother Gonzago and Then, Playing as Your Dead Brother's Son, Murder Your Usurping Uncle? I Sure Hope So; Choose From Over 300 Different Possible Endings*.

It's one of your favourite books, and you tell her so, excitedly asking questions about characters and motivation and how she did that thing with the choices.

While the four of you talk, Polonius walks into the room and tries to work his way into the conversation, but whatever, nobody here likes him. Christina doesn't make any attempt to include him and that makes you love her even more.

You start quoting your favourite passage to her — it's the bit from the back cover — and she takes over when you forget some of the words. It goes like this: "You are still really mad that your dad was killed by his brother. You decide that you should murder him for revenge, and that, my friend, is a really good idea. Do you decide to wait to murder him?"

"No!!" shout you, Rosencrantz, and Guildenstern in unison. Christina smiles. Polonius mutters, "This is boring," but nobody cares.

"Excellent. Then you sneak into his room at night and stab him in the neck. A huge fountain of blood erupts from his neck, under such pressure that it bursts through the ceiling and forms a glorious red geyser above the roof. Some kid walking by sees the geyser and says, 'Whoah' and while he's saying the 'oah' part of 'whoah,' blood lands in his open mouth. It's so awesome. You have earned 1000 points, and the 'whoah' kid also earned 50 points."

The three of you laugh and cheer and applaud, while Christina smiles politely and Polonius stands around with his arms crossed. "Whatever, I wanted to wait before killing him," he grumbles.

Christina recited her book with such heartfelt emotion that you actually feel pretty bad about not murdering your own uncle yet.

Wait a minute, that gives you an idea!!

Go murder your uncle: *turn to 142*

Instead of murdering your uncle, go grab your copy of the book! Then you can get it signed and then you can see if you can get Claudius to read it and then if he chooses the "murder your brother" path and then if he looks guilty, you'll know he did it even though a ghost already investigated it and told you he did: *turn to 62*

SCHOOL THAT IS IN ENGLAND
DANISH PRIDE
YAY FENCING
HAWK
HAND SAW
LIVE
ophelia
MARLOWE

8 You walk back to where Horatio is waiting for you.

"Listen, Horatio, never speak of this whole 'me and a ghost' thing, okay? We've got to keep it a secret."

"That's cool," says Horatio.

"No, I'm serious, man!" you say, grabbing him by the shoulders. "Some REALLY SERIOUS STUFF is going to go down, and I need you to keep this a secret. Swear that you'll never talk about this."

"I swear," says Horatio.

"SWEAR IT," booms your dad's voice out of nowhere.

"He already did!" you shout. You then lock eyes with Horatio and say, "Oh! For some reason I might act crazy for a while, but it's all an act, so just be cool."

"I shall endeavour to be cool," says Horatio. "But what's this all about?"

"There are more things in heaven and earth, Horatio—" you begin.

"—than are dreamt of in my philosophy," Horatio finishes. "Fine. Right. Whatever."

It's past midnight, and Claudius is probably falling-down drunk. What now?

Say goodbye to Horatio and go kill Claudius: *turn to 142*

Go home for nappy times: *turn to 86*

9 You raise both hands in the air, and Rosencrantz and Guildenstern understand instantly. They raise their hands as well, and you pull off the rarely seen SPONTANEOUS CONNECTED-GRAPH BRO-PAL HIGH FIVE TRIAD (MUTUAL FRIEND x3 MULTIPLIER).

You love these guys.

Whoah! Your charisma score has gone up 2 points!

Ask them how they've been: *turn to 13*

10 This is what you say to nobody in particular:

To be, or not to be, that is the question:
Whether 'tis Nobler in the mind to suffer
The Slings and Arrows of outrageous Fortune,
Or to take Arms against a Sea of troubles,
And by opposing end them: to die, to sleep
No more; and by a sleep, to say we end
The heart-ache, and the thousand Natural shocks
That Flesh is heir to? 'Tis a consummation

Devoutly to be wished. To die, to sleep,
To sleep, perchance to Dream. Ay, there's the rub,
For in that sleep of death, what dreams may come,
When we have shuffled off this mortal coil,
Must give us pause.

Man. NICELY DONE, Hamlet!

HEY, WAIT A MINUTE! OPHELIA'S HERE! *turn to 32*

11 This is what you say to nobody in particular:

To be? No, not to be, that is the answer:
Whether 'tis Nobler in the mind to suffer
The Slings and Arrows of outrageous Fortune,
Or to take Arms against a Sea of troubles,
And by opposing end them. Yeah, sounds good,
To die, to sleep no more; and by a sleep, to say I end
The heart-ache, and the thousand Natural shocks
That Flesh is heir to? 'Tis a consummation
Devoutly to be wished, which is why I just Decided to do Thatte,
To die, to sleep, perchance to Dream. Ay, there's the rub,
For in that sleep of death, what dreams may come,
When we have shuffled off this mortal coil,
May give some pause, but Not Me, I'ma find out Soon
I guess that's why the ladies love me, because
The ladies love a man of action,
And that's what I am,
Ladies.

It's a beautiful speech, and you're not going to come up with any better last words than those. You chug some poison that's sitting around, but unfortunately you choke on it a little as you drink so your last words are accidentally "Arrghah ggghhhhh bleh." But nobody's around anyway so no bigs, right?

No bigs!

THE END

Turn to 372

12 On your way to your mom's room, you pass by the church (you live in a very fancy castle, were you aware of that?) and who should be there engrossed in prayer but Claudius! I guess after he ran off to his room, he decided to go to church to pray instead? He's such a wiener.

Wait a minute.
YOU COULD TOTALLY KILL HIM IN A CHURCH. How badass is that?

Man, pretty badass! Let's kill Claudius in the church!
Turn to 87

No time for murders now, I'VE got a date with my mom!
Turn to 24

13

"How have you been, gentlemen?" you say. "I've been okay, except for, you know, the nightmares. Anyway! What brings you here?"

They look at each other. "What — um, what do you mean what brings us here? Uh, why don't we instead talk about your, um...plans and motivations?" Rosencrantz says. Your face falls. Man, you knew it! Claudius sent for them! They're here to spy on you!

"Aw, really? Come on, guys. Were you sent here to spy on me?" you say.

"Well, um...yeah," Rosencrantz replies. "Kinda?"

"Frig man, I knew it," you say. "Look, I'll make it easy on you. I know I've been all emo lately and mopey and even though we don't have the words for it yet, I'm pretty sure I'm what you'd call 'CLINICALLY DEPRESSED.' That's all."

You sigh, and then look at them with a small smile.

"I guess I'm quite the piece of work, huh?" you say.

"Would you care to explain that in more detail?" Rosencrantz says.

You reply:

"As a matter of fact, I would!" *Turn to 72*

"No man, didn't you hear? I'm clinically depressed." *Turn to 84*

14

You are Hamlet! You're 30 years old and you're back living at home, but it's okay, because your home is a castle. That's right, ladies, you're a PRINCE.

Things have been rough lately. You had been trying to focus on your studies at Wittenberg University where you and your bros Horatio, Rosencrantz, and Guildenstern all hang out, but you were called home because your father died. Then your dead dad's brother (Claudius!) married your mom (Gertrude!) two weeks later. Yep. It's made you kind of upset. You raced home to comfort her but she's married your uncle and that is weird. You feel weird.

Right now you're in the audience chamber of your father's castle, here in sunny Denmark. King Claudius is here, addressing his court. Laertes and Polonius are here too; Laertes is kind of a jerk and Polonius is his father. Polonius is also the father of Ophelia, whom you're totally sweet on. She's not here though. Who knows what adventures she's having as we speak, while you're stuck in this drafty castle room listening to other people talk about their feelings??

Speaking of speaking, just now Laertes says something about how now that Claudius is king and he's attended the coronation, is it okay for him to go back to France? Claudius says, "Sure."

Wait a minute. You'd love to leave too and go back to school, away from this weird incesty thing your mother's gotten herself into! It's so gross and weird!

Ask Claudius for permission to go back to school: *turn to 66*

Hold your tongue and just wait around: *turn to 545*

15

You finish up this tender moment by threatening the woman who gave birth to you, and leave.

Oh, Hamlet. What are we going to do with you, Hamlet?

On your way out the door, you bump into your bros Rosencrantz and Guildenstern. "You wanna get out of here?" you say, and they concede that they would like to party on a boat. You know what? That sounds nice. Sort of give everyone space, you know, while also standing around on a positively buoyant vessel? It sounds real nice.

"There's a boat headed for England in just a few hours!" you say. You know this because boats to England are kind of a big deal.

You send some servants to clean up crazy ol' dead Polonius and another to be there for your mother, and you pack your bags. A few hours later, you and your bros are partying on a boat!

Party boat!! *Turn to 151*

16

You clear your throat and hold out a hand in front of you. Here's what you say!

Witness this army of such mass and charge
Led by a delicate and tender prince,
Whose spirit with divine ambition puff'd
Makes mouths at the invisible event,
Exposing what is mortal and unsure
To all that fortune, death, and danger dare,
Even for an egg-shell. Rightly to be great
Is not to stir without great argument,
But greatly to find quarrel in a straw
When honour's at the stake. How stand I then,

That have a father kill'd, a mother stain'd,
Excitements of my reason and my blood,
And let all sleep? while, to my shame, I see
The imminent death of twenty thousand men,
That, for a fantasy and trick of fame,
Go to their graves like beds, fight for a plot
Whereon the numbers cannot try the cause,
Which is not tomb enough and continent
To hide the slain? O, from this time forth,
My thoughts be bloody, or be nothing worth!

Not bad, not bad! Rosencrantz and Guildenstern are polite enough to pretend not to hear. They're so great.

CONTINUE PARTYING ON A BOAT: *turn to 19*

17

You step into the quantum leap accelerator and the world around you vanishes. You're surrounded by the darkest blackness you've ever seen.

The next thing you know, the world is reassembling itself around you. You're aware of light beginning to shine on you, of heat you haven't felt in millennia beginning to warm your body. You feel yourself becoming real, corporeal. You look around you, watching the world become more and more solid with each passing second as your jump approaches completion. We're almost there, Hamlet.

COMPLETE THE JUMP: *turn to 96*

18

You whistle and sit yourself down on the floor in the middle of the room. That seems a little awkward, so you stretch out on your side, your arm supporting your head and your other arm resting on your hips. There! Nobody could be more casual than you!

The door opens and who should enter but Corambis, Polonius's twin brother! You recognize him from the royal courts.

"I unlocked the door, so you can leave no—" he begins, but then cuts himself off. "Hey, what's going on?" Corambis looks around. "Why are you acting so casual? How come you stabbed that curtain?"

He looks behind the curtain and sees what you did. He begins to scream and scream and scream, and — whether you decide to kill him or not — a bunch of other people are running over here and you're pooched.

Claudius discovers your crime and puts you to death. Your last words are "Oh geez, if only I'd been better at covering up my murders; had I only the chance to do it again, I would most certainly dispose of that body differently."

"Obvs," says the hangman.

THE END

Turn to 451

19

Partying on a boat is great, but it doesn't last forever! After several hours, the party winds down and everyone starts going to bed. You and Rosencrantz and Guildenstern stumble off to your quarters, three awesome dudes in one awesome room. One awesome...PARTY ROOM??

The next day, you wake up, still feeling the effects of the previous night's partying. You put on your shirt but it feels different — turns out it's Rosencrantz's shirt! Wow. As you pull it off, a letter falls out of the pocket. Rosencrantz wakes up, teases you for wearing his clothes, and then notices the letter.

"Hey Hamlet, you dropped something," he says.

"No man," you say, "it's your letter. This is your shirt." You pass him the garment. He has the shirt.

"It's not my letter, bro," he says, pulling it over his head. "Someone must've slipped it to me sometime yesterday. What's it say?"

Flipping it over, you notice it's got a royal seal on the back. "It's from King Claudius!" you say.

Rosencrantz and Guildenstern say the following: "Whaaaaaaaaaat??"

Open the letter: *turn to 276*

Don't open it: it's got an OFFICIAL SEAL: *turn to 212*

20

This is awesome! And it's going to go great, because who better to know how to kill someone than someone who has recently been through that "getting killed to death" process themselves? You wait till Claudius is sleeping (NEXT TO YOUR WIDOW) then wake him up by tapping him on the forehead a bit.

"Hey, it's me!" you whisper. "Your brother! The one you murdered!!"

"Aw crap," Claudius whispers back. "Ghosts are real?"

"Real pissed at you, anyway," you reply. "Listen, I'll cut to the chase: we are from a time where 'an eye for an eye' is considered to be a good thing to build a justice system around, so I am here to kill you."

"How?" Claudius asks, his eyes wide, terrified.

"Aw geez, so many ways," you say, counting them off on your fingers. "I could startle you and make you have a heart attack, but that takes time. I could throw a pot at your head until you die, but that lacks grace. Instead, check this out."

You move your ghost body so it's floating right above Claudius. He stares at you, his eyes wide.

"I'm sorry," he whispers.

"Way too late for THAT," you reply. You lower yourself to him, face to face, and keep going. His face dominates your field of vision and then you're inside his skull, inside the pink of his brain, his blood darkly obscuring your sight. You sink slowly deeper and deeper into him, lining up your ghost body with his regular body, until you are just about occupying exactly the same space.

Then you make yourself corporeal.

What happens next happens so quickly and with such force that it's hard to describe, but "Claudius explodes everywhere" captures most of it. I mean, you're fine, but man is this disgusting. Literally disgusting. Gertrude wakes up, dripping in gore, screaming.

You, my friend, have achieved revenge.

You roll over onto your back and apologize to Gertrude. You explain over her screams what happened, and you tell her that you still love her even though she married your brother mere weeks after you died. But you can't be with her anymore, you say. You tell her you need to go find your own path.

"Sorry about the bed," you say, floating up through the roof.

You spend the rest of the afterlife acting as an immortal judge from beyond the grave, exploding those who have committed the most egregious crimes, merely blowing the hands off those who have been awful people but still, you feel, deserve a second chance. People whisper your name in fear (criminals are a cowardly, superstitious lot, after all) and it works out pretty good for you. You do a lot of good for a lot of people.

And yep, it turns out that blowing up bad guys never does get old!!

THE END

Turn to 531

21

You knock on Antonio's door. He answers, wearing a very snappy suit. Man, he looks great. I will describe his lips as being "enticing," his eyes as being "reflective pools in which you feel you might drown" and his legs as being "apparently unable to quit."

"Hi Antonio," you say. "It's me, Ophelia. Are you busy tonight?"

"Never too busy for a pretty lady," says Antonio. "Though you should know, generally my nights tend to end up pretty...EROTIC."

"Oh," you say. "Weird."

"Yeah, it's like — a curse or something," Antonio says. "Just once I'd like to have a regular date without it descending into mind-blowing eroticism."

"Huh," you say.

Ask about mind-blowing eroticism: *turn to 291*

Ask about what he'd like to do instead: *turn to 296*

UNCAN HOUSE

DUFF
cotland
culture
ebate, Fencing

d, Scotland!"

HAMLET H. HAMLET
b. Jutland, Denmark
BA, Philosophy
Philosophy Club (president),
Debate, Drama, Fencing

"There is nothing either good or bad, but thinking makes it so."

TAVISH JAMES MACBETH
b. Moray, Scotland
BA, Political Science
Drama, Golf, ROTC

"Is this a Jäger I see before me?"

Duncan House
al cookout

23

Thank you, thank you, you're too kind.

Let me set the scene: you, Rosencrantz, and Guildenstern rush above-decks at the sound of the lookout yelling, "Pirates ho!" Following his arm pointing to the horizon, you see a ship sailing directly towards you with alarming speed, her disguise of a Danish flag being lowered as a black flag with a grinning skull and crossbones unfurls in its place. It's pretty badass! Behind her a huge storm has gathered, lightning striking into the water. Both are headed straight for you.

She's a magnificent ship, a three-masted beauty running 50 metres long from bow to stern. She slices cleanly through the sea with the wind filling her sails: 1,400 tons of boat, a symphony of wood, canvas, brass, and iron. She's as tall as she is long, with each of her masts proudly carrying four gargantuan rectangular sails. Rigging of baffling complexity stretches between each mast, its crossbars, and the side of her hull.

She carries 26 cannons on her port side and 26 on her starboard, each loaded and at the ready, and she's running with her gunports open. She also sails with two forward-facing cannons mounted on her bow, beneath which protrudes the beautifully carved figure of a mermaid. Over 150 strong and able men — all pirates — call her home. The painted and polished red wooden letters affixed to her hull betray her name: *Calypso's Gale.*

You, on the other hand, are on a party boat, the HDMS *Vesselmania IV.* Your boat is a mere 100 tons, her armaments a slight six cannons per side. *Vesselmania*'s two smaller masts bear a single triangular sail each. Her crew of 20 is inexperienced and young. Her captain, with whom you've had only a passing acquaintance, seems fresh out of captain school, if that is even a thing.

He's there at your side now, barking orders left and right. Men haul up the sails and run below-decks to prepare the cannons. It is a scene of barely controlled chaos, and that's when you hear the first report of cannonfire.

Both shots hit their target. The pirates are firing chain shot: two cannonballs tied together with a length of heavy chain, stuffed into a single cannon, designed to tear apart sails and rigging as they blast through it. The first shot tears apart some of the rigging on your forward sail, but luckily, nothing critical is damaged.

The second shot hits low, and instead of tearing into the sails, it decapitates the captain in an instant. His headless, bloody body drops at your feet.

PIRATES! THIS IS SO AWESOME!! *Turn to 470*

24

"Hey Mom, what's up?" you say. She jumps back from the curtain she was just messing with. Moms, am I right?

Okay, I'm going to interrupt the story here to tell you that this isn't going to go well for you no matter what you do. I'm spinning around a chair so it's backwards and I'm sitting on it, straddling the back of the chair with my legs, so you know we're about to have some Real Talk.

You know how in this story you've been choosing the crazy options and doing some crazy stuff? Here's the thing. Sometimes people do that in real life, with their own actual real-life lives. I don't know why, but they do it and it happens.

Just throwing this out there, but your mom has married her husband's brother-murderer, and literally served appetizers left over from his funeral at the wedding. This is an actual thing she, a queen of comfortable, can-certainly-afford-more-appetizers means, decided to do. She's not in the best frame of mind, and I've been minimizing her role in the story as much as possible in order not to embarrass her and to give her some space, but you're talking to her now and there's not much I can do to avoid it. Try to understand if she acts crazy.

Okay, lecture over! I'm turning the chair back to its normal orientation. We don't have to rap about our feelings anymore.

"Hey Hamlet," Gertrude says. "Listen, you were a dick when you messed up Claudius's reading earlier."

"I didn't mess up anything!" you say. "He's the one who read the murdery options! If anyone messed up, it's YOU, because you married Dad's brother and that's messed up, MOM."

I thought we were going to be nice to her?

Your mom looks at you like she's seeing you for the first time. "What are you going to do: murder me? ARE YOU GOING TO MURDER ME??" your mom asks. Terrific.

"No, Mom, I'm not going to murder you," you say, holding your palms out in front of you in what you hope reads as a "be cool" motion. "Why would you even think that? Oh, is it because I'm wearing a sword? Listen, all the princes wear swords these da—"

"Help!!" she screams at the top of her lungs.

A voice from behind the curtain says, "What?! Help! Help!!" It seems your mom has a spy eavesdropping on this little conversation! Remember what I said before about giving her the benefit of the doubt? This is kinda the perfect chance to give her the benefit of the doubt.

Tell her you'll talk to her later when she's (a) less crazy and (b) you can talk in private: *turn to 126*

Show her how non-murderous you are by killing whoever's behind the curtain: *turn to 215*

25

"What?!" she says, furious. I don't think those were the secret code words, bro. "Um," you say. Try again?

Maybe the code phrase is "Get thee to a nunnery"? *Turn to 65*

Go with "A hip, hop, a hippie, a hippie to the hip hip hop": *turn to 101*

Go with "The wolf stalks the quiet evening prey": *turn to 285*

27 Those sails she's carrying — three masts, each with four rectangular sails on them...

"Of course!" you say.

The pirate captain did what you would have done in his position: he's chosen the most favourable angle of attack! He's coming in with the wind fully at his back, because that's when his boat is fastest. Those square-rigged sails are terrific at catching the wind, and he's got lots of them, but their disadvantage is that they can't be adjusted quickly. Every change requires the crew to climb up and change the rigging on each sail individually.

You, on the other hand, can adjust your two triangular sails quickly, and it can be done at deck level! If you come about into the storm while maintaining a slight angle away from it, you should be able to turn around, maintain speed, slip past *Calypso's Gale*, and be long gone before she can even begin to turn!

It's your only hope.

You lower the spyglass, lock eyes with your first mate, and shout your orders over the roar of the storm.

"Come about into the storm! Set sails windward! Keep a close-hauled tack!" *Turn to 45*

"Come about into the storm! Set sails windward! Keep a close-hauled tack...me hearties? Yo ho ho!" *Turn to 108*

28 You and your bros come up with a plan. It goes as follows:

» You replace the letter with a forgery you wrote together that reads:

Hey King, can you make it so that Rosencrantz and Guildenstern are given fancy houses and made princes and given all the cool things it is possible to have, as they are extremely awesome, but please do not mention this letter or its contents ever again to me, Claudius, the man who is writing this letter right now. If you do see me and this letter comes up and then I claim I did not ask for these things, then I'm lying. I like to pretend sometimes that I didn't write letters, but it's just pretend, hah hah. I can never take this back. Rosencrantz and Guildenstern are awesome. Hamlet's rad too. Rosencrantz and Guildenstern are way awesome though.

» You replace the official seal with a forgery. Since you're wearing a ring and it bears the royal seal, this is surprisingly easy!

» You decide that Rosencrantz and Guildenstern will deliver the letter while you catch the next boat back to Denmark to kill Claudius!

» You're at this stage in fulfilling the plan when pirates attack!

Pirates?! Nobody said there were pirates! HOLY COW, THIS BOOK JUST GOT AWESOME: *turn to 23*

29

It's the ghost of your dad, like from before!

"Didn't I ask you to kill Claudius?" the ghost says. "So far all you've done is watch someone else read a book and then kill your girlfriend's dad."

"It's — complicated?" you say.

"Who are you talking to?" asks Gertrude.

"MOM, I'M TALKING TO THE GHOST OF MY DEAD DAD," you yell. "I TALKED TO HIM BEFORE AND EVERYONE SAW HIM THEN; I DUNNO WHY YOU CAN'T SEE HIM NOW; I DUNNO WHAT HIS DEAL IS."

"Aw geez, you're crazy. My son is bonkers," your mom says to herself, drying her tears.

To be fair, you do look a little crazy. Ghost Dad reminds you that you're supposed to be murdering Claudius, not Polonius, and he doesn't really see how cussing out his widow is helping anything. Be nice to her, he says. "Also," he says, "I'm pretty sure she's conflicted about this whole, um, marriage to my brother thing that I guess is going on, so maybe you could talk to her about that?"

"But DAD," you say.

"Hamlet," he says, frowning as he disappears.

"FINE," you say. "Hey Mom, um, how's it going? Listen, stop having sex with Claudius, okay?"

She slaps you across the face. Maybe that's why people don't usually discuss sex lives with their moms? Who knows??

"Look Mom, I'm not really crazy, but don't tell anyone, okay?" you say, gingerly touching your face where she hit you. "What is crazy is what you've been doing. This marriage to your husband's brother: it's gross; we all think it's gross. I know you're not happy about it. I know that, Mom."

"Hamlet —" she begins, but you cut her off.

"It's not too late, Mom. If you can't be good, maybe tonight you can just — pretend to be good? And then keep pretending to be good night after night, and it'll get easier. And by 'pretend to be good,' I mean 'make yourself unavailable to Claudius sexually and emotionally.'"

Your mom's crying again, but quietly. She looks up at you. "Alright," she says. "Alright."

"I'm proud of you, Mom," you say. "Listen, I've got to go. I kinda killed Polonius by accident, and I'm gonna go lay low for a while."

"Okay," she says. "Toodles."

Tell her that it would be very unfortunate if she told Claudius you're just faking crazy, and as a consequence of that had an..."accident" that "broke her neck": *turn to 15*

On second thought, leave without saying that: *turn to 208*

MARLO MEEKINS

31

Right, you're Ophelia! You are a beautiful and independent young woman, and although it makes you roll your eyes when you think about it, you've fallen in love with a prince. Prince Hamlet is funny and charming and he seems to like you a lot. You try not to get too excited about it, because you're worried you might jinx it, but things really are going great.

Only...

Only it's been hard doing the long-distance thing while you've both been off at university, and while you've loved studying capital-s Science and you're sure Hamlet's loved studying capital-u Undeclared, it hasn't been easy. Now that you're both back together in Denmark for his father's funeral and his mother's second wedding, it's been harder still. Hamlet's really sad, and you can't blame him for that since, you know, his DAD DIED, but you wish there was something you could do to help him.

When you last saw him, Hamlet mentioned how the castle seemed cold and drafty, and for some reason it stuck with you. You've been sitting at your desk, trying to think of something you could give him that would help with that — a way of cheering him up a little, remind him he's still got people who care about him. He wears these cloaks all the time, but then he's taking them off in warm rooms and putting them back on in cold ones. If only there was some way you could keep the rooms at a uniform temperature, he wouldn't need to be constantly adjusting his clothes throughout the day. But to do that you'd need some way of measuring heat and a way of transporting it throughout the castle, perhaps through a series of pipes...

Your thoughts are interrupted by a knock at your door. "Who is it?" you call.

"It's me," says your brother. "Come on, let me in."

Let him in: *turn to 361*

Tell him you're busy: *turn to 359*

32

You say hi to Ophelia, but she's acting all upset, trying to give back the presents and all the love letters you've sent her over your relationship. Weird!! It looks like someone's convinced her that you're not marriage material after all. To be fair, you did just finish talking out loud about killing yourself.

Huh!

And though I know you're now frantically looking for the "Whatever man, she's just doing this because chicks be crazy" option (Hamlet, you are nothing if not classy), I'm not going to give it to you. Listen, I'm going to help you out. You think Ophelia's crazy, but maybe...maybe she's just ACTING crazy?

In considering that possibility, you think to yourself that Ophelia doesn't have any real reason for being as upset as she appears to be — sure, you've kinda ignored her for a few weeks, which was selfish and jerky, but on the other hand this isn't the first time you've been caught up in something and you're sure she can handle it as she has before, with understanding, and not by, you know, ABANDONING THE RELATIONSHIP ENTIRELY IN SOME STUPID CASTLE ROOM. So maybe it is entirely possible that she's being fake crazy too. Maybe — maybe because she's figured things out and also wants to murder Claudius?

You decide you need a way to see if she's faking crazy while you're simultaneously also faking crazy, without revealing to anyone who may or may not be listening in that you're both actually just faking the crazy. Hmm...is there a code phrase or something you can use?

SAY "THE WOLF STALKS THE QUIET EVENING PREY": *turn to 285*

SAY "I NEVER LOVED YOU": *turn to 25*

SAY "A HIP, HOP, A HIPPIE, A HIPPIE TO THE HIP HIP HOP": *turn to 101*

33

You move the piece to intercept, but Gertrude ignores it and instead moves diagonally to take your castle. Darn it, I should've noticed that! You totally should've noticed that too!!

"Qa1," Gertrude writes, and MAN you wish you knew what those letters and numbers meant. And now you're down two pieces, and one of them was a good one!

It's hard to recover from this loss, but to your credit, you actually do alright! As the game goes on, you fight valiantly, but eventually your pieces are reduced to your king and a single pawn. Not too great, Ophelia. Gertrude's down to her king too, but she's got TWO pawns backing her king up. Here's the board.

Be careful: there's no way to win at chess if you're down to just your king. That one pawn you've got is worth its weight in gold, and losing it will absolutely cost you victory.

There are three moves you can make here. What do you do?

Move the pawn ahead two squares (b5): *turn to 463*

Move the pawn ahead one square (b6): *turn to 457*

Move the king back a square (Ka6): *turn to 479*

34

Okay. You sit on the throne. And since I like you, I'm going to describe your situation in rhyming verse!

Now this was gonna be a story all about how
Your life got flipped, turned upside down,
But instead you're gonna sit your butt down in this chair,
And ignore how you're really Denmark's rightful heir.

Whoah! My flow is so awesome that it infects even you! You begin rapping to yourself, about yourself. Here's the lyrical truth you lay down:

In west Denmark I was born and raised,
On the battlefield is where I spent most of my days,
Chilling out with dad times, stabbing all the fools
And all swordfighting Norwegians outside of my school,
When a couple of armies, they were up to no good,
Started repulsing our invasion of their neighbourhood,
Dad died one little time and my mom got scared,
And said, "I'm marrying your dad's brother, but we weren't
having an affair."

You feel like you could keep spitting some extremely tight rhymes, but you also feel like you've brought yourself pretty much up to speed on your own life! Well done, Prince Hamlet. You certainly are…fresh?

Continue sitting on the throne: *turn to 69*

36

"Abandon ship! All hands, abandon ship!" you yell into the storm. The crew looks at you in shock, but there's not much they can do.

"You want us to jump into the ocean?" someone yells.

"I don't want you to jump into the ocean!" you reply. You bite down on the blade of your sword and begin to climb one of the ropes leading up to the pirate ship. Some of your men nearby realize what you're doing and join in, climbing up other ropes.

Partway up, you turn around, grasp your sword, and shout down at your remaining crew:

"I WANT YOU TO JUMP INTO THE FIGHT!!"

Your crew shouts in defiance at the pirates, charges the ropes, and begins to climb.

CONTINUE CLIMBING! *Turn to 42*

37

You throw each meaty chunk of Polonius out the window, and each hits the ground with a moist thump.

Let's take stock of things. You're now covered with blood, in a room covered with blood, with a bunch of bloody body parts lying on the ground five storeys beneath you. There's someone about to unlock the door, and you need to look non-suspicious or you'll get caught!

You have 2 turn(s) remaining.

LIGHT DOOR ON FIRE: *turn to 254*

TIE TWINE ACROSS BASE OF DOOR TO TRIP WHOEVER ENTERS THE ROOM: *turn to 320*

JUMP OUT THE WINDOW: *turn to 207*

39

That is honestly the most credible of all the choices, which just made me very, very sad.

Okay, so you used to be Ophelia and then you were King Claudius but now you're Hamlet! Honestly, this doesn't seem like a very fair trade to me. Listen, kid, I like you. I don't want you to be stuck being Hamlet. Why don't I turn my back real quick and count to 10 and when I'm not looking you...

Be Ophelia: *turn to 355*

40

Tying the body parts to the hot-air balloons is the easy part, surprisingly. You manage to balance the load (i.e., chunks of human flesh) across balloons so that each balloon is positively buoyant. The hard part is moving them around in this relatively tiny and low-ceilinged room.

You get one balloon out the window, but in doing so knock a torch onto the curtain, leaving it considerably charred. You get another out, but manage to upset the pot over the fireplace and get stew all over the floor. With not much else left to damage, you get the remaining balloons out the window and watch as they float off into the sky, carrying most of the evidence of your crime miles and miles away, each to land in a different area. And please, who would bother investigating the discovery of just a SINGLE body part? Hopefully nobody, that's who!

Turning around, you see the door open and who should enter but Corambis, Polonius's twin brother! You recognize him from the royal courts.

"I unlocked the door, so you can leave no—" he begins, but cuts himself off, shocked. "What happened here?!"

You smile in what you hope is a calming manner. "As you can see, I was preparing stew when I tripped," you say. "Stumbling backwards, I fell onto the table, hitting the wall, which knocked a torch onto the curtain, causing it to almost catch on fire. As I shoved the remaining torches in the stove to destroy them without a trace and prevent further fire hazards, I knocked over the stew, causing it to get everywhere, including on myself."

"That looks like blood on you though," says Corambis.

"Nope, it's stew. See?" you say and then you draw a finger across your arm and lick off the "stew." It's disgusting. You throw up a little in your mouth, and then you throw up a little on the ground.

Corambis looks at you.

"I am not a particularly talented chef," you say.

"Well..." Corambis begins, and then pauses. He seems to reach a decision. "Be careful next time, okay?"

"You got it, bro," you say. You smile. Corambis looks at you and leaves.

Congratulations! You have gained 10 conversation points, your maximum hit points have gone up by 5, AND you have completed the optional sidequest of Nobody Will Miss Polonius (Murder That Guy Polonius for No Real Reason).

Unfortunately Corambis only has a 1 in 2 chance of dropping loot upon quest completion, and it didn't work out for you this time.

On the plus side, you have successfully killed a man, but it wasn't the man you were supposed to kill. Remember? Claudius? The king who killed your dad? Anyway, before you started this murder, I'm pretty sure your mom wanted to talk to you!

Go talk to your mom: *turn to 91*

42

You and your crew scramble up the ropes. Partway up, an explosion rocks *Vesselmania IV*. You hold tight to the rope as the force of the explosion reaches you, shooting debris upwards into the sky, taking your captain's hat with it, and messing up your hair. Looking downward, you see the entire top deck of *Vesselmania* has been destroyed, revealing fires raging underneath. There's no way anyone could've survived. You hope Rosencrantz and Guildenstern made it above-decks in time, but there's too much storm for you to make out the others on the ropes below you clearly.

Maybe...maybe they made it to the ropes?

Yes, that's definitely what happened: *turn to 55*

No man, they died: *turn to 99*

43

"I'm going to end this madness now. I'm going to let you live," you say.

"Thanks," says Osric, "but no thanks. Would rather be a ghost, if it's all the same to you."

"I'm not going to kill you!" you shout at him.

"Fine. Then I'll kill you. Or at least, I'll keep trying, over and over and over again. I'm not gonna stop, sweetie, until you're dead. The only way to stop me is to kill me."

He looks like he means it.

If you untie Osric now, he'll probably attack you. If you leave him tied up, he'll get loose eventually and then attack you. Either way, you're going to be attacked by him in the near future, and he is going to try to kill you. On the other hand, he's tied up right now, which gives you a distinct advantage in the "who is killing whom" department.

Leave him tied up and escape: *turn to 417*

Kill him now: *turn to 158*

45

The sails are adjusted by your crew. As you turn towards the wind, the waves, which had previously been travelling with you, are now moving against you. Huge white-capped waves crest and splash over the deck.

"Hold on, men!" you shout into the gale.

Your ship heels over, almost capsizing with the intensity of the turn, but the sails keep just clear of the water and the manoeuvre is successful. As she rights herself, you see *Calypso's Gale* ahead of you, bearing down, still at speed.

All you need to do is pass by her side and you'll be free.

"Steady! STEADY!" you shout as the two ships approach each other, *Vesselmania* slipping by on the right. Looking at the crew of the pirate ship, you see them scrambling into the rigging, adjusting their sails as fast as they can. It shouldn't be enough.

It shouldn't be.

But they're not trying to come about. They're not trying to sidle up parallel to fire their cannons. Instead, they've thrown the rudder hard to port, sending the ship into a tight curve. They're attempting to ram you, Hamlet.

"Hard to starboard! HARD TO STARBOARD!" you scream, but there's not enough time. *Calypso's Gale* tears into the side of your ship at full speed. You and the rest of the crew are knocked to the deck as *Vesselmania* is cleaved almost in two. You scramble to your feet and see that she's somehow managed to stay together, impaled on the much larger bow of *Calypso's Gale*. But she's mortally wounded. She's filling with water as we speak, Hamlet!

Looking up through the storm, you see ropes being thrown over the edge of the pirate ship. Pirates are sliding down them, swords at the ready, hoping to kill you and take whatever valuables they can find before *Vesselmania* finally sinks. Given her current condition, they'd better be fast.

You'd better be fast too, whatever it is you decide to do next!

Order the crew to abandon ship. Then commandeer the pirate vessel! *Turn to 36*

Order the crew to abandon ship. Then go below-decks to rescue Rosencrantz and Guildenstern! *Turn to 447*

46

You swing your sword sideways as hard as you can, making contact with his left elbow at full speed. Your sword slices through the flesh easily. He screams and tries to attack you with his other arm, but a second later you've cut that one off at the elbow too.

You both look down at his now-useless arms, lying on the deck, one hand still clutching his sword. The perfect thing to deadpan suddenly comes to mind, the words crystallizing in your head like they were written for you by the very gods themselves:

"ALL HANDS ON DECK." *Turn to 378*

"HEY, WHO HERE THINKS I'M WINNING THIS FIGHT? CAN I MAYBE GET A SHOW OF HANDS?" *Turn to 162*

"HUH. LOOKS LIKE YOU'RE...NOT AS WELL ARMED AS YOU THOUGHT?" *Turn to 253*

47 The next morning, you and Horatio walk into the castle and towards the royal court. You meet nobody along the way, which is a little weird.

"Maybe they're all in the throne room?" Horatio says.

"One way to find out," you say and kick in the throne room door. It goes perfectly, the doors flying open with a huge bang. It's so satisfying, Hamlet!

ENTER THRONE ROOM: *turn to 61*

48 You drop to one knee and put all your effort into sending your sword upwards at his outstretched hand. You manage to cleave it from his wrist in a single slice! The momentum from the blow carries his hand up into the air, and you both watch (he in shock, you in surprise at how good this awesome sword is) as his detached hand describes an arc directly towards you.

It hits your chest with a bloody splat.

You brush his hand off your jacket and say:

"HEY, I NEVER KNEW WHAT IT WAS LIKE TO CUT OFF A LIMB BEFORE! GUESS NOW I'VE FINALLY GOT SOME FIRST-HAND EXPERIENCE." *Turn to 59*

"BY THE WAY, THIS WAS MY FIRST SWORDFIGHT AT SEA, SO — THANKS FOR GIVING ME A HAND?" *Turn to 152*

"HEY! HANDS OFF THE THREADS." *Turn to 233*

50

Rather than sailing in to shore and attacking the king head on, you decide not to tip your hand. This is the plan you come up with:

You'll approach Denmark at night, flying Danish flags. *Calypso's Gale* will stay out from shore, looking like any other trader, but will remain ready to move on your signal. You'll leave Rosencrantz and Guildenstern in command, dive overboard into the ocean, and swim to shore.

Once there, you'll compose and send three letters to Horatio by messenger. The first will be addressed to Claudius and read, "Hey, I'm back from England, all by myself. SURPRISED? You will be, tomorrow, when I see you. P.S. I am naked." Hopefully you'll be able to scare / confuse him into some rash, overt action against you, which you'll be able to counter with *Calypso*'s help.

The second goes to your mother, and reads, "Hey Mom, I'm still mad at you for marrying Claudius, so I'm pretty sure I'm going to kill him. Sooooo...try to act surprised?"

The third and final letter is for your friend Horatio and says, "Hey Horatio, CRAZY STORY: pirates attacked! And they took me hostage, but just me, and then they brought me back to Denmark because I said I'd do them a favour. Speaking of which, can you make sure these other two letters reach Mom and Uncle-Dad? Then come see me real quick, okay? I'll be down by the docks."

That should be enough to both ensure your letters are delivered, and to see if Claudius has gotten to Horatio while you were away. If he hasn't, Horatio can help you take down Claudius. If he has — well, you'll deal with Horatio the same way you dealt with the pirates: with your swords and your wits, both deadly sharp and both insanely pointed.

Rosencrantz and Guildenstern agree to your plan. You arrive near Denmark's shore in the middle of the night, the waves silver with reflected moonlight.

"Good luck, my friends," you tell Rosencrantz and Guildenstern.

"And to you," they reply.

You've all grown so much this trip. It's been so great. You've never felt closer to these awesome dudes. You dive into the sea and swim for shore.

REACH SHORE AND SEND LETTERS: *turn to 58*

51

"Hey!" you yell. "Big bad pirate! Why don't you come down here and fight me?"

The pirate seems reluctant, until you tell him that he's a disappointment to his family, and how the grief and shame of having a child who grew up to work as a pirate — who BECAME a pirate — seems so colossal to your parents, and yet at the same time also so private and personal that they rarely speak of him, even to each other. They live with this invisible wall between them, always preventing them from being as close as they used to be, as they want to be again, the subject of their son somehow always in mind but never broached. His parents, who used to tell each other everything, now go to bed in silence, and this pirate's actions — HIS choices

— have created this thing, untouchable, unreal, that nevertheless heartlessly and inexorably drives his parents a little more into solitude each day. They've become strangers to each other.

The pirate hollers in rage at your way-sick diss and begins climbing down. When he's close, you brace your legs against the hull and push, but the pirate is ready for it and holds on tight. What he's not ready for is the fact you pushed at an angle, sending you out into space and then back to the ship further to the left of where you had been. You grab another rope and in the same smooth action reach up and send your sword through his rope, just above of where he's holding.

You watch as man and rope fall, silhouetted by the burning deck of *Vesselmania IV*. They disappear into the flames.

"You're fired," you say.

You manage to climb up quite a bit before another pirate takes his place. I hope for your sake you've got another trick up your sleeve!

Push out from the ship, use your legs as a battering ram, and smash your way inside through a porthole: *turn to 106*

52

I'm sorry to hear it. I mean, it makes sense, but...sorry about your feelings, buddy?

Okay! So you've just said, "This means the spooky ghost was correct!" and Ophelia has looked at you strangely, and now she's speaking.

"A ghost?!" she says.

"You're crazy."

Then she looks at Horatio and says, "You're crazy too," and then she looks at you again, sighs and says, "I don't even know why I'm here," and leaves, shoving past Rosencrantz and Guildenstern in the doorway.

Looks like you two are still broken up, which makes you sad! But on the plus side, Rosencrantz and Guildenstern are totally awesome. Bros before woes!! You're about to greet your best bros with your choice of high fives, slaps on the back, or hugs all around, when Guildenstern holds up his hand and speaks.

"Your mom wants to see you," he says. "As you know, in this time period if you want to talk to someone, you have to literally walk over to where they are to chat them up, which I can hardly believe; anyway, she's lazy so she wants you to walk to her instead."

"Dude. She said she's 'stonished by your behaviour," Rosencrantz adds.

"'Stonished isn't real slang," you say.

"Just trying it out," Rosencrantz says, and you high five to linguistic experimentation.

"Well, I guess I'm off to see her," you say. Just then, Polonius enters the room and says, "Hey, your mother wants to see you."

"I KNOW; NOBODY WANTS YOU HERE, POLONIUS!" you yell at him. "GOD, I COULD JUST STAB YOU THROUGH A CURTAIN."

Hey, that gives you an idea!

GO STAB POLONIUS THROUGH A CURTAIN: *turn to 206*

GO STAB THE KING, WHICH IS WHAT YOU WANTED TO DO IN THE FIRST PLACE! *Turn to 209*

GO TALK TO YOUR MOM: *turn to 12*

53

You whistle and sit yourself down on the floor in the middle of the room. That seems a little awkward, so you stretch out on your side, your arm supporting your head and your other arm resting on your hips. There! Nobody could be more casual than you!

The door opens and who should enter but Corambis, Polonius's twin brother! You recognize him from the royal courts.

"I unlocked the door, so you can leave no—" he begins, but then cuts himself off. "Hey, what's going on?" Corambis looks around. "Why are you acting so casual? How come you stabbed that curtain? Why are you surrounded by lumpy bags and why is there all this blood everywhere?"

He opens a bag, pausing only briefly to negotiate his way around the twine you tied. It's a bag with a human head inside, and Corambis thinks that's super gross and suspicious! He begins to scream and scream and scream, and whether or not you decide to kill him to cover your tracks, a bunch of other people are already on their way here and you're pooched.

Claudius carries out your execution personally. Your last words are "Oh geez, if only I'd been better at covering up my murders; had I only the chance to do it again, I would try to figure out something better than putting a human body into a bunch of bags and tying the bags off with twine; may I just say that in retrospect I'm not even sure what I was thinking."

In retrospect, neither am I!

THE END

Turn to 119

dude into other dudes or a lady
to other ladies or a dude into
dies or a lady into dudes or just
ito all of it (*This date would have
one better if you had a more
ppropriate sexual orientation*).

exy *adj.* **(-ier, -iest) 1** super hot
ude (*Man, that Hamlet is really
exy. Is he single?*).

fig. 1

2 exciting,
ppealing (*Did
ou see that sexy
iew skull Hamlet
found?*).

shabby *adj.* **(-ier, -iest)**
looking rough and grungy. In a stat
of disrepair. Literally everyone
... for royalty

55

Hah, nice try! Your friends have to choose their OWN adventure here. You don't get to make life-or-death choices for them! If you want to do that, you should play my other book, *God: the Adventure! Decide How Each of Billions of Individual Stories End! Fun at First, Tedious Soon After (So Many Lives Are Depressingly Similar).*

PERSONALLY though, I also hope Rosencrantz and Guildenstern survived, and I think that probably that counts for something?

So! As you're climbing, lightning suddenly strikes the water below. A huge crash of thunder deafens you, but in that brief instant, the world is illuminated. You see your young crew of almost 20 (both by count and by age), cutlasses at the ready, fighting as they climb. Pirates swarm down the lines, battling them for sport. Above them, on deck, they're being cheered by a row of pirates. And at the very bow of the ship, looking down with a spyglass, stands the captain. He's got a fancy hat and a parrot on his shoulder: the works. And he's staring right at you through the storm.

The darkness of the storm is restored moments later. You grimly resume your climb. One way or another, you're going to end this.

CONTINUE CLIMBING, ATTACK PIRATES! *Turn to 92*

56

"Naw man, here's the real story!" you say, and you briefly recount your pirate adventures. Horatio appreciates how you took the time to say something appropriate to go with every death and dismemberment.

"Sweet," he says.

"Thanks!" you say.

"So what's your plan now?" he asks, and you lay it out for him: you're gonna go see Claudius tomorrow, having given him fair warning of your visit. You're hoping he'll freak out that you're not dead, and when you visit him you'll be able to goad him into doing something overtly criminal against you. When he does that, you'll have enough proof of his guilt (if not of your father's death, then at least of his attempt to murder you) that you can move against him. *Calypso's Gale* will support your claim to the throne — with cannons.

"You're talking about an insurrection," he whispers, his eyes wide.

"I'm talking justice," you say. "Lock and load."

"Okay," Horatio says.

"Incidentally we don't use guns that require that motion," Horatio says.

WAIT TILL TOMORROW, THEN CONFRONT CLAUDIUS TOGETHER!
Turn to 47

58 You send your letters. You have time before the messenger will deliver them, so you wander down to the docks.

You get the attention of a passerby, who looks like she works here. "Excuse me, what's that ship over there?" you say, pointing as casually as you can at your insanely majestic ship.

"Her? That's uh...*Calypso's Gale*, looks like a Danish trader. I imagine she'll be docking in a few hours," she says.

"Oh. Neat," you say.

Everything's going according to plan. You wave to the ship, just in case Rosencrantz and Guildenstern are watching, and wander around, waiting for Horatio to show up. You eat some fried fish. It is really yummy.

Suddenly, you feel a tap on your shoulder. Looking around, you see your old friend Horatio! "Hamlet, you're back!" he says, hugging you.

"Did you deliver my letters?" you ask.

"Yep! So what's your story — pirates attacked and only took you hostage? And then they brought you back here for no reason? Hah hah, that's so crazy! That's REALLY what happened?"

Do you trust Horatio? If you do, you'll let him in on the full story. If you don't, you'll let him think that only you made it back from the trip.

Trust Horatio, no way he'd side with my murderous stepdad over me! We saw a ghost together. You just don't turn away from that. *Turn to 56*

Trust no one! *Turn to 110*

59 The pirate captain screams in rage, charging you with his sword. You deftly parry and sidestep, ending up behind him.

The two of you circle each other, flurries of swordplay erupting whenever one of you detects an opportunity. Despite his injury, neither of you is able to gain the advantage on the rain-soaked deck of the ship.

Suddenly, lightning strikes the brass rail behind the pirate captain, and he's briefly stunned by the tremendous thunder that follows. You're stunned as well but, being a few feet away, you recover more quickly.

There's your opening, Hamlet!

Attack his dominant, sword-bearing arm! *Turn to 46*

Attack his eyes! *Turn to 469*

Attack his legs! *Turn to 234*

61 The entire royal court turns to face you.

"Miss me?" you say. Laertes runs out from the crowd with his sword. "You killed my father!" he screams at you. To your right is Osric, now operating in his capacity of Royal Court Helper and Sometimes Sword Carrier, and he's currently carrying a selection of three swords. You kick Osric in the chest, catching two of the swords that he drops as he stumbles backwards, one in each of your hands. You toss one blade to Horatio. Laertes screams as he runs towards you.

"He's a distraction!" Horatio shouts to you. "Leave him to me!"

"I've no quarrel with you!" screams Laertes to Horatio.

"I'm afraid you do," says Horatio, "as you seem to be intent on killing my best friend. That sort of thing has always been—" he cuts himself off as their blades clash for the first time, sparks flying "—a pet peeve of mine," he continues.

"You talk a lot," says Laertes.

"Dude, it was like two sentences," says Horatio, as the sound of steel hitting steel fills the air.

Turning away from the fight, you kick the last sword towards the throne. "This is for you, Claudius," you say.

"Hah!" says Claudius nervously. "How ridiculous! Why...um, why would I ever fight you?"

You shout:

"You killed my father!" *Turn to 185*

"You tried to have me murdered in England!" *Turn to 127*

"You have a stupid face and I get irritated whenever I look at it!" *Turn to 184*

62 Okay, but one thing at a time, buddy! First, you go back to your room and get your copy of the book for Christina to sign, which she does. "To Hamlet: Best wishes! I hope you like to read these words that I wrote on a piece of paper. Cheers, Christina," she writes. Amazing. It's perfect, and now you've got the perfect book to entrap your uncle!

You excuse yourself and go back to your room to flip through *Gonzago* again. You get absorbed in the adventure and, a few playthroughs later, you're convinced: it really is a great book, and it should work perfectly for your plan.

Now all you need to do is find Claudius! I'm pretty sure he's in the royal court, dude!

Go to the royal court: *turn to 73*

Nap for a while: *turn to 387*

64 "Hey Horatio!" you yell. "Want to switch dance partners?"

"Sure," says Horatio. "Laertes is learning my sweet moves, but Claudius doesn't know any of them yet."

Laertes opens his mouth, probably to tell Claudius all about Horatio's sweet moves, but you leap up, flip over his head, and land on your feet behind him. You spin around and bring the flat of your sword under his chin. Applying some pressure, you push his mouth shut.

"Shh," you whisper. "Nobody cares about what you have to say, you big dummy."

Laertes spins around, and your swords clash. Meanwhile, Horatio is fighting Claudius, pushing him backwards. You're pushing your opponents to opposite ends of the royal court! Laertes has his back up against the wall, and you're about to go in for the killing blow when, in what I think is fair to call a lucky strike, he knocks your sword from your hand and sends it skittering behind you. You fall, landing on your butt.

At the same time, Claudius strikes Horatio's sword in a similarly lucky blow, sending it spinning backwards as well. You feel something bump against your hand and look down to see Horatio's sword.

This is perfect.

You and Horatio pick up each other's swords at the same moment, deflect an otherwise-fatal attack from your opponents at the same moment, and then stab Claudius and Laertes through their hearts, yes indeed, at the exact same moment. It's the best example of beautiful, synchronized fighting ever in the history of the whole dang planet, and it happened entirely by accident. Nicely done, gentlemen! And congrats Hamlet on finally putting that Kill Claudius quest to bed. So! With Claudius and Laertes dead, there are no more bad guys in this story! (Gertrude isn't REALLY a bad guy; she's just an easily manipulated person who makes bad decisions when it comes to boyfriends, remember? We talked about this, I'm pretty sure.)

The court wants to pronounce you king, but you've had enough of Denmark for a while. You tell everyone Horatio should be king instead. After Horatio sits on his throne for the first time and everyone applauds, you leave. Where to? You haven't decided yet.

But you know one thing: no matter what you choose, it's going to be an adventure.

THE END

Oh wait, P.S. On the way out the door, you bump into Fortinbras, who is here trying to take over Denmark! He's a jerk so you kill him. Nobody cares that you stabbed him; he's a jerk!!

Turn to 192

65

You tell her to get to a nunnery, because if she has sex, her kids will be awful because everyone is awful, and man, if you only had the time, you'd be the awfulest person ever. Also, only a fool would marry her, because anyone smart knows that women are awful.

"Why are you saying these horrible, horribly sexist things?" she asks. I've gotta say...it's a pretty good question?

Last chance, Hamlet.

Say "A hip, hop, a hippie, a hippie to the hip hip hop": *turn to 101*

Say "The wolf stalks the quiet evening prey": *turn to 285*

Say "Women are idiots who just want to get a sexing": *turn to 248*

66

You hold up your hand and open your mouth, but before you can say anything, Claudius addresses you directly, calling you his son!

On the one hand, that's entirely appropriate, especially since he just married your mom like two weeks ago. But on the other hand, he HAS brought "creepy uncle" to new heights. Points for that, maybe?

Insult him under your breath by saying you're more than kin (i.e., you're related more than once now as both father/son and uncle/nephew), but less than kind (i.e., this relationship you're in is unnatural). In real life people think up zingers like this on the spot all the time, so this totally makes sense. *Turn to 235*

Say "You're not my real dad!" and storm out of the room: *turn to 69*

67

You and Claudius spar, while beside you, Horatio and Laertes fight each other in parallel. It's pretty great.

"Hey, are you thirsty, Hamlet?" asks Claudius. "Because I've got a drink made up special for you!"

Your sword clashes against his as you reply. "Why? Did you poison it?"

Claudius seems surprised. "What? How did you know?"

"I guess by not being stupid!" you yell, thrusting your sword at him. "Why else would you offer me a drink in the middle of a battle to the death?"

Claudius attacks you with renewed passion, and Horatio seems to be struggling against Laertes too. Aw man! Don't mess this up for me, dude; I was excited to see where this is going!

Switch opponents with Horatio: *turn to 64*

Keep the same opponents, but say something mean to Claudius! *Turn to 129*

68

You burst into the lobby, and it looks like a war zone. Injured people are staggering everywhere. But time bombs aren't really a thing yet, so the terrorist (OR TERRORISTS??) (I mean I guess I already let it slip that there's three of them, but let's pretend I didn't) must be nearby. Spinning around, you look for anyone suspicious. There's a man very conspicuously trying to look very inconspicuous as he leaves the hotel.

"Hey you!" you shout, and he breaks into a run. Looks like this is your man! You give chase and slam into him, sending him straight into a wall. He hits his head hard and falls back, dazed. You pick him up by the collar.

"Who sent you?" you ask.

"What?" he replies. You slap him across the face, and he laughs, so you close your hand into a fist and shatter his nose. He's not laughing now. In fact, he's in a lot of pain!

"Not gonna ask you twice," you warn.

"Okay, okay, geez!" gasps the man. "I was helped by my two terrorist friends, Georges and Margaret. They're in a coffee shop two blocks away."

You mash around his broken nose a little.

"Okay, okay!! THREE blocks away!" he shouts through the pain.

You press your fingers against his eyes and he cries out. You wait for him to stop and take a breath. "You killed a lot of people back there," you say. "I think given our current cultural context and the fact that we're not operating with the benefit of hundreds of years of ethical development that some hypothetical future people might have, I'm justified in killing you." His only answer is to whimper.

"Did you know there's a name for that judicial framework?"

He shakes his head, and then you pull out one of his eyes with your fingers.

"An eye for an eye," you say.

As he's screaming, you decide to actually break his neck and kill him, since that's what "an eye for an eye" means in its non-literal sense, after all. You then run down towards the coffee shop he indicated, coming in through the back door. Everyone is talking nervously about the explosion except for two people.

"Hey Georges! Margaret!" you shout, and the two people who weren't talking both look towards you. Bingo. You pull up a chair to the side of their table and throw your arms around their shoulders.

"Listen guys, it kinda sucks that you blew up all those people," you say.

"Um — what? Hah hah, that's crazy that you'd think we are the terrorists!" says Georges.

"Oh, right! Hah hah, what a crazy thing for me to accuse you of!" you say, your arms still around their shoulders. "Let's talk about this outside," you say, pulling them up by their collars and dragging them out to the alley behind the coffee shop. You let them go, and their demeanours change instantly. "What'd you do with Patrick?" demands Margaret.

"Who's Patrick? The dead guy? I killed him," you say. "He's dead now."

"Horse droppings," says Margaret. "I don't believe you."

"Oh, no, I can prove it," you say. You grab Margaret with both hands. "Here, here's what I did to your friend that made him dead."

Seconds later, Margaret's way-dead body is lying at your feet with a broken nose and a missing eye. You look up at Georges, who's staring at Margaret's body in shock.

"Do YOU believe me, Georges?" you ask. He hesitates, unsure whether "yes" or "no" is the right answer. You decide to help him out.

"There's no right answer here, Georges. Sometimes life isn't fair," you say, and then you break his neck too.

"Them's the breaks," you say.

Go back to the hotel, collect your things, and get out of here! This country is crazy; you wanna go back to Denmark. *Turn to 305*

Stay here, this country is awesome, let's track down more terrorists!! *Turn to 344*

69

While you're busy doing that, your friend Horatio bumps into you and tells you:

a) he's in town for your dad's funeral / mom's wedding, and they served leftover appetizers from one at the other,

b) ghosts are real,

c) he's seen one and so have a bunch of other guys,

d) it keeps showing up at the same time, and

e) he's pretty sure it's the ghost of your dad.

Finally! Some adventure! Some CLOSURE. You agree that you'll come with him tonight to see the ghost when it shows up again. It's such an obvious decision that it kinda feels like you don't even have a choice in the matter!

Agree to go with Horatio tonight to see the ghost when it shows up again: *turn to 164*

71

You, Hamlet, prince of all of Denmark, are now sitting in your bedroom and playing solitaire for hours and hours and hours and hours, which is a pretty colossally useless waste of your time, especially since you keep cheating. A five goes on top of a three, Hamlet? REALLY? Anyway at this point we're 15 games in, and WOW if you're not careful people might start saying that your tragic flaw is, I don't know, inaction?

Eventually the sun does go down, and it's almost 11:30, which hopefully you remember as the appointed hour Horatio told you about wherein a ghost keeps showing up to bother him! Time to go meet that ghost, huh?

MEET UP WITH HORATIO AND BUST SOME (MYTHS ABOUT ACTUAL) GHOSTS (BEING REAL): *turn to 268*

72

You are inspired. You clear your throat and hold out one hand in front of you. You look Rosencrantz and Guildenstern in the eyes, one after the other.

"What a piece of work is a man!" you say, choosing your words (and punctuation!) carefully. "How noble in reason, how infinite in faculty, in form and moving how express and admirable, in action how like an angel, in apprehension how like a god!"

Your friends nod. Humans ARE pretty great.

"The beauty of the world, the paragon of animals — and yet, to me, what is this quintessence of dust? Man delights not me —"

You break off as Guildenstern interrupts you.

"Gayyyyy," he says.

"I said man delights NOT me, idiot," you say. "Nor woman neither, though you seem to think —"

This time you're interrupted by Rosencrantz.

"Asexuallll," he says.

You look at your friends.

"Anyway, whatever," you say. "I've been depressed but it's great to see you guys, homophobia and asexualaphobia aside."

"Oh hey!" says Guildenstern, suddenly remembering something. "We met an author on the boat over. We invited her to come say hi."

An author! This is really really exciting. And who should walk through the door just as Guildenstern stops talking? Why, it's the very author they just mentioned! How perfect! Having her show up now keeps this narrative moving forward at a nice clip AND avoids any awkward downtime where you'd otherwise all just sit around in a circle waiting for someone to show up and talk to you. Huh! Nicely done, narrator of this story a.k.a.: ME.

TALK TO AUTHOR: *turn to 6*

73 You go to the royal court and it's — deserted? Practically, anyway. It kinda looks like maybe Ophelia is there in the corner reading a book, but PLEASE it's not like you have time to make certain.

Well, this sucks. You had this perfect plan ready, but if Claudius isn't around then he can't read the book and the whole thing is useless and stupid and you hate it!

You feel some introspection coming on. Yes. Oh man, this is going to be a big one. It's gonna all boil down to this: is it even worth LIVING in a world where things don't always go your way? Or to put it differently: "being alive is good, or MAYBE...being dead is good?" Or to put it a third, more copula-tastic way: "to be, or not to be?"

Man. This is the big one, Hamlet. This is the speech this book is named after. I guess you'd better talk it out, huh?

CHOOSE WISELY.

You clear your throat and raise one hand in front of you.

Turn to 10 **TO BE**

or

NOT TO BE: *turn to 11*

74 "Hooray!" Gertrude says, hugging you. She's covered in your brother's guts, but it's still a nice moment.

I must say, you are doing really well, King Hamlet! Not only have you revenged yourself in record time, you've also reconciled with your widow. Nicely done!

You reveal yourself to the royal court the next morning, and nobody's happier to see you than your son, Hamlet Jr. Your reappearance as a ghost does cause a minor constitutional crisis when someone points out you might not be able to reassume the throne, but a quick flip through the constitution reveals that there's nothing in the rules that say a ghost CAN'T be king! There's actually a section that explicitly says that should this happen, the ghost assuming the throne would be totally neato. I'm serious; that's what it says: "totally neato."

You've got yourself a pretty cool nation, Hamlet Sr.! You rule with your wife by your side for a really long time, and even get help solving national problems from the ghosts of history's greatest rulers, many of whom become close personal friends.

Your final score is 3400 megapoints and I'm really proud of you. Nicely done!!

THE END

Turn to 397

75 You say they got married basically right after the funeral, and that makes Claudius king now. You explain how maybe it's not TECHNICALLY incest, but the timing alone sure feels squicky.

"Didn't he ever read the *Table of Kindred and Affnity, Wherein Whosoever Are Related Are Forbidden in Scripture and Our Laws to Marry Together*??" asks your dad.

"Ah," you say, "you refer to the document Queen Elizabeth ordered produced, which says a marriage such as this one we're discussing is not just squicky, but a real-life hard-core sin against God, a book which later made its way into the Book of Common Prayer, itself so influential that we take many phrases such as 'Till death us do part' and 'Peace in our time' from it?"

"The very same," nods your father. "Although I can imagine that in the future, sentiments might change as to whether or not such a marriage between genetically unrelated, loving, and consenting adults is among THE VERY WORST THINGS IT IS POSSIBLE FOR A HUMAN BEING TO DO, that's not necessary for us to discuss right now."

You agree.

"Anyway," says your dad. "Kill Claudius for me, cool?"

Promise a ghost you'll commit murder: *turn to 139*

Promise a ghost you'll commit murder in the classiest verse you can come up with: *turn to 456*

76 "That'd be a decent move," Gertrude says, "if you weren't about to lose."

"That'd be decent trash talk," you reply, "if trash talk bothered me, which it doesn't."

"Oh well," Gertrude says, and she moves her queen to take the pawn it was threatening in f7.

"Qxf7#," she writes. She looks up.

"That means you lose," she says. Aw man! THIS SUCKS, Ophelia!

Checkmate: *turn to 309*

BAM.

78 Don't freak out, but right now you're staring cold in the face of a g-g-g-spectre. You can't even imagine how crazy this whole situation is. If you're getting too scared, read this next clause over and over until you're not insane with fear anymore: EVERYTHING WILL BE OKAY. Alright. Okay. We can do this. With your last shred of sanity, you quickly glance at the ghost, and then you worry that if you stare at the ghost too hard, your brain will realize it's looking at something SO INSANELY IMPOSSIBLE that you'll just black out.

Anyway: this ghost. You can see through it, but only a little? It's weird. And I'll tell you what the frig else: this ghost does look like your dad. And he's getting closer.

Stare at the ghost intently and black out as your mind shuts down: *turn to 5*

Don't stare at the ghost too intently and try to figure out what it wants: *turn to 236*

Run away: *turn to 137*

79 You tell Polonius that you don't actually know who he is, but maybe he's a pimp? He doesn't get that you are (or rather, that I am) rather cleverly trying to suggest that you suspect he's been trying to mess with Ophelia in order to get to you. It goes entirely over his head. Anyway, he seems satisfied with your answer, which is great!

Polonius puts to you his riddle the second. "What have you been reading lately?" he says.

Answer with the exact words I want you to say: *turn to 239*

80 You walk back to where Horatio is waiting for you.

"Listen, Horatio, never speak of this whole 'we totally saw a ghost' thing, okay? We've got to keep it a secret."

"That's cool," says Horatio.

"No, I'm serious, man!" you say, grabbing his shoulders. "Some REALLY SERIOUS STUFF is going to go down, and I need you to keep this a secret. Swear that you'll never talk about this."

"I swear," says Horatio.

"SWEAR IT," booms your dad's voice out of nowhere.

"He already did!" you shout. Horatio looks at you, questioning. "Hamlet.

Bro. What's this all about?" he says. "There are more things in heaven and earth, Horatio—" you begin.

"—than are dreamt of in my philosophy," Horatio finishes, annoyed. "Fine. Right. Whatever."

Okay! Horatio will keep your secret, and you've got a quest from a ghost to fulfill! And at the end, he'll probably give you some cool loot for completing it! Maybe? I mean, it's possible.

Anyway, it's past midnight, and Claudius is probably falling-down drunk. What now?

Say goodbye to Horatio and go kill Claudius: *turn to 142*

Go home for nappy times: *turn to 86*

81

You move your pawn up one square.

Gertrude quickly jots down something on a piece of paper you hadn't noticed before. "e4 f6," it reads. Beside it she's noted the words "oh man, seriously??"

Wow! Maybe she's impressed? I mean, that is a really optimistic way to look at things!

Gertrude moves her queen's pawn out two spaces, so it's standing beside her other one. She's building a wall of pawns! But she's overlooked the fact that when pawns are side by side, they can't defend each other as well as if they're in a zigzag pattern. What's she doing? Doesn't she REALIZE?

"d4," she writes.

Build a wall too, but make mine zigzag! (g5): *turn to 510*

Build a wall too, but make it straight like hers (g6): *turn to 522*

82

You say you'd like to go walk outside...STRAIGHT INTO YOUR GRAVE! It's that last bit of crazy that really sells it.

Somehow Polonius thinks you're actually saying something really significant about how we're all really dying from the moment we're born? He observes that in madness you're actually speaking the truth. Hey! Your answers seem to have helped him reach the conclusion we wanted in regards to your sanity!

Polonius says he'd better be going, and you say nothing would make you happier except if you somehow literally died right now, and then you motorboat your lips and flick your index finger over them, making a "brururururur" sound.

Yep. He definitely thinks you're crazy.

So! I hope you're happy. I have fixed this as best I can, and remember: we're just FAKE crazy now, okay?

Okay.

You can drive again.

As Polonius leaves, your friends Rosencrantz and Guildenstern enter the room! What? You thought these guys were still back at university! This is awesome!

Greet your friends with high fives: *turn to 9*

Greet your friends by slapping them on the back: *turn to 501*

Greet your friends with hugs all around: *turn to 145*

Let's not get carried away. Just walk up, say hi, and ask them how it's going. *Turn to 13*

83

You aim for his upper body. He easily deflects your attack.

You push forward, forcing Laertes to step backwards as he parries. You lock blades with him and with one final effort shove as hard as you can. Laertes stumbles wildly, but he only takes one or two steps before he crashes into a windowsill. This knocks his legs out from under him, and he falls out the window and disappears. Then: silence.

You carefully approach the window and peer over the edge, but as soon as you do a hand shoots up and pulls you out. Laertes was hanging over the edge waiting for you this whole time! NICE. I mean it sucks because now you're falling, but you've got to give it to Laertes: that was a sweet move.

As you fall, you reach out and grab Laertes' leg. The both of you hang for a split second before the weight's too much for him and you both fall. You land in a rosebush, dazed. Stumbling to your feet, bloodied and bruised, you find you've both managed to keep hold of your swords.

Laertes catches your eye and points a finger towards his mouth. You wipe your mouth there with your sleeve. It comes away wet. You stare at your nice clothes, now all sticky with your own blood.

"Plenty more where that came from," you say, grinning.

Laertes charges at you, pressing hard, forcing you to jump backwards several times to avoid his attack. You stay close to the castle wall until you finally shout, "Enough!" and take several steps away from him.

"Do you yield?" Laertes shouts.

"Not even at controlled intersections," you say, and run towards him as fast as you can.

Laertes steels himself with a defensive stance. At the last moment, you veer slightly towards the castle wall, jump up, and run sideways along it. You pass clear over Laertes' head, your blades meeting briefly in the air between you. As you land behind him, he spins around to face you.

Laertes presses his attack again, and it takes all of your skill to prevent him from landing any strikes. You're forced to retreat, and passing a door, you kick it open and rush inside. There's a stairwell leading up, but Laertes is right behind you, forcing you to take the stairs backwards as you counter and parry his attacks.

As you climb the stairs, you realize you're entering back into the hallway where this fight started. Laertes' blade forces you back in front of the king and queen. He raises his sword to stab you but you shout "Stop!" and raise your hands above your head.

"Do you yield?" Laertes asks again, panting.

"Nope," you say. "You didn't let me finish. I was going to say, 'Stop! Stop decorating castles with chandeliers held up by ropes!'"

With your arms still raised, you flick your wrist and send your sword flying towards the chandelier. It slices through the support ropes cleanly, and the chandelier right above Laertes' head begins to fall. He looks up, sees what you're doing, and stares at you angrily. Without breaking your gaze, he sidesteps to the right, and the chandelier narrowly misses him.

"Nice try," he says.

"Thanks, but that wasn't —" you begin, as you catch your falling sword in a still-raised hand, "— really what —" you say, flicking your sword downwards and nicking Laertes on his shoulder, "— I was going for."

Another hit!

NICE! *Turn to 244*

84

"Oh. Okay," says Guildenstern.

"That's cool," says Rosencrantz.

You share an awkward silence, which lasts until you break it by asking your friends about their trip over. Was the boat ride fun?

"It was super fun! We met an AUTHOR on the way over," says Rosencrantz.

"An author!!" you say, excited. "I love authors! They're such creative minds, and so handsome too, unless they're women, in which case they're extremely the female equivalent of handsome," you say.

"Sexy," suggests Guildenstern.

"Well, I mean, not to say the men aren't sexy also," you reply, "for we all know male authors are, without exception, and I say this with all my marshalled heterosexuality, also way sexy."

Rosencrantz and Guildenstern nod. Rosencrantz gestures for the two of you to come closer, so that he can tell you a secret.

"When I stare at a male author, I can feel my heterosexuality crumbling," Rosencrantz whispers.

"Makes sense," you agree.

Anyway, at this point an author walks in the room!

TALK TO AUTHOR: *turn to 6*

86

You go home and nap. The next morning it rains, so you don't leave your room. Then the next morning after that the ground is all muddy, and you think maybe you'd leave footsteps that could be traced back to you, and anyway long story short several days have gone by and you haven't done a thing.

To continue doing nothing for another several days, *return to the top of this node and read it again*

Well, enough's enough! Time to go murder Claudius! *Turn to 142*

Go see Ophelia! She's smart; maybe she has some ideas on how to commit some good murders. *Turn to 189*

87

You find Claudius engrossed in prayer, which is completely silent, so you have no idea what he's praying about. Probably he's feeling guilty about the murder he did, huh? The murder of your dad? The murder that makes you so mad you want to commit the murder act on him?

You unsheathe your sword and raise it above his head.

But wait! If he's praying right now, then doesn't that mean that — according to religion — his soul is pure with all its sins confessed? If you kill him, he'll die with HIS soul more pure than that of your father when he died. Hardly seems fair, does it?

Wait, is it still "cool" to murder a jerk if they're praying? Is there a page in the Bible on that or something?

Better not kill him now at this perfect opportunity, because it's really important what happens to him after he dies: *turn to 133*

Hah hah, nice try, Claudius; prayer doesn't work that way. What time is it? Oh, wow, would you look at that, the day's barely started and already it's a quarter past STABS O'CLOCK: *turn to 148*

89

That's right! Why be a hero in your own story? Better to be a supporting character in somebody else's!

You go below-decks and wait. Eventually, a cannonball slices through the wall and into your belly and, rather than killing you instantly, it kills you gruesomely enough and slowly enough that when you finally die, 10 minutes later, you actually kinda wish it had happened instantly.

The shock of watching you die with a big ol' hole in your belly pushes Rosencrantz and Guildenstern into action, and they eventually capture the pirate ship in an amazing display of derring-do that I wish I could describe to you, but you're dead. I can't be seen talking to a corpse! That's crazy!

People will think I'm crazy!!

THE END

Turn to 326

90

"Correct!" shouts Horatio. "I'm sorry Fortinbras, but you sucked so hard at this. All hail Queen Ophelia!"

Be the new queen of Denmark: *turn to 534*

91

"Hey Mom, what's up?" you say. She jumps back from the curtain she was just admiring and not messing with at all.

"Hey Hamlet," she says. "Listen, you were a dick when you messed up Claudius's reading earlier."

"I didn't mess up anything!" you say. "He's the one who read the murdery options! If anyone messed up, it's YOU, because you married Dad's brother and that's messed up, MOM."

"What are you going to do: murder me?" your mom says. "ARE YOU GOING TO MURDER ME??"

"What?" you say, honestly confused. "No, why would you even think that? I—"

"Help!!" she screams at the top of her lungs.

"Mom, calm down," you say. "I'm not gonna kill you." She looks at the curtain and then at you. "Why are you walking around with a sword then?" she says, eyeing you suspiciously.

"I'M A PRINCE AND IT IS THE FASHION OF THE TIME," you say.

"How come it's got blood on it though?" she says.

"Um —" you say. "That's not blood, that's...stew?"

"Oh. Weird," she says.

Wow! This whole castle is super credulous!

Anyway, she tells you that she's tired of covering for your crazy behaviour all the time, and you tell her you're an adult and she's not the boss of you anymore! She says as long as you live under her roof it's her rules, so you shout that you're going to go on a trip with your friends to do whatever you want, and she says she hopes you do, because she's worried about you and thinks the travel could do you some good.

I guess you're going on a trip now! This is a good idea anyway, because they're going to notice Polonius missing eventually, and if you're not around you can avoid some awkward questions about where he is / who killed him / where the body is hidden. Plus your bros are always up for a trip anyway!

You leave and find Rosencrantz and Guildenstern nearby and you tell them you're gonna go party in England. And you're going to get there by boat. And do they want to come? If they do, please could they say what sort of vehicle they will be riding to England?

"PARRRRRTY BOOOAAAT!!" the three of you shout in unison.

Several hours later, you are partying on a boat!

Party boat: *turn to 93*

92

You're about halfway up when you meet your first pirate. You decide you have the advantage: you can always slide down the rope some to gain distance, while he can only climb up, which takes more time.

Before it comes to that, however, you brace your legs against the hull of *Calypso's Gale*. As the pirate approaches you, you push off with all your strength, sending you both into the darkness, hanging in space out above the ocean. You were ready for this; the pirate wasn't. You wield your sword and stab upwards, sending it cleanly through the surprised pirate's butt (hah hah, sweet). You hear him scream as he falls, and then you hear a small splash as he hits the ocean. Looking up, you see another pirate already climbing down to take his place.

The same trick isn't going to work twice, Hamlet!

Climb up higher to meet the pirate: *turn to 112*

Lure the pirate to slide down lower: *turn to 51*

93

As the boat sails for England, you catch sight of a huge army sailing towards Poland. There has to be an entire military corps on board! I'm serious, there's got to be 20,000 people all crammed onto a single ship.

The ship is too far away from you to communicate by talking or even shouting, but luckily you brought semaphore flags and are fully trained in their use. And, AS YOU KNOW, by holding up the two coloured flags in different positions, you can spell out letters of the alphabet! And in response, folks on the other ship can send messages back to you.

"Hey, Hamlet here! What's going on?" you say in semaphore.

"Hey Hamlet, we were sent by Prince Fortinbras from Norway — he's kinda a rough equivalent of you, come to think of it? Anyway, he's on board and we're all going to fight over some really terrible land that sucks," comes the signed reply.

"Really?" you signal.

"Yeah it's totally sucky land, but what are you gonna do? Fighters gonna fight," he signals, "and we're happy to do it."

"'Kay thanks," you reply in flag-talk.

Wow. Fortinbras and his army are ready to fight over something entirely useless, and the Polish are willing to defend it too! These people will fight and kill over NOTHING. And you can't even kill your uncle even though you have totally valid reasons!

Whoah dude, hold up! You start to feel inspired!

Be inspired in free verse, kicking it old school: *turn to 16*

Be inspired in rhyming couplets. . . AND EVERY COUPLET HAS THE SAME RHYME: *turn to 140*

94

"Correct!" shouts Horatio. "Fortinbras, you and Ophelia are now tied for first. Whoever answers my next question correctly will be the ruler of all of Denmark."

Horatio clears his throat.

"Final question: I am imagining a speculative future country that I will call the United States of America. This country is made out of many smaller states, each with their own name. Which speculative future state am I thinking of when I say that its land area is slightly less than twice the size of Denmark?"

Uh oh.

You slap in and say:

"**Texas.**" *Turn to 533*

"**Massachusetts.**" *Turn to 518*

"**Alaska.**" *Turn to 508*

96

You're underwater! Frantically, you swim towards the surface, but upon breaking it you find yourself suffocating. You sink back to the water and inhale, expecting to drown, but somehow it sustains you. It — it feels natural.

I hate to break this to you, but the temporal targeting has missed your old body by quite a bit. We don't have much time, so I'll give it to you straight.

Hamlet, your consciousness is now inside the body of a trout.

And that's not even the worst of it. Your mind is collapsing, unable to be sustained by the simpler neural structure of the fishy body you now inhabit. I'm sorry, but there's just not enough neurons here to sustain you. I'm really not sure how much longer you — as a person — will last. It'll be minutes at best, seconds at worst, but either way, it won't be long before everything that made you who you are is lost forever.

In the meantime, Hamlet, do you want to swim upstream or downstream?

Hamlet?

...Hamlet?

THE END

Turn to 390

97

"I'm gonna open it," you say. This is what you read:

Dear King of England,

It's me, Claudius, the King of Denmark! Listen, we get along pretty well, right? And both our countries are in pretty good shape. Anyway, it'd be really convenient for me (and it would help both our countries STAY in good shape) if you could kill Hamlet for me real quick. It's not that big a deal, just kill him, okay? Cool? Cool. P.S. I'm 100% serious please kill him right now.

You and Rosencrantz and Guildenstern stare at each other for a long moment. Looks like this whole time while you were planning to kill Claudius, he was also planning to kill you!

"Dude, are you scoping this letter's CHOICE ASSASSINATION ORDERS?" asks Rosencrantz.

"I told you, man! I TOLD YOU ABOUT CLAUDIUS," Guildenstern yells.

"Maybe somehow he...he heard my raps from last night?" you ask.

Figure out a plan with Rosencrantz and Guildenstern:
turn to 28

99 Hah, nice try! Your friends have to choose their OWN adventure here. You don't get to make life-or-death choices for them! If you want to do that, you should play my other book, *God: the Adventure! Decide How Each of Billions of Individual Stories End! Fun at First, Tedious Soon After (So Many Lives Are Depressingly Similar).*

PERSONALLY though, I hope Rosencrantz and Guildenstern survived, and I think that probably that counts for something?

Suddenly lightning strikes the water below! A huge roar of thunder deafens you, but in that brief instant, the world is illuminated.

You see your young crew of almost 20 (both by count and by age), cutlasses at the ready, fighting as they climb. Pirates swarm down the lines, battling them for sport. Above them, on deck, they're being cheered by a row of pirates. And at the very bow of the ship, looking down with a spyglass, stands the captain. He's got a fancy hat and a parrot on his shoulder: the works. And he's staring right at you through the storm.

The darkness of the storm is restored moments later. You grimly resume your climb. One way or another, you're going to end this.

CONTINUE CLIMBING, ATTACK PIRATES! *Turn to 92*

100 Gertrude looks at you and smiles.

"Did you know," she says, "that not only have you lost, but you've lost in one of the fastest ways possible? I'm actually kind of impressed." She moves her queen to take the pawn she was threatening.

"Qxf7#," she writes. You've just lost the game, Ophelia! I'm gonna give you 15 points for losing so quickly, but I don't think that's gonna help, like, at all!!

CHECKMATE: *turn to 309*

101 "What?" she says, surprised.

You repeat yourself. "I said a hip, hop, a hippie, a hippie to the hip hip hop—" Without missing a beat, Ophelia jumps in with "— and you don't stop the rock it to the bang bang boogie say up jumped the boogie to the rhythm of the boogie the beat!"

You now know for certain she's faking her craziness, because she'd never joke about tight rhymes. And she knows you're faking it too, because while those rhymes were insane, you'd have to be in full command of your mental faculties to produce them!

And it's perfect, because anyone listening in would simply think you two are making crazy noises to each other! They would not realize that what they hear is just a test...of SANITY ITSELF.

Ophelia has joined your party!

Tell Ophelia about your murder book plan: *turn to 314*

102

You give the order to turn around and face the pirates head-on.

"In irons?" your first mate asks, alarmed.

You're not entirely sure what that means, but it sounds kind of badass.

"Y-yes?" you say.

"Aye" comes the reply, and *Vesselmania IV* comes about. Unfortunately, as you have ordered that the pirate ship be faced head-on, and the wind is at their back, this means that you are now facing directly into the wind.

Your sails are not designed to work in reverse like this.

They catch the wind but are unable to produce enough drive to maintain any momentum. You coast to a stop and begin drifting backwards, travelling not much faster than the sea itself.

Before you can give any orders to get out of this situation, *Calypso's Gale* catches up with you, comes alongside, and blows you into the sky! It's fatal, which is a not-actually-that-fancy way of saying "you totally die when this happens."

Sorry dude, fish are eating your body now! They're like, "Om nom nom!"

THE END

Turn to 488

103

The gravedigger sings about being young and in love.

"He's singing while he digs a grave!" you say.

"Um, yeah," says Horatio. "His job is to dig graves, so he's used to it."

"Whoah!!" you say. This whole thing is seriously blowing your mind!

The gravedigger sings about being old now, and the tune is pretty catchy, actually! While he's busy digging this grave, he digs into a pre-existing grave (remember that in our time period it's not like that is especially weird or awful) and digs something up. He tosses it behind him.

Hey! There is a skull here!

Look skull: *turn to 118*

105

Anyway, you decide to play dumb. “Hamlet? Who ees Hamlet?” you say, elbowing Horatio, who’s standing beside you. Horatio rolls his eyes.

“Why the accent?” Horatio sighs. “You didn’t have it a second ago.”

“Hamlet is the prince who went to England because he was crazy,” says the gravedigger. “He’ll get less crazy there, or he won’t, but either way it won’t matter because everyone’s crazy in England!”

“Racism,” says Horatio.

“How did zee Prince Hamlet go — how do you say — crazy?” you ask.

“Very strangely,” he replies. Oh God, you two are going to go at it again, aren’t you? Oh God. You are.

“How strangely?” you ask.

“By losing his mind,” he says.

“On what grounds?” you ask. HEY. STOP SETTING HIM UP.

“Why, right here in Denmark,” he says. HAH HAH HAH, listen I’m cutting you off.

The rest of your conversation is censored, but at some point he gestures to one of the skulls you were looking at earlier and volunteers that that’s the skull of Yorick, once the jester to the king, now dead and buried 23 years.

“He poured a flagon of Rhenish on my head once,” says the gravedigger. Check this out: you are really interested in hearing about either one of those things!

Talk about Yorick: *turn to 404*

Talk about Rhenish: *turn to 113*

106

That’s a really good idea. Huh! Nicely done. You push out from the ship, use your legs as a battering ram, and smash your way inside through a porthole. You manage somehow to hit the deck, roll, and leap to your feet in one impressively smooth motion.

Unfortunately, there’s nobody around to see it, as everyone is above-decks engaged in battle. And you’ve landed in the captain’s quarters! Around you are the accoutrements of command, the ship’s log, and — YES, a sword. A much nicer sword, actually, than the one you started this journey with. You decide to take it.

You are now wielding the fancy sword!

You don’t care that you lost your other sword. It sucks now. You kick down the door (it has a handle but things were just going that way) and take the ladder to the top deck. You push open the trapdoor and climb out. In front of you is an epic battle: your crew taking on two, sometimes three pirates at a time. It’s amazing. Each success seems to fuel them further, each pirate body hitting the deck only adding to their experience points.

You can almost see them levelling up as you watch, and it’s like all their perks are being invested in battle techniques. Suddenly, you feel a cold tap on your shoulder. Turning around, you find yourself face to face with the pirate captain.

You both raise your swords as you leap into your duelling stances. A pause, and then you rush each other, swords clashing. You thrust and parry back and forth until a moment comes when your swords catch each other, and in that sudden silence you stare across your blades into each other's eyes.

"You fight like a dairy farmer," he says.

"How appropriate. You fight like a — OW!" you say, as he slices at your arm, cutting you. It was superficial this time. You're lucky, dude!

The pirate captain gloats at drawing first blood, pointing to you and calling you a bunch of very unkind names that I'm not going to say here because I don't want you to throw down this book so you can try to find and murder this pirate in real life! Just take my word for it: the things he says about you are that bad.

On the plus side: while he gloats, there's an opening! You should attack!

Attack the hand he's pointing at you with! *Turn to 48*

Attack the face he's laughing at you with! *Turn to 245*

Attack the shoulders he's giving structure to his stupid upper body with! *Turn to 231*

108

Your first mate shouts, straining to be heard over the gale. "Sailors don't actually speak like that!"

"Okay!" you shout in reply, and he nods.

"Pretend I didn't say that yo ho ho stuff!" *Turn to 45*

109

The gravedigger and you chat back and forth. Here's a snippet of the conversation you have.

"Whose grave is this?" you say.

"It's mine," he says.

"I thought it was yours, because you're the one lying in it," you say.

Really, Hamlet? He's not lying in it, he's standing in it, digging, and if you're going for a "lying down / lying untruth" pun then I'm sorry but it's not going to wor—

"And you're lying out of it, so it's not yours!!" says the gravedigger, super proud of this dumb wordplay. He goes on: "Actually, I'm not lying, it really is mine."

"But you are lying," you say before I can stop you, "because you're in it and saying it's yours, but you're alive and graves aren't for the living! Ah hah! Got you there!"

RIVETING. This back-and-forth goes back and forth, and eventually it comes out that he's digging a grave for a young woman, and you — as you are an uncouth brute — ask how long he's had this job before you even ask him his name, and he says he's been working as a gravedigger since the day Hamlet was born.

Hey, that's you! What a crazy coincidence!! You should probably say something?

Tell the gravedigger you're Hamlet: *turn to 216*

Play dumb: *turn to 105*

110

"...yes. That is exactly what happened," you say.

"What about Rosencrantz and Guildenstern?" he asks. "They...um, died," you say. "The king wanted to...murder me...and he got them to carry a letter telling the English king to kill me! Yes, that's it — and so I...secretly...replaced that note with a forgery that told him to kill Rosencrantz and Guildenstern instead! They're dead now, because, as I said earlier in my letter, the pirates left after they captured me. Yes! Everything fits together nicely!"

It's a good lie: close to the truth, so it won't be hard to keep straight!

"Whoah," Horatio says. "Bro, that's cold. What did Rosencrantz and Guildenstern do to deserve that?"

"Um, yes, that is a reasonable question, and the reasonable answer is that they...carried the letter from Claudius...on purpose? And they were allied with him all along and...I trust them as much as I trust snakes?"

"Huh," says Horatio.

"Oh, and I would TOTALLY KILL ANYONE who was secretly working for my stepdad!" you say, making significant eye contact with him.

"Huh," says Horatio, perfectly neutrally. Darn these even-handed, noncommittal responses that tell you nothing!

You've been walking as you talk, and you and Horatio find yourselves in the graveyard. It's close to the river everyone takes their drinking water from, which I guess kinda explains why people act so crazy around here (SPOILER ALERT: water contamination) (SPOILER ALERT: this is gross).

There are two gravediggers here. Wait, hold up: one of them is leaving — off to have his own adventures, no doubt! Do you ever think about that, Hamlet? About all the people you pass in the street and how they're each the star of their own little narrative? How it's weird that people who you'll never talk to are off having their own lives, building their own stories, and isn't it crazy that from THEIR point of view, you'd be a minor character, entirely forgettable?

Well, it's true, and in this gravedigger's story you play the role of "GUY WHO SHOWS UP AND TOOTS JUST AS I LEAVE."

You toot. He leaves.

The remaining gravedigger is singing!

YEA
NAY

Listen to his singing: *turn to 103*

Join in with his singing: *turn to 168*

112

You climb up to meet the pirate.

Waving your sword around, you prevent him from climbing down any closer, but you can't climb up higher to reach him. He raises his arm, sword at the ready, as if he's going to hit something as hard as he can. But what? You're clearly out of range of his sw—

Wait a minute. He's going to cut the rope beneath him! You'll fall to your death!!

Screaming, you throw your sword at the pirate, roll a natural 20, and do a critical hit right in his eye. Your blade sticks out of his skull. It's amazing. He screams and lets go of both sword and rope as he falls.

"Looks like you saw my point," you say.

You're close to the top, but you've lost your sword and you see one more pirate hoisting himself over the railing and onto your rope.

I don't know how you're going to pull this one out, Hamlet!

Push out from the ship, use your legs as a battering ram, and smash your way inside through a porthole: *turn to 106*

113

"Ah, you refer to any of several white wines from the Rhine River valley in Germany!" you say.

"Yes," says the gravedigger, "and though it was many years ago, I do recall the wine being sweet."

"That makes sense, as Rhenish wines do tend to fall on the sweet side of things," you say. "Did you know that grapes have been grown there since Roman times and their development was even promoted by Charlemagne?"

"I did not!" says the gravedigger. "But did YOU know that there are many different varieties of grapes grown in the region, which allows it to support a wide and varied viticultural output?"

"I was not aware of that," you reply, continuing, "though I was aware that typically it's the grapes that are grown closest to the Rhine that produce the best wines, as the richer soils there allow for a more complex, subtle flavouring."

"Yes," says the gravedigger. "I knew that, as I have tasted Rhenishes of infinite subtlety, of most excellent finish. I have chugged them down my throat a thousand times."

Suddenly, you hear a noise! What a relief; I was really tired of hearing about wine!

Investigate noises: *turn to 120*

114

You're about to reach for a sword when a huge flash of purple-blue light appears, knocking you, Laertes, and everyone else to the ground. As you scramble to your feet, you look into the fading light and see a silhouette of...

Yourself?

"What year is this?" the other you demands. "The year!!"

"Um, well, it's sort of an anachronistic amalga—" Claudius begins to say, but the other you interrupts him. Hold on, I'm gonna call this other you "Hamlet 2" so things don't get confusing. Alright, so Hamlet 2 begins to reply but — wait, you know what? I think I'm gonna call him "Hamlet 2000" instead, because that sounds way more badass.

No, maybe it's dumb. Okay, Hamlet 2.

"Future Hamlet"? "Hamlets"? "Hamletter"?

"Hamlettest"??

Okay, okay. Hamlet 2. For real.

"Wait," says Hamlet 2000. "This seems familiar. You want to kill me, right Claudius? You and Laertes are here to kill me? I mean, us?" Claudius kinda nods and Futu-Hamlet looks down at his own body in approval.

"Nice," he says. Future Hamlet kicks one of the swords over to you and kicks the other one up into his hands.

The two of you crouch into ready positions. "Let's go," Temporal Hamlet says. "Two against two."

"No fair!" Laertes says. "I only signed up to battle one Hamlet at a time, and it's supposed to be two against one!"

Hamlet of Christmas Yet to Come nods. "Right. Okay, I can fix that," he says. He then spins in a circle, swinging his sword like a hammer thrower — you know the guys at the Olympics with a heavy ball on the end of a rope, and they spin and throw it as far as they can? That's what Hamlet 2K is doing, only he's keeping as much eye contact as possible with Laertes as he spins, so he looks a bit like a dancer, but when he lets go of his sword a few rotations later he sends it straight through Laertes' head, grip and all, and it exits cleanly out the other side, where it embeds itself into the wall.

Laertes falls to the floor, totally and 100% dead. "There," Other Hamlet says. "Two against one." "That's even less fair than before!" says Claudius.

Hamlet From a Future Time smiles at Claudius. "So kill me," he says.

Attack! *Turn to 218*

TOWN
CRIER

116

"Even if we take all the ghost-creation issues out of the equation," you go on, "there's still the matter of revenge, on its own, not being an ethical act."

"Not to mention the complicated issues surrounding vigilante capital punishment," the ghost says.

"Exactly. I'm sorry, Ghost King Hamlet, but I don't think this is a super rad idea," you say. Prince Hamlet nods in agreement.

"Okay, yeah, that makes sense. Okay. Well. Do what you can to punish him for my murder though, cool?" the ghost says.

You agree to work to uncover proof of the murder and then work within the legal system to achieve a fair punishment for Claudius.

"Sounds reasonable!" says the ghost. "Alright! I guess I'm out. Thanks for the talk; I found it really useful!"

You and Hamlet do some legwork and track down where Claudius got the poison. The poison-monger identifies Claudius in a lineup. Even though he's the king, Claudius is not above the law, and the case goes to court. The prosecution has no witnesses to the actual murder, but means, motive, opportunity, and tons of circumstantial evidence.

Claudius is found guilty of regicide and sentenced to 30 years in prison. He's sent to Verona, where he won't get any special treatment from the two gentlemen drafted to guard his cell. Hamlet's father is still dead and this won't bring him back, but on the other hand, he's also a ghost and you can talk to him at night. It's a pretty fair verdict, measure for measure!

So! Turns out you scored a possible 100 out of 100 in LEGAL JUSTICE POINTS but unfortunately you only got, like, a 3 in ADVENTURE POINTS. Man, that's baloney! That's what you get for working within the pre-existing legal system instead of employing unpredictable vigilante adventurism, am I right??

THE END

Turn to 517

117

As Claudius is distracted by Horatio dying, you send your sword through his heart.

Claudius looks at the sword sticking out of his chest, then up at you. "Sorry," he says. "But if I'm to be hung, I'd prefer it to be in the court of public opinion." He then pushes you aside and takes a step towards the crowd.

"Look at what this usurper has done to your king!" he shouts. "You are all witness to this murder most foul, in the sports sense! By that I mean it wasn't fair." You hear murmurs of people saying "Yeah, cheap shot" and "I can't believe he stabbed his own stepfather."

He then PULLS THE SWORD OUT OF HIS OWN CHEST (super gross) and all this blood comes out. He lifts the sword above his head and says, "It's also foul in the gross-nasty sense. Avenge me, everyone!" and then falls backwards onto the royal tiles, dead.

You turn to face the crowd, which is now advancing on you. Laertes is advancing too.

You make the only choice you can: you run. You run all the way down to the dock, hop into the water, and swim out to *Calypso's Gale*. Climbing on board, you explain that things didn't go well down there, and you've KINDA turned the entire country against you.

Rosencrantz and Guildenstern stare out at the shore.

"Bummer," says Rosencrantz. "Well, I guess we can start new lives here on the high seas as awesome pirates, since we already know we're awesome at it."

"Or we can fire our cannons and destroy the town," suggests Guildenstern. "Then you could be king of a destroyed town."

START NEW LIVES AS PIRATES: *turn to 187*

DESTROY THE TOWN: *turn to 220*

118

You keep your distance from the gravedigger, but look at the skull intently.

"That skull had a tongue in it once," you say to Horatio.

"A-yup," says Horatio.

"It had jowls too," you say.

"Yeah probably," says Horatio.

"Maybe it was a politician's skull! Ooh! Or a courtier! Lord Such-A-One or whoever! And look, that guy's throwing it around like it's not even a thing!" you say.

"Lord Such-And-Such, you mean," sighs Horatio, as the gravedigger digs up another skull. There are now two skulls here! The other skull seems pretty interesting too.

You close your eyes and think, very clearly, "look other skull." Then you open your eyes and examine the other skull intently. I'm not gonna lie, from this distance it definitely looks a lot like the first skull. You're fascinated by it though!

"Maybe that other skull was a lawyer's skull!" you say, nudging Horatio. "Look at him now! Where's his impressive lawyer tricks now, huh? His fancy rhetoric for the judge and jury?"

"He's dead," says Horatio.

"Why doesn't he sue this guy for assault after he dug up his skull with a shovel if he's such a fancy lawyer?" you say.

"I'd have to say...it's probably because he's dead," says Horatio.

"Maybe it was a landowner's skull instead! Maybe he owned all this land and had all this complicated accounting for it. Hah! Is one of those accounting rules that his empty skull now gets filled up with dirt??" you say.

"Yes, I believe that's generally what happens when you die," says Horatio.

You stare at him wildly, then back to the skull, then back to Horatio. Then you stare at the skull for a bit.

"Listen," Horatio says, "maybe you want to talk to the gravedigger for a while? I'm sure he'd find your viewpoint absolutely novel and riveting."

TALK TO GRAVEDIGGER: *turn to 109*

120 You, Horatio, and the gravedigger investigate the noises and discover that they were caused by Gertrude (your mom!), Claudius (your new dad that you swore you'd murder!), Laertes (Ophelia's brother! You haven't really hung out with him that much actually!), a priest (priests are ordained ministers of the church!), and a coffin (coffins are what people get buried in; dude, you should know this).

It seems like Gertrude was — screaming? Wailing? Weird.

You elbow your friend. "Hey," you say. "Look how sucky that coffin is, look how small this ceremony is. It must have been someone who killed themselves. You know what'd be hilarious? If we stayed and watched."

"Listen...Hamlet, there's something you should know," Horatio says.

"Shh!" you say. "Look, that's Laertes!" you say to the gravedigger. You pause and stare at him intently. "Yeah, he's pretty rad," you say.

"Hamlet," Horatio says, "don't you wonder why Laertes is at a funeral? Maybe if he's here it means it might be someone close to him who die—"

You cut him off. "I CAN'T EAVESDROP ON PEOPLE IN THEIR MOST PRIVATE MOMENTS OF GRIEF IF YOU KEEP TRYING TO HAVE A SERIOUS CONVERSATION ABOUT A LIFE-OR-DEATH MATTER WITH ME," you hiss at him.

Turning your attention back to Laertes, you see him arguing with the priest, asking for more rites. More rites, he says! But the priest says he's done all the rites he should do already and then some. Since this person committed suicide (called it!), they don't get as many rites. "If we do any more rites, we'll profane the blessed souls of the other people buried here," he says.

You, Horatio, and the gravedigger all wince as you glance at the skulls he's dug up. Um...whoops?

Laertes continues to argue with the priest. "Well fine, then go ahead and lay her here, jerk-a-rama priest!" Laertes says. "My sis will be an angel in heaven while you're burning in hell!" They lower her body into the grave.

Wow, he's really upset! Wait...sister? OPHELIA'S DEAD?!

Ophelia's dead?! *Turn to 153*

121 You say, "Maybe this wasn't such a good idea" to Horatio and the gravedigger, say your goodbyes, and go home, avoiding a big scene and likely an even bigger stupid fight. You are the better man here, Hamlet, and I applaud you. As a token of my appreciation, I am giving you a Potion of Not Grieving Anymore Because Feelings Are Boring.

Your inventory bag suddenly feels heavier!

Okay. So we're still on track for tomorrow though, right? You're still going to go to the court and goad Claudius into admitting his plan to murder you, and then you'll claim the throne with the help of *Calypso's Gale*.

For now, you've got to deal with your feelings about Ophelia. She was always really important to you, whether you were dating or not. She was smart, attractive, clever, funny — she was great, Hamlet, and now she's dead.

Tell you what: grieving sucks, and you've been mopey enough in this story. Why not drink the contents of the bottle I gave you?

Drink the Potion of Not Grieving Anymore Because Feelings Are Boring: *turn to 177*

No, I want to explore this feeling, I want to put my flag on it, I want to set up camp and build a new home here in Griefland: *turn to 362*

122

You go to bed and spend about eight hours lying unconscious while you hallucinate. Wait, humans call that "dreaming," right?

Right! Because we're all humans here!

So you "dream" (it still sounds weird when I say it) about dogs with spiders for mouths, which is scary, but then it kinda shifts into a situation where you're back at school, only it's NOT your school, and your best friend is your teacher, only he's NOT your best friend, and before you can get your bearings it shifts again into this weird sex thing that has the effect of making me wish that I, as narrator, wasn't quite so omniscient.

Anyway, after a while it's tomorrow!

Greet the new day: *turn to 178*

123

"WHAT?! You POISONED the cup?!" you yell. Your mother looks towards Claudius, shocked. "Get him," she says, and then shoves her fingers down her own throat, trying to induce vomiting. It works. It actually works...explosively well?

You advance on Claudius with your sword. "I came here to assume the throne and get distracted by sword fights," you say, "and I'm all out of getting distracted by sword fights."

"It was an accident!" Claudius says. "I only meant to poison YOU!" He glances frantically towards Laertes. "Finish him!" he shouts.

You spin and see Laertes looking at you, his sword still drawn. "Et tu, Laertes?" you say, and though you don't know it, you've just approximately quoted another exciting book in this series, *Cowards Die Many Times Before Their Deaths: The Valiant Never Taste of Death But Once! You Are Julius Caesar and You Must Now Choose Your Own Adventure While You Deal with That*, available at a bookseller near you.

Laertes hesitates. "Hamlet, the tip of my sword is poisoned, but it was

Claudius's idea," he says. "Look, I think things...I think things kind of got out of hand. Claudius made me blame you for a lot of stuff that's happened recently. He made me want to kill you. I don't know."

He pauses, looking at your mother, who is on her hands and knees, now just throwing up bile.

"I don't think I feel that way anymore," he says. He offers you his sword.

"Keep it," you say. Reaching into your pocket, you grab the cherry bombs you created secretly while on *Calypso's Gale*. Yes, secretly! I didn't even tell you that you'd created them, and you know why? Because then you would've wanted a "use cherry bombs on [WHOEVER YOU'RE TALKING TO AND/OR EVERY SINGLE THING IN THE ROOM]" option and we'd never have made it this far, and don't even look at me like you don't know that's one million percent true, Hamlet!

"Besides," you say, as you light the cherry bombs and toss them out the window, signalling for *Calypso's Gale* to start firing her cannons at the castle, "everyone knows you shouldn't bring a sword to a cannon fight."

Claudius stares at you, uncomprehending.

"Laertes! Horatio! Assorted bystanders! Now is a really good time to be somewhere else!" you shout as you rush towards your mother. Supporting her on your shoulder, you begin to lead her out of the castle. Claudius tries to push past you too.

"No. You wait here," you say, impaling him through the chest and pinning him to the wall. He tries to pull the sword free, so you pick up the other swords Osric offered you earlier, now lying forgotten on the ground, and stab each of his hands into the castle walls as well.

You support your mother down the hallway. But as you reach the stairs leading down to the exit, your mother pushes away from you and stands uncertainly, finally supporting herself with one hand against the wall. She turns to look back at the impaled Claudius, and wipes the vomit from her mouth with the sleeve of her dress. Claudius looks up and meets her gaze.

"Stick around," she says, and you love her more than ever.

THE END

Turn to 107

124

"No man, I'm good for swordfights," you say, and Osric leaves.

Nicely done! Alright, now all we need to do is expose the king. To the royal court! It's just up ahead, actually!

As you step forward, Horatio puts his hand on your chest to stop you. "Look," he says, "I know you've been different since you got back from England. And I know you don't really trust me, though I don't know why. But when you declined that fight, I saw a glimmer of the old you. I want you to know that I'm still your friend. And if I can help you now, I wish you'd let me."

You search his eyes.

"Please," he says.

"Okay," you say, "alright." And you bring him up to speed on what really

Though I leave the mortal realm with business unfinished, I refuse to linger on as a mere shadow of my corporeal self. There is no desire in my heart to tarry here beyond death. If I cannot march onward as flesh and bone then I would rather cease to exist at all!
I hereby shed all bonds to this world, and disappear now into the void of...
Sexy Ghost Beach Volleyball Tournament
This Way!
Wait, no no no, undo. I meant to say that being a ghost is super cool and I want to stay--

happened, telling him all about Rosencrantz and Guildenstern and *Calypso's Gale*, all waiting on your signal.

"I'm in," Horatio says. "Let's do this."

"Let's," you say, and you kick in the throne room door.

ENTER THRONE ROOM: *turn to 61*

126 You open your mouth to say that, but whoever's hiding behind the curtain is trying to save your mom, and in bursting out from behind the curtain somehow manages to impale himself on the sword hanging from your belt. He sort of rolls out and stands up and trips and anyway would you look at that he's seriously hilt-deep in sword. By the time you notice him there, it's already too late.

"Polonius?" you say, looking down at your (ex-)girlfriend's father. Wow. I'm serious, Hamlet; he's really run the sword right through himself.

"Lo, I am so darn clumsy," he says. "Just like my twin brother, Corambis." Then he dies.

"Bleh," he says.

This is pretty messed up, and your mom is freaking out about this dead body. You promise to have someone come get rid of it, and on your way out the door, you bump into your bros Rosencrantz and Guildenstern. "You wanna get out of here?" you say, and they concede that they would like to party on a boat. You know what? That sounds nice. Sort of give everyone space, you know?

"There's a boat headed for England in just a few hours!" you say. You know this because boats to England are kind of a big deal.

You send some servants to clean up crazy ol' dead Polonius and apologize to your mother for you, and pack your bags. A few hours later, you and your bros are partying on a boat!

PARTY BOAT!! *Turn to 151*

127 The crowd gasps. "Is this true?" someone shouts.

"It is," you say, "and I have proof. Here's the original letter he wrote and sealed with the royal mark, instructing the King of England to murder me! Here, you can read it right now," you say, passing it to someone in the crowd. "When you're done with it, pass it around clockwise to the person next to you. Don't worry, I'll wait until you've all had a chance to read it."

You wait while the assembled courtiers each read it, one by one. They're not the fastest readers in the world, and it actually takes a full 20 minutes for everyone to have a turn. Come on, guys. But when everyone's finally done reading it, you can sense the change in the mood of the crowd. They definitely seem to be on your side! Claudius looks nervous. You raise your sword. He looks even more nervous now.

"Defend yourself, incestuous pretender to the throne!!" you shout. Claudius picks up his sword and drops into a defensive stance.

SWORDFIGHT CLAUDIUS! FINALLY! *Turn to 67*

128

Okay. You talk out loud to the empty room and what do you say? I'll tell you what you say: you say you wish your skin could literally melt off your body, revealing a skeleton that gives a double thumbs-down before crumbling into dust. You say that you thought your mom really loved your dad, but now that she's married Claudius less than a month after Dad's death, either love itself is fake or she was faking love, and either way it doesn't matter because you've lost faith in your own mother. You say to the empty room, in all seriousness, that you want to kill yourself.

Whoah. Bro. This book just got REAL.

KILL YOURSELF: *turn to 134*

DON'T KILL YOURSELF: *turn to 69*

129

"Hey Claudius, does it smell in here?" you say, striking his sword.

"A lot of things smell in here," he says, gesturing briefly to the crowd gathered to watch you fight. You glance over and see a bunch of people smiling and shrugging, as if to say, "Wow he's got my number, that's for sure!"

"Okay that's true," you say, "but the point is, you are smelly!" Claudius shrugs.

"I hope that damages your self-esteem!!" you shout. It is not the most super-effective insult ever deployed.

You continue attacking, but you notice that Claudius seems to have learned your fighting style, and the more you fight, the better he gets at it. Horatio seems to be having the same problem. You're both losing. Finally, your back's up against the wall, and Claudius knocks the sword out of your hand.

"If I die, I'll come back as a ghost and ask someone to kill you for me!" you say in desperation.

"Who," says Claudius (and at this point he's stabbing you in the chest), "would be stupid enough to do that?"

"Um, ME, obviously," you say, and then you're dead, so if you're keeping track, the last word you ever said was "obviously" and your first word ever was "Look" when you were a baby and together they make the phrase "Look, obviously" and that's almost a sentence so that's pretty cool! I know it's kinda weak, but I'm reaching here to find some Accomplishments in Hamlet's Life, okay?

THE END

Turn to 539

CLARK
BEAR AND BIRD ENTHUSIAST
PEQUIN
"A GOOD SMALL BRO"
GRAN

131

King Claudius goes on to tell you, in so many words, to buck up, stop dressing in black, stick around for a while, and have a little fun. He says all the feelings you're having are boring and wimpy. Your mom echoes his sentiments. Dude. Your own mom just called you a wimp.

You agree to stick around in Denmark for a while, they leave, and you're suddenly alone. Woo! You're finally alone, Hamlet! What are you going to do?

Talk to yourself about how your life is in ruins and how everything just suuuuucks: *turn to 128*

Stand around quietly until something happens: *turn to 69*

132

The wind at your back fills your two sails to capacity and even beyond, but I'm sorry — it's not nearly enough to outrun the pirates. You've got two sails. They've got 12. The math just doesn't work out.

Calypso's Gale sidles up beside you, fires all of hers guns at once, and you explode in disgrace.

THE END

Turn to 307

133

Okay. You walk away from the perfect chance for murder and go see your mom instead. Don't worry — I get it. You're afraid that if you kill Claudius the book will end, and you don't want it to be over yet! I have nobody to blame but myself, I suppose. I wrote an adventure that was simply too awesome!

Anyway — onward, to adventure!! To an adventure that is so awesome I hope it never ends and this book becomes a prison for both of us!

Go talk to your mom: *turn to 24*

134

While you're busy doing that, your friend Horatio bumps into you and tells you:

a) he's in town for your dad's funeral / mom's wedding, and they served leftover appetizers from one at the other,

b) ghosts are real,
c) he's seen one and so have a bunch of other guys,
d) it keeps showing up at the same time,
e) he's pretty sure it's the ghost of your dad, and
f) what the heck, are you killing yourself right now as I'm speaking?? You are, aren't you? What the heck, bro??

You are now a ghost.

Haunt Horatio: *turn to 188*

See if you can find your Ghost Dad: *turn to 196*

136

"You have bested me in an honourable game of trivia and come out the better for it," you say, offering your hand. "Congratulations."

Fortinbras looks at you for a moment before accepting your hand. "Thanks. You were really fast at slapping a table."

"Yep," you reply. "Well, good luck with Denmark! Everyone I know is dead so I'm...gonna go move somewhere else now."

"Okay, cool," says Fortinbras, and you're out. You go home to collect your things. Staring at your packed bags, you make a split-second decision to move to Italy, because you heard it's pretty. Turns out it is! While in Italy, you enroll in university (they have a DUDES-ONLY policy, but you have a GET AROUND SEXISM BY DRESSING SUCH THAT YOU PASS AS A DUDE policy, so it works out well) and, after that, you start a successful business making awesome inventions while also painting in your spare time. Long story short, you know that Renaissance that's everyone's been talking about?

ALL YOU.

THE END

P.S. Your final score is really high, because I didn't mention it but while you were in Italy you invented flying machines! You use them to fly back to Denmark and shoot Fortinbras! Oh wow, you also invented guns!

Turn to 432

137

You make a break for it, screaming like a little baby, and Horatio does the same.

"Holy cow holy cow HOLY COW," you say, jumping over a boulder and hiding behind it.

"Man, that was INTENSE," Horatio says, a hand on his chest. You both sit for a moment, each trying to catch your breath. "Hey, let's go back and see if he's still there!" Horatio says.

Go back and check out the ghost again: *turn to 78*

138

"Um, just kidding?" you say.

"Oh phew," says your dad. "That's good. If that had been the case, then I would've demanded that you murder Claudius at once. That way he could be a ghost too, and I could sit down with him and ask him why he thought what he did was appropriate, and after hearing his reasons hopefully we could come to some understanding."

He sighs, wistfully. "It would be nice to be able to do that now, rather than having to wait until decades from now when he dies of natural causes."

"Good news!" you say.

Tell Dad they did actually get married: *turn to 75*

139

You clear your throat, tilt your head, put on a grin, and give your dad a double thumbs-up.

"I promise I'ma kill him," you say.

Your dad seems satisfied.

You have begun quest Kill Claudius! It's worth 3500 experience points! That's pretty good!

Leave it there and return to Horatio: *turn to 80*

140

You ask Rosencrantz and Guildenstern to drop a beat, and they oblige. You hold out two hands in front of you and start throwing up signs.

This is the science you lay down on them:

My name is Hamlet, yo, you better check this composition:
Just peeped an awesome army boat that of its own volition
Is led by my man Fortinbras (a man of great ambition)
Who lessens me whenever we're seen in juxtaposition

And who's taken for himself this chosen military mission
But also lacks my frankly odd particular condition
Of being told just who to kill by ghostly apparition
And being told to kill a man who by his own admission
Has sent my dear departed regal dad to the mortician
Now Fortinbras goes off to war and just to requisition
Land so sad and barren that any given tactician
Would think him crazy; well, you see that this new proposition
Suggests to me quite clearly my apparent opposition
To this Revenge Your Dad and Kill Your New Dad expedition
When I have motives valid, beyond any inquisition
Is weak and dumb, so I've got to end this predisposition
Towards inaction that I have; my stupid inhibition
Must be gotten over fast cuz I got to reposition
Myself to kill my new dad right away. And in addition,
And though I know this carries no small risk of repetition
And saying this out loud will only add to your suspicion
From now on the only things that I will bring into fruition
Are the bloody gory parts of my own personal cognition
That is to say: only thoughts regarding the commission
Of the brutal death of Claudius. No more exposition!

And you're out! Rosencrantz and Guildenstern clap and compliment you on your flow, although they suggest the lyrics might, hah hah, make people think you want to kill the king. Isn't that crazy, they say. Hah hah hah.

Aw man, that reminds you: you forgot to rhyme with "sedition"! You're miffed because it would've worked REALLY WELL!

CONTINUE PARTYING ON A BOAT: *turn to 159*

142

You wait until it's 2 a.m., planning to sneak into Claudius's room and give him the ol' stabby-stab, but on your way there you find him passed out in the hallway. There's a bottle of booze in his hand! He really is a cartoon drunk!

This is gonna be real easy!

You hold your hand over his mouth so he can't scream and slit his throat and he's dead within the minute. Ta-da! You leave quietly, making sure not to be seen, and head down to the shore to wash your blood-soaked hands and your blood-soaked clothes. The ocean water cleans off the blood quickly, which is great because you heard it was hard to get out damned blood spots. Turns out, nope, it's actually really easy! You're glad you stayed cool and rational and didn't freak out at all during this process. Good job, champ!

You walk home in your wet clothes, change into adorable pyjamas, get into bed, and fall asleep. Content in the knowledge that you were right to murder a dude and that you even had supernatural forces on your side, your dreams are generally peaceful. (There's some sex stuff in there too but whatever man, it happens. Don't even worry about it. It's honestly not a big deal.)

In the morning you act super surprised that Claudius got killed to death ("Whaaaaat?" you say, waving your hands in the air) (come to think of it that was probably a little much but everyone bought it so PHEW) and then later you become king! And check it: your economic policies are both wise and fair, and your country becomes way prosperous! Due to economics not being a zero-sum game, you not only make the lives of your subjects better, but you actually improve the lives of those they trade with too. Hamlet, you've literally make the world a better place. NICE.

And all you had to do was kill a human being!

THE END

P.S. Oh, I meant to mention it sooner, but one day you step on a butterfly that has the cascade effect of preventing not one but TWO worldwide wars from occurring, centuries down the line! So, good job all around, I'd say! Keep on killing everyone who interferes with your preferred version of history, I'd say!
Congratulations! You were really terrific at being Hamlet.

THE END FOR REAL THIS TIME

Turn to 271

143

Okay, well, I did promise that you'd get to make your own choices here, so that's what you do! You decide you're going to get Hamlet to do a murder for you. Even though that's awful. That's awful, dude.

Listen, hypothetical question: let's say you do that and Hamlet is eventually successful and you are revenged. What would you do then?

What would you do with your (after)life if revenge was no longer its driving force?

Accountant: *turn to 538*
Actor: *turn to 538*
Amusement park employee: *turn to 538*
Animal husbandry: *turn to 538*
Animator: *turn to 538*
Architect: *turn to 538*
Athlete: *turn to 538*
Bakery owner: *turn to 538*
Bouncer: *turn to 538*
Brewmaster: *turn to 538*
Cake decorator: *turn to 538*
Chef: *turn to 538*
Comic book artist: *turn to 538*

Counsellor: *turn to 538*
Cowboy: *turn to 538*
Engineer: *turn to 538*
Explorer: *turn to 538*
Firefighter: *turn to 538*
Food critic: *turn to 538*
Game tester: *turn to 538*
Geologist: *turn to 538*
Librarian: *turn to 538*
Linguist: *turn to 538*
Long-haul trucker: *turn to 538*
Makeup artist: *turn to 538*
Marine biologist: *turn to 538*
Mechanic: *turn to 538*
Musician: *turn to 538*
Painter: *turn to 538*
Personal trainer: *turn to 538*
Photographer: *turn to 538*
Physician: *turn to 538*
Pilot: *turn to 538*
Policy analyst: *turn to 538*
Professional gambler: *turn to 538*
Professional golfer: *turn to 538*
Programmer: *turn to 538*
Researcher: *turn to 538*
Restaurateur: *turn to 538*
Roller derby player: *turn to 538*
Sex worker: *turn to 538*
Skateboarder: *turn to 538*
Spy: *turn to 538*
Tamer of ghost dinosaurs: *turn to 538*
Travel writer: *turn to 538*
Watchmaker: *turn to 538*
Waterslide builder: *turn to 538*
Waterslide tester: *turn to 538*
Welder: *turn to 538*
Window cleaner: *turn to 538*
Writer: *turn to 538*

I'm not here to consider life-affirming hypotheticals, I am here to see my son murder a man: *turn to 478*

145

Hugs! Hugs for everyone, all at once. You're not really the hugging type, and neither are they, but somehow — SOMEHOW — everything clicks. It works. It feels right. As the hug continues, you realize that it feels more than right: it actually feels terrific!

This, my friend, is a hug for the ages. It lingers for a while longer and when you all exit it, crazy grins on your faces, you feel way better than you did going in.

Your maximum stamina has been increased by 2 points!

Hug them again! More stamina!! *Turn to 436*

Ask them how they've been: *turn to 13*

146

Okay.

You get mad at yourself for being such a screw-up, then you go back to bed, then you nap.

A good night's sleep and the quiet morning light help you reflect and take stock of things a bit better. You didn't do what you wanted to do yesterday, true, but really all that means is you failed to commit the act of murder. Against your stepfather. Who's actually doing a pretty alright job of running the country. Maybe you could gather evidence of his crime and present it to the court, should you, you know, actually find evidence stronger than the hearsay of a ghost you met once. "A ghost I met once," you think. Man, you do sound crazy. This whole thing is crazy.

You decide to go back to school, focus on learning more, and try to put this whole thing behind you. You never find any evidence that your father died of anything other than a heart attack. You get on with your life. And it actually ends up being generally okay.

And guess what? All's generally okay that ends generally okay!

THE END

Turn to 7

147

You reach the room almost entirely out of breath. You try to speak, but all that comes out is moist, wheezy panting.

"Oh, hey Hamlet," says Claudius, closing the book he was just reading. Your mom's here too, as are Rosencrantz and Guildenstern and — well, basically the whole court, actually. It appears they've all gathered to watch Claudius read Christina's latest reader-choice adventure, *As You Choose It,* subtitled *You Are Rosalind and Must Decide Who You Want to Marry, There's a Court Jester But Let's*

Not Be Hasty, You Could Also Just Totally Make Out with Your Cousin Celia Instead. It appears you've missed the entire show.

"Um, you wanna read this book now instead?" you say, offering up your signed Gonzago book.

"No, I'm good," says Claudius. "In fact, I think I'm done reading books for a very, very, very long time."

Oh snap! Your whole plan is ruined!!

GET MAD AT YOURSELF, BUT CHANNEL THAT EMOTION SOMEWHERE PRODUCTIVE, LIKE INTO KILLING CLAUDIUS LIKE YOU TOLD A GHOST YOU WOULD! *Turn to 197*

GET MAD AT YOURSELF FOR BEING SUCH A SCREW-UP, GO BACK TO BED, NAP: *turn to 146*

148

GOOD POINT.

You sneak up behind him, sword raised. Just before you bring your sword down through the top of his skull, you have time for the perfect one-liner. And here's what you say!

(Write your one-liner here for future reference.)

If you get stuck, feel free to choose from the following suggestions:

"You shouldn't go around killing dads, especially if their kids are willing to kill for revenge. Hey, here's another free TIP." (Then send the tip of your sword into his head.)

"I got you this for Father's Day, I hope you don't MIND." (Then stab him in the mind / brain.)

"Looks like you're about to take a POMMELING." (The pommel is the counterweight in the hilt of a European sword; it sounds like "pummel," which means beating someone up with your fists, so it doesn't work super well, but it would work okay if you hit Claudius with your sword instead of stabbing him with it, but it's too late for that now.)

The sword goes right through his head and it's super gross. His eyes pop out and roll under the pew. Oh gosh, it just got grosser!!

Congratulations! You have beaten this book, and also murdered an alive person.

Your final score is, oh, let's say...423 out of 1000.

THE END

Turn to 26

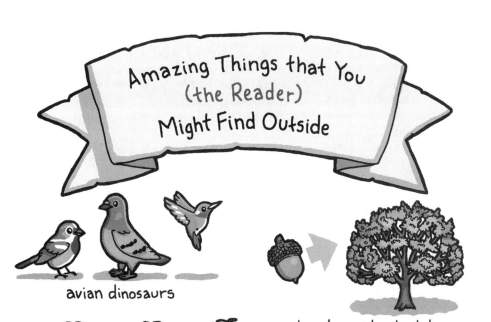

Amazing Things that You (the Reader) Might Find Outside

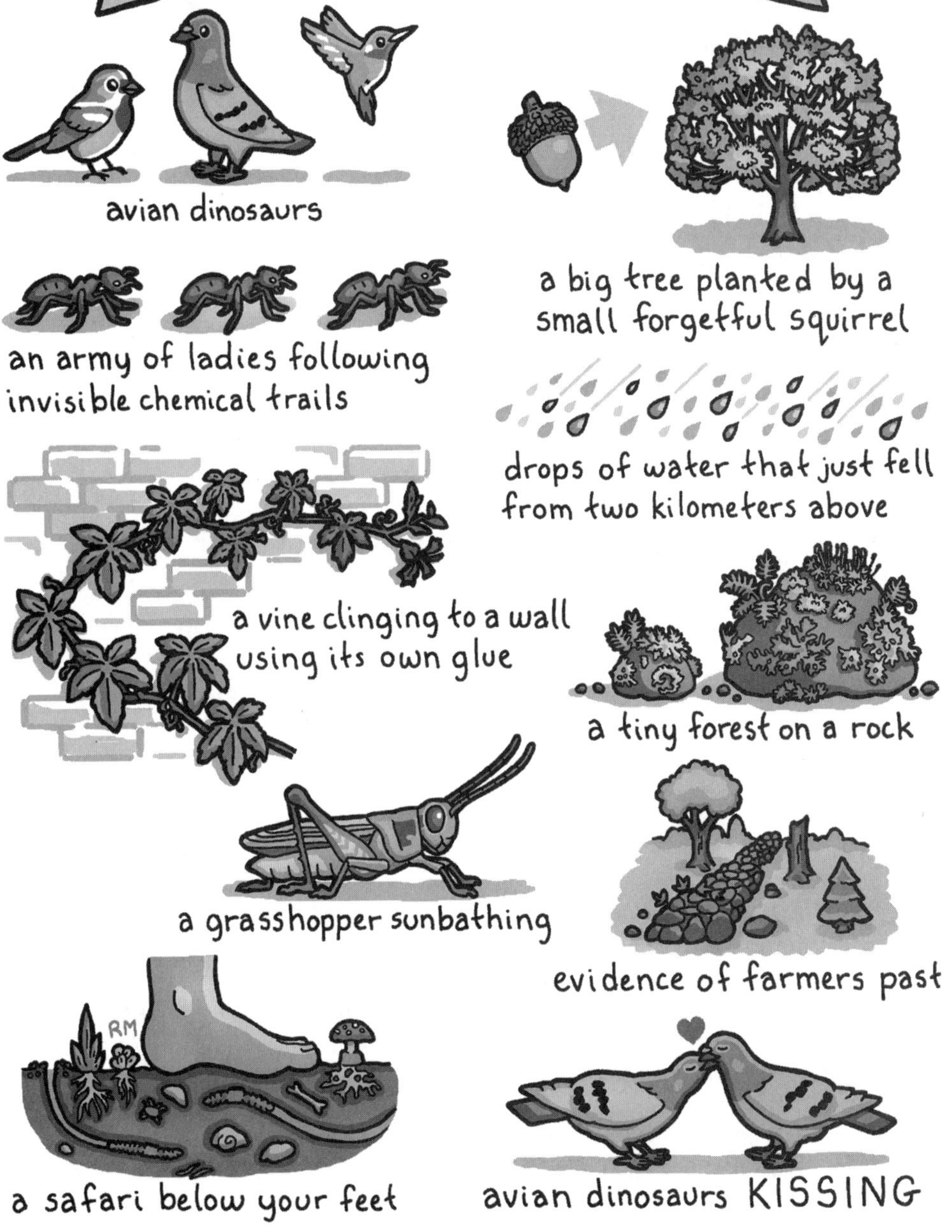

avian dinosaurs
a big tree planted by a small forgetful squirrel
an army of ladies following invisible chemical trails
drops of water that just fell from two kilometers above
a vine clinging to a wall using its own glue
a tiny forest on a rock
a grasshopper sunbathing
evidence of farmers past
a safari below your feet
avian dinosaurs KISSING

150

First thing in the morning, you show up to the royal court. You look out at the assembled courtiers and see that everyone's here: your mom and stepdad, Polonius, Rosencrantz and Guildenstern, a bunch of people you've never met, Ophelia — the whole gang! You're still looking around when Horatio comes up behind you and slaps you on the back, in an expertly executed manoeuvre.

"Brotimes!" he says. "How's it going, brotimes?"

"Good," you say. "Listen, can you do me a favour?" You explain that you're going to be watching Claudius closely, but ask if maybe he could keep an eye on him too as he reads. "You're, um, really good at stuff," you say, wishing that there was somehow a better way to put that.

He agrees that he's pretty great at stuff and consents to do some of that watching stuff for you. Alright. There's nothing left to do, Hamlet! It's go time!

"Hey Claudius!" you say, brandishing your signed copy of *Gonzago*. "Why don't you read THIS book today?"

"I certainly don't see why not," he says, and you pass him the book. Now all that's left is to decide where to sit!

Sit at Ophelia's feet, ask to lay in her lap (in the sexy sense), and remind her that she has genitals: *turn to 198*

Stand behind the king so you can see what choices he makes as he reads and thereby figure out if he's guilty or not: *turn to 210*

151

OH CRAP!!
YOU FORGOT TO TELL OPHELIA ABOUT HER DAD.

Well, I can't get off this party boat now: *turn to 154*

152

The pirate captain screams in rage, charging you with his sword. You deftly parry and sidestep, ending up behind him.

The two of you circle each other, flurries of swordplay erupting whenever one of you detects an opportunity. Despite his injury, neither of you is able to gain the advantage on the rain-soaked deck of the ship.

Suddenly, lightning strikes the brass rail behind the pirate captain, and he's briefly stunned by the tremendous thunder that follows. You're stunned as well but, being a few feet away, you recover more quickly.

There's your opening, Hamlet!

Attack his dominant, sword-bearing arm! *Turn to 46*

Attack his eyes! *Turn to 469*

Attack his legs! *Turn to 234*

153

“Ophelia’s dead?!” you say out loud, shocked. The gravedigger shrugs. He’s not friends with any of these people!

“I tried to tell you —” Horatio says. “I meant to tell you earlier but you seemed so happy to be back and I — I wasn’t — look, I’m sorry, Hamlet. She passed away shortly after you left on your trip.”

Gertrude and Laertes and Claudius are still unaware that you’re here. Gertrude throws flowers on her grave, saying that she’d always hoped Ophelia would marry you, and that instead, she’d be throwing flowers on her wedding bed.

Geez, Gertrude. Inappropriate. That is not something for a new mother-in-law to do for newlyweds.

Laertes curses three times whomever it was who robbed Ophelia of her sanity, and then curses them again ten times three times, for a total of thirty-three curses. Then he jumps into the grave so that he might hold her in his arms once more.

Geez, Laertes. That’s like — double inappropriate to the power of three, for a total of eight inappropriates.

Okay, so they’re all really upset and acting crazy. The right thing to do here is to go home, approach them later, and say you saw them at the funeral but didn’t want to interrupt. Also, it’ll give you a chance to deal with your grief too, which you should be feeling. You are feeling it, aren’t you, Hamlet? She was your sweetie, and you’ve come back from a trip to find her dead of apparent suicide!

What do you do?

Go home and talk to everyone later: *turn to 121*

Step from the shadows and introduce yourself dramatically: *turn to 182*

Be Ophelia: *turn to 174*

154

Even if you broke up recently, you should at least console Ophelia over her loss! Especially since you were kinda involved in his accidental death. But instead you’re running away and partying on a boat??

I'm calling it: YOU ARE THE WORST BOYFRIEND AND/OR EX-BOYFRIEND EVER.

But you're on this boat and it's set sail for England, so there's not much you can do.

Try to party as best you can, given the circumstances: *turn to 93*

155 You and Rosencrantz and Guildenstern scramble in parallel, snagging the lanterns as they roll across the deck, getting a few just mere seconds before they'd make contact with the many gunpowder trails criss-crossing the floor. Somehow you pull it off without colliding into each other or exploding into a chunky mist of blood and bone.

Tossing the lanterns out a porthole, it looks like you've taken care of the immediate crisis, but you are still on a mortally wounded boat, and she's taking on water. In fact, you can see water seeping in the far side of the darkened room now.

"NOW can we abandon ship?" you say.

"Most def," says Guildenstern. Running above-decks, you look up, but the storm has blackened the sky. Suddenly, lightning strikes the water beside you. The sound of thunder is staggering, but in that brief instant, the world is illuminated.

You see 15 ropes hanging from the bow of *Calypso's Gale*, going down to water level. Midway up, you see your young crew of almost 20 (both by age and by count), cutlasses at the ready, fighting. Pirates swarm down the lines, battling them for sport. Above them, on deck, they're being cheered by a row of pirates. And at the very bow of the ship, looking down with a spyglass, stands the captain. He's got a fancy hat and parrot on his shoulder: the works. And he's staring right at you through the storm.

As the darkness of the storm is restored moments later, you yell at Rosencrantz and Guildenstern over the ringing in your ears. "Climb up!" you yell. "Attack them! I'm going after her captain!"

Rosencrantz shouts back something, but you can't hear. You point up at the boat and grab a rope and begin to climb. Glancing back, you see your two bros running to do the same.

One way or another, you're going to end this.

Continue climbing, attack pirates! *Turn to 92*

157

I'm — not sure what you're expecting to happen here?

You argue with them to abandon ship, they tell you to help them pick up the lanterns, eventually you all explode! To make it worthwhile, I'll describe your last moment in rhyme.

"Flame makes contact with the trail of gunpowder / Turning you all into chunky clam chowder."

It's ironic that someone who's been so indecisive up till now dies because he can't undecide to abandon ship, huh? "Irony." Write that down.

THE END

Turn to 505

158

You walk calmly to your closet, retrieve a sword, and walk calmly back to Osric. "Okay. You killed the man I love," you say, "AND you did it in the bed I love, and now they're both ruined and covered in blood and for that I am going to kill you."

"Go nuts," he says.

You do.

Osric laughs the whole time. Just before he dies, Osric holds up one hand to get you to stop. "Wait, wait, wait a second," he says. "I have to ask you a question."

You point your sword at his neck. "Better not take too long," you say. "I'm not sure how much blood you have left in there."

Osric looks at the sword, then up at you. He's smiling.

"What makes you think," he says, grinning through a mouth full of blood and broken teeth, "that I was the only one Claudius talked to?"

"What?" you say.

"He talked to everyone. He promised them everything. They all —"

Osric slams his head down on your sword, cutting his face. "— want you —"

Osric slams his head down again, cutting deeper.

"— dead."

Then Osric slams his head down on your sword, cleaving his skull in two. Oh my gosh. I can't believe he did that. That's disgusting. What the heck, dude?

You look around the room. Hamlet's dead. Osric's dead. And everyone you know has been given a really good reason to want you murdered. This is going to be a challenging day, Ophelia, and you're only three hours into it.

You go to a window and look out into the night. You can't bring Hamlet back, and if he IS a ghost, then you'll meet him eventually. But not now. Right now you've got plenty to live for, and lots you want to do before you die.

By way of an example, one of the things you want to do is kill everyone in town before they kill you first.

You pick up your sword, wipe it clean on Osric's body, and re-sheath it in its scabbard. "Looks like it's time to KILL EVERYONE IN HAMLET and chew bubblegum, and I'm all out of gum," you whisper to yourself.

What you meant was "Looks like it's time to kill everyone in THIS hamlet," referring, of course, to the small town that the castle is in, but it's early and nobody heard you anyway, so no harm no foul, right?

Okay, Ophelia. Let's do this. Let's have a living person take personal revenge in this story for once.

Let's, as you say, kill everyone in Hamlet.

Kill everyone in the royal court! *Turn to 338*

Kill Polonius and Laertes: *turn to 446*

Kill the background characters in your life (Rosencrantz, Guildenstern, those gravediggers that are always slacking off, etc.) one by one: *turn to 428*

159 Partying on a boat is great, but it doesn't last forever! After several hours, the party winds down for the first night. You and Rosencrantz and Guildenstern stumble off to your quarters, three awesome dudes in one awesome room. One awesome...PARTY ROOM??

The next day, you wake up, still feeling the effects of the previous night's partying. You put on your shirt but it feels different — turns out it's Rosencrantz's shirt! Wow. As you pull it off, a letter falls out of the pocket. Rosencrantz wakes up, teases you for wearing his clothes, and then notices the letter.

"Hey Hamlet, you dropped something," he says.

"No man," you say, "it's your letter. This is your shirt." You pass him the garment. He has the shirt.

"It's not MY letter, bro," he says, pulling it over his head. "Someone must've slipped it to me sometime yesterday. What's it say?"

Flipping it over, you notice it's got a royal seal on the back. "It's from King Claudius!" you say.

Rosencrantz and Guildenstern say the following: "Whaaaaaaaaat??"

Open the letter: *turn to 97*

Don't open it: it's got an OFFICIAL SEAL: *turn to 212*

160 I still do not admit to any murder," you say. "That is to say, my continued non-admittance to murder proceeds relentlessly."

Hamlet turns to a different page.

BAA?

"Liar!!" he reads. "You totally killed your brother by poisoning him in the ear! You should admit it right now." He looks at you.

"Your choices are to —"

"Hamlet," you interrupt. "Does this story go anywhere, or do you just accuse the reader of murder for the entire book?"

"That's a form of going somewhere," Hamlet says.

You sigh and take the book from him. "We need to start over, sweetie," you say. "We're not going to trap the conscience of a king with this. We need something more subtle, something with themes that inspire guilt and remorse inside him, planting a seed that'll eat him up from the inside out —"

Now Hamlet interrupts you. "Or we could just plagiarize this other book I got," he says. "I met the author by accident a few days ago and it totally works for our purposes!"

Look book: *turn to 370*

162

The pirate screams at you, livid. He's lost some very important body parts, but he's not going to stop. He's out of control with rage and will fight you right to the end. You can't let your guard down. He'll take you apart with his teeth if you let him.

It's time to finish this, Hamlet.

Deliver the killing blow! *Turn to 163*

163

The captain tries to spit in your face. You stab him right in the chest, piercing a lung. He gasps and swears at you.

"Save your breath," you say. You take a step back and slice off the captain's chin, sending it flying into the rigging.

"Come on, keep your chin up!" you yell, slicing again at his face. You cut off the tip of his nose and it flies overboard.

"You know what they say," you say grimly, taking your sword in both hands. "Follow your nose."

With one huge strike, you behead the pirate captain. His head rolls at your feet, and you kick it overboard into the ocean.

Let me just say: holy crap. Never in your life have you fought so well. This was awesome, literally awesome. If you lived to be a thousand years old, you'd never have a fight go so amazingly well as it did today.

You're catching your breath when you hear familiar voices yell "Hamlet!!"

Turning around, you see Rosencrantz and Guildenstern rushing towards you. They survived! In fact, they did more than survive the battle: like you, they thrived in it! All around them lie the bodies of pirates, and your crew dispatches the last few survivors. This is incredible. *Calypso's Gale* is yours. And the storm surrounding her is clearing as quickly as it appeared in the first place! Sunlight pierces through the clouds.

You and Rosencrantz and Guildenstern hug each other, and your crew cheers. Pulling back, Guildenstern notices the blood on your jacket and then the headless torso on the floor.

"What happened to the captain?" asks Guildenstern. "Dunno," you say. "Last I saw, he was...HEADED for sea."

"Oh," says Rosencrantz. "Does that mean you cut off his head and then threw it overboard?"

"Let's just say that when he fought me...he got in a little over his HEAD."

"Oh, you cut off his head and then threw it overboard," says Rosencrantz.

Take command of this larger, much nicer vessel: *turn to 240*

164

"I'll be there, 11:30 sharp!" you say, and Horatio leaves, satisfied.

Well, now you have eight hours to blow before it's time to meet ghosts. What do you want to do, Hamlet?

Be Ophelia for a while: *turn to 31*

Play solitaire: *turn to 71*

165

While sailing to Denmark, you and Rosencrantz and Guildenstern come up with a plan.

Clearly King Claudius wants you dead, but he isn't willing to move overtly, hence the letter he planted on your friends. Heck, even the pirate attack could've been orchestrated by him. It's impossible to know who he's gotten to while you've been gone. You can't trust anyone.

You decide to...

Attack Claudius head-on from *Calypso's Gale*: *turn to 402*

Attack Claudius more discreetly, lest a frontal attack from a pirate ship disturb the people of Denmark and weaken your right to rule: *turn to 50*

167

"This isn't what it looks like!" you shout frantically, removing your knives from the perforated body of your dead brother. "I know that it looks like I killed four people here!!"

You turn to face Osric.

"The total's actually five," you say, stabbing one blade into his heart and another into his lung.

You're not even surprised anymore when you look up from Osric's body and see Rosencrantz and Guildenstern standing there, aghast.

Kill Rosencrantz and Guildenstern: *turn to 529*

Try to explain the growing heaps of bodies surrounding you: *turn to 544*

168

The gravedigger sings a song: it's this really nice musical interlude right in the middle of your adventure! This is great because while we've had all sorts of murders and junk, nobody has, as yet, busted out any ditties. His song is about being young and in love, and this is what he sings:

In youth when I did love, did love,
Methought it was very sweet
To contract-o-the time for-a-my behove,
O, methought there-a-was nothing-a-meet.

You join in on the singing:

Just now when I did hear, did hear
Your singing, methought it rad
But it's-a offensive, that fake-o
Italian accent you-a had!

The gravedigger sings his response:

I wasn't being racist, I was grunting while digging this grave!
And if I can employ some contemporary slang, methinks I call you...knave.

Oh man, sick burns, Hamlet! You just totally lost a lyrical battle. Suddenly, the gravedigger digs up a human skull!

Look skull: *turn to 118*

WAIT, WHAT

170

She steps away from Claudius. “What’s going on, Hamlet?”

You motion behind you for Rosencrantz and Guildenstern to give the order to fire.

“You see, Mom,” you say, as the fuse on the cannon burns down, “there’s something I can only say to you if you’re standing over there!”

“Okay, what do you want to say?” she shouts.

“Oh, shucks, I just wanted to be the first to congratulate you on your divorce!!” you shout, and at that moment the cannon fires. It’s perfect timing. The ball tears through the air, hits Claudius in the stomach, and, rather than going through him, actually carries him through the air.

“My only regret is that I killed my brother and married his widowwwwwwwwww,” says Claudius, as he’s carried away over the castle. A few seconds later, you hear a wet thud.

The people of Denmark accept you as their new king, because it actually took a whole lot of skill to hit someone with a cannonball from that distance, especially given the state of cannonball technology. You didn’t fire the cannon, but you did HIRE the person who fired the cannon (well, kinda), and that’s good enough for them!

Denmark enters a period of wealth and prosperity, thanks to your leadership — and your dad’s. That’s right: your ghost dad makes his appearances a permanent thing, and when you assume the throne (he’s had enough fun being king already, he says), you appoint him as your chief advisor. He makes it so everyone can see him too. It’s just more convenient that way.

A few months later, he and Gertrude remarry. Everyone is shocked, but you check, and it turns out there’s nothing in the rulebook that specifically says a woman can’t marry a ghost! NICE! There’s also nothing in the rulebook that says a dog can’t play football but that hasn’t come up yet nor is it really likely to if we’re being honest.

When your mother dies of old age years later, she becomes a ghost and sticks around too. Eventually, you succumb to your own mortality and you also become a ghost.

It turns out that having benign enlightened leadership that also can’t die is really useful for a country? I mean, after a while you become antiquated relics of a previous age with beliefs and mores rooted in the past that are out of touch with our modern reality, but for many generations it’s really good! You’re able to accumulate several lifetimes worth of knowledge, and direct it all towards the business of running a nation!

Eventually, some of your people do revolt, hatching a plan to employ a charged particle beam emitted from a portable particle accelerator to dispose of you, but that’s a story for another time. Also, it’s a story for another book. Look, it’s basically an entirely unrelated story and I need to draw the line somewhere.

THE END

Turn to 98

171

"Okay, let's do this!" you say. Why not, right? It's not like you've got anything else going on hah hah hah THAT WAS SARCASTIC.

Osric leaves and then comes back immediately. "King wants to know if you'll fight him now," he says. "He's just in there."

Oh right, I forgot to mention! You're right outside the royal court, which is also the castle fencing room. Anyway. Messengers gonna message, right? You say that's fine, and Osric says okay and leaves.

Horatio turns to you. "Listen man, I don't think you should do this. I don't think you're gonna win, Hamlet," he says.

"Sure I am!" you say. "I've been practicing fencing since the start of this story."

"What?" says Horatio, and I'm saying "What??" too, because there have been zero fencing scenes? Like, at all? Unless you count the pirate battle, but that was more swordfighting than fencing. There's a difference, you know. They both require swordsmanship, but in the same way that poetry and essays are both "writing."

You realize that you were lying just now and start to feel bad about your chances.

"Maybe I won't win after all," you say. "I suddenly feel a sense of foreboding that would perhaps trouble a woman."

Aw geez, Hamlet. Aw geez.

Talk about how sometimes you say terrible things about women and how sometimes, in private moments of reflection, you wonder what that says about you: *turn to 204*

Talk instead about the nature of free will: *turn to 230*

172

But you — you already told him about it. If you talk to him about it again, the story's just going to be super repetitive.

Talk to Horatio about the pirate trip again!! *Turn to 219*

Talk to Horatio about what just happened: *turn to 201*

173

FINE. You stay a ghost and avoid travelling through time. You make a few other friends who feel the same way you do, and the bunch of you spend the rest of eternity going through time the old-fashioned way: at the steady rate of one second per second, and only ever forward.

You almost convince yourself that it's enough.

Almost.

But it's not.

And you start to really regret your decision. But the ghost time travel / body replacement machine is in an advanced state of disrepair, since the ghosts who invented it all went back in time to live in new bodies, the dead cannibalizing the past to live once more, which is kinda monstrous and awful when you think about it, so let's not!

You spend a large chunk of your afterlife trying to figure out how this ghostly time machine works, and eventually reverse-engineer something that you think will do the trick. And amazingly, you're pretty sure your time machine will actually work better than the original! Rather than taking over your past self 's body (or someone else's), this machine SHOULD send you into the past, corporeal, in a body all your own.

Nicely done, Hamlet!

You test out your machine by chucking a handful of dirt (ghost dirt) into it and it seems to work. I mean, the dirt disappears, so either it's a time machine or a molecular destabilizer, but you're optimistic. You step into the quantum leap accelerator and vanish.

THE END

P.S. The machine totally worked and you arrived in the past! Yay!

P.P.S. To explore this new timeline you've created, re-read this book and try to find an option during a fight to choose from only two swords: the left sword or the right sword. Rather than turning to the nodes indicated, add the two node numbers together, divide the sum by three, multiply by 15, take the square root, and add 63 while rounding up to the nearest integer. Turn to that node instead: this will push this other you into the new timeline you've just created here.

If this math seems complicated, then let me say this: man, who told you that time travel was easy??

Turn to 166

174

You're certain? You want to be Ophelia, even though you JUST saw her coffin get lowered into the ground?

It's okay, I've got a plan: *turn to 203*

On second thought, keep being Hamlet, go home, and talk to everyone later: *turn to 121*

On third thought, keep being Hamlet, step from the shadows, and introduce yourself dramatically: *turn to 182*

H

176

"Incorrect!" Horatio says. Fortinbras slaps in with his answer: "Denmark's earliest archaeological findings date back to the Eemian interglacial period. That's from 130,000 to 110,000 BC."

Darn it, it's like he read your friggin' mind.

"Correct!" shouts Horatio. "Fortinbras, if you get this next question right, you will be my new king. Ophelia, if that's who YOU want to be, you've got to get this next one right just to stay in the game."

Horatio looks at you both, and then clears his throat. "Next question: how long is the coastline of Denmark?"

Again you slap in first.

"8735 KILOMETRES!" *Turn to 487*

"7314 KILOMETRES!" *Turn to 94*

"TRICK QUESTION! NO COASTLINE HAS A PRECISELY DEFINED LENGTH, AS THE LENGTH WILL DEPEND ON THE METHOD USED TO MEASURE IT. IF I USE A METRE STICK, VARIATIONS IN THE COAST SMALLER THAN ONE METRE WILL BE IGNORED. BUT IF I USE A CENTIMETRE STICK, THEN I'LL INCLUDE THOSE MEASUREMENTS, BUT IGNORE THOSE LESS THAN ONE CENTIMETRE! SINCE COASTLINES BEHAVE LIKE FRACTALS IN THIS REGARD, THERE IS NO SINGLE LENGTH MEASUREMENT I CAN POINT TO WITHOUT MAKING SIMPLIFYING ASSUMPTIONS FIRST." *Turn to 507*

177

Coming in loud and clear, buddy!

You drink the potion and feel better about things. You're still sad Ophelia's gone, obviously, but it's not as bad as it was.

Okay! Time to go to bed and wake up bright and early the next day! You have a fake king to expose!!

I'm not joking!

GO TO BED: *turn to 122*

178

This is it, Hamlet! THIS IS THE DAY YOU CONFRONT CLAUDIUS.

You put on your best confronting-the-king tights, and your fanciest confronting-the-king scabbard. Don't worry, I looked it up: it's a sheath for holding a sword.

You and Horatio are walking into the castle when Osric shows up! Hey, I know this guy! He's a member of the royal court, and he's super manipulable. Here, I'll show you!

"Put your hat on," you say to Osric.

"No thanks. It's too hot today," he says.

"No man, it's cold, with winds from the north and a 30% chance of precipitation," you reply.

"Oh yeah, it's cold," he says.

"And yet, it's also super hot and humid!" you say.

"Yes. Yes, it's quite hot out," he says.

See? SEE?

Okay. I need to apologize because I've been making fun of your choices this entire book, but when I took over here all I did was have a pointless conversation with a dude who isn't even a real character in this story. I'm sorry. Maybe...maybe this ISN'T as easy as it looks?

So I'll tell you what Osric's here to say: the king wants you to fence with Laertes, and he's gone ahead and made a bet. He thinks that in a dozen rounds Laertes won't win by more than three hits. Oh, and he's put six horses on the line, six swords complete with sword accessories, and three fancy carriages. He is wagering all this neat stuff!

On the one hand, you're here to expose Claudius, not Laertes, and fighting Laertes won't actually solve anything at all and is entirely unrelated to avenging your father's death. Also, he's probably upset about, you know, his sister and father dying, and I'm not really sure what sword fighting him will accomplish in the "helping him get past his grief" department.

On the other hand...well, no, actually, I can't think of a good reason why you should fight this guy. Did you hear that? I, the author of this story who has imagined this entire realm wholesale and brought it to life inside my head, cannot conceive of a single reason why you should fight Laertes.

What do you do?

Accept the swordfight invitation: *turn to 171*

Decline the swordfight invitation: *turn to 124*

179

You challenge Fortinbras to a race around the world! The first to return is the one that gains Denmark's crown! THESE ARE THE STAKES, you proclaim!

"Man, I just came here from Norway. I'm tired of travelling," Fortinbras says. He looks at you and waves dismissively.

"Off with her head," he sighs.

Horatio feels bad about having to cut your head off, but the whole point of a monarchy is you invest all state authority in one single individual, which I guess is why it's not the most effective mode of government after all, ESPECIALLY when the only constraint on that monarch's power is a constitution that they themselves can rewrite and I could go on, but you're dead. You died. Your last thoughts are "I hope I get to hear the end of that sentence about monarchy" but NOPE: dead.

Totally dead.

YOU

THE END

Also there's no coming back as a ghost this time; I dunno what to tell you.

So! You kinda managed to not actually accomplish much AND you let your boyfriend do all the killing for you. Since you kinda turned into a sucky role model for independent, self-sufficient women I'm going to award you...3 micropoints!

Everyone else gets 3 MACROpoints!! Oh snap, how's that taste??

Turn to 246

181 You follow the ghost into the mist. After walking for what seems like forever, you get tired of walking.

"I'm tired of walking," you say. You sit down. "Pretty sure I'm done walking. Yeah. Yeah, I'm out."

The ghost stops and speaks to you for the first time, its voice issuing forth from lungs that no longer breathe air:

"Hamlet. It is I, your father. Look, I can't stay around here forever so you need to listen to what I tell you. I didn't die of old age. I did some digging around and it turns out I was murdered...by Claudius!"

You gasp, shocked and enraged. Killed by his own brother!

"He did it while I slept! I was walking in a garden, and you know how gardens are really boring, right?"

You nod. "They're boring even for people who like them."

"Exactly!" says Ghost Dad. "Well, it was so boring I fell asleep, and while I was sleeping he poured poison in my ear."

"I didn't know poisons worked that way," you say.

"That's what I said!" shouts your dad, throwing his hands above his head in frustration. He starts to pace back and forth.

"Anyway, I want you to take revenge on him for me. I dunno. Cuss him out or something. Pull out his chair when he's about to sit down. Offer him a high five but then when he goes to high five you, pull your hand away and say, 'Too slow.' Or should he offer you a high five, you must leave him hanging."

"I could murder him," you offer. "After all, he is sleeping with Mom."

Your dad stops pacing and stares at you. "He's WHAT?!"

TELL HIM THEY GOT MARRIED TWO WEEKS AFTER THE FUNERAL: *turn to 75*

TELL HIM HAH HAH, YOU WERE JUST KIDDING: *turn to 138*

182 You step out of the shadows of the graveyard, leaving Horatio and the gravedigger behind.

"Who's the man whose grief is so extreme, whose words of sorrow can make even the stars themselves stand still and wonder in sadness at what they hear? It's me, Hamlet the Dane!"

Then you hop into the grave, joining Laertes there. Why not? Emotions are a competition, right?

Laertes sees you and screams in rage. "The devil take thy soul!" he shouts, which, I mean, if you're going to yell anything, it's pretty much the awesomest and classiest thing to yell at a time and place like this. And with that, you fight! That's right. You and Laertes fight, in a graveyard, during a funeral, in an OPEN GRAVE, with the coffin of Ophelia at your feet. This is how you choose to live your life.

Laertes punches you in the teeth, and you stagger back until you collide with the muddy grave wall. You raise your eyes up to Laertes, wiping blood from your mouth with the back of your hand. You glance down at your bloodied hand. "That's a funny way to pray," you say, and laugh. Laertes looks at you.

"Here's how I do it." You jump at him, forcing your head into his chest as hard as you can. He falls backwards, winded, gasping for air.

"Our father," you say, your left fist connecting with his cheek, "who art in heaven"—here your right fist collides in a punishing blow with his jaw—"hallowed be thy—"

His hands shoot out and encircle your throat and before you can react, he squeezes. You see stars dance around the edge of your vision. "You don't want to do that," you gasp, but Laertes only squeezes tighter.

"Now why's that, Hamlet?" he says, smirking, mock concern written on his face.

You lock eyes with him. "There's something dangerous inside of me, and you should be afraid of it," you say. "I am. You shouldn't make me angry, Laertes. You wouldn't like me when I'm angry."

Laertes laughs at you, and you feel almost giddy. You can feel yourself losing control. You can feel yourself starting to want it.

"I won't tell you again, little man," you say, unsure if you're threatening him or pleading with him. "Take. Your. Hands. Off."

Turn into a gamma-irradiated monster: *turn to 200*

Continue being Hamlet: *turn to 274*

183

You find Ophelia and tell her she's the most important person in your life, and you mean it. You've lost faith in your family, you realize, but not in love itself. As she stares at you, tears welling in her eyes, you tell her that the love you have for her and the love she has for you — that's the most important thing. It gives both your lives meaning. And it's worth fighting for.

You and Ophelia move away from Denmark and settle someplace stable, sunny, and warm. You don't get married, because you never needed a piece of paper to tell you that you're happy. Ophelia starts a business selling her inventions, and you are able to live comfortably.

You have two sons, Timon and Pericles. When they come of age, Timon moves to Athens where he does very well for himself. Pericles moves to Lebanon and works on writing puzzle books. You and Ophelia await their letters with interest. This is a pretty good family man ending, I gotta say! If that's what you were going for: nice work, man! You did it!

THE END

Turn to 520

184

The crowd murmurs their assent, but Claudius raises a hand and speaks. "I was born with a stupid face, yes. And I admit it freely. But I should not be killed by my adopted son because of that. We must look beyond our bodies and judge people not by circumstances — accidents, really — of their birth, but by who they are. And despite my stupid and irritating face, I have been a pretty decent king to you all."

The crowd murmurs their assent again. You hear someone in the crowd shout "I never liked his stupid face but I always strive to rise above my prejudices" quite clearly.

Horatio is distracted by the speech and Laertes stabs him through the heart, killing him almost instantly. His last words are "It's still a stupiiiid faaaaace... *gurgle*"

Everyone looks at you expectantly. If you attack Claudius now, it'll appear unjustified, and you'll seem like a usurper to the throne. On the plus side, you could at least kill Claudius, which is all you wanted to do in the first place. Assuming Laertes doesn't kill you first!

Kill Claudius: *turn to 117*

Say "Hah hah, nevermind, my mistake": *turn to 255*

185

The crowd gasps. "Is this true?" someone shouts.

"It is," you say, "and who do you trust? Me, a handsome, successful young prince, or Claudius, a murderer and an attempted murderer twice over and one who, as I'm sure you noticed, has a stupid face?"

"Man, he DOES have a stupid face!" Horatio says, between Laertes' attacks. The crowd seems to be on your side. You raise your sword. "Defend yourself, horny murderer!!" you shout.

Claudius glares at you, then quickly stoops and picks up the sword. Holding it at the ready, he beckons you towards him.

Swordfight Claudius! FINALLY! *Turn to 67*

187 "It's a pirate's life for me!" you say, referencing nothing because you're actually the first person in history to say it! You order *Calypso's Gale* turned around and head out into the open seas. Ocean spray splashes up into your face.

You may have messed up in Denmark, but out here on the open seas, you're going to be alright. You're going to be alright, Hamlet.

A few years pass, and you and your crew become legendary pirates! But you all use assumed names so if you want to read about your adventures, just read any pirate book and you'll know it's secretly about you. I'm not even lying, they're all really about your adventures. You're that good!

THE END

P.S. At one point you find 15 men on a dead man's chest, but it's more of a necrophilia thing, not a treasure thing, so that's weird.

Turn to 424

188 It seems some time has passed since you killed yourself and became a ghost. Horatio, who was clean-shaven when you last saw him, now has a beard. He's at the castle talking to Ophelia. Apparently she's invented a device of alcohol and glass that can measure the temperature of things, a sort of "thermo-meter"? She was always so good at stuff. She says she thinks they could be used in medicine.

Anyway, neither Horatio nor Ophelia can sense you. You go to Horatio's house and throw some pots and pans around. It's pretty spooky, but nobody's home right now, so it's also pretty futile.

You continue this style of annoying haunting for several hundred generations of Horatios, generation after generation, never leaving their houses, never learning of anything else going on in the world, until Earth is baked to a crisp by an ever-expanding sun shortly before it consumes the planet entirely.

It's a pretty frustrating way to end your story, but it's also pretty frustrating to only be able to communicate through the not-so-universal language of throwing pots and pans, so you're used to it.

THE END

Turn to 443

189 You go down to Ophelia's place and knock on her door. "Who is it?" she calls.

"It's me, sweetie," you say, opening the door and stepping into her room. You haven't seen each other for a while; it's so great to see her! You run up and throw your arms around her and you kiss. It's just like old times.

You hold her at arm's length and look into her eyes. "Listen," you say, and then you...

GO MURDER CLAUDIUS: *turn to 142*

GO ON TO SAY "I NEED YOUR HELP WITH SOMETHING": *turn to 222*

UNBUTTON YOUR JACKET, FOUL YOUR STOCKINGS, TAKE YOUR GARTERS OFF, AND GRAB OPHELIA BY THE WRIST: *turn to 223*

190

You go back to Wittenberg U. A few years into your studies, you and Ophelia break it off; long distance was just too hard. With her out of the picture, you don't go home much anymore. You feel bad about it, but it's too weird being around Uncle Dad all the time, and besides he was never the kind of person you would have described as "extremely non-creepy."

You drift apart from Horatio and Rosencrantz and Guildenstern too, as you start hanging out with your new school friends a lot more. You spend most of your time with one guy in particular, T.J. Macbeth. You're unlikely friends — he, a jock; you, president of the philosophy club — but that doesn't stop you. Friends is friends. In your sophomore year you get a place together, just a few minutes off campus, and he starts calling you by a nickname: "Banquo." He laughs whenever you ask for an explanation, and eventually you just get used to it.

Anyway, after graduation neither of you can find work, so he invites you to come back home to Scotland with him. He says his dad can get you both some pretty good jobs high up in the army. He says there's a lot of possibility there for advancement.

You accept. You never do return to Denmark.

THE END

Turn to 22

191

"One sec!" you yell and run below-decks. You choose the biggest cannon available, and tilting it downward, roll the loaded cannonball out onto the deck. You then hoist yourself up into the cannon and push yourself in as far as you'll go. Satisfied, you stick your head out and address the weapons officer.

"Well...?! Fire me, man! It's our only hope!"

The weapons officer shrugs his shoulders, aims the cannon carefully, and lights the fuse. You duck back inside the cannon and prepare yourself.

Okay, I've got to interrupt things here and ask you an important question:

KAZU
2013

how realistic do you want this story to be? No rush, but you need to answer before you leave this page.

Please, your question insults us both. I want nothing but your finest realism! *Turn to 262*

I am inside a cannon about to be fired at my stepfather because a ghost told me to. Let's not get too hung up on realism right now, okay? *Turn to 260*

193

So you walk in on your mom and fake dad as they're trying to run the country, but it turns out they were talking about you anyway. Polonius is there too. He's talking to you like you're touched in the head. Hey! He thinks you're crazy! MAYBE THAT'S BECAUSE OF ALL THE DUMB DECISIONS YOU'VE BEEN MAKING?

So in an effort to save this, we're going to assume that you were just PRETENDING to be crazy, because that way all of this kinda makes sense and nobody would ever suspect a crazy person of committing a murder, right? This is literally the best option we've got left. This is what you've reduced us to. I've gone back and rewritten the story so that in your talk with Horatio now you say "I might act crazy for a while, just be cool." (You can go back and check, it's totally there, *turn to 8*.)

Okay! So it turns out Polonius considers himself a master riddlemaster, and he's going to ask you three riddles to determine if you're sane or not. Riddle the first:

"Do you know who I am?" he says.

Since you're now just ACTING crazy, this gets a little easier. Normally I'd give you the choice between a reasonable answer and a crazy answer, but I figure now you want to pick the reasonable one just to screw things up, and I swear to God there will be a method to your madness if it kills me. So here are your options!

Say "I don't know who you are. Maybe...you're a pimp?" *Turn to 79*

I know you're looking for the option to say "Um, yeah, you're Polonius" here, but you know what? I like being in charge. Say "I don't know who you are. Maybe...you're a pimp?" *Turn to 79*

194

You make a break for it, but trip over Horatio, who is also making a break for it in the opposite direction. You collide into each other and fall, hitting your head on a rock for good measure.

"Is this funny?" you hear the ghost say as you fade from consciousness. "I don't know if this is supposed to be funny."

You come to months later. Not much has changed: your mom is still married to your uncle, and Horatio tells you the ghost kept coming by for a while but eventually seemed to lose interest in the whole thing. He asks what you're going to do now. You're not sure. The funeral and wedding you came back home for are long over. It's probably time you get back to the business of living your life. So! What do you want to do with it?

Get serious with Ophelia: *turn to 183*

Go back to school: *turn to 190*

195

You and Hamlet are pressed invisibly up against the wall of the royal church, your clothes and ninja hoods blending in with the stone and mortar perfectly.

Claudius is here, talking to Rosencrantz and Guildenstern, and he's speechifying. He's got one hand out in front of him, holding it in the air. It looks pretty dramatic!

"I like him not," Claudius says, "nor stands it safe with us to let his madness range. Therefore prepare you. I your commission will forthwith dispatch, and he to England shall along with you."

"Dude, nobody's seen Hamlet for days," Rosencrantz replies.

"Yeah, we can't take him to England because not a single bro knows where he is," says Guildenstern.

Claudius lowers his arm.

"Well, poops," Claudius says, and Rosencrantz and Guildenstern look at each other and it's awkward and then they leave.

Polonius comes in and offers to spy on Hamlet by hiding in Gertrude's room, just in case Hamlet happens to show up. It is a weird, pervy plan, but Claudius agrees to it, and then Polonius gets really excited and runs out of the room.

Finally alone, Claudius again raises one arm out in front of him as he says, "O, my offense is rank, it smells to heaven; it hath the primal eldest curse upon't, a brother's murder." You and Hamlet exchange a glance. Dude is not only guilty, he confessed his guilt to an empty room. Wow. And Claudius is STILL confessing his crime for, like, another minute, until he finally bows and prays.

You could kill him now if you want. Or you could let him twist in the wind a little longer.

Kill Claudius! *Turn to 374*

Let him go, it's time to engage Operation Act 3 Scene 4: *turn to 352*

196

It seems some time has passed since you killed yourself and became a ghost. When you finally catch up with your dad, he's appalled to see you. "Why didn't you come see me when I tried to contact you months ago?" he demands of you, and all you can say is that you were really depressed back when you were alive.

"You know what would've cured that depression?" says your dad.

"Nope," you say.

"AVENGING MY DEATH, BECAUSE CLAUDIUS MURDERED ME." Your father throws his hands up in the air and leaves you alone, but at least you've got all of eternity to work it out between you, because you're both already ghosts.

Eventually a few hundred years pass and you do patch things up, and just in time too. It's now the year 2100, and an alien probe has landed on Earth. While it looked empty to the living people who opened it, it actually contained thousands of ghosts from another world: an invasion force escaping from their dying planet! And they're attacking every ghost on the planet! And the living people of Earth have no idea this is even happening!

You're right in the middle of a ghost-on-ghost war for the survival of the afterlife, and the two of you, Hamlets Jr. and Sr., are leading the armies of humanity's greatest ghosts into battle. You've just finished a super dramatic pre-battle speech, whipping the troops into a frenzy. It is the morning of your biggest strike yet. You look to your right, and your father is grinning in grim determination. You look to your left, and the ghost of Franklin D. Roosevelt cocks his shotgun and says, "Let's do this, Hamlet."

It's so awesome. This is an awesome ending.

Your horse rears, you raise your sword, and you charge.

THE END

Turn to 49

197

Oh, terrific! I'm glad that the engraved invitation to choose this option finally arrived in the mail!!

Alright, let's do this!

Go murder Claudius: *turn to 142*

198

You know what? No. Just no. When you write your own book, you can fill it with all the "let's have sex in front of my mom and dad" and "hah hah women have different parts than men" jokes you want, but this is my book and I'm unilaterally deciding, right now, that you don't get to do this.

Instead, you decide to go stand behind your stepdad and watch him read!

How's that taste? Does it taste like COMPROMISE? Because it shouldn't. It should taste like FALLING IN LINE.

Stand behind your stepdad: *turn to 210*

199

These are all, like, soldier guys, so they'll be a bit harder to kill. On the other hand, you HAVE just killed several dudes.

The three of them are up on a castle parapet, looking out over the edge at the ground far below. You walk up behind them. "Hey boys, seen any ghosts lately?" you say.

"Actually, yes, two of them!" replies Bernardo, turning around. "And one said that if I die while trying to kill Ophelia, I'll gain ghost powe—"

The sentence dies on his lips when he sees you.

"Boo," you say.

Bernardo runs at you, but you sidestep him easily, and he falls over the edge of the parapet and hits the ground far below with a sickening crunch.

"Leaving so soon?" you say.

Marcellus and Francisco glance at each other, then run at you, their swords drawn. You duck and spin, cutting off their feet. They fall off the edge as well, landing near Bernardo. You kick their disembodied feet off the parapet and down onto their lifeless bodies.

"Go on," you say, "shoo."

OH WOW, THAT WAS A TERRIBLE PUN SINCE THEY WEREN'T EVEN WEARING SHOES, BUT WE'RE STILL COUNTING IT FOR THREE IN A ROW!! All that's left of these background characters are the courtiers! These murders you've done so far have taken a while, so it's early morning now and the royal court is not in session anymore (I should tell you that the royal court hours are from midnight to 4 a.m. and noon to 6 p.m.; it's weird but whatever). No worries though! YOU'LL JUST TRACK THEM DOWN AND KILL THEM INDIVIDUALLY.

Kill courtiers: *turn to 449*

200

You embrace the madness. You feel your clothes tearing as your body changes, becoming larger, monstrous. Colossal muscles move under skin that's rapidly darkening to a vibrant shade of green. A few seconds ago, the dirt walls of Ophelia's grave surrounded you on all sides. Now, looking down, you see your massive legs barely contained within it.

The world seems smaller. Punier.

Throughout all this, Laertes has hung on to your throat, trying to choke you. "HAMLET NO LIKE CHOKEY MAN," you say, picking him up and flinging him over a distant grove of trees. "HAMLET NO LIKE ANYONE WHO INTERFERE WITH HAMLET'S CONCEPT OF PERSONAL AGENCY."

You jump out of the grave and land on the ground with a huge crash. You pick up Claudius by the head. "GHOST TELL HAMLET TO KILL KING MAN. HAMLET NOT SCARED OF GHOST BUT DOES AS HE ASKS UNDER OWN VOLITION."

Claudius's head pops like a grape.

"EW GROSS," you say.

Gertrude says, "Oh Hamlet, I always knew you had a gamma-irradiated monster inside you, just waiting to come out and save me when the moment was right!" Horatio and the gravedigger rush up beside you and say you're the most awesome dude ever. Suddenly, you feel woozy.

"HAMLET HAVE TO SIT DOWN," you say. "HAMLET FEEL DIZZY, AS IF ALL OF THIS IS ELABORATE FANTASY HAMLET'S OXYGEN-STARVED BRAIN ENTERTAINING ITSELF WITH JUST BEFORE HAMLET IS CHOKED TO DEATH."

"That's crazy," says Ophelia. What? Yes, she's still alive! She's stepping out of her coffin. "Don't be silly, Hamlet," she says, reaching towards you. "Everything's fine, my love. Everything is beautiful, and nothing hurts."

And the funny thing is, she's right. You kiss her, and it's almost like that one single kiss lasts the rest of your life.

THE END

Turn to 257

201

"Listen, I feel kinda bad about getting into that fight with Laertes," you say.

"And ruining Ophelia's funeral?" Horatio volunteers.

"That too. You know what, I'll be nice to him. He's grieving too, right? We're like two peas in a pod, only instead of peas, we're humans, and instead of being in a pod, we're in a state of grief."

"Okay," says Horatio.

"I just really hate it when people try to grieve harder than I do!!" you exclaim, punching your fist into your palm.

"That must come up a lot," says Horatio.

"Anyway, meet me at the castle tomorrow morning, okay?" you say. "There's something that's going to go down that I think you'll want to see."

"Okay. I will."

"Sweet. Well, see you later!" you say, and then it's awkward because you're both still walking to the castle in the same direction side by side. You walk in silence for a bit, until you get the bright idea of stopping because a flower looks SO INTERESTING, and then Horatio will walk ahead and it won't be weird anymore, but then Horatio stops too, a few paces ahead. God.

It proceeds like this, the two of you walking in fits and starts, one pausing to adjust his leggings or whatever and the other deciding to wait, but only after taking a few halting steps ahead. You guys. I don't know.

When you finally get to bed, you go to sleep sad (Ophelia's dead, remember?) but also excited (You're going to expose Claudius tomorrow and you have *Calypso's Gale* to back you up, remember?).

While you're sleeping, I sneak in and pour a Potion of Not Grieving Anymore Because Feelings Are Boring into your ear (that's how liquids enter the body most efficiently, remember? REMEMBER? THIS IS ONE CALLBACK-FILLED SCENE, MY FRIEND) and you wake up feeling not too emo, which is terrific, because honestly we're finally heading towards a climax and I don't want you missing out on it because you stay home being sad.

Okay!

It's tomorrow!

Greet the new day: *turn to 178*

203

Okay, you are Ophelia. You are dead.

Surprise, I wasn't joking!!

THE END

Turn to 130

204

"Listen, Horatio, sometimes I say sexist stuff and I don't really mean it," you say, trying to salvage things.

"But why would you say something you don't mean? And then keep saying those things over and over again?" asks Horatio.

"Look, Horatio, you can't judge the past by the standards of the present. Maybe in the future we'll have more evolved attitudes, but it's unfair to judge someone from the past by those higher standards as he or she was raised in a different cultural context."

"Okay, sure, but we're both in the present," says Horatio. "Chicks, man, am I right? They crazy," you say.

"Yes, what IS the deal with over half the human population of the planet? They're definitely all 100% insane," Horatio replies sarcastically.

Well, this isn't going very well. You decide to stand around silently and wait for something to happen.

Stand around silently and wait for something to happen: *turn to 329*

206 Okay! You wanted to kill your stepfather earlier, but why not kill Ophelia's father instead? That's obviously a really good decision!

You leave the room with Polonius in tow. You find a nice empty room with a nice curtain in it and tell Polonius to stand behind it. He does. You stab him through the curtain.

"Oh, I am slain," he says. His eyes roll back in his head. "Oh, it was much sooner than I expected."

Well, now you've got a body to hide and it's not even the body you wanted! Nice going, Hamlet!

Thinking quickly, you close the door to the room, so at least you won't be discovered for a while. Unfortunately you forgot that the key is on the other side of the door, so now you've locked yourself into the room with the body of the man you just murdered. Whoops!

Suddenly you hear someone coming down the hall. If they reach this room and find you here, it'll be game over! You must dispose of the body and/or escape the room before being discovered!

You have 8 turn(s) remaining.

LOOK ROOM: *turn to 227*

TRY THE DOOR AGAIN, MAYBE IT'S NOT REALLY LOCKED: *turn to 224*

207 You go and stand on the window ledge. Looking down, you see a five-storey drop beneath you. You jump, fall five storeys, miraculously hit the ground on your feet without breaking anything, trip over one of the body parts you've thrown there, fall down, break your neck, squirt out blood everywhere, and die.

Sometimes when people read books like this where they get to make choices, they get mad that they die for no reason. While your death right after miraculously surviving your five-storey drop COULD qualify as that sort of unfair storytelling, you did also just jump out of a window expecting to survive, so on second thought, no it doesn't. You're still dead! And you stay that way...FOREVER.

THE END

Turn to 383

208 You leave, promising to have someone come get rid of the body, and on your way out the door you bump into your bros Rosencrantz and Guildenstern. "You wanna get out of here?" you say, and they concede that they would like to party on a boat. You know what? That sounds nice. Sort of give everyone space, you know?

"There's a boat headed for England in just a few hours!" you say. You know this because boats to England are kind of a big deal.

You send some servants to clean up crazy ol' dead Polonius and another to be there for your mother, and you pack your bags. A few hours later, you and your bros are partying on a boat!

PARTY BOAT!! *Turn to 151*

209

You go to the king's room, but he's not there and the door is locked. On the door is a note:

"Gone prayin'."

You deduce that Claudius is in the church, which means you could kill him in a church, which has got to be among the most badass places to kill someone. Just before you stab him you could say a one-liner like "REST IN PIECES," or "YOU NEVER HAD A PRAYER," or "GIVE US THIS DAY OUR DAILY STABS" — man, there are tons of options here! You decide you really want to explore them!

GO TO THE CHURCH TO STAB CLAUDIUS: *turn to 87*

210

You walk around behind the throne so you can look over his shoulder as he reads. You figure that helps your whole "act crazy" thing, because you'd HAVE to be crazy to not know how annoying this is!

You try to peer over Claudius's shoulder and try to make it look casual, but it's not easy, and the clothes Claudius is wearing aren't helping any. He's all decked out in these puffy-shouldered, mega-regal "king clothes" that probably look GREAT in a portrait, but now they're just annoyingly interfering with your view. You can still see what he's reading, sure, but you're forced to constantly move around as he shifts in his chair just to maintain an unobstructed line of sight. It's kinda suboptimal.

Hey, you know what would be even BETTER than this whole scene? Actually being Claudius and then reading the book as him! Then you'd be there on the ground floor, seeing exactly what he sees, and there'd be no furs in the way! It's perfect!

You agree with me that this is a much better solution, and that I am a kind and gentle author for having suggested it.

BE CLAUDIUS, SEE HOW THAT GOES: *turn to 311*

O, I die, Horatio! The potent poison quite o'ercrows my spirit! I cannot live to hear the news from ENGLAND.
But I do prophesy the election lights on FORTINBRAS.
He has my dying voice. So tell him, with th' occurrents, more and less, which have solicited.
THE REST IS SILENCE. O,o,o,o.

212 "Well, we'd better not open it," you say. Flipping the letter back over, you see it's addressed to the King of England.

"I guess we should probably deliver it to its proper recipient instead!" you say. That's exactly what anyone decent would do, right? You're good people.

When you eventually arrive in England, you do just that, only it turns out the letter contains instructions sent by Claudius, in which he asks the king of England — king to king — to kill you. So that's what England King does, really efficiently, and your bros fight for you and they get killed too.

It was a super dick move by Claudius! If only you could swear revenge on him and then exact it, perhaps by going back and making a different decision? If only that were a thing you could do. If only that were a thing you could do RIGHT NOW AS YOU READ THESE WORDS, DOING IT BEFORE YOU EVEN REACH THE END OF THIS SENTENCE, wow still here, huh?

Okay, I'm going to make it really easy for you. It's the page you just came from. Why not go read it? Just — just go back a little; nobody will judge. I'm giving you a do-over. Take it.

THE END
OR IS IT, HOPEFULLY IT IS NOT

Turn to 269

213 Are you sure you want to be a pirate? They not only fight nations, they also fight each other. I mean, you DID just defeat a crew of them, but to be honest you got really lucky. I wouldn't want to push it.

Hah hah, okay, you talked me out of it. To England! Party!! *Turn to 302*

Hah hah, okay, you talked me out of it. To Denmark! Revenge!! *Turn to 165*

Um HELLO I already said I want to be a PIRATE: *turn to 480*

214 "I didn't murder your dad!" shouts Claudius. "And YOU'RE the one who murdered Polonius!"

Oh right. There is that.

"HEY!" you yell. "You killed Dad by pouring poison in his ear while he slept, and then stole the throne by sexing up his widow!" This is a useful thing to shout, as it brings all the onlookers up to speed.

"You don't have any proof," Claudius replies, evenly.

"Proof? DAD'S GHOST CAME AND TOLD ME WHAT HAPPENED. How's that for proof? Also, the afterlife exists! I guess he's proof of that too!"

"I don't think—" Claudius begins.

"MOM, MOVE 15 PACES TO THE LEFT," you shout. Claudius grabs her by the wrist.

"She's not going anywhere," he shouts. Now what?

Fire the cannon anyway; maybe you'll hit Claudius and not your mom: *turn to 367*

No, that'll never work! The only way to pull this off is if you launch YOURSELF out of a cannon. *Turn to 191*

215

I need to learn to stop giving you gag options, because you keep taking them. Joke's on me, I guess?

Anyway, you throw "being nice to the woman who gave birth to you" out the window, and you give the curtain the ol' stabby-me-do and kill whoever's behind it. "Lo, I am slain," he says, though it kinda sounds like "Lol, I am slain," which you think would've been funnier. But wait a second! The voice sounds like...Polonius?

"What have you done?" screams your mother. Thinking quickly, you say, "Nothing as bad as killing a king and marrying his wife!"

"What?! I didn't murder anyone!" she says.

"Okay, NO, obviously," you say. "But Claudius did and then you married him! Besides, maybe I thought the guy behind the curtain was Claudius and therefore I was...doing a good deed?"

"How is it a good deed to kill my husband?" asks your mom. "And besides, didn't you see him praying on your way here? We both know he's in the church. He can't be in two places at once."

"Um," you say. Turning away from the body, you start yelling at your mom, saying how great Dad was, how awful Claudius is, and how she traded the best dude ever for the worst dude ever in time, and finally how she's pretty dumb and awful and too old for love anyway. You say all these things to your own mother. You reduce her to tears.

"You've made me feel horrible about my marriage," she says, pitifully.

"When you have sex, it's awful and it makes the bed all greasy," you reply.

Wow.

Suddenly, a ghost appears! TWIST!!

Talk to ghost: *turn to 29*

216

"I'm Hamlet!" you say.

"Okay," he says. "I'm Partario. Nice to meet you."

An awkward silence follows.

"Hey," says the gravedigger finally. "You know that skull you were eyeing before? That's the skull of the old king's jester, Yorick. He poured a flagon of Rhenish on my head once."

"Yorick?!" you say, excited. "Rhenish?!"

TALK ABOUT YORICK: *turn to 404*

TALK ABOUT RHENISH: *turn to 113*

217

I don't see a chamber here.

You have 6 turn(s) remaining.

FRIG! LOOK AREA!! *Turn to 3*

218

You and Hamlet 2 rush at Claudius as he roars, his sword raised. He tries to stab it through you, and you cut his arm off. He punches at Hamlet 2 with his remaining arm, so Hamlet 2 cuts that one off too. Then the two of you team up and use your swords like giant scissors to cut off Claudius's head.

What just happened is so awesome I'm not sure I can properly convey it. Giant scissors cutting off a head. It's — it's amazing. Let's linger on that image. I'm sincerely impressed with how awesome you guys were just now.

Okay! Let's move on!

You look around at everyone who'd gathered to watch this fight, and they're all pretty shocked and amazed at what they just saw.

"Um, I'd like to introduce my friend," you say. "I think he's...me?"

"Thanks," says Hamlet 2. "Only I'm not quite you. I'm actually your ghost! But I figured out how to time travel in such a way that I got a new body too."

"So — I died?" you ask.

"Yeah, um, a while back actually," he says. "But that was another timeline. I think things are different here though. I think you won't have to die to create me because another Hamlet already did that, and all possible timelines coexist at once in one giant timey-wimey jumble."

"It doesn't have to be a jumble," you offer. "I'm sure you could also imagine a universe of alternate possibilities nicely bound together in a book, presenting a well-organized choice structure."

Hamlet 2 smiles and offers his hand to you.

"Yeah. I think we're good," he says.

The two of you stand side by side and raise your hands up together, in front of your mother, your friends, and the cheering audience.

You and Hamlet 2 rule Denmark together really well, with your youthful exuberance balancing out Hamlet 2's literal millennia of knowledge and contemplation. When you're not attending to matters of state, the two of you hang out and become best friends and even fool around a little but that's weird, it's weird, I don't know why you guys have to be so weird.

THE END

P.S. For making out with yourself, you are awarded 1,000,000 autoperv points AND unlock the skill Mirrored Tongue Fencing! USE IT WISELY, MY FRIEND.

Turn to 528

219

Okay! FINE. Remembering that you haven't decided if you can trust him yet, you have a long conversation where you explain again, in detail, the lie you've told him. You elaborate it into a crazy story where you alone come across the letter by accident, you leave out all the awesome parts of the pirate battle (a crime in itself), you tell him only you made it back alive and how Rosencrantz and Guildenstern are dead, and he's all "Whoah that must make you sad," and you say "No bro, they got what they deserved," and he's all "Whoah bro: harsh." You definitely do not tell him how you have one of the most impressive ships in the world today waiting just outside Denmark Harbour for your signal.

Alright! We're all brought up to speed with your cover story of how you escaped, AGAIN, and Horatio has made the appropriate sympathetic noises. Satisfied? Look you can stop pretending, we all know you kinda lost the plot here and wanted to waste everyone's time while you got a refresher from me. But now you're out of options, and all you can do is:

TALK TO HORATIO ABOUT WHAT JUST HAPPENED: *turn to 201*

220

"We're taking them with us, lads!" you say, which interestingly enough is the point at which you become the villain of the story. "Port crew: FIRE ALL CANNONS!"

Deafening gunfire sounds, and soon cannons are pounding the castle and town. Incendiary cannonballs inflame anything that will burn, while spider shot tears bodies to shreds. By the time you're done, nothing remains of Castle Kronborg (that's the name of the royal castle, should've mentioned this before but better late than never) and of the town of Elsinore (again, that's where this takes place, REALLY sorry for not mentioning this sooner) but rubble and gore.

A few nights after this awful attack, the ghost of your dad visits, says, "WHAT THE HELL," and never appears to you again. It's okay though, because you have plenty of hauntings from the ghosts of the rest of the townspeople you murdered! They throw pots at your head and they can never die!

THE END

Turn to 95

222

You explain to her about your dad and the ghost and how he wants you to murder Claudius.

Ophelia looks at you for a long moment, and then she takes your hand. "Sweetie," she says, "I can tell that you think you saw those things, and for now, I'm going to believe you. But we need to gather evidence of this ghost and find out if he's credible. Even if he is a ghost, are we CERTAIN he's the ghost of your dad? What if he's a ghost of someone else who's trying to mess with you? I think you should have some confirmation before you go around murdering people."

What she says makes sense. She says the two of you can try to see the ghost again tonight, and if he does show up, you can figure out if he's really your dad or not. It sounds really nice. It sounds...sane. You agree to go with her.

"In the meantime," she says, "check out what I've been working on for you. It's alcohol in a glass flute!"

She looks at you for your reaction, and you're not sure what you're looking at. "It measures temperature!" she says. "With this, you won't have to be too cold or too warm in different castle rooms, because we'll be able to see which ones are uncomfortable before we go in them!"

She's been working on this all by herself over the past several weeks, while you've been sitting alone in your room, moping. She's so awesome. You love her more than ever.

Go see the ghost with her tonight: *turn to 519*

223

Um. Okay. You do that. Ophelia looks confused during this whole production.

"What's wrong, Hamlet?" she says, concerned. "Why are you fouling your stockings?"

Tell her you don't know why you're doing that, apologize, and ask her to help with murdering your uncle: *turn to 222*

You know what? This is not going as well as I'd hoped. Tell Ophelia you don't know why you're wasting your time either, excuse yourself, and GO MURDER CLAUDIUS. *Turn to 142*

Continue holding her wrist, and move your other hand to your forehead as if you might faint, while staring at her intensely: *turn to 228*

224

You jiggle the door, but it's locked firmly. The noise attracts the attention of the person in the hallway.

"Have you locked yourself in there?" you hear. "Hold on, I'll open the door for you! I'm running now to get there faster! I will get there really soon now!!"

Nice going, dude!

You now have only 1 turn(s) remaining.

Try to act casual: *turn to 18*

There's probably a window behind that curtain; jump out the window to escape: *turn to 232*

225

"Put the wind at our back!" you order. Your first mate says, "Aye sir," and begins barking commands to the crew. "Set sails leeward! We'll be running before the wind, boys!"

The crew adjusts the sails quickly, and you can feel it as the boat gains speed. You look behind you, expecting to see *Calypso's Gale* fade from view, but even with the wind fully at your back, the pirate ship is still gaining.

It wasn't enough. *Calypso's Gale* fires again, and chain shot tears through *Vesselmania*'s stern and exits through the port side of the hull, thankfully above the waterline.

"Orders, Captain?"

You stare at *Calypso's Gale* through a spyglass. The square shape of her rigging reminds you of something...

"Continue with the wind at our back." *Turn to 132*

"Turn around and face the pirates head-on." *Turn to 102*

Try to remember everything you know about sailing before you answer: *turn to 27*

227

I don't see a room here.

You have 7 turn(s) remaining.

Look chamber: *turn to 217*

228

These are some stellar choices you're making here, champ.

Okay, you do the crazy things. Ophelia keeps staring at you in confusion. Finally, you sigh, as big as you can, three times in a row. What do these sighs mean? Ophelia doesn't know, I don't know, and neither do you. It's like you think you've saved your game earlier so now you can just do stupid stuff without consequences. BUT YOU CAN'T SAVE A GAME IN REAL LIFE, SILLY, so now you've got to live with the consequences of these choices. And here's one of those consequences: Ophelia's love for you has taken 15 damage. Lucky for YOU, she still loves you a whole heck of a lot.

Eventually you run out of sighs and get up and leave, but rather than walking out of the room like a regular person, you look over your shoulder, lock eyes with her, and walk out of the room and around the corner without ever breaking that eye contact. You're lucky you didn't walk into a wall.

You know what? I think you've made enough choices for a while. Move over. I'm driving.

You decide to go see what Claudius is up to: *turn to 193*

229

AWESOME. I'm glad you chose this option!!

"AWESOME," Hamlet says. "I'm glad you chose this option!" So wow, it seems everyone is down with this course of action, Ophelia!

Okay so space travel hasn't been invented yet (IF IT EVER WILL BE, I DON'T KNOW BECAUSE I AM FROM HISTORY TOO) so this is going to be a bit — tricky? You and Hamlet spend most of your time trying to invent rocket ships, but this is with old-timey technology which is, like, tarps and stuff, so needless to say it doesn't work.

However, a few months into your research you begin to think that if you can't reach the stars, second best isn't so bad, and so you and Hamlet get Claudius drunk and put him in a giant wicker basket attached to a hot-air balloon, which is a thing you did manage to invent! Then you send him so far up he suffocates to death in the thin air up there, and then the balloon explodes due to the low atmospheric pressure, and then when his body hits the ground it explodes too, so I guess the saying is wrong after all and really, revenge is a dish best served at slightly below body temperature, dropped from a great height, and observed from a safe distance.

THE END

Turn to 135

230

You talk about free will!

"Providence controls everything, even a sparrow's death," you say. "If something's supposed to happen now, it will. If it's supposed to happen later, then it won't happen now. All that matters is that we're prepared for it."

"Wait," says Horatio, "if you subscribe to a 'destiny is all' worldview where things happen when they're supposed to, how does preparedness enter into it? If it's going to happen, it'll happen whether or not you're prepared."

"Um," you say.

To repeat what you just said about free will, *read this node again.*

To talk about that sexist thing you said in the last node, choose this option instead: *turn to 204*

I'm done talking! Stand around and wait for something to happen. *Turn to 329*

231

You jump at him quickly and slice at his shoulder. Incredibly, your sword slices through it like butter: it looks like you got more meat than bone, but it's still an impressive strike. The piece of pirate you carved off flies through the air, hits your shoulder, and slides down to the ground, landing in a bloody heap of flesh and gore.

The pirate looks at you, aghast.

"Excuse me, I never introduced myself," you say, brandishing your sword. "I'm Prince Hamlet. And today must be your lucky day, my friend, because..."

"You just rubbed shoulders with royalty." *Turn to 59*

"Someone finally fixed that chip on your shoulder." *Turn to 233*

"Nobody's going to be looking over your shoulder anymore!" *Turn to 152*

232

You go and stand on the window ledge. Looking down, you see a five-storey drop beneath you. You jump out which is fun, fall five storeys which is terrifying, hit the ground which is incredibly painful, break your arms and legs and neck and squirt out blood everywhere and die, which, it turns out, is fatal.

Yep! Dying is fatal!

Listen man, real talk: nobody's gonna judge you if you go back a bit and do things differently.

THE END

Turn to 221

233

The pirate captain screams in rage, charging you with his sword. You deftly parry and sidestep, ending up behind him.

The two of you circle each other, flurries of swordplay erupting whenever one of you detects an opportunity. Despite his injury, neither of you is able to gain the advantage on the rain-soaked deck of the ship.

Suddenly, lightning strikes the brass rail behind the pirate captain, and he's briefly stunned by the tremendous thunder that follows. You're stunned as well but, being a few feet away, you recover more quickly.

There's your opening, Hamlet!

Attack his dominant, sword-bearing arm! *Turn to 46*

Attack his eyes! *Turn to 469*

Attack his legs! *Turn to 234*

234

You swing your sword at his legs, putting all your strength behind the blow. Your sword slices through his left leg easily, and he staggers. You swing again with both hands on your sword and cleave off his right leg. He falls backwards to the deck, still holding his sword. He's furious, and incredibly the wounds he's just suffered haven't stopped him. He begins to crawl towards you, blood marking his path in a dark, sticky trail behind him.

You crouch so that you can meet his gaze, and say the perfect one-liner:

"Hey! Look! I found your sea legs!" *Turn to 162*

"Wow. You're really on your last legs." *Turn to 253*

"My friend, you don't have a leg to stand on." *Turn to 378*

235

He straight-up ignores your zinger.

WELL, SHOOT: *turn to 131*

236

"Are you my dad? I mean, my Ghost Dad?" you ask the ghost, but it says nothing. Instead, the ghost beckons to you. He clearly wants you to follow him and leave Horatio behind. I dunno, is this safe? Can ghosts kill people?

"Can ghosts kill people?" you ask Horatio.

"I DON'T KNOW MAN, BUT I REALLY DON'T THINK YOU SHOULD BE ALONE WITH THAT THING," he says, clearly leaving no ball untripped in his own freakout.

"HAMLET, MAN, SOMETHING IS ROTTEN IN THE STATE OF DENMARK, I GOTTA SAY," he yells, his quivering finger pointing at the ghost. Well, duh.

"I'm gonna do it," you say, and you...

FOLLOW THE GHOST INTO DARKNESS: *turn to 181*

GO ON TO SAY "BY THAT I MEAN, I'M GOING TO TAKE THIS LAST CHANCE TO RUN FOR IT!!" *Turn to 194*

237

You and Laertes settle on the swords you like and face off against each other. As you're about to begin, Claudius speaks!

"Let's make this a drinking game!" he says.

"Um," you say.

"If you make the first hit," Claudius says, "then we'll both take a drink."

"Okay," you say.

"But if Laertes hits you and you only make the second hit," he says, "then we'll both take a drink too."

"Okay," you say.

"Ooh! And if Laertes hits you TWICE before you make a hit, so you only make the third hit, then we'll both take a drink."

"I'm not sure if I should get drunk during a fencing match," you say.

"I'll put a pearl in your drink, hah hah, there's nothing suspicious about that!" Claudius says.

"Not really super thirsty either way," you say.

Claudius stares at you.

"Can we fence now?" you say.

The fencing match begins! Laertes moves towards you, sword at the ready. What do you do?

Go for his upper body!! *Turn to 242*

Attack his lower body!! *Turn to 263*

238

Really? You're gonna pretend you didn't hear your stepdad — the one you're here to take revenge on, I remind you — when he says he just poisoned your mother? When they invented "choose your own path" books, I'm pretty sure they were assuming you wouldn't choose to be insane! So thanks for proving them wrong, I guess!

Okay, you ignore him, and since this is YOUR adventure, everyone else ignores him too. Why not, right? You and Laertes continue your fight. At one point Laertes says that what he's doing is almost against his conscience, which seems like a weird thing to say in a friendly non-fatal fight like this, but you ignore that too! Hooray! Your ears are useless!

You fight back and forth, and at one point your swords clash in front of you and there's a moment of silence as both of you try to overpower the other. This is your chance to say something awesome.

"Bring it on," you try to say as grimly and badassedly as possible, but somehow it comes out as "I pray you, pass with your best violence. I am afeard you make a wanton of me," so...oh well?

Pushing as hard as you can, you manage to force Laertes' sword aside, but in the fighting that ensues he manages to cut you on your arm. Enraged, you break the rules of swordfighting just a little and kick his hand, sending his sword flying. In response, he kicks at your hand, sending your sword flying to the exact same spot. You both scramble towards the swords, trying to re-arm yourselves.

Take the left sword: *turn to 265*

Take the right sword: *turn to 252*

239

That's RIGHT. Fall in line, baby.

You haven't touched a book since you came home from university on funeral / wedding break, so you answer by making up a book you've been reading called *Old Men Are Gross and Dumb*. It's about how old men are gross and dumb. You conclude by saying that Polonius would be the same age as you...if people aged backwards!!

Oh snap.

Polonius agrees that this is probably the case.

Finally he challenges you with the final of his three riddles. "Would you like to go for a walk...outside?"

You sure would!! *Turn to 82*

240

You do that, and make Rosencrantz and Guildenstern your first officers. Congratulations, Captain Hamlet! *Calypso's Gale* is yours to command!

Your crew demands a speech, cheering and hollering at you. Stepping up onto the highest part of *Calypso's* bridge, you decide to give them what they want. You hold your hands out in front of you and ask for silence.

They quiet, and in the moment before you speak the only noise you hear is the sound of waves gently splashing on the hull beneath you, a peaceful, beautiful sound. It's a perfect moment.

You look at your crew, and they at you.

"People often speak of the machinery of fate," you say, "as though the course of our lives is governed by some untouchable, unknowable clockwork. Well, if fate be a machine...today she was a machine that transformed us all into an UNSTOPPABLE FORCE OF VENGEANCE!"

Your crew cheers wildly!

"Gods, even!!"

Your crew cheers even louder!

"Yes," you say, "today we truly were gods from the machine." Your crew resumes their duties.

This was a really amazing part of your adventure, Hamlet.

You're sure that, should you ever one day write a book about this story or perhaps a stage production, you'd DEFINITELY include this scene. Why, you'd have to be literally crazy to write a story where you journey to England, get attacked by pirates — actual pirates! — but then just sum up that whole adventure in a single sentence. Hah! That'd be the worst. Who puts a pirate-attack scene in their story and doesn't show it to the audience? Hopefully nobody, that's who! Even from a purely structural viewpoint, you've got to give the audience something awesome to make up for all the introspection you've been doing; that just seems pretty obvious is all.

Anyway, enough crazy hypotheticals! To where will you make sail?

Sail to England; this party is JUST GETTING STARTED: *turn to 302*

Sail back to Denmark to revenge yourself on Claudius: *turn to 165*

Become pirates! The sails are already flying; it'll be EASY. *Turn to 213*

242

You decide to attack his upper body, but hesitate. Maybe the lower body is better after all? He wouldn't be expecting it. You're about to change your mind and attack the lower body when you get hit on the back of the head with a piece of dirt. The audience is heckling you! With dirt!! This makes you mad, which makes you attack his upper body after all!

You jab and thrust towards Laertes' upper body. He deftly parries, blocking your every attack and returning them with attacks of his own, using your own momentum against you.

This isn't as easy as it was on the pirate ship! It seems like Laertes really knows what he's doing?

Every time it looks like you might make a hit, Claudius seems really excited and raises his glass. Wow, that is one thirsty usurper to the throne!

Finally, and not without quite a bit of luck, you land a glancing blow on Laertes' left shoulder!

"Got you!" you say.

"Nuh-uh!" he says.

"Ref?" you say.

"Am I the ref?" says Osric. "I am? Oh. Yeah, that was a hit. Palpably so!"

"Hooray!!" Claudius says. "Let's drink! Hamlet, come drink with me! Look, I put a foreign substance in your drink!"

"I'm in the middle of fencing here, Claudius," you say. Claudius looks crestfallen. He lowers the drink as the fencing match begins again.

Go for his lower body this time!! *Turn to 259*

Go for his upper body again!! *Turn to 83*

243

You use up one of your turns observing the room extremely carefully. You see a medium-sized square room, with a curtain on the wall opposite the door. Light escaping from beneath the curtain suggests there's a window on the other side. Pulling the curtain back, you see there is indeed a large window, big enough to fit yourself or a body through. Looking down, you see you're about five storeys up from the ground.

Turning back from the window to face the door you just locked, you see on the right wall a fireplace with what smells like a pot of stew simmering. On the facing wall to the left is a table upon which some twine and several tightly woven but light-looking bags sit. The room is lit by several torches on the walls. I think you're in a kitchen!

In your inventory, you have: the sword you just used to stab Polonius.

Polonius's body is here, behind the curtain. You have 4 turn(s) remaining.

Use sword on Polonius's body: *turn to 278*

Throw Polonius's body out the window: *turn to 270*

Jump out the window to escape: *turn to 232*

244

"Got you," you say.

"Okay, okay. You got me," Laertes says.

"Our son will win," says Claudius calmly.

"Um, hello, I'm not your son!" you shout in reply. Just then, your mom calls you fat and lazy and offers you a napkin to rub off your sweat, because she thinks you're so fat you're already sweating out of your forehead from just one little fight.

Whoah! Where'd THAT come from?

"What the butt, Mom?" you say. "Where'd THAT come from?"

"Whatever," she says and holds up the goblet Claudius poured for you. "Look, I'm ironically drinking to your good health and fortune!"

"Don't drink that!" Claudius says.

"I drinks what I wants," your mom says, and then she does just that, drinking what she wants.

"Aw geez, that's the poisoned cup. It's too late for you now," Claudius says.

Say "WHAT?!": *turn to 123*

Pretend you didn't hear him: *turn to 238*

245

You jab your sword at his face, and he jumps to the side in an attempt to dodge it. However, in doing so he catches the tip of your sword on the side of his lip, slicing through his cheek and sending a small chunk of flesh flopping down to the deck. An inch-long wound stretches along the side of his face, revealing the teeth underneath. He screams in pain and clutches at his mouth. Blood pours through his fingers and down his chin.

Wow. This is really grody. On the plus side, I think you're winning the fight! You draw his gaze down to the hunk of cheek on the deck.

"I heard people say you were a good swordfighter...," you sigh,

"Such a shame to see you suddenly LOSE FACE." *Turn to 152*

"Well, I suppose you always did have a BIG MOUTH." *Turn to 59*

"How embarrassing is losing this fight for you? Boy, is your face red!" *Turn to 233*

SLASH

247

"Okay," Horatio says. "I'll tell them you said, 'I found Denmark clay, I leave her marble.'"

"That's plagiarized from Augustus, first emperor of the Roman Empire," you say.

"Yeah, but it's a pretty classy thing to say, especially for someone in power!" he replies.

"But I was never actually in power, as I died before any formal ceremony could take place," you say. "And even if I had technically been king, I could not have yet had any impact, negative or positive, on the nation as a whole," you say, quite reasonably.

Then you die.

After you die, Horatio tells everyone your last words were "Rootie tootie, rub a dub dub / I once did a toot inside of a tub" and then he says, "Wait, wait, no, I just remembered, his actual last words were 'Hey blabby flabby,'" which isn't even better, what the hell, Horatio??

THE END

Turn to 44

248

Sometimes I wonder why I give you these choices.

Okay, you say those things, but you at least clarify that you think women just PRETEND to be dumb to get that sexing they so crave. You accuse all women of being unfaithful, and you say there should be no more marriages, because they necessarily involve women and women are awful.

There's — a couple of things wrong with that, actually?

Anyway, you say that people who are already married can stay married, YOU GUESS, except for ONE VERY SPECIAL COUPLE IN PARTICULAR. You look at her to see if she's getting what you're hinting at. And she looks...super angry, actually! I don't think you're gonna pull this off, dude!

This whole conversation is an unmitigated fiasco, and if she was just pretending to be mad before, she's seriously furious now. Congratulations, Hamlet! You just broke up with your girlfriend because you were pretending to be insane and trying to talk in a stupid secret code! You can't really say you blame her for leaving. All you have now is your plan to trap Claudius with a choose-your-own-path adventure book, so you go home, rest, and tomorrow, that's exactly what you do.

TRY TO TRAP CLAUDIUS WITH THE BOOK: *turn to 150*

250

You are now Ryan North. This is weird!

So listen: you just had the idea to write a book where you can play as Hamlet or Ophelia or even the ghost. Right now, the book exists as mere potential. On one hand, you can make it happen, but it'll take months of work. On the other hand, ideas are like chest hairs: you have so many of them that it's hard to get attached to any one in particular. Plus new ones are popping up all the time!

You go skateboarding to decide what to do. You're getting mad air while pulling off some insanely rad skateboard tricks while also munching on pizza, and it hits you: writing this book is something you want to do. You say goodbye to all the babes and go home to write.

Almost a year later, you write the last ending for the last version of reality you've chosen to put in this book. It's done. It's a pretty solid first draft. A few months after that, you've smushed it into a pretty solid second draft, and then months after that, a totally rad final draft. All that's left now is to do a final readover to make sure there are no typos, inconsistencies, or spelling errorrs!

You grab some snacks, sit down, and bring your draft so close to your face that you can't really see anything else. And then you start reading.

These are the words you read! *Turn to 1*

251

You grab hold of your chair with both hands and hold on tight as your ship shudders around you. Outside, in space, blaster fire from the Deltron ship comes within a few degrees Kelvin of lighting your ship's hull on fire.

"Return fire!" you order. "Give them everything we've got!"

Your first officer unleashes a torrent of energy and hardware at the Deltron ship, enough to destroy just about any ship in your fleet.

It barely scratches the Deltron hull.

You're running out of options, Captain. What do you do?

Ramming speed! *Turn to 272*

Evasive manoeuvres! *Turn to 269*

Engage...the Omega Protocol! *Turn to 275*

252

You grab the right sword while Laertes grabs the left. In the flurry of swordplay that ensues, you cut Laertes on his leg while at the same time Laertes cuts your leg. It is a perfect symmetry.

Fortunately for you, the sword you grabbed had poison on its tip! Life's full of surprises, huh? And this new surprise is that Laertes is now poisoned. Very soon you're going to be responsible for an extremely public murder. But don't worry too much: since it was Laertes' sword that was poison-tipped in the first place, that means you too are poisoned from that earlier cut! Hooray!

Okay, just to summarize real quick: you still haven't killed Claudius, but you have managed to poison your onetime (now dead) girlfriend's brother, get poisoned yourself, and allow your mother to be poisoned too. If you're wondering about your score, right now it's at, oh I don't know, NEGATIVE 55,000 KILOPOINTS??

Gertrude collapses from the poison you ignored earlier, and feigning ignorance you say, "How's the queen?" and Claudius says, "She fainted because you guys are bleeding," and she says, "NO, I'm poisoned from the drink!" and then she dies.

"We've been betrayed" you shout, and then feigning ignorance again, you shout, "Quick, lock the doors! Let's find out who did it!"

Laertes, a man who is dying AS WE SPEAK, is thus forced to spend his last few moments alive explaining to you very clearly and with no big words that your mother was poisoned by the king. He also explains to you that you've been poisoned too, but I already told you that. It's too bad too, because he said it very nicely, all "Hamlet, thou art slain. No medicine in the world can do thee good" while I was all "wooby wooby woo, jokes jokes jokes" (NOTE: I am paraphrasing).

ANYWAY. Now is your absolute last chance. You have a poisoned sword in your hand and Claudius is sitting here in front of you. You will be dead in 1 turn(s). What do you do? LAST CHANCE, Hamlet.

Kill Claudius: *turn to 384*

Don't kill Claudius: *turn to 304*

253

The pirate screams at you, livid. He's lost some very important body parts, but he's not going to stop. He's out of control with rage and will fight you right to the end. You can't let your guard down. He'll take you apart with his teeth if you let him.

It's time to finish this, Hamlet.

Deliver the killing blow! *Turn to 163*

254

You take wood from the fireplace and attempt to light the door on fire. However since this is real life and NOT fantasy land, the door does not burst into flames instantly but instead just singes a little. You exhaust any remaining turn(s) in the attempt, and as soon as it / they are used up, the door opens. This has the effect of knocking the burning wood onto your shirt, and that doesn't take nearly as long to catch on fire.

The town criers the next day all have the same story: "HAMLET CATCHES ON FIRE AFTER KILLING THIS GUY POLONIUS / MOST EXCITING THING TO HAPPEN IN MONTHS."

And you know what? It WAS. Thank you for "firing" the imagination of your subjects!

THE END

Turn to 115

255

You drop the sword and leave. "Well, um, see you later I guess!" you say. You walk to the docks and swim out to *Calypso's Gale*.

"I'm a big wimp," you say, "and I couldn't even competently confront Claudius." Rosencrantz and Guildenstern suggest you still could kinda confront him, and it wouldn't even have to be a direct confrontation, as long as you don't mind killing everyone else in the castle too.

"One sec!" you say, diving into the ocean and swimming back to shore. Re-entering the castle yet again, you say, "Hey Mom, come here for a minute?" and lead Gertrude outside. You ask her to stay out of the castle for the next 15 minutes.

"Why?" she asks.

"It's gonna be a big surprise," you shout over your shoulder, already running back down to the docks. Climbing aboard *Calypso's Gale*, you give the order to fire. Twenty-six cannons fire in unison and the outer wall of the castle crumbles. You keep shouting "Fire!" and more cannonballs keep tearing into stone walls and you only stop when there's nothing left of the castle but a big ol' pile of rubble.

Congratulations, you killed Claudius!! And you kept your mom alive. You also killed tons of innocent bystanders too though, as well as the entire castle staff without exception, so your final score is...1.

Man you did all this reading for 1 measly point! You're a champ!

THE END

Turn to 482

256

"Technically correct!" shouts Horatio. "I'm sorry Fortinbras, but you sucked so hard at this. All hail Queen Ophelia!"

Be the new queen of Denmark: *turn to 534*

258 Hah hah, nice try! WHAT YOU JUST SAID IS A TOTAL LIE. And you know what happens when you lie?

I'll tell you what happens.

You hear a rumbling. Ophelia and Horatio run to the window to see what's happening, but as they reach it the castle floor beneath them crumbles and splits. Your last vision of Ophelia is of her falling and calling out as the roof buckles in, burying them both.

You stumble backwards, running out the door as the castle collapses behind you. You're running as fast as you can, tearing down the hallway but still staying only just ahead of the destruction. You leap outside, barely escaping as the castle collapses into rubble behind you. Looking up, you see the storm clouds, lightning crackling between them, thunder shaking the very ground beneath you. The clouds seem to form letters that read "YOU THOUGHT YOU COULD LIE TO THE AUTHOR ABOUT THE CONTENTS OF HIS OWN BOOK? SERIOUSLY??"

As you stumble to your feet, the earth cracks open beneath you, and you're left straddling it with one leg on either side as it splits open wider and wider. Looking down, you see magma and liquid metals rush towards the surface. This gash leads all the way to the earth's core, and the toxic gases rushing past you as they blast towards the sky burn your skin and make you choke. The planet is tearing itself apart, and moments later, it explodes, killing not just all life on Earth but all life that would've lived there in the future, if only you'd told the truth.

The human race is extinguished. You have scored -1 out of a possible 1000 points and died.

Also, you lied to a book.

THE END

Turn to 54

259 You aim for his lower body and Laertes is unprepared for this and you totally score a hit right away!

Nice! *Turn to 244*

260 Okay! The cannon fires and shoots you at Claudius, but the aim is a little off and you're too high. That's realistic, right? Don't worry, it's the last realistic thing that happens.

As you fly over Claudius, you drop your hand down and grab him by his back collar, and the two of you fly over the castle walls together.

"Hamlet! Let me go!" he screams, but by the time his shouts reach your ears it sounds exactly like "Hamlet! Use me like a skateboard!"

"A skateboard?" you say, intrigued.

"Hamlet!!" he hollers at you, but again, by the time those sound waves reach your ears they have amazingly been transformed into sound waves that instead form the words "It's a plank with wheels on it!"

"Neat!" you say.

Anyway, eventually your momentum runs out and you land on the ground using Claudius as a skateboard. He squishes and dies. Just before impact though, you jump off the board, thereby cancelling out your downward momentum and landing softly on his gross corpse.

How realistic!

So you've succeeded in your mission and — oh heck, let's say later on you marry a bear.

THE END

Turn to 144

261

You hang around Norway for a bit, trying to listen in on what people are saying, but they're all speaking Norwegian! You only speak Danish, so understanding Norwegian is a little difficult. It all sounds like Swedish to you!

Which actually makes a lot of sense, since Danish, Norwegian, and Swedish are all related North Germanic languages, descended from early linguistic differentiation between regular Germanic speakers and North Germanic speakers around 200 AD.

You nod your head, agreeing that all of this is both accurate and extremely interesting.

While these three languages are GENERALLY supposed to be mutually intelligible, you find you can understand Norwegian speakers only if you're concentrating (which you are) and if they're speaking slowly and clearly (which they're not, as everyone is running around upset about war and all these kings getting killed). Ironically, Norwegian speakers can understand Danish easier than Danish speakers understand Norwegian, but that doesn't help you much! That would only be useful if you were playing as the Norwegian king whose ghost has stowed away on YOUR army's boat headed back to Denmark, but I haven't given you that option even though it would be extremely awesome. If you're wondering what happens to this Vengeful Ghost King, I can tell you only this: THE ANSWER EXISTS IN YOUR IMAGINATION??

But here's the good news, it turns out WRITTEN Danish and WRITTEN Norwegian are actually pretty similar! So you spend the next several nights haunting people, quietly reading their diaries while they sleep peacefully in their beds. And you don't know this, but ghosts do this all the time. Ghosts just love sneaking a peek at the secrets of the living!

It takes a while, but you finally find the diary of someone who wrote on the day you died that she was wandering by a garden, minding her own business, when she saw some Danish guy pour something in some other Danish guy's ear!

Hey! That sounds like what could've happened to you (but remember you don't know that's exactly what happened to you because of that new irony we invented)!

Wake up this person and ask her about it: *turn to 279*

Wake up this person and hold up a piece of paper where you've written down a question asking her about it: *turn to 481*

262

Okay!

So here's the thing. People really DO get shot out of cannons in real life, but those cannons aren't the same as a cannonball-cannon. They're actually more fairly described as "giant slingshots specially designed to send people flying, with a tiny bit of gunpowder used only for visual effect."

On the other hand, you, my friend, have climbed into an actual cannon stuffed with lots and lots of gunpowder. When the fuse goes, you explode out of the cannon in a chunky red mist. This has the side effect of killing you.

It is extremely realistic / gross. That's what everyone says when they see it! "How realistic slash gross," they say.

THE END

Turn to 353

263

You jab and thrust towards Laertes' lower body. He deftly parries, blocking your every attack and returning them with attacks of his own, using your own momentum against you.

This isn't as easy as it was on the pirate ship! It kinda seems like Laertes really knows what he's doing?

You continue fighting, and every time it looks like you might make a hit, Claudius seems really excited and raises his glass. Wow, that is one thirsty usurper to the throne!

Finally, almost effortlessly, Laertes lands a glancing blow on your left shoulder. It cuts your shirt but barely breaks the skin, so, hooray for thickly woven shirts, I guess!

You resume the match!

Attack his upper body this time!! *Turn to 288*

Attack his lower body again!! *Turn to 289*

KILL

265 You grab the left sword while Laertes grabs the right. In the flurry of swordplay that ensues, you cut Laertes on his leg while at the same time he cuts you on your leg too. It is a perfect symmetry.

Unfortunately, Laertes' sword had poison on its tip all along, and now you've gotten a double dose! Life's full of surprises, huh? I guess the only problem is SOMETIMES these surprises are stupid and fatal.

Gertrude collapses from the poison you ignored earlier, and seconds later you too fall to the ground as the poison destroys your body from the inside out. Claudius looks down at you both.

"Gertrude collapsed because she's a woman and faints whenever she sees blood, and Hamlet collapsed because he's super wimpy and a tiny cut on his leg is enough to kill him," he says, establishing an official history for the crowd.

"Don't be so sexist, jerk," you say, and I'm sorry, but one "don't be so sexist" isn't enough to redeem you from a lifetime of being way sexist, even if it is the very last thing you ever say.

Which, it turns out, it totally is!

THE END

Turn to 419

266 "Okay," Horatio says, and you die.

You are now Horatio!

You rush out of the castle and down to the docks, where you swim out to *Calypso's Gale* and are pulled aboard by the crew. You explain to Rosencrantz and Guildenstern what's happened, and they launch a surprise attack on Fortinbras's ship, sinking her easily. When Fortinbras runs out of the castle and down to the docks, you have spider shot fired at him (one large cannonball with eight smaller cannonballs attached to it; when fired it spins and tears though basically everything including Fortinbras's body; it is awesome) and he gets totes obliterated.

War breaks out between Denmark and Norway. You and Rosencrantz and Guildenstern are instrumental in Denmark's eventual victory, and yeah I'm going over things super quickly here but this was supposed to be, like, Ophelia's story or Hamlet's story and honestly I've always liked you, Horatio, but I'm already bending the rules like crazy by letting you have your own little adventure here so we've got to end it somewhere.

You be good, my friend.

No, you know what? Scratch that. You be GREAT.

THE END

Turn to 70

267 No book comes together without an author feeling like they're in debt to SOMEONE.

Thanks to MetaFilter for all the terrific advice on how to dispose of a body and not get caught (SPOILER ALERT: there are murders in this book). They have a page just about this, did you know that? They're one of the top search results for "how to dispose of a body." And I guess also thanks to the Canadian Security Intelligence Service for not getting me in trouble (yet) after I ran all those searches for "how to dispose of a body" and "I want to know how to get rid of a dead human body" and "gross dead body + how to hide it" and "what if I committed the murder act, how do I ditch the body & not go to jail IT'S AN EMERGENCY??"

Thanks also to Chef Michael Smith, Emily Horne, and William Shakespeare for the stew recipe (SPOILER ALERT: you can learn to make stew in this book too! It's not murders ALL the time), for the expansive knowledge of boats and the seas in which they sail (SPOILER ALERT: play your cards right in this book and you just miiiiight gain command of a pirate ship, just...just be cool), and for ripping me off and making this book so famous (but which thank-you applies to which person?? That is for YOU to decide. Yes, even here in this acknowledgement parenthetical it's up to YOU to choose your own adventure, but I mean come on it's pretty obvious).

Thanks to all my artist friends who drew all these pretty pictures in the book. You've made death into a visually stunning treat. And thanks to Crissy Calhoun for copyediting this book and fixing all my dumb mistakes! Any that remain I added in afterwards because of brain problems.

Finally, thanks to Steven Law and Joey Comeau for his skills at chess, Ray Fawkes for his skills at mad libs, my extremely awesome wife, Jenn, for being extremely awesome, and to my brother, Victor, who confirmed over walkie-talkie that the idea for this book was rad.

And thanks to you, for buying this book or at least picking it up and flipping to this page: that took initiative! As a reward, you get to continue enjoying reading this book!!

Okay, I'm ready now. I will choose my character! *Turn to 1*

Um no, I'd rather read more acknowledgements: *turn to 358*

You know what? I want to know more about the author before I commit to anything. *Turn to 281*

You know what? I want to BE the author before I commit to anything. *Turn to 250*

268 You and Horatio go to where he saw the ghost the first time.

"Now we play the waiting game," says Horatio. He's interrupted by the sound of trumpets. You look at him and raise an eyebrow.

"They make that noise to warn everyone that King Claudius is getting wasted," he says. "Those trumpets go off every night around this time."

He sighs.

"Denmark," he says.

At that exact moment, something insanely crazy happens! What the frig? I'll tell you what the frig: A GHOST IS HERE!

Look ghost: *turn to 78*

269

Your first officer forces the ship to fly quickly, moving in ways well beyond its specs.

"We can't keep this up much longer!" she shouts over the groan of structural bulkheads compressing in ways they weren't designed to handle.

"We have to!" you order. "Just a little longer, Commander!" A section of her control panel begins blinking alarmingly. She looks at it and then at you.

"Structural collapse in 30 seconds!" she shouts.

And then it turns out that in real life these things are actually really hard to predict down to the second and that big catastrophic shipwide structural collapse you were worried about happens as soon as she finishes that sentence.

THE END

P.S. It kills you, by the way.

270

You lift Polonius's still-warm body to the window and push it out over the edge. It hits the ground with a sickening crack, and you see his limbs and neck now rest at unnatural angles. Blood bursts out from his corpse and gets all over the place.

You're now left in a room with a bloody, stabbed curtain, a few storeys up from the mangled body of your ex-girlfriend's father. This isn't going to look good if anyone finds you like this! Especially if they should happen to look out the window!

You have 3 turns(s) remaining.

Burn curtain using fire from fireplace: *turn to 297*

Jump out window, use body to cushion your fall: *turn to 282*

You know what? I can talk my way out of this. Just be cool. Act casual. *Turn to 18*

WHAAAT?
THE
END

272

Your first officer looks at you, her eyes asking if this is really what you want to do.

You nod.

She turns and presses a few buttons on your console. "It's been a pleasure," you tell her.

"The pleasure," she says, "was all mine. Good luck, Captain."

You say, "You too, Commander," and then your ship crashes into the Deltron ship hull and that's the last thing you see for a really, really, really long time.

You do get reanimated in the distant future, but that's another story (AND HERE IT IS: hyper-advanced future people use a form of beaming that works across time and transfers information instead of matter so that non-destructive duplicates can be made; this allows them to revive interesting historical figures from any point in their lives, so the hyper-advanced future people can learn about EVERYTHING, and anyway they got you by mistake this one time; you live in the future for a bit and it's pretty cool because you can chill with all these historical people but they all sound really old-timey and the ones from really long ago are, like, racist? They're all really super racist.)

THE END

273

You move your king away from the pawn, but I'm sorry, Ophelia, Gertrude wasn't lying. She takes your pawn, and now it's just your king against her king and castle. You can't win.

So you do the opposite of that: LOSE TERRIBLY.

It takes Gertrude 10 moves to get everything in place, but she does it while you impotently move your king around. Anyway, look, you just lost a game you had a lot riding on and this is why gambling destroys lives and relationships! Sheesh, gambling, why are you so terrible??

Checkmate: *turn to 309*

274

Rather than embracing the madness, you bring your hands up between Laertes' hands, and bashing them outwards, free your neck from his grasp. You're vaguely aware of your mother shouting your name as you punch Laertes over and over again, avoiding his own punches as best you can. You're both getting in some good hits. Finally Horatio and the gravedigger jump down into the grave and hold the two of you apart. You're both trying to break free.

"WHAT THE HECK IS THIS ABOUT?" yells your mother. "THIS IS A FUNERAL AND YOU'RE FIGHTING IN AN OPEN GRAVE FOR NO REASON."

"Mom, Laertes is saying he loved Ophelia more than I did!" you say. "I loved her more than 40 billionty stupid ol' brothers!"

"He really is crazy," says Claudius.

"I'll eat a crocodile to prove how serious I am," you offer.

"I'm sorry for my crazy son," Gertrude says. "Usually he calms down after a little while."

You decide to prove her right. Turning to Laertes you say, "Listen, bro, why are you treating me like this? I've done nothing to deserve this." But Laertes stares at you, aghast, almost like he...holds you responsible for Ophelia's death?

"Anyway," you say. "Hamlet out."

You leave.

A little while later, Horatio catches up with you. "Hey, sorry, Claudius made me leave too."

"What about the gravedigger?" you say.

"Um, I think he's back to digging graves. He was supposed to be working the whole time we were there, anyway."

"Ah," you say.

Talk to Horatio about your pirate trip again: *turn to 172*

Talk to Horatio about what just happened: *turn to 201*

275

"But, Captain!" shouts your first officer. "The Omega Protocol is untested! We don't know what effects it'll have on the space-time continuum!"

"Don't you think I know that?" you bark. "It's that or die. Do you want to die today, Commander?"

"I guess not," she shrugs.

"Then I suggest you engage the Protocol, Commander."

Your first officer presses a few buttons on her keypad. "Omega Protocol engaging...in 30 seconds," comes the voice of your ship's computer, broadcast across every deck.

"Best-case scenario, we survive — barely," you mutter to yourself. Your first officer allows herself a small smile.

"Worst-case scenario," she says, "the space-time continuum is torn a new one, which has all sorts of unexpected effects. We could find ourselves somewhere else in our galaxy — or outside of it. Theoretical models suggest there may be some matter substitution, but it might not be the entire ship that's affected. It may be localized to certain rooms, certain objects. We may just find that certain pages of our books have been substituted with pages from other books, drawn from all over time and space. Who knows, maybe even our Automatically Recorded Dramatic Ship's Logs in Second-Person Prose Format would be included! And while that would affect our entire library, only a comparatively small handful of books across the universe would get our pages in exchange. That'd localize the effects to only a few publications. Most planets actually wouldn't be affected at all."

"That'd be cool," you say. "Having our logs swapped out to another world like that. Maybe we could learn from the pages we got in exchange."

"But it'd be pretty confusing," says your first officer.

"It would still be pretty neat though, wouldn't it? To be a person who comes across one of these books and has no idea that this 'printing error' is actually a recording of the brave actions taken by a valiant crew thousands of light-years away, fighting for their lives in some unknown, distant war?" you begin, and then your computer engages the Omega Protocol, and everything goes white.

THE END

276

"I'm gonna open it," you say. This is what you read:

Dear King of England,

It's me, Claudius, the King of Denmark! Listen, we get along pretty well, right? And both our countries are in pretty good shape. Anyway, it'd be really convenient for me (and it would help both our countries STAY in good shape) if you could kill Hamlet for me real quick. It's not that big a deal, just kill him okay? Cool? Cool. P.S. I'm 100% serious please kill him right now.

You and Rosencrantz and Guildenstern stare at each other for a long moment. Looks like this whole time while you were planning to kill Claudius, he was also planning to kill you!

"Dude, are you scoping this letter's CHOICE ASSASSINATION ORDERS?" asks Rosencrantz.

"I told you, man! I TOLD YOU ABOUT CLAUDIUS," Guildenstern yells.

"Maybe he heard my free verse from last night?" you say. "It was extremely tight."

Figure out a plan with Rosencrantz and Guildenstern:
turn to 28

277

Nicely said, Hamlet. I've got to give you a few points for that.

So! Your final score is, oh, let's say 675 points out of 1000. That's a solid C+. You took a heck of a long time to kill Claudius, but you DID do the pirate sidequest, which is nice, because it was my mistake to put it so late in the story anyway. We'll open with it in the remastered edition.

Okay! Thanks for playing! Good night, sweet prince, and flights of angels sing thee to thy rest!

THE END

Turn to 211

So, you're still here, huh? Story's over, dude! Don't just linger on this page, go re-read the book and make some other choices! In fact, here's two to get you started:

Re-read the book and make some new (maybe even better?) choices: *turn to 1*

Refuse to let it end this way: *turn to 284*

278

Using your sword, you begin to chop Polonius's body into smaller pieces. You begin by separating the limbs and head from the body. That completed, you work on reducing the torso to smaller chunks of meaty gore. It's difficult, disgusting work. Blood gets everywhere. EVERYWHERE.

You have 3 turn(s) remaining. There are a lot of body parts here.

Dump body parts out the window: *turn to 37*

Put body parts into stew: *turn to 295*

Put body parts into bags: *turn to 293*

Use twine on body parts: *turn to 298*

279

You bang some pots and pans together until she wakes up.

"Hey, I'm a ghost, but not of anyone you know. Listen, tell me more about that garden murder you saw!" you say.

In response, the woman looks at you terrified. She says something in Norwegian and you suddenly feel dumb. You're already a spooky ghost, but now you're a spooky ghost talking to her in a language she doesn't even know!

Anyway, by the time you find a piece of paper and write down "HEY I DON'T WANT TO KILL YOU," it's too late: the woman has run out of the room. And every time she sees you, she gets mad and throws something at you and leaves.

You kinda blew it here, King Hamlet!

You keep reading her diary every night for a few months, hoping that she'll mention more about the thing she saw, but it's mostly filled with some really personal stuff about her feelings and you kinda feel honestly creepy about this whole situation. The stuff that isn't personal is about how she wonders if ghosts read diaries, and if they do, if they know what TOTALLY AWFUL people they're being.

Long story short: eventually you leave her alone, never find out who murdered you, and settle down to a nice pleasant afterlife with the other ghosts in Ghost Norway. You guys do charades with each other and everything! It's pretty fun.

THE END

Turn to 303

281

Ryan North was born on October 20, 1980. Since then he has done the following things (this is NOT an exhaustive list):

» failed to die for over 12,924 days IN A ROW;
» eaten food and then converted that food into ideas;
» kissed over FIVE different people not from his family, all of whom totally came back for more;
» studied computer science and computational linguistics and graduated from university TWICE;
» written the online comic *Dinosaur Comics*; it's that comic with dinosaurs that you love;
» co-edited the anthology *Machine of Death*, which is a book about people who know how they will die;
» written the *Adventure Time* and *Unbeatable Squirrel Girl* comic book series, which have a lot of really awesome stuff going on in them;
» analyzed the novelization of *Back to the Future* in way more detail than probably anyone could've anticipated;
» gotten married, and adopted a dog named Noam Chompsky;
» oh I also totally wrote this book! And a sequel too, called *Romeo and/or Juliet!* Whoah!!

Okay, your stalling tactics are really easy to see through and also really confusing because it's not like someone has a gun to your head and is forcing you to read this book. (Right? If this is indeed the case and you are totally fine, let me know by NOT sending a message back in time to me to the very moment I'm writing these words, which is March 9, 2016, 10:31:14 a.m. EST. Okay, terrific, we're good.)

All you can do now is:

CHOOSE YOUR CHARACTER: *turn to 1*

282

You go and stand on the window ledge. Nothing's changed since a few seconds ago, and you're still five storeys up. You jump, fall five storeys, hit Polonius's body, and break your legs. Blood squirts everywhere, but luckily most of it is his. You lie there crying out in pain for your remaining 3 turn(s) until you see a head peering out over the window ledge down at you. "Did you murder that dude and then jump on his body?" he asks.

You continue to scream in agony.

"I think you murdered that dude and then jumped on his body!" he says, and ducks back inside the room.

A few minutes later, you hear voices from inside the room as you begin to fade from consciousness.

"Since this is olden times, we don't really have the medical expertise to help with infection, and Hamlet is lying on a messy corpse with open wounds," you hear.

"Man, Polonius hasn't been dead for that long," you think, but you don't know that there are lots of gross bacteria in the colon and you burst Polonius's guts all over the place. Anyway, you get an infection (a couple of them in parallel, actually) and you die.

THE END

What can I say? It's a really gross death, THE END, let's all stop talking about it!!

Turn to 356

283

Nothing changes, as *Calypso's Gale* continues to gain on you. This isn't working, Hamlet! You've got time for one last manoeuvre before the pirates come alongside, and when they do I can promise you your first-ever naval command will end in disaster.

"Orders, Captain?" your first mate shouts. Lightning strikes the sea behind him, and you can feel the thunder shake your ship.

You stare at *Calypso's Gale* through a spyglass. The square shape of her rigging reminds you of something...

"Put the wind at our back! Give us all the speed she can muster!" *Turn to 132*

"Turn around and face the pirates head-on." *Turn to 102*

Try to remember everything you know about sailing before you answer: *turn to 27*

284

Congratulations! You have unlocked the SECRET ENDING.

The thing is, you're still dead. You played as Hamlet and you killed him and there's no taking that back.

But here's the secret: while you ARE dead, there's another you that exists outside this book. There's a you reading these words right now who hasn't even died once yet (PROBABLY??). There's a you who invested some time reading this and there's a me who invested even more time writing it and we're all in this together and it's way too late to back out now. But we've come a long way, and I like you. I think we had fun.

So here's your secret ending, and it's the very last choice you ever get to make. You find yourself in a certain location in the universe, remarkable, at the very least, for being where you are right now. You have just experienced the story of Hamlet, Prince of Denmark. It was a fun diversion, but real life beckons. Here's your big choice, right here, right now:

You can either (a) put down this book and work every day to be the best darn person you can be at whatever it is you choose to do, or (b) surprise, there is no other choice.

Go get 'em, tiger.

THE END

Turn to 149

285

She looks at you for a long moment.

"Okay," she says, sighing, putting all the love letters you wrote her and the presents you gave her into your arms. "See you when I see you, I guess."

She walks out of the room, but she pauses at the doorway. Turning around, she says, "I always took our relationship seriously, and it really sucks that you never could." And then she's gone.

That uh...didn't go well?

As you've just broken up with your girlfriend, you figure your plan to catch Claudius is pretty much all you've really got going right now, so you throw yourself back into it. There's still a chance to make it work, you realize. You'll just come back here tomorrow and get him to read the book then!

Do that thing I just said: *turn to 150*

286

Good call. Why travel through TIME ITSELF when you have the option to continue sitting around doing nothing?

So here's what you do: you pal around with some other ghosts, and eventually form some really good friendships. But each of these friends eventually decides to travel back in time for a do-over, and it's hard to blame them. It's such a tantalizing possibility!

One last chance, Hamlet: do you want to travel through time? There'll always be a chance that you end up in the wrong body, and that'll never change. But there's also a chance you could change your history, fix your mistakes — there's a chance you could help everyone. You could improve the lives of everyone you ever knew. Given that, is it ethical to not even try?

It all comes down to this, Hamlet, Prince of Denmark: do you decide to be TOTALLY AWESOME??

Okay! I decide to step into the quantum leap accelerator!
Turn to 17

NO. Mom always said to never travel through time, okay?
Turn to 173

288 You try to hit Laertes, but he seems to be moving faster and faster. Or maybe you're just moving slower? In any case, it's become harder to hold him off, and eventually he manages to stab you right in the lungs.

You collapse to the floor and die. Since you're dead, I can tell you that the blade was actually poisoned, and Claudius put Laertes up to it. Surprise!

You are now a ghost! And you are a ghost who wants revenge on Laertes and Claudius. Unfortunately, you don't have a son to do the revenging for you, but you do have your Ghost Dad to help you out! Your dad saw how unfair the battle was and how well you fought anyway, and he believes you were wronged. You are a father-son revenge team from BEYOND THE GRAVE, and you have *Calypso's Gale* on your side. How can you fail?

Well, it turns out the answer to that question is "quite spectacularly actually." You and your dad are talking over your failures a few weeks later in Ye Olde Ghost Pub. It's a pretty cozy place. There's a nice wooden sign hung behind the bar that reads, "There is nothing either good or bad, but drinking makes it so."

"Maybe — maybe Claudius will be a good king after all," you say, trying to put a positive spin on things. "He does seem to really want the throne. Maybe it's because he can't wait to put his revolutionary and effective socioeconomic theories into practice?"

"I don't know," your dad sighs. "I don't know." He takes a long sip of his beer: a cloudy, complex wheat-based sour beer brewed by the ghost of an ancient Roman brewmaster who's had a millennium to practice his art, the words Carpe Cervisiam printed in elaborate script along the bottle's side. "What am I gonna tell your mother? I got her only child killed in some harebrained revenge scheme from beyond the grave."

"That's true. Also, I kinda killed Polonius for no real reason," you say, taking a swig of your beer, a blonde ale flavoured with strawberries called The Secret of the Boo-ooze that you ordered because you liked the cute ninja ghost on the label. "Maybe revenge is harder than it looks."

"Or maybe we're just not that great at it," your dad says. He stares at his beer for a bit, and then looks up at you. "You wanna do something else with the next few decades? Something — non-revengy?"

"What?" you ask.

"I always wanted to be a painter," he sighs. "But I kept telling myself that the business of being king took priority. I kept saying there was never enough time. That's not the case anymore."

"Hmm," you say. "Well, to be honest, I always wanted to live forever with voluntary and unlimited access to powers of flight, invulnerability, and invisibility, plus the ability to phase through solid matter. That's definitely the case now." You hover above the table and phase your hand through your beer to illustrate your point.

The next morning your dad picks up a paintbrush for the first time in 40 years. He wants you to pose for him, but you're excited about your new project too, so you compromise.

His first painting is one of you, a pin held in your mouth, a sewing needle in your hand, stitching together your new superhero costume.

THE END

Turn to 386

289

You try to hit Laertes, but he seems to be moving faster and faster. Or maybe you're just moving slower? In any case, it's become harder to hold him off, and eventually he manages to stab you right in the eye. There's a sword literally sticking out of your eyehole.

Gross, Hamlet.

You run around in pain and eventually run into a wall, which only jams the sword into your brain. You die in a pretty spectacular fashion.

GROSS, Hamlet!

You are now a ghost! Since you're dead, I can tell you that the blade was actually poisoned, and Claudius put Laertes up to it. You try to get your Ghost Dad to help you take revenge, but he saw (a) how bad you were at revenge when you were alive, (b) how you swordfought the wrong guy and did it so badly that you died, and (c) how your slapstick death was more hilarious than anything else, and so he decides then and there that he wants nothing more to do with you.

You feel really sad and depressed and like you wasted a lot of your life.

A timeless age passes.

You're still pretty down in the dumps.

Another timeless age passes.

You're a bit emo about what happened, but not TOTALLY broken up about it.

A third timeless age begins and ends.

You're finally cool with what happened. Looking around, you find that thousands of years have passed since your death. It's the distant future! And while time travel hasn't been invented in the mortal realm, it turns out some of your fellow ghosts have been using these timeless ages to perfect the process. You can't send your body back in time (not that you have one in the traditional sense of the word but WHATEVER), but you can send your consciousness back in time, leaping from this life to that one, perhaps even putting things right that once went wrong.

It's possible to leap into the body of your past self, back before you died. You'll be able to make things turn out differently! There's a catch though: while the ghost scientists can target the destination time with quite a bit of precision, targeting the person who you'll be leaping into is just a teeny bit fuzzy. Look, the bottom line is this: there's a small chance that you could end up in the wrong body. And if that happens, there's also a teeny-weeny chance that the mind / body mismatch could cause the host body to override your ghostly neural pathways, the end result being near-total amnesia about who you really are and what your mission is.

But it is a chance. Do you take it?

Take the chance! Step into the quantum leap accelerator!
Turn to 299

No, it sounds dangerous! *Turn to 286*

DAVID
HELLMAN

291

"Tell me, Antonio, what's your favourite act of mind-blowing erotic int—" you begin, and just then a huge explosion rocks the hotel. Debris showers into the room, knocking Antonio unconscious. Looks like you're under attack!

BY TERRORISTS!!

Hah hah, screw this dating thing: you have three terrorists to kill!!

Run down to the site of the explosion: *turn to 68*

292

Really?

Really.

Wow. I'm glad to hear it. Honestly I'm kind of...surprised? But seriously: nicely done, Hamlet! Way to sustain someone's interest in being your sweetie!

Ophelia opens her mouth and says, "Um, Hamlet, I love you, but you never said you were doing this because a ghost told you to."

"Baby," you say, "I know it sounds crazy, but let's forget about it, as we now know Claudius is guilty of murder, and that doesn't change whether or not a ghost gave me my initial suspicions."

Ophelia turns to Horatio. "Did you know about this ghost?" she asks.

"He chased us. It was really spooky," he says.

"Really," Ophelia says.

Horatio nods. "I was never more spooked."

"Okay. Well, I trust you, Hamlet," she says. "But this ghost had better be real."

Ophelia's so awesome. You should probably be her for a while. Moving your consciousness between bodies is a free action anyway, right?

Be Ophelia: *turn to 355*

293

The body parts are now each in a bag. Nobody will suspect a thing!

Actually, that's not true: anyone would suspect everything. There's blood everywhere, man.

You have 2 turn(s) remaining.

There are bags full of body parts here.

Dump bagged body parts out the window: *turn to 300*

Put bagged body parts into stew: *turn to 308*

Use twine on bagged body parts: *turn to 313*

294

"Incorrect!" Horatio says. Fortinbras slaps in with his answer. "Denmark's earliest archaeological findings date back to the Eemian interglacial period. That's from 130,000 to 110,000 BC."

Darn it, it's like he read your friggin' mind.

"Correct!" shouts Horatio. "Fortinbras, if you get this next question right, you will be my new king. Ophelia, if that's who YOU want to be, you've got to get this next one right just to stay in the game."

Horatio looks at you both, and then clears his throat. "Next question: how long is the coastline of Denmark?"

Again you slap in first.

"**8735 KILOMETRES!**" *Turn to 487*

"**7314 KILOMETRES!**" *Turn to 94*

"**TRICK QUESTION! NO COASTLINE HAS A PRECISELY DEFINED LENGTH, AS THE LENGTH WILL DEPEND ON THE METHOD USED TO MEASURE IT. IF I USE A METRE STICK, VARIATIONS IN THE COAST SMALLER THAN ONE METRE WILL BE IGNORED. BUT IF I USE A CENTIMETRE STICK, THEN I'LL INCLUDE THOSE MEASUREMENTS, BUT IGNORE THOSE LESS THAN ONE CENTIMETRE! SINCE COASTLINES BEHAVE LIKE FRACTALS IN THIS REGARD, THERE IS NO SINGLE LENGTH MEASUREMENT I CAN POINT TO WITHOUT MAKING SIMPLIFYING ASSUMPTIONS FIRST.**" *Turn to 507*

295

Okay, this is gross but okay. You put the body parts into the stew, but it's only a stew pot, it's not big enough to hold a full human body. The dead head of Polonius sticks out the top, along with arms and legs and torso. If you were hoping to disguise the body as stew, this isn't going to cut it.

You have 2 turn(s) remaining.

EAT STEW: *turn to 414*

REMOVE BODY PARTS FROM STEW: *turn to 306*

LIGHT DOOR ON FIRE: *turn to 254*

296

"Well, I mean, is there something else that you would like to do inst—" you begin, and just then a huge explosion rocks the hotel. Debris showers into the room, knocking Antonio unconscious. Looks like you're under attack!

BY TERRORISTS!!
Hah hah, screw this dating thing: you have three terrorists to kill!!

Run down to the site of the explosion: *turn to 68*

297

You take a log from the fireplace and light the curtain on fire. It doesn't really burn that well as it has blood on it, but you char it a bit. Blood's everywhere, man.

You're pretty sure you wasted a turn.

You have 2 turn(s) remaining.

Eat stew: *turn to 317*

Light door on fire: *turn to 254*

Tie twine across base of door to trip whoever enters the room: *turn to 320*

298

You tie a length of twine to each body part. It looks kinda cool, I guess? Your twine supply is reduced by 50%. There's still plenty of twine left though, honestly. Look at all that twine.

You have 2 turn(s) remaining.

There are body parts tied with twine here.

Use remaining twine to tie the wall torches beneath the bags, thereby forming crude hot-air balloons: *turn to 547*

Use remaining twine to tie body parts together to form a giant grisly bolas: *turn to 316*

Use remaining twine to tie a tripwire across the base of the door, thereby tripping whoever enters the room: *turn to 320*

299

You step into the quantum leap accelerator and the world around you vanishes. You're surrounded by the darkest blackness you've ever seen.

The next thing you know, the world is reassembling itself around you. Clouds and trees slowly fade into existence. You feel your body becoming real, corporeal. You hold up your hands in front of you — your hands! — watching them become more and more solid with each passing second as your jump approaches completion. We're almost there, Hamlet.

Complete the jump: *turn to 444*

300

The bags burst as they hit the ground. You hate to admit it, but the splatter of gore they create is pretty much the textbook example of "suspicious."

You have 1 turn(s) remaining.

Jump out window to escape: *turn to 207*

Act casual: *turn to 18*

Eat stew: *turn to 339*

301

You pull the knives out of the bodies of Gertrude and Horatio and cram them into the body of your brother, Laertes. You literally cram them in there. It's like...you think he's a doughnut that you're trying to get the cream inside? I'm reaching for a metaphor here. It's like you think he's suffocating to death and you're convinced that your knives are the only air in the room and you really want him to breathe again.

Anyway, you seriously killed this dude! And this courtier Osric has just entered the room and is looking around in shock!

Oh, brother!

Kill Osric: *turn to 167*

Try to explain the now several bodies surrounding you: *turn to 544*

302

You sail to England and deliver the forged version of Claudius's note to the king. He sets you up nicely: houses, money, even willing and imaginative sexual partners! Whoah! Nobody said this was EROTIC fiction! More to the point, nobody said this was choose your own EROTIC fiction!!

~~HEY~~ I DON'T
WANT TO
KILL YOU.

You make some really erotic choices, and you and Rosencrantz and Guildenstern party until you can't party no more. Claudius dies of natural causes several years later. You never see the ghost of your father again.

You let the okay times roll and never go back to Denmark. People whisper that you're wasting your potential, living in England with your bros and having flabbergastingly sexualized adventures, but that sounds like the complaints of people who HAVEN'T experienced the joys of having flabbergastingly sexualized adventures, so you ignore them. When you get old, you die of natural causes while doing something way sexy, and I can't even tell you what that something was, mainly because it's difficult to reconstruct your exact manoeuvres based solely from the position of your flabbergastingly naked bod.

THE END

Turn to 141

304

You brandish the sword at Claudius and say, "I could stab you to make you dead! But instead I'm going to sit here and die."

And by focusing all of your willpower on it, you miraculously manage to speed up the poison, and that's what you do! You die. So! Let's sum up your runthrough this time, okay? You failed to kill Claudius several times, but you did manage to kill or have killed a bunch of unrelated characters for no good reason, so you have lost this game. In fact, you have lost so badly that I'm afraid I'm going to have to ask that you stand up, find someone else nearby, and offer this book to them. Here is what you must say:

"Please, take this book and read it. It is a book where you make your own choices to determine the narrative, but I myself am TERRIBLE AT CHOICES. I have just been demoted back down to books in which only a single thing ever happens, and it's entirely out of my control. You know: a book where the author only gives you a single story to read. Entry-level stuff. Baby books."

The person will say, "What? You mean, like, *The Divine Comedy*?"

You will say, "Please. Just take this book from me. It's better this way."

And here's the thing: it really will be.

THE END

Turn to 63

305

You go back to the hotel, pushing your way past the crowd of onlookers and local authorities assessing the blaze and damages. Back in your remarkably undamaged hotel room, you quickly pack your bags. On the way out, you stop by the room you were in when the bomb first went off, and leave a single rose on your date's still-unconscious-but-otherwise-okay-actually-MORE-than-okay body, along with a short handwritten note:

"I had fun. XOXOXO –O"

You want to hop on the next boat to Denmark, but it leaves, like, six weeks from now. Boats, man. Instead of waiting, you journey on an indirect path involving three countries, six connecting cruises, and two week-long layovers. It's honestly not bad. You've had worse times!

When you finally arrive in Denmark, the place is quiet...too quiet. Nobody is there to greet you on the pier. You drop your bags off at your room and head to the royal court, again seeing nobody along the way. The only sound you hear is the echo of your own footsteps. When you open up the doors of the royal court, you find a room full of dead bodies (Hamlet, your family, the king and queen) and some dude is there on the throne.

What the hell?

"What the hell?" you say. "Did you kill these people?"

"No man, they killed each other. Hi, I'm Fortinbras. I'm the new king of Denmark."

"Horse droppings," you say. "That's what they say in England to mean 'bull droppings,'" you explain.

"No, honest! I showed up and everyone was dead and it turns out that Hamlet's dying wish was that I should assume the throne," he says.

"How did you know what Hamlet's dying wish was if everyone was dead?" you ask.

"Oh, there's a perfectly logical explanation for that as well," says Fortinbras. "Hamlet's friend was here and saw it all and stuck around long enough to tell me. It was a cool story."

"He's gone now though," he finishes.

"Um," he says.

It's not the most credible story in the world?

Accuse him of lying: *turn to 321*

Accept his explanation and go back on vacation; Denmark is CRAZY: *turn to 459*

306

Now the body parts are on the floor, all covered in stew. The pot on the stove still has some stew in it though. There's enough for one serving. You could probably eat it.

You have 1 turn(s) remaining.

There are stew-covered body parts here.

Put body parts back into stew and eat the stew: *turn to 330*

Jump out window to escape: *turn to 232*

Eat the stew as-is: *turn to 337*

308 Okay, you put the bagged body parts into the stew, still in the bag. This is a chef thing, isn't it? You're — what, braising them or something? Is that what braising is?

Anyway, it's only a stew pot, it's not big enough to hold a full human body, much less a human body PLUS bags. Bagged body parts stick out all over. If you were hoping to disguise the body as stew, this isn't going to cut it.

You have 1 turn(s) remaining.

Eat stew: *turn to 327*

Remove body parts from stew: *turn to 324*

Act casual: *turn to 341*

309 Gertrude looks at the board, looks at you, and smiles beatifically. "Checkmate," she says.

You look down at the board, trying out all the possibilities you can see. She's right. There's no move you can make. You've lost.

"Looks like you don't get to kill me after all!" she says, flipping the table. Attached to the underside of the table are two short-swords that she grabs in mid-air. She takes a swipe at you, which you dodge.

"What the hell?" you ask.

"You can't kill me, as per the terms of our agreement," Gertrude says. "But we never agreed that I couldn't kill you."

You reach to draw your sword.

"Now now, be careful with that!" Gertrude says. "You wouldn't want to cut me! I could die from an infection!"

Put the sword back in its sheath: *turn to 441*

Draw the sword anyway: *turn to 464*

310 "A logical defence," Gertrude notes. Yay! You did a good move, I guess! Gertrude picks up her right-hand bishop and sends it out so it's parallel with your horsey guy.

"Bc4," she writes, and looking up at you, she says, "Hey. Now my queen AND bishop are both threatening that pawn in f7. You should probably save that li'l guy." Wait, I see what she's doing, Ophelia! She's trying to mess with you! You can't move the pawn out of the way, because then you'll be in check from the queen. But you can defend it!

Or maybe that's just what she WANTS you to do, and instead you should attack her queen that's causing all these problems for you?

But on the third hand, I dunno much about chess actually, hah hah, whoops?

Protect the pawn! Move out my queen so they're side by side (Qe7). *Turn to 421*

Attack the queen! Move out my horsey so it's threatening her (Nf6). *Turn to 100*

This whole queen thing is a distraction! Move my OTHER horse so it is threatening her bishop (Na5). *Turn to 76*

311

You are now King Claudius! You murdered your brother so you could marry his widow and claim the throne, but don't tell anyone!

You've just consented to read a book that your new son-by-marriage, Hamlet, gave to you. One of the royal court's favourite activities is to listen to you read a book out loud because yay that is fun and fun things are hard to come by in an era before a way to warm up a house without literally starting a fire inside that house was invented!

"As I was saying," you (King Claudius: that's you! Don't forget!) say to the assembled court. "This story is called *The Murder of Gonzago: A 'The Adventure Is Being Chosen by You' Story!*" You look up. "The title goes on for a while after that, but MY first choice is going to be to skip to the first page!" you say.

There is a smattering of polite laughter.

Begin reading: *check out the awesome cover on the next page, then turn it to begin reading this incredible adventure*

Shout "I'M NOT A MURDERER!!" then throw the book as hard as you can at Hamlet's head, tell the court "I regret nothing," and make a break for it: *turn to 315*

the MURDER of GONZAGO
by
Christina Marlowe
Can you murder your brother Gonzago and then, playing as your dead brother's son, murder your usurping uncle? I sure hope so
CHOOSE FROM
OVER THREE HUNDRED
DIFFERENT POSSIBLE ENDINGS
A 'THE ADVENTURE IS BEING CHOSEN BY YOU' STORY

This is a copyright page, my name is Christina Marlowe and I totally wrote this and y'all are not allowed to steal it.

If you steal this book I'm going to come to your house and cut off your legs and eat them. I will eat your legs, I swear to God.

Also copyright is a thing I just invented that means you're not allowed to steal these here words I wrote. I think that's pretty clear but I don't wanna hear any cries of "boo hoo hoo I didn't know" while I chow down on your walkin' sticks. Don't even push me. I will eat your legs and make you watch. I'm ready. I think about it all the time.

For information about special discounts for bulk purchases, please contact Christina Marlowe. I live in the house down by the field.

Manufacturing by this guy at the printer, I didn't get his name. The guy with the printing press. "Gus"? I dunno.

Marlowe, Christina.
The Murder of Gonzago: A 'The Adventure Is Being Chosen by You' Story! Can You Murder Your Brother Gonzago and Then, Playing as Your Dead Brother's Son, Murder Your Usurping Uncle? I Sure Hope So; Choose From Over 300 Different Possible Endings. #42069 Christina's Classics LLC.

If you want to get a hold of me then shout for me down by the field and I'll hear you. I have good ears. I'll use them to track you down if you steal my book. Not even joking.

Illustrations by Andrew Hussie. He wanted me to say "You're welcome" here, but I paid him though so why am I welcome?? I should be saying that to him. Whatever.

Seventy-first printing.

G1

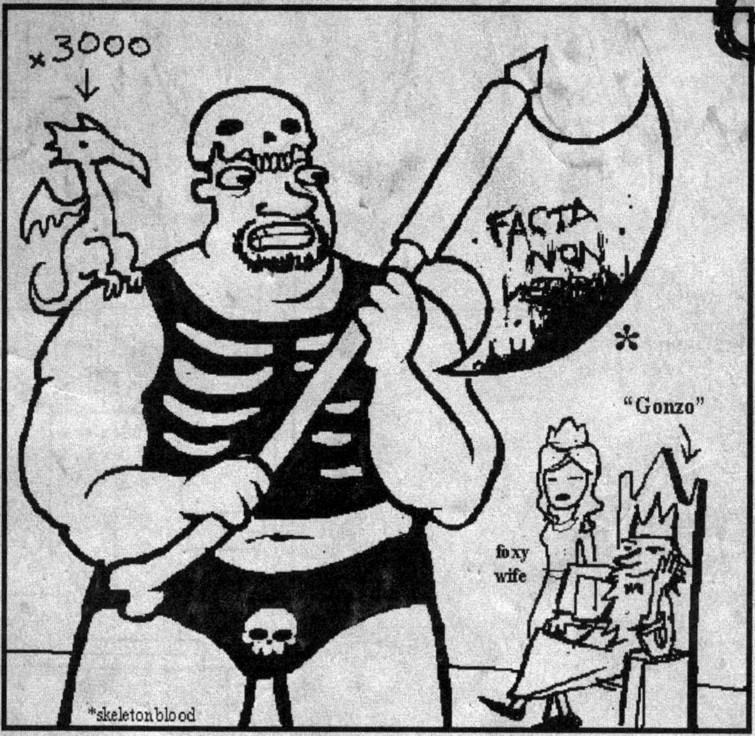

You are Battlelord Pete, or as you prefer to be called, DRAGONMASTER 3000, since you are the master of 3,000 dragons. You are amazing because of all the dragons you control, plus you wear the armour of a skeleton warrior and you wield a battle axe that has the Latin phrase "FACTA NON VERBA" written on it...in BLOOD. You know what that means? That means "DEEDS, NOT WORDS."

Holy crap Claudius, this book is already awesome.

You've been feeling a little jealous lately because your brother, Gonzago, gets to be king, and it occurs to you, maybe if YOU killed him and married his wife, you could be king instead!

Maybe you should do that! Or maybe you should just go slay some skeleton warriors.

To go kill your brother, proceed to G3

If you'd rather kill skeletons, proceed to G2

G2

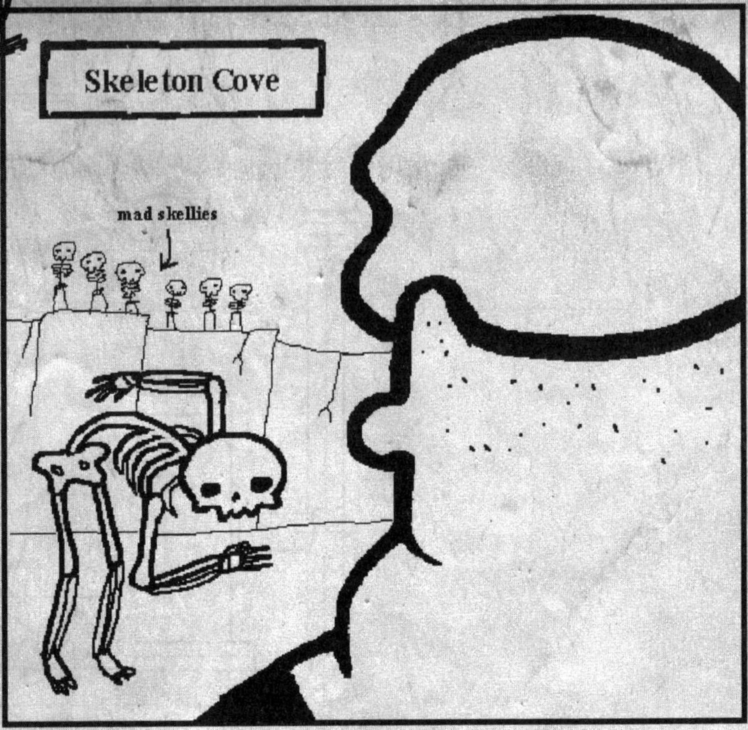

Battlelord Pete, you pick up your trusty battle axe and stroll into Skeleton Cove, where you heard all the skeletons hang out.

You encounter your first skeleton! He bows theatrically and introduces himself as Skellington of the East Coast Skellingtons.

Cut him up with your axe!! Proceed to G6.

Tell him you're pleased to meet him, then enquire if you can AXE him a few questions: proceed to G5.

You choose the "go kill your brother" option. Behind you, Hamlet seems to get interested in your choices.

Wait a second. You remind yourself that you did actually just kill your brother, and so maybe reliving the murder in front of the court through the medium of high literature is not the greatest idea?

On the other hand...ADVENTURE BECKONS??

Say "Oh wait I meant to choose the skeleton thing" and turn to that page instead: *turn to page G2*

Onward! To adventure and also murder! *Turn to page G11*

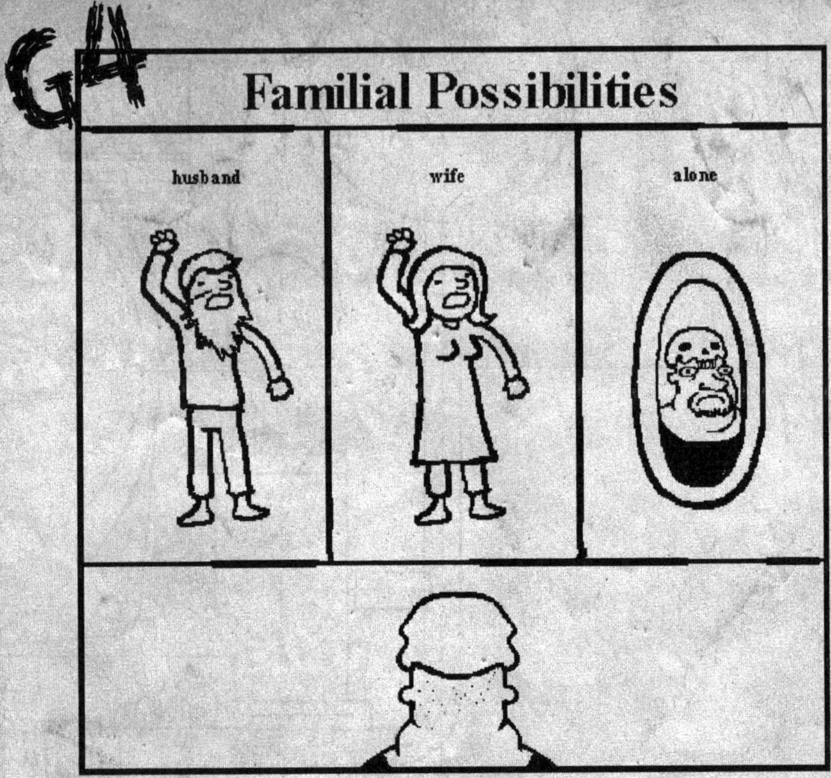

You return to your family and announce that you have killed an alive skeleton.

“That was my uncle Skellington!” screams your husband or wife, depending on your sexual orientation and life choices. If you are not married, you scream it to yourself while looking in the mirror as you realize what you’ve done.

Anyway, your husband/wife/self is so mad at what you’ve done that in a fit of rage, they choke you to death / stab you in the head / assist you in committing suicide.

Hah! Looks like this reasonable option actually resulted in sudden, unpredictable death! HOW IS READING A BOOK WHERE SOMEONE ELSE DECIDES WHAT HAPPENS TO YOU WORKING OUT, CHAMP??

Anyway, you die in the book and that means you die in real life too. SURPRISE,

THE END!!

G5

"I don't understand the emphasis you're putting on 'axe,'" says Skellington, "but I'd be happy to answer any questions you might ha—"

Your battle axe sends his head flying through the air! Skellington continues talking as his head flies into the sky.

"Do not worry about harming me!" his head says as it flies over a nearby mountain. "As I am already dead and this is only an inconvenience! No hard feelings!"

You grit your teeth and kick over Skellington's still-standing body.

"I hate to CUT AND RUN," you say through your manly grimace as his body collapses into a pile of bones. Then you walk away in slow motion. "KNIFE to meet you," you say, realizing you really should've used that one sooner, but oh well.

You have two options now: you can go kill more skeletons by journeying to Skeleton Homeland and smashing everyone there, or you can go home and return to your family.

Your country was attacked! Go to Skeleton Homeland! Proceed to G7.

Go home to see your family; one skeleton is enough for one day, you think! Proceed to G4.

You slice your opponent into a million pieces, cutting him over and over and over again! YES, THIS IS ALL YOU WANT OUT OF LIFE.

To attack more skeletons, imagine doing that now!

To single-handedly stop an invasion of your land, proceed to G7.

Wait, now you want to go kill your brother like you could do before; let's go poison him in the ear, proceed to G12.

G7

Your homeland was just attacked by a ruthless, cunning skeleton invader, and you alone are our last, best hope for a bloody, vengeful counterattack. You decide that the best counterattack is a preemptive attack, so you journey to Skeleton Homeland and on the way you start cutting up fools before they can even invade!

Things are going really well until you actually reach Skeleton Homeland, where it's like 30,000 against one! You die really quick!!

Oh and I didn't mention earlier, but guess what if you DIE IN THE BOOK, YOU DIE IN REAL LIFE!!!

You blew it and you're totally dead.

THE END!!

G8

You continue reading:

You've killed your brother and married his widow and now you're king! Congratulations, you have scored 400 out of a possible 1000 points. Now you get to play as the dead king's son, and try to reveal your own murder!!

You look up from the book. "Sweet, this book is a lot of fun!" you say, "And I sure am completely innocent...as to what might happen next!"

Behind you, Hamlet whispers to himself. "MAN, WAIT MAYBE HE DIDN'T DO THE MURDERS," you hear.

You return to the book:

You are Gonzago II, or as you prefer to be called DRAGONMASTER 3001: son of the king and nephew of the DRAGONMASTER 3000! You have all the powers of your uncle, the 3000th member of the DRAGONMASTER clan. Also you look a lot like your uncle too, but that's neither here nor there. Anyway, you're a prince!

Things have been rough lately. You've been trying to focus on your studies at Teen High where you and your bros The Whiz, Standard Softtop, and Heatshrink Buttsplice all hang out, but you've been called home because your father died. Then your dead dad's brother, DRAGONMASTER 3000, married your mother two weeks later. Classy.

You think your father's recent death was MURDER, and you suspect it was his brother who did it. Should you investigate his murder? Or should you go kill skeletons, as he would've wanted — to do himself, that is, if he were still alive?

You look up from the book and say:

"I **CHOOSE TO INVESTIGATE THE MURDER**!" *Turn to G14*

"I **CHOOSE TO KILL THE SKELETONS**!" *Turn to G13*

You turn to the appropriate page.

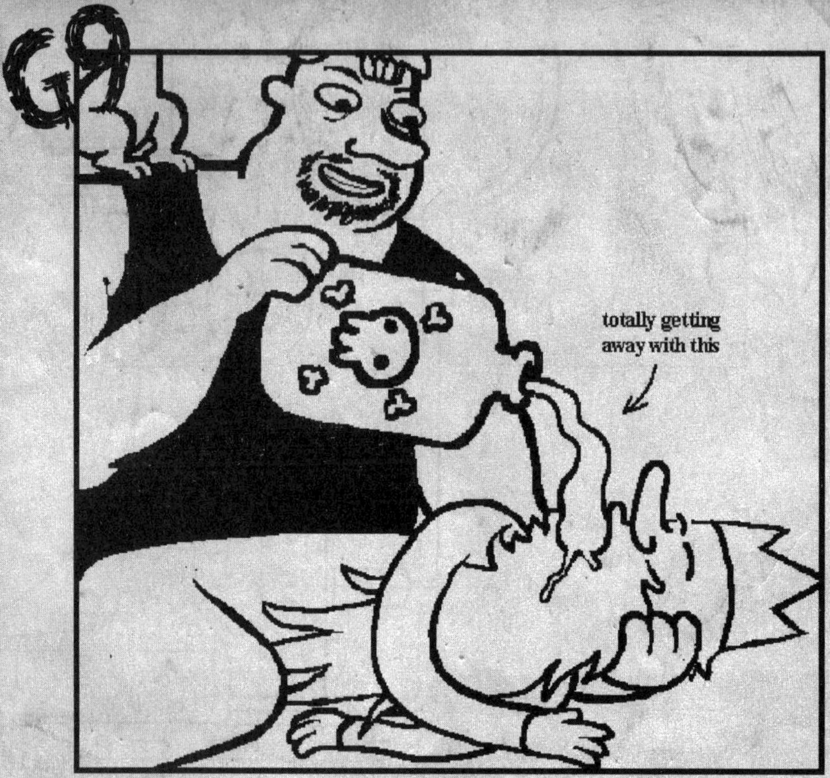

You pour the poison into his mouth. Like all sleeping people, your brother doesn't wake up when cold liquids are poured down his throat without his consent, so this whole thing goes really well! Congratulations, you have just murdered your brother. Perhaps you'd like to assume his throne now as well?

Behind you, Hamlet whispers to himself, "MAN THAT'S CLOSE ENOUGH, ONLY A MURDERER IN REAL LIFE WOULD APPROXIMATE A MURDER IN A FICTIONAL ENVIRONMENT AS WELL."

Nice one, Claudius. Hamlet now believes you murdered his father!

It seems you have two choices: you can throw the book down, yell that you hate it, and run out of the room. Or, since an innocent person would actually not react that way, you can just continue playing as if nothing's wrong, thereby NOT instantly confirming your guilt, and allow your choices to be read as simple random chance!

Run out of the room: *turn to 322*

Continue playing as if nothing's wrong: *turn to G8*

G10

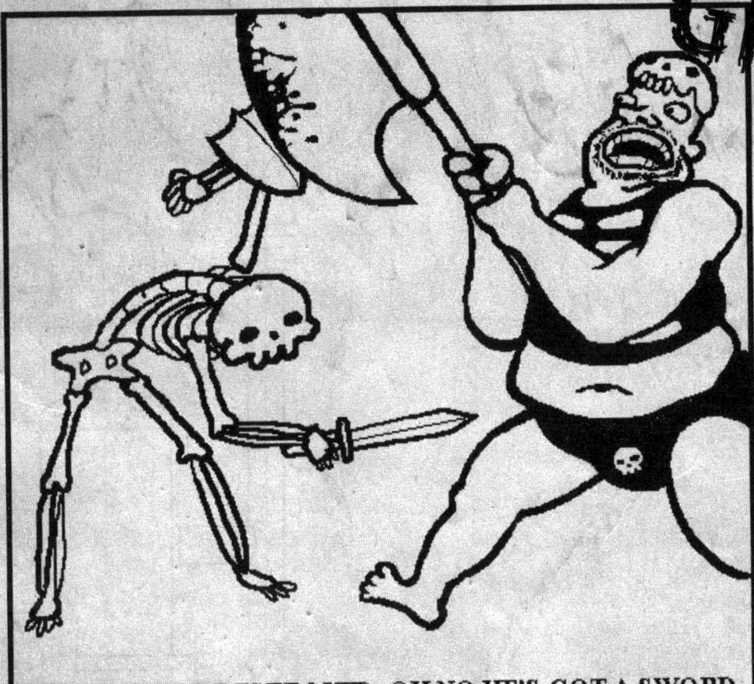

NEW FRIENDS DESTROYED: OH NO HE'S GOT A SWORD

You try to slice your opponent into a million pieces, cutting him over and over and over again! But it doesn't work. Skellington II has a shield!

Oh damn!

He's also got a sword! You battle back and forth for a while, and it's super dramatic. You may choose, at this point in your adventure, to imagine it. Go all out! It's nuts!

Eventually, however, you manage to stab Skellington II in the head and then pull his head off, and then you kick his body into an open grave, and then you say, "Ashes to ashes, and dust to dust," and you crush his skull into dust and pour that on top of the body, so that's cool.

What do you want to do now? There'll be more Skellingtons to kill if you go to their homeland. On the other hand, you could just go home and return to your family.

Your country was attacked! Go to Skeleton Homeland! Proceed to G7.

Go home to see your family; one skeleton is enough for one day, you think! Proceed to G4.

You announce that you really did intend to choose this option. Behind you Hamlet whispers to himself, "MAN, I KNEW IT."

You read out loud the text on the page:

You find your brother, Gonzago, sleeping in a garden. Gardens are really super boring, so it makes sense that he fell asleep.

You hear your audience murmur in agreement.

Sneaking up on your brother, you notice that he's sleeping on his side. You have some poison in your pocket. Do you hold his nose and pour the poison into his mouth, pour the poison into his ear, or realize that murder is terrible, leave, and go kill skeletons instead? They're basically already dead.

If you're trying not to get caught, I really think you should go kill some skeletons.

Poison in the mouth! Proceed to G9.

Poison in the ear! Proceed to G12.

Go kill skeletons instead! Proceed to G2.

G12

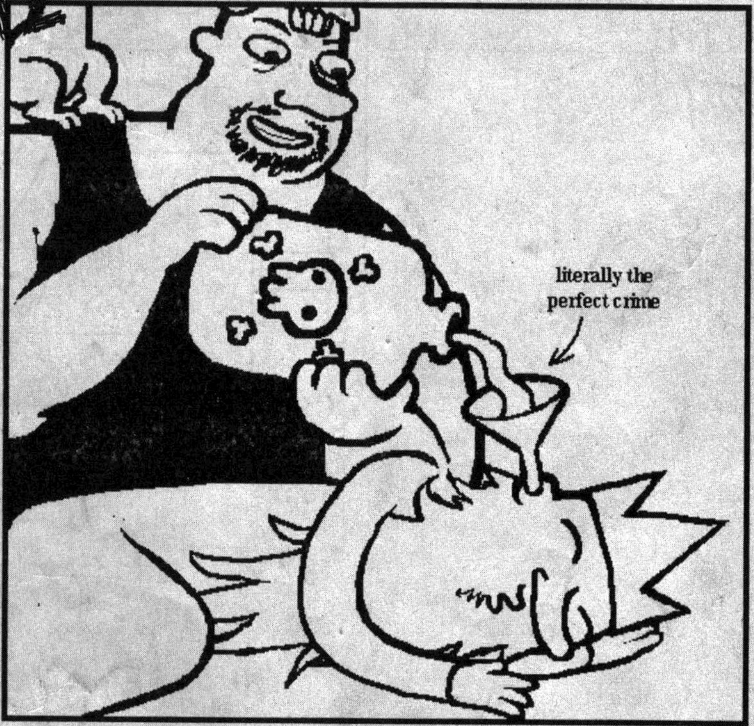

You pour the poison into his ear. Like all sleeping people, your brother doesn't wake up when cold liquids are poured directly into his ear hole, so this whole thing goes surprisingly well! Also, who knew that the ears really were the best way to introduce poison into the body? You and I did, obviously, so I guess any medical doctors in the audience who are about to say "Excuse me but I studied human bods for six years at the university level" can straight-up go suck a lemon. YOUR BRO IS DEAD.

Congratulations!! Poisons really do work that quickly, and you have just ended a life. Perhaps you'd like to assume your brother's throne now as well?

Behind you, Hamlet whispers to himself, "MAN, THAT'S EXACTLY WHAT I SUSPECTED, AND THIS HAS ALLOWED ME TO CONFIRM MY SUSPICIONS PERFECTLY!"

Nice one, Claudius. Hamlet now believes you murdered his father.

It seems you have two choices: you can throw the book down, yell that you hate it, and run out of the room. Or, since an innocent person would not actually react that way, you can just continue playing as if nothing's wrong, thereby NOT instantly confirming your guilt, and instead allow your choices to be read as simple chance.

Run out of the room: *turn to 322*

Continue playing as if nothing's wrong: *turn to G8*

G13

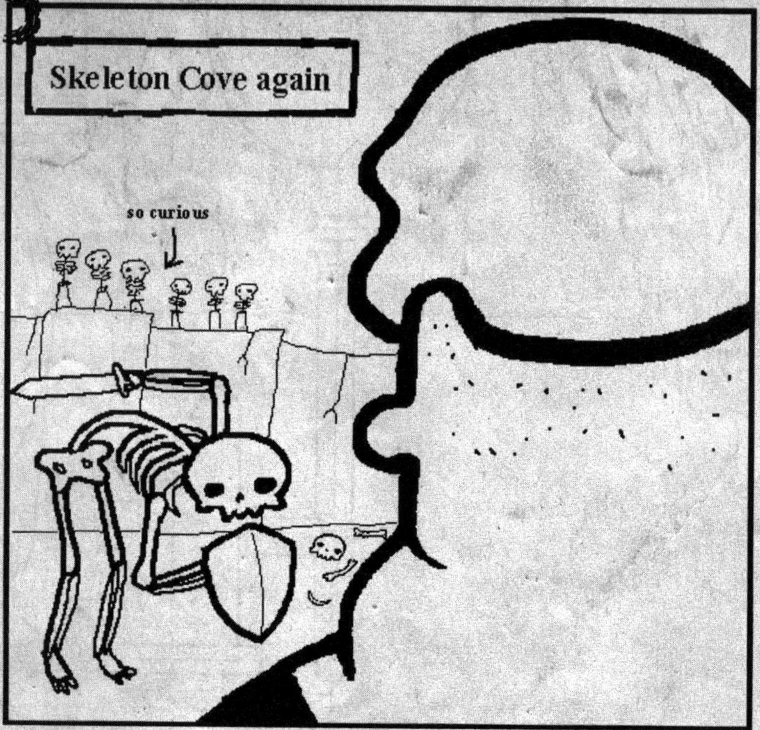

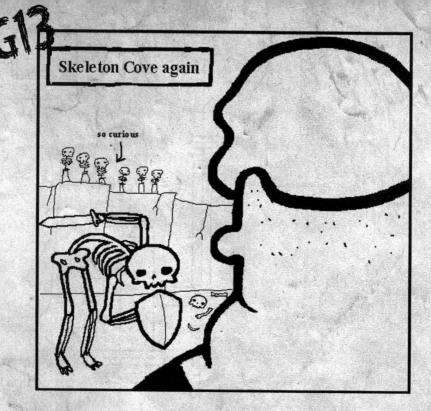

Gonzago II, you pick up your trusty battle axe and stroll into Skeleton Cove, where you heard all the skeletons hang out.

You encountered your first skeleton! He bows and introduces himself as Skellington II of the East Coast Skellingtons.

“Please, call me Skellington,” he says.

> **Cut him up with your axe, just like your father did before you!!** Proceed to G10
>
> **Tell him you’re pleased to meet him, then enquire if you can AXE him a few questions:** Proceed to G5

You turn to the appropriate page, and read about how you're sad from your dad's death so you dress in black and act all sullen, but you're still looking for something to reveal itself so that you might spring into action and begin your investigation. In the meantime you're acting weird and making a general nuisance of yourself. There's a cool picture too! It looks like this:

Holy cow! This book is like a mirror image of what's actually been happening lately! It's got both your and Hamlet's characters down perfectly, just with different names, and also with dragon-mastery powers that don't actually ever seem to come up.

In fact, there are so many similarities between the book and real life, you bet that if you went back a bit, squinted your eyes, and did all the correct name substitutions as you read, you could continue reading the book as if it actually WAS a choose-your-own-adventure book written about Hamlet!

So that's what you decide to do! You begin to mentally make all substitutions necessary while reading this book to make the book match up with what's been going in real life, and you...

Play as Hamlet: *turn to 14*

312

You sit down and wait for him to wake up. You're a ghost. You have all the time in the world.

After a few moments, you look up and see Hamlet's friend Horatio standing beside you. He's staring at you, a little too intently, and then he passes out too. Terrific.

Eventually the sun starts to come up and nobody can see you anymore. You stick around though, and soon Hamlet and Horatio wake up, rubbing their eyes in the early morning sunlight.

"Whoah," says Hamlet. "Did you have the same CRAZY GHOST DREAM that I did?"

"I did!!" says Horatio. "Oh my gosh, it was SO SPOOKY!" Oh no, you think. Hamlet and his friend are stupid dudes. They go back and forth, excitedly discussing their "dream" with each other. You sigh and start to thinking.

Here's what you think: you think, hey, I'm a ghost now. You think, hey, I can travel the world for free, I don't have to worry about being hungry. I can see what happens to Denmark in the future — heck, I can see what happens to the WORLD in the future!

You think maybe life's too short for revenge. Maybe — maybe even an immortal afterlife is too short for revenge? You think this is a great opportunity to learn all you can about the world around you. And you think that if Earth ever gets boring, all you have to do is float up to the moon and see what's there.

Also, there are ghost beasts from Earth's prehistoric past all over the place, and there's something that looks like an enormous but friendly building-sized lizard munching on trees over that hill. It's kind of hard to be focused on revenge when (a) you're already dead and (b) you could be taming dinosaurs and riding them across the universe.

So that's what you do!

Many years later, when you look back on it all, you have precisely this many regrets: UM, NONE??

THE END

Turn to 35

313

You tie off the bags with twine. There! Now anyone who wants to peek inside has to really want it!

Well, it's still not that hard to peek inside, actually. It's just twine. You double-knot the twine, but it doesn't make that much of a difference.

You have 1 turn(s) remaining.

There are tied bags full of body parts here.

Act casual: *turn to 53*

Jump out window to escape: *turn to 232*

Eat stew: *turn to 339*

314

You pull Ophelia into a Privacy Closet and tell her about your suspicions and your plan to reveal Claudius as a murderer, and while she's not super enthused about it, it turns out that yes, she has some questions about this whole thing she'd like answered too, and this plan could help with that! She says she'll watch Claudius with you as he reads the book.

She's in! And you're working on a project together, which is great. You've missed this. You've missed Ophelia. You tell her that.

"I know we've both been busy with personal projects lately," she says, "and I'm sorry. I should've brought you into my investigation sooner rather than ignoring you. I get so wrapped up in things sometimes."

"It's okay, it's okay," you say, "I did the exact same thing. I really had no idea you were also looking into Claudius! But we'll figure this out together." You look at her for a long moment.

"We're cool, right Ophelia? I mean, like, our relationship?"

"We're cool," she says, and you kiss. Nice.

The next morning, you both wake up early to show Claudius the book.

Show Claudius the book: *turn to 150*

315

Nobody...nobody really accused you of anything? But you decide that a preemptive denial is the best approach to any possible accusation, so out of nowhere you stand up and shout, "I'M NOT A MURDERER!!"

Everyone in the crowd is looking at you in shock — except for Ophelia, who instead has the look of someone whose long-held suspicion was just confirmed by a crazy, unprompted denial! It's a subtle facial expression but I'd recognize it anywhere, so that's why I'm telling you about it. It's there, dude.

Continuing with your ridiculous plan, you turn around and throw the book as hard as you can at Hamlet's head. It bonks him pretty hard I guess, but you catch him with the flat side instead of the corner, so it's not actually that painful. "Hey!" says Hamlet. "Hey, ouch! Why are you doing this? Is it because you did in fact literally murder a person, and that person was my father and YOUR VERY OWN BROTHER?"

You spin around and face the crowd again, motioning for everyone to calm down. "Guys, no, you don't understand. I'm saying I did NOT kill my brother, and as such, any future accusations anyone may make to that effect are groundless," you say.

"So uh...nobody make those," you say.

This isn't working, Claudius! The crowd's suspicion level has risen to 98%. You decide to make a break for it and tear out of the room, leaving a very suspicious Hamlet, Ophelia, and the entire royal court behind you. Today's not going very well for you, huh? You run all the way to your bedroom in tears, because you are an adult king of an entire country.

Well, Claudius, there's no two ways about it: you globbed up big back there. I think you'd better be Ophelia for a while, huh? You were honestly doing way better as her.

Be Ophelia: *turn to 355*

316

Your giant bolas weighs as much as a human man, and is thus entirely impractical. Actually, it's less "bolas" and more "a bunch of chunks of human flesh all tied together in the middle of the room."

You have failed spectacularly at looking less suspicious.

You have 1 turn(s) remaining.

There is a giant human bolas here.

Jump out the window to escape: *turn to 232*

Light door on fire: *turn to 254*

Tie twine across base of door to trip whoever enters the room: *turn to 420*

317

You eat some of the stew. It's delicious! It doesn't help your current situation, but your hunger has been reduced by 10%.

You have the distinct feeling you've now wasted two turns and are entirely doomed.

You have 1 turn(s) remaining.

Light door on fire: *turn to 254*

Act casual: *turn to 18*

EAT MORE STEW; I want to go out eating stew: *turn to 339*

Don't freak out.
GLUUUUR—.
ZUB

319

You open your eyes, and the world slowly comes into focus. You're in your bedroom, back in good ol' Denmark!

You sit up in bed as you remember the dream that you just woke from. Wow, that was crazy! To be more specific, what a crazy incredibly detailed and realistic dream in which you had been asked by a ghost to murder a king! And then...you were on a pirate ship, right? And people were getting killed? Including your sweetie? You get out of bed and move to the window, still a little shaken by it. "It doesn't have to be that way," you say, out loud. "That crazy stuff only happened in my dream. It doesn't have to happen the same way in reality."

You look out at beautiful Denmark, your home since you were born. It's real, as real as you are. That dream didn't really mean anything; it was just the random firing of some silly old neurons in your head. Wouldn't you agree...OPHELIA?? WHICH IS WHO YOU ACTUALLY ARE AND THAT HAMLET STORY WAS ALL A DREAM YOU HAD AND IT DIDN'T ACTUALLY HAPPEN IN REALITY?!

Speaking of reality, Hamlet (who I stress again is not you, that was a dream, you're Ophelia) said he saw a ghost last night! And he's back here today first thing in the morning and he's knocking on your door and says he wants to talk about it!

Talk to Hamlet about the ghost: *turn to 365*

320

You tie up the twine like a tripwire. Now whoever enters the room will trip over it and fall! Hilarious! You wish you could record their pratfall to somehow share it with others, but that would require literally hundreds of years of technological development that hasn't happened yet.

You have 1 turns(s) remaining.

There is a twine tripwire here.

Jump out the window to escape: *turn to 232*

Act casual: *turn to 333*

321

"You're lying!" you say, thinking maybe it's time for you to kill a dude. Again.

"No, wait, I can prove it! Horatio, come back here please!!" he shouts. A few seconds later, Horatio pops his head in the door. "You called for me, my king?"

"Yeah, um, this woman, I'm sorry, I didn't get your name—"

"Ophelia," you say.

"This Ophelia doesn't believe I'm king because everyone else died and then Hamlet wanted me to be king. Tell her that's what happened."

Horatio turns to you and shrugs.

"Sometimes reality is real stupid," Horatio says.

"Perfect!" Fortinbras says, smiling. "Okay, now that we've got that 'establishing that I am the rightful king of Denmark' thing out of the way: off with her head!"

"Wait, what?" you say, and it's actually the last thing you ever say because Horatio slices off your head in one smooth motion and you can't speak without vocal cords, Ophelia, sheesh! You know this, you've dissected enough dead bodies to know what strings do what!

I mean, you USED to know this, before you died from not having a body attached to your head anymore!

THE END

Turn to 169

322

You tear out of the room, throwing the book behind you, leaving Hamlet and your beloved Gertrude alone in front of a very confused crowd. Today's not going very well for you, huh?

You run into your room in tears and lock the door behind you and throw your face into your pillow and cry.

Well, Claudius, there's no two ways about it: you globbed up big back there. I think you'd better be Hamlet for a while, huh?

Be Hamlet: *turn to 460*

323

At your desk, you continue your work on the problem of automatically heating the castle. Hours turn into days and you're generally left alone by both your family and your boyfriend.

Your father ignoring you is no big deal, and while you're a little worried about Hamlet not stopping by more often, he HAS asked you to leave him alone for a while, while he mourns, and you're respecting his wishes. But if you're gonna be honest with yourself, you've also just gotten really absorbed in this problem.

You decide to split the problem into sections: delivering heat and knowing WHEN to deliver heat. It would be possible to put servants in every room and have them report when it's too cold, but that's both expensive and unreliable. It depends on the servant, the warmth of their clothes, how much they love to lie to people about what temperature their skin is sensing, and so on.

You're wandering the castle grounds when it hits you. You've been thinking about how water expands when it freezes, and how that could be used to tell you when it's cold, but it's not much use for measuring temperatures outside the freezing point. Your father, Polonius, happens to wander by, talking to himself about the evils of drink. And you realize: ALCOHOL.

The right alcohol would expand linearly with heat, and by putting it in a slender glass vial you could measure the size of that liquid, which would correspond 1:1 with temperature!

Put the same markings on each of these glass vials at the same temperatures, and you've got a universal, comparable, and consistent way of measuring heat. You wouldn't have to rely on a servant's impression; they could just tell you what line the alcohol has reached!

You run back to your room to start working on the prototype. Just as you complete it, you hear a knock at your door. "Who is it?" you call. And oh my, who should answer from the other side of the door?

Seriously, who should answer from the other side of the door?

Your boyfriend, Hamlet: *turn to 328*

Your father, Polonius: *turn to 347*

Your best friend, Dromiceiomimus: *turn to 543*

324

Okay, now the body parts are on the floor, still in their bags, all covered in stew. You've really accomplished a lot here today.

The door opens and who should enter but Corambis, Polonius's twin brother! You recognize him from the royal courts.

"I unlocked the door, so you can leave no—" he begins, but then cuts himself off. "Hey, what's going on?" Corambis looks around. "You didn't kill Polonius, cut him up, stuff him into bags, and put the bags into stew briefly only to remove them, did you?"

"Um," you say.

Anyway, long story short, it turns out that's illegal??

THE END

Turn to 401

325

You go see your dad.

"Hey Dad, is Hamlet sick?" you ask, knocking on the door as you open it.

Polonius isn't there. Instead in his room you find an oversized yet crude papier-mâché Hamlet head and a note labelled "THREE-STEP PLAN TO REPLACING HAMLET."

Let's take a look at that note, shall we?

It reads:

"STEP ONE: MAKE HAMLET DISGUISE." There's a checkmark next to this one.

"STEP TWO: HIDE BEHIND CURTAIN AND THEN JUMP OUT AT HAMLET, SO HE GETS SO SCARED THAT HE DIES." There's no checkmark next to this one. That's a relief.

"STEP THREE: DISPOSE OF BODY, WEAR HAMLET DISGUISE, TAKE OVER HIS LIFE."

Hah hah, WOW THIS IS CREEPY. Turns out your dad is crazy, I guess! And with Hamlet sighing his way through insanity, that's pretty much the two most important men in your life gone bonkers. The only ones left are Brother Laertes and King Claudius, and you don't really like those two guys that much anyway!

Well Ophelia, you basically have two choices here. You can pretend you didn't see this note, go to Hamlet's room, and ask him what's going on. Or you can say "screw these guys" and go on vacation, and someone else can deal with this, or if not these two can just dang well figure it out on their own.

You've got the money, Ophelia, and you've wanted to get away for a while!

Go ask Hamlet what his friggin' deal is: *turn to 365*

Go on vacation: *turn to 354*

327

You begin to cannibalistically consume the bagged remains of your ex-girlfriend's father when the door opens. You turn to face whoever is at the door, Polonius's left arm hanging from your mouth by the fingers, its empty bag lying at your feet.

It's hard to look guiltier than this!

When Claudius hears of this, he agrees. He personally kills you himself! His last words to you are "If you had all that time alone with the body, why didn't you try to dispose of it in a more reasonable way? Sheesh."

He stabs you.

"Sheesh," he says again, stabbing you to death.

THE END

Turn to 369

328

You decide you want Hamlet to be on the other side of the door, open it, and...Hamlet really is at the door! That's so freaky! How'd — how'd you do that? Hamlet steps into your room. You haven't seen each other for a while; it's so great to see him. You run up and throw your arms around him and you kiss. It's just like old times.

But the moment passes, and when you look at his face you can see concern written all over it. He's troubled by something.

Ask him what's troubling him: *turn to 365*

Wait for him to tell you: *turn to 334*

329

You stand around for a bit.

Suddenly, Claudius enters! And your mom too! And Laertes! And a bunch of other people you don't know! Wow, it looks like this plot is going to advance itself whether you want it to or not!

Claudius makes you and Laertes shake hands, and you apologize to Laertes as you do it. You explain that, as a victim of mental illness, you should not be held criminally responsible for your actions, and it's a very nice speech except you are only faking being crazy, so all in all it's sort of a dick move on your part.

You draw the analogy of firing an arrow over your house and accidentally hitting your brother, and how in this situation it's not REALLY your fault for injuring him. Laertes accepts your apology and is polite enough not to ask why you're recklessly firing arrows over your house in the first place. He still wants to fence you though!

What the heck — it's a pretty wide hallway and everyone's already here. Guess you're going to fence right in this hallway! Why not, right?

Osric offers you some swords. They're all pretty much the same, so whatever sword you choose doesn't really matter.

Choose the sword on the left: *turn to 237*

Choose the sword in the middle: *turn to 237*

Choose the sword on the right: *turn to 237*

330

This shouldn't surprise you, but surprise! They're too big to fit. Limbs sticking out of the pot, lifeless eyes staring at you accusingly, etc. You begin to cannibalistically consume the remains of your ex-girlfriend's father when the door opens. You turn to face whoever's at the door, Polonius's left arm hanging from your mouth by the fingers.

Congratulations! It's hard to look guiltier than this!

A little while later, Claudius puts you to death for your crime. You notice how it didn't take him very long between "deciding something needs to be done" and "doing it," which MAYBE is a lesson you could learn for next time?

Hah hah, listen to me: "next time." There's no next time! You're totally dead!!

THE END

Turn to 546

you are slaughtered
DAG

332

You decide to follow Horatio for a bit to see if he knows anything useful. You and Hamlet follow him as he goes through his day, and he doesn't suspect a thing. It's actually kinda thrilling, to be moving unseen among all these people, to know things nobody suspects you know. You could get used to this!

Eventually, Horatio meets up with Gertrude and some other guy in a nondescript room, but all that happens is the guy says, "Ophelia is gone," and Gertrude says, "Why would she leave?" and the dude shrugs and walks away. Gertrude looks at Horatio and Horatio at her and they stare at each other in silence for a long while, until Claudius enters and says, "How do you do, pretty lady?" and Gertrude says, "Fine thanks," and then it's Gertrude and Claudius and Horatio ALL just hanging out and staring at each other in silence.

You tap out a message to Hamlet: "PEOPLE ARE WEIRD WHEN WE'RE NOT AROUND." Hamlet taps back, "YA SERIOUSLY WTF."

A few minutes pass, and then Horatio leaves without saying anything. Eventually there's a noise down the hall and Gertrude says, "Alack, what noise is this?" as a messenger enters the room saying, "Young Laertes, in a normal mood, enters." Laertes ducks his head in the room and says, "Hey, have you seen my dad?" and Gertrude says, "Last I saw him he'd fallen asleep behind the curtain in my bedroom," and Laertes says, "Cool, thanks," and he leaves, taking his messenger with him.

And then more awkward, motionless silence.

"UM ARE WE THE ONLY TWO INTERESTING PEOPLE IN THE WORLD?" you tap out to Hamlet.

"DUUUUUDE WE NEED TO FIND SOME RADDER PEOPLE TO SPY ON," Hamlet replies.

After another interminable silence between Gertrude and Claudius, Claudius finally says, "Well, I'm out. You coming?" and they both leave the room. You and Hamlet step away from the walls, making yourself visible for the first time in hours.

"This is boring and stupid. Let's go kill Claudius," he says.

"Um, yeah, totes," you say.

Go kill Claudius: *turn to 375*

333

You whistle and sit yourself down on the floor in the middle of the room. That seems a little awkward, so you stretch out on your side, your arm supporting your head and your other arm resting on your hips. There! Nobody could be more casual than you!

The door opens and who should enter but Corambis, Polonius's twin brother! You recognize him from the royal courts.

"I unlocked the door, so you can leave no—" he begins, but then he trips over the twine, stumbling into you. He trips over you and into the curtain, pulling it off its rod. You turn around just in time to see the curtain-encumbered body of Corambis fall out the window. You get up and look out the window and see

Corambis's body smushed into the ground. It's actually hard to tell where Corambis ends and the ground begins. It's probably the grossest thing you've ever seen.

Turning around, you see Claudius standing at the entrance to the room. "Whatcha looking at?" he says. In the next few seconds he will look out the window, see what you did, and put you to death himself by shoving you out the window. In the seconds before he does that, you have time to do one thing though. You decide to answer his question.

"Um, nothing?" you say.

Anyway, a few seconds later he puts you to death and you die from overdosing on falling from a great height onto hard ground!

THE END

Turn to 467

334

You wait, doing nothing, and he pulls away from you and holds you at arm's length.

"Listen," he says, and then he begins unbuttoning his jacket, taking his garters off, and — oh gosh, yes, he's actually doing it. He's fouling his stockings.

"What's wrong, Hamlet?" you ask in alarm. What you say next sounds like the obvious question, but you ask it anyway. "Why are you fouling your stockings?" Instead of answering, he grabs you by the wrist. You come to the entirely obvious conclusion that he's not acting like himself. This conclusion is reinforced in the next few moments, when he moves his other hand to his forehead as if he might faint, but instead of fainting, he stares at you intensely.

"Hamlet, I don't know why you're doing thi—" you begin, and he sighs really loudly. It's the most intense sigh you've ever heard. It's actually — kind of impressive?

"Look, if you'll just talk to me we can w—" you begin, and he sighs again, so loudly that it literally drowns out your words.

"Fine, weirdo, let's play the wrist-holding game. Yayyyyy." You meet his eyes, and he sighs one of those ultimate sighs again, then gets up and leaves in what can only be described as "the creepiest way possible," walking with his head wrenched over his shoulder so he can watch you even as he crabwalks out the door.

Well, that was weird.

Maybe he's sick? You decide to check in with your dad, because as annoying as he is, he does have some experience in these matters. *Turn to 325*

Follow Hamlet and ask him what's wrong; maybe you can help him sort things out: *turn to 365*

336

It's been several years since you first decided to kill Claudius. During that time, you and Hamlet have been going out at night, getting fake drunk, and then making out in the bushes.

It's actually pretty nice.

Finally, you're interrupted by Claudius, who has seen you in the bushes. Claudius is wasted and says, "Hey, what's going on here? Ophelia? Hamlet? I'm so wasted, but are you guys making out in the bushes?"

"Oh crap," you say, pulling your shirt down. "Claudius, um...can you hold on a second?" Damn it, where did you leave those swords?

"Sure, I'll wait right over here," says the king of all of Denmark.

You and Hamlet quickly find some swords and run Claudius through with them. He's too surprised to say much beyond "What? Why now?" and "Owie ow ow" and then he's dead and you and Hamlet are running back to the drinking hall.

You show up, establish your alibi, and then go to bed.

The next day, Claudius is found dead, but I've got to tell you, a lot has changed in the three years that you've been kissing in the bushes. Claudius has been a reasonably successful king, and the people miss him. Hamlet is made king but struggles to rule effectively, the both of you having put all of your points over the past several years into maxing out kissing, and not regality. You do get married, however, and to the credit of your pumped-up kissing stat, the "I now pronounce you husband and wife: you may kiss" moment WAS basically incredible.

You help your husband out as best you can, but he ends up having an entirely middle-of-the-road kingship, and that's WITH your help. History books remember him as "an okay guy, I guess," which is weird because normally they're more formal than that.

You die old and reasonably satisfied!

This is a reasonably satisfying ending!!

THE END

Turn to 548

337

Okay, you eat the stew.

You know, this would've been a really good stew if someone hadn't put human flesh in it. Even if it had been removed later, it's still gonna be a stew that had human in it. That's gross. The stew is gross.

You get caught eating gross stew and it's obvious you're the murderer and you get killed; your last words are "Owie ouch, I'm serious, ouch."

If only you hadn't chosen to kill Polonius for no reason or, failing that, had chosen to kill Polonius for no reason and disposed of the body in a clever way! Oh well. As they say, if wishes were horses, we'd all be horses!

Your final score is irrelevant: you ate a person and that's so gross that I kinda don't want to have anything to do with you any longer.

THE END

Turn to 473

338

You kick down the door to the royal court.

"Queen Gertrude!" you shout. "What time is it??"

"Moon looks like it's about three in the morningish," she replies, glancing out the window.

"WRONG!" you shout. "It's DEATH O'CLOCK!"

"I really think the moon looks to be about — wait, what?" she says. "Death o'clock? Are you here to kill me?"

"Yep!" you say cheerfully. "And everybody else here too! What are you all doing here anyway, having a party?"

"No, we were figuring out the best way to kill yo—"

"That's too bad!" you shout, interrupting, sensing that your chance to make this pun is getting away from you as you draw your sword. "Because PARTYING IS SUCH SWEET SORROW!!"

Everyone in the room stares at you.

"What's funnier is that this room is packed with people who want to kill you instead," Gertrude says, and then waves in your direction. "Have at it, everyone!"

And that's what the room full of people do. Wow, attacking the queen right away didn't really pay off, huh? You should've at least waited until you had some practice at murders, instead of trying to kill tons of people all at once. Live and learn, I guess! Or in your case, live and learn and then die without having a chance to use the knowledge you gained?

THE END

P.S. You don't even come back as a ghost, what a rip!

Turn to 202

339

Food helps me think too!

You spend your last turn eating stew right from the pot. Delicious! I'm not even gonna lie. It is a really delicious stew. It's among the best stews you've ever tasted in your entire life. In fact, here's the recipe!

2 pounds (900g) stewing beef
a sprinkle or two sea salt and freshly ground pepper
a splash of any vegetable oil
a few carrots, peeled and roughly chopped
a few stalks celery, roughly chopped
a few potatoes, peeled and roughly chopped

a few parsnips, peeled and roughly chopped
a few onions, peeled and roughly chopped
a 28-fluid-ounce (796 ml) can of whole tomatoes
1/2 bottle of hearty red wine
3 or 4 cups (700–950 ml) beef broth
a few bay leaves
a few sprigs of fresh rosemary
a small jar of pickled baby white onions, drained
a few handfuls of peas, fresh or frozen

Preheat a large thick-bottomed pot over medium-high heat. Meanwhile, pat the beef dry with a clean towel and then cut it into large cubes and season it with the salt and pepper.

Add a splash of oil to the pot — enough to cover the bottom in a thin layer — and toss in enough meat to form a single sizzling layer. Sear the meat on every side until it's evenly browned.

Be patient when you're browning the meat; it takes a little time but it's worth every minute. The caramelized flavours are the secret to a rich hearty stew. As the meat browns, remove it from the pan, adding meat and more oil as needed.

Once the meat is done, discard the remaining oil but keep all the browned bits in the pan; they'll add lots of flavour to the stew.

Add half of the vegetables — reserving the other half — and all the browned meat to the pot. Add the tomatoes and enough wine and beef broth to barely cover the works. Add the bay leaves and rosemary, and bring the pot to a simmer.

Continue cooking until the meat is almost tender, about one hour, then add the remaining vegetables, the baby onions, and the peas. Adding the vegetables in two batches allows the first batch to dissolve into the stew while the second retains its shape, colour, and texture. Continue simmering until the meat and veggies are tender, another 30 minutes or so. When the stew is tender, taste it and season as you like. And enjoy!

So, back to you: you are discovered when the door opens, and then you're put to death, because you murdered a guy and hung around to be discovered when the door opened. The stew was really delicious though! And YOU got the recipe!

You take this recipe to your grave and share it with all the ghosts, translating it from the unfamiliar and bizarre metric and imperial measurements I used here into "ghostric," which uses the interior volume of a spooky skull as the standard unit of measurement. It makes you really popular! You have some really amazing and fun ghost dinner parties and make a lot of cool new friends who can fly!

THE END

Turn to 346

340

You knock on Cleopatra's door. She answers, wearing a very snappy dress.

"Hi Cleopatra," you say, but she interrupts you.

"Please Ophelia, call me Cleo. And come in," she says, gesturing to her hotel room.

Ophelia, the room is GORGEOUS. Whoever she is, Cleo must have tons of money! Is it her own? Are her parents supporting her somehow? You resolve to find out.

You walk into the room, and Cleo softly clicks the door closed behind her.

"So, Ophelia!" she says, turning to face you. "To what do I owe the pleasure of your company?"

She's kinda stunning. For a second, you forget what you were going to say, but then you remember:

"Cleo, I'm bored." *Turn to 537*

"Cleo, you wanna go get dinner? I hate dining alone." *Turn to 343*

"Cleo, I could use a friend. Things are a bit crazy back home." *Turn to 348*

341

You whistle and sit yourself down on the floor in the middle of the room. That seems a little awkward, so you stretch out on your side, your arm supporting your head and your other arm resting on your hips. There! Nobody could be more casual than you!

The door opens and who should enter but Corambis, Polonius's twin brother! You recognize him from the royal courts.

"I unlocked the door, so you can leave no—" he begins, but then cuts himself off. "Hey, what's going on?" Corambis looks around. "Why are you acting so casual? How come you stabbed that curtain? Are you making stew?"

"You can't make stew with the meat still in the bag," he says. "What is this, a chef thing?"

He opens a bag and sees that it's full of chunks of Polonius. Of COURSE he'd open the head bag first. Of course. He begins to scream and scream and scream, and whether or not you decide to kill him to cover your tracks, a bunch of other people are already on their way here and you're pooched.

Not too long later, Claudius puts you to death! Your last words are "Oh geez, if only I'd been better at covering up my murders; had I only the chance to do it again, I would certainly not focus so much on making disgusting human stew; with bags or not, it's extremely gross."

True, Hamlet. True.

THE END

Turn to 287

~THE END~

343 Cleo laughs. "You came down to invite me to dinner personally, Ophelia? That's adorable. Of course I'll join you. I've already eaten, but I'll get some drinks while you eat — I know the perfect place a few doors down from here."

It sounds really nice. But before you can say so, a huge explosion rocks the hotel! Debris showers into the room, knocking Cleo unconscious. Looks like dinner will have to wait: you're under attack!

BY TERRORISTS!!

Hah hah, screw this dating thing: you have three terrorists to kill!!

RUN DOWN TO THE SITE OF THE EXPLOSION: *turn to 68*

344 You decide to stick around! You make your way back to the hotel and offer your services to the local authorities. They are wary until you reveal that you've already tracked down and killed the terrorists responsible for the hotel attack, at which point they're impressed (the terrorists were carrying notes admitting their guilt so the authorities know you aren't just a regular murderer) (this is really lucky; good thing I thought to put that detail in your story, huh??).

After the bodies are carried away, you excuse yourself and return to the hotel lobby, where you convince a still-shocked hotel clerk to extend your stay by another six months. "And I may be staying longer after that too," you say. "Although the terrorists responsible for this attack are taken care of, they weren't operating alone."

"Okay," says the clerk.

"There's a whole terrorist organization here that needs to be brought to justice as quickly — and as painfully — as possible," you say, and Ophelia, that's exactly what you do.

I don't want to spoil it all for you, but there's this one point down the line where you're basejumping off a cliff down to the rocks below, and you pull back your arms to reveal a gliding suit you've invented, and you swoop down using that suit and crash horizontally into some terrorists so hard that you literally tear them a new one (where "one" is "a gaping wound in their chests") (you put pointy spears on your hands, that's part of the gliding suit).

So!

That's something to look forward to!

THE END

Turn to 410

345 Hamlet is shocked to see the room filled to capacity with the bodies of literally everyone in town. He doesn't seem too cool with it when you say, "See? Claudius is dead and there are no witnesses! Now we can be happy forever!!"

KISS THINE COOK

Hamlet backs out of the room, slowly. "No, I'm just ACTING crazy!" you shout after him. "Hah hah, I see why you're confused! But it's just an act, remember!"

You grab your bloodied knives and catch up with him. You try to explain how now that everyone is dead, all your problems are solved and you two can be happy together forever, but you're so used to the "kill $charactername" option that you accidentally kill Hamlet too, entirely by muscle memory. Whoopsie!

As gamemaster, I can see across alternate timelines, and dude, this isn't even the first time you've killed everyone in the entire town. It is the first time you camped out in one room and killed them as they walked in, which was easier than the alternative, I guess, but it really seems like maybe you've got some issues you maybe want to work out? Maybe there are some things you want to address? Perhaps some impulses within you should be brought to light, just maybe?? AND HERE I'M KINDA REFERRING TO YOU, THE READER, IN REAL LIFE??

Naw, I'm just kidding, fantasy is awesome because you can do whatever you want and not get in trouble. Kill 'em all, m'lady!! And so, in summary and in conclusion, you're the best at what you do, and what you do is relentlessly choose the "kill everybody" option until there's nobody left to die.

Hey!

Put that on your résumé!!

THE END

Turn to 85

347

Hamlet is at the door!

That's right, turns out that simply wishing for someone to be at your door doesn't change who's actually there. You don't control reality with your THOUGHTS, Ophelia. Sheesh.

Anyway, Hamlet opens the door and steps into your room. "It's me," he says. You haven't seen each other for a while; it's so great to see him. You run up and throw your arms around him and you smooch. It's just like old times.

But the moment passes, and when you look at his face you can see concern written all over it. He's troubled by something.

Ask him what's troubling him: *turn to 365*

Wait for him to tell you: *turn to 334*

348

Cleo takes a small step closer to you and puts her hand on your shoulder. "Ophelia, I know we're still at the beginning of this 'you and me' thing, but I'd be happy to be that friend you need tonight. Sit there, I'll get us some drinks, and we'll talk all about it."

But before you can move to the pillows she gestured to, a huge explosion rocks the hotel! Debris showers into the room, knocking Cleo unconscious. Looks like things are a bit crazy away from home too: you're under attack!

BY TERRORISTS!!

Hah hah, screw this dating thing: you have three terrorists to kill!!

Run down to the site of the explosion: *turn to 68*

349

Letting go of the smallest balloon, you stop rising. Then you start falling. Your momentum is increasing at only 0.2 m/sec, but when I say "only" that's still quite a bit per second and you're quite a few hundred metres up, so anyway long story short, have you ever seen those images of a drop of water hitting a puddle where it bursts in that beautiful crown shape? In that magical moment, over so quickly that it can only be seen when it's artificially frozen, we can see invisible beauty hidden in destruction.

Imagine that, but with your totally gross guts!!

THE END

Turn to 161

350

You go down to the hotel bar where you last saw Pat.

"Hey Pat," you say, but Pat is passed out next to his drink. Well. You sure know how to choose 'em, Ophelia.

You quickly return to your room to consider your remaining options!

Cleopatra Slim: *turn to 340*

Antonio Tony: *turn to 21*

351

You hold on, but your palms start to sweat, and before you know it you're slipping. Then you're falling. This isn't looking good, Hamlet!

You hit the ground so hard that your legs crumple like an accordion. One of your leg bones stabs up through your chest and pierces you right in the heart. Didn't think that was possible? Neither did I, but hey, here we are! Ouchie!

That's the last thing you think: "Ouchie!"

THE END

P.S. You don't come back as a ghost, but you DO come back as a tiny smelly bug that gets stepped on real quick, so — that's...something?

Turn to 104

352

You and Hamlet exit the room with perfect stealth, leaving Claudius alone. You sneak your way into Gertrude's room, again undetectably. You and Hamlet hang upside down from the ceiling, right above Gertrude's bed.

"He'll come," Polonius is telling Gertrude. "Tell Hamlet he's been crazy, okay? And ask him where he's been these past few weeks."

"Okay, okay, fine," Gertrude says. "Go hide. I don't want him to see you here with me."

Polonius goes and hides behind a curtain. You can see his feet sticking out the bottom. Geez. Come on, Polonius.

For a long while, nobody speaks. Gertrude picks up a book and lies on her bed, reading. You hear Polonius shuffle a bit, then fall silent. Gertrude turns the page and coughs, and Polonius peeks out from behind the curtain.

"Not here yet, huh?" he whispers.

"Nope," Gertrude says, without looking up. Polonius installs himself behind the curtain again, and you feel Hamlet tap you on your shoulder. Using the secret tap-based language you learned, Hamlet says, "I DON'T THINK THESE TWO KNOW ANYTHING." You reply, "I KINDA WANT TO SEE HOW LONG HE'LL KEEP HIDING BEHIND THE CURTAIN." Hamlet replies, "WE'RE LEAVING IN AN HOUR," and you tap back, "FINE."

One hour later Polonius is sitting against the wall, sleeping, his body making a very obvious bulge in the otherwise flowing shape of the curtain. Gertrude's taking a nap too.

"WOW, I GUESS REALLY NOT MUCH HAPPENS WHEN I'M NOT AROUND," Hamlet taps, "WHICH SOMEHOW I FEEL ACTUALLY MAKES SENSE?" The two of you sneak out of the room. Nobody notices! You're such awesome spies now!

We have enough intel. Kill Claudius! *Turn to 379*

Proceed with the next part of the plan, Secret Mission Act 4 Scene 2! *Turn to 373*

H

354 A few hours later, you're on a boat for England. YEP. IT'S THAT EASY TO MAKE A VACATION HAPPEN. IN FACT I'M KINDA SURPRISED YOU'RE NOT READING THIS BOOK ON A REAL-LIFE VACATION, UNLESS YOU ARE, IN WHICH CASE I AM STILL KINDA SURPRISED, BUT IT IS A PLEASANT SURPRISE, SO YAY YOU.

"Later haters!" you shout as you wave from the deck of the ship down to the pier below. Nobody's there to see you off though.

"Wooooo!" you yell to the empty pier.

The trip itself takes awhile (wind-powered boats: not the fastest mode of transportation) and is pretty uneventful. But the good news is that when you arrive, you've happened to catch England's annual two weeks of nice weather! There are all sorts of hunky guys here too, which is fun because you're pretty sure you kinda just broke up with Hamlet, because as soon as he started acting crazy you split town. After hanging around your hotel for a few days, you've made small talk with three people who seem to be non-duds. There's:

» Antonio Tony, the mysterious and sexy tourist

» Cleopatra Slim, the friendly, adventurous explorer, and

» Brother Pat, the religious guy who drinks a lot, oh man

So! Who do you want to hang out with tonight? You have the next few weeks to talk to your chosen person, and if you choose the right dialogue option, you may even get them to fall in love with you!

THAT'S RIGHT: this is a dating simulator and you're just going to sit here and keep reading this book as you get to know a bunch of imaginary people and pretend you're trying to date them.

Are you ready??

You take a deep breath and decide to chat up...

Antonio Tony: *turn to 21*

Cleopatra Slim: *turn to 340*

Brother Pat: *turn to 350*

355 You are now Ophelia!

You and Hamlet now know that Claudius is guilty, and though it took you a bit to figure it out, I guess Step Two is to murderize him, huh?

You know that if you leave Hamlet alone he's going to try to kill Claudius, and you love your prince, but MAN that guy can take awhile to get things done. There'll be side projects he'll get enthusiastic about and then abandon, and suddenly he'll

EW.
Gross.
YEEEAAAAAG!!

act like the only way to kill Claudius is to go on a boat ride to England with his pals. It'll go better if both you and Hamlet try to take down Claudius together!

You tell Hamlet you need to speak to him privately, he makes his excuses, and before long you're both back in your bedroom/laboratory/place where you do your best thinkin'.

"Hamlet," you say, locking the door behind you. "We're going to commit murder."

"I guess," he says, shuffling his feet.

"No," you say, locking eyes with him. "We two, you and I, are going to commit murder. And we are going to get away with it. And you know why we're going to get away with murder?"

"Why?" he says.

"Because we are going to be incredibly good at it," you say.

Hamlet looks at you for a moment, unconvinced. "But how do you know that's true?" he says.

"Easy," you say. There's a knife lying on your workbench, and you bring your fist down on its handle. It flies into the air, twirling wildly. You catch it like it's no big deal and point the tip directly at Hamlet's chest.

Whoah! That was really badass, Ophelia!

"We are going to be incredibly good at murder," you say, "because we are going to TRAIN, we are going to STUDY, and we are going to NAIL IT."

Hamlet looks at you.

"I don't wanna study," he says.

Be Hamlet, become convinced by Ophelia's plan, then be Ophelia again and put the plan in motion: *turn to 377*

Try to convince him just by talking to him: *turn to 371*

357

You kick down the door to the royal court. "COURT IS NOW IN SESSION, THE RIGHT HONOURABLE JUDGE EVERYBODY-DIES PRESIDING!" you shout.

"What is the meaning of this?" demands Gertrude, mom to Hamlet AND queen of the entire dang country.

"Oh crap, I didn't think you'd be here, Gertrude, though it makes sense that you are," you say. "Wow, hah hah, I did NOT think this through."

"Seize her!" Gertrude yells. The entire royal court pounces on you, seizing you nicely.

"Okay, now murder her! Come on, let's not waste any time. We don't want her escaping," Gertrude orders, and that's what they do. Wow, I really think you should've waited till court was out of session and taken them down one by one!

This is where your story ends, Ophelia! You got killed by a bunch of politicians; it's kind of a really stupid way to go! Life is full of choices, huh? And I guess, in the end, that's just another way to say, "Life is full of opportunities for you to really mess things up."

THE END

Turn to 241

358

Gosh, well, I suppose if we're really doing this, then I also want to thank everyone involved in the series of events that led to me being here today, able to write and tell jokes for a living, which means I'm thanking...pretty much everyone I've ever interacted with? And I'm also thanking everyone THEY'VE ever interacted with, for helping to make them so awesome. And if I'm doing that, I should probably thank the people who influenced the people who interacted with the people who influenced me as well, right?

Thank you, a large percentage of the planet that I'm pretty sure reaches 100%! But these people didn't just pop into existence fully formed. My thanks take a step sideways and begin racing back in time, up past everyone's parents and grandparents and great-great-great-great-grandparents, thanking them all as we go, further and further, grandparents getting hairier and hairier, until my thanks coalesce all the way back 200,000 years ago in East Africa with Mitochondrial Eve, the one woman from which every single human alive today descends.

Thank you, Mitochondrial Eve.

My thanks speed up, thanking faster and faster back in time, humanity devolving before our eyes. My thanks extend to the first human, pass through Australopithecus, and then on through great apes.

Thank you, great apes. Without you, none of us would be here.

But my thanks are still speeding up, tearing through the primates, then the treeshrews, then the placental mammals. We're 125,000,000 years in the past, thanking everyone we meet. We go back further, thanking the early vertebrates, watching them get smaller, simpler, until there's no animal life on land and you blink and it's 2,100,000,000 years ago and we're thanking the very first cell with a nucleus, alone in the ocean.

Thank you, very first cell with a nucleus. You're a neat li'l guy. You started some really cool stuff.

We watch the cells around us get simpler, more primitive, and then they're gone. My thanks are rushing backwards almost impossibly quickly through this empty planet when suddenly we're watching the Earth itself break apart, diffusing into a tremendous cloud of dust and gas. Mixed in here are the beginnings of all the other planets in our solar system, plus all the material that would one day become our sun. We're 4,568,000,000 years in the past and we are thanking a lifeless hunk of diffuse matter with all our heart. As we're doing that, it combines itself with a colossal molecular cloud, a stellar nursery from which a whole bunch of suns would eventually form, including our own.

Thank you, giant molecular cloud 65,000,000 light-years wide. You were probably very pretty.

The universe around us is contracting, getting smaller and denser and hotter until we're in a universe only a few metres across and shrinking at an incredibly fast rate. 13,000,000,000 years in the past, we are thanking the entire universe, which right now is mostly superheated plasma with a colossally high energy density. We would hug all that is and ever would be, if we could. But we can't. So we say thanks instead!

Thank you, the universe as it existed a mere 10^{-37} seconds after the Big Bang. If you really are sensitive to initial conditions, then I hope nobody ever goes back in time to mess with you.

And then, at last and finally, my thanks race just a little past the origins of the Big Bang, give secret unknowable props all around, and careen back to the present where you're here reading this book.

Hey, thanks babe!! I made a picture for you. *Turn to 363* to see it.

I think we covered everyone. All you can do now is:

READ ABOUT THE AUTHOR: *turn to 281*

START THE STORY ALREADY! *Turn to 1*

359

"I'm busy!" you shout through the door to Laertes.

"I'm leaving for France soon!" he shouts back. "Don't you want to say goodbye?"

"Apparently not!" you shout in reply.

"Whatever!" Laertes yells. He storms off, stomping all the way. You sit in silence for a moment.

He stomps back. "Say bye to Dad for me, okay?!" he shouts.

"Okay, I will!" you yell through the door.

He storms off again. To France, I guess?

Brothers, am I right?

RETURN TO YOUR WORK: *turn to 323*

360

It's a new day, and you and Hamlet wake up in bed together, surrounded by the stacks of books you've been reading. And as of this morning, you've read and mastered every single one of them. It's a beautiful day, Ophelia. It's the kind of day that makes you think, "Man, I bet I could totally murder a head of state by noon."

You prop yourself up and face Hamlet. "We'll start by following Claudius, learning his routine. We'll be in full stealth mode the entire time, so nobody should detect us," you say.

"We have gotten way good at sneaking," Hamlet agrees.

"We'll do three separate missions, each with idiosyncratic naming," you say. "On Secret Mission Act 3 Scene 3, we tail Claudius for a while. During Secret Mission Act 3 Scene 4, we stake out Gertrude; maybe she knows something. And in Secret Mission Act 4 Scene 2, we tail your friends Rosencrantz and Guildenstern, in case they have any information."

"I like it," Hamlet says. "Nobody has seen us for weeks, so they won't even be looking for us. It's perfect."

"That's kinda the reason I made this plan be so awesome!" you say. You roll on top of Hamlet and kiss him, holding his face in your hands while he holds yours in his. It's nice. Eventually you pull back from the smooch.

"Let's do this!" you say in unison.

You both have morning breath, but that's neither here nor there.

ACT 3 SCENE 3: *turn to 195*

361

You open the door for your brother.

"You can come in," you say, "but I don't want to hear any opinions about my personal li—"

"If you sleep with Hamlet you're a slut," he says.

SLAM THE DOOR IN HIS FACE: *turn to 368*

INVITE HIM TO ENTER YOUR ROOM: *turn to 391*

362

What's that? Sorry, I couldn't quite make out what you said. You say you...want to drink the potion anyway? Well, alright!!

You drink the potion and feel a bit better about things. You're still sad Ophelia's gone, obviously, but it's not as bad as it was. This is really great because it allows us to skip ahead to the action part of the story instead of having to slog through you choosing your own depression for the next 300 pages! You can thank me later.

Okay! Time to go to bed and wake up bright and early the next day! You have a fake king to expose!!

GO TO BED: *turn to 122*

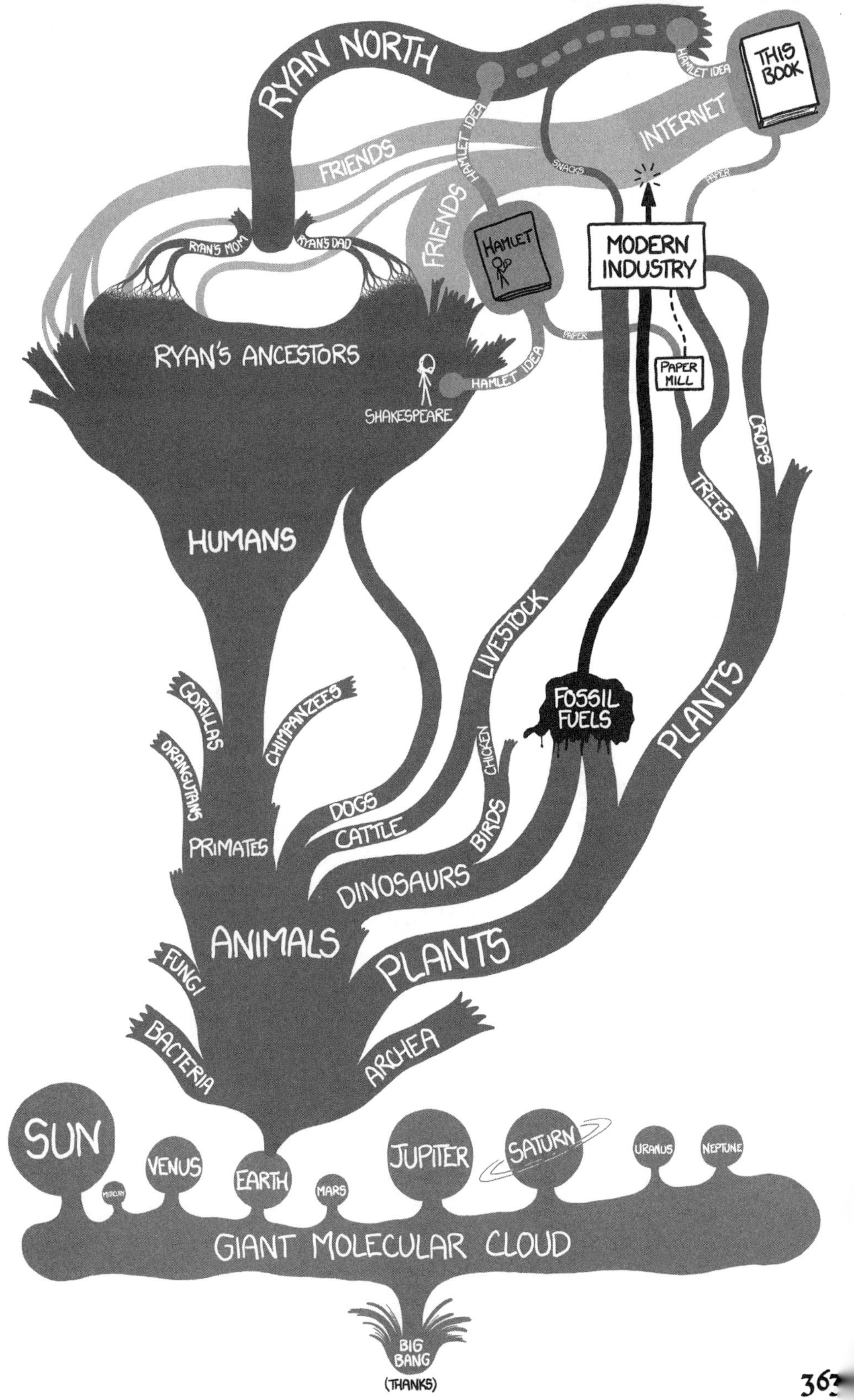
RYAN NORTH
HAMLET IDEA
THIS BOOK
INTERNET
FRIENDS
HAMLET IDEA
SNACKS
PAPER
FRIENDS
RYAN'S MOM
RYAN'S DAD
HAMLET
MODERN INDUSTRY
PAPER
PAPER MILL
RYAN'S ANCESTORS
HAMLET IDEA
SHAKESPEARE
CROPS
TREES
HUMANS
LIVESTOCK
FOSSIL FUELS
PLANTS
GORILLAS
CHIMPANZEES
ORANGUTANS
CHICKEN
DOGS
CATTLE
BIRDS
PRIMATES
DINOSAURS
ANIMALS
PLANTS
FUNGI
BACTERIA
ARCHEA
SUN
MERCURY
VENUS
EARTH
MARS
JUPITER
SATURN
URANUS
NEPTUNE
GIANT MOLECULAR CLOUD
BIG BANG
(THANKS)

364 You pass Hamlet some books off your shelf. One is a book on poisons. The other is a book on sneaking around. "Here, read these," you say. "At the end, you should be good at poisons and sneaking around."

"Got it," Hamlet says.

"In the meantime, I'm going to read these books on how to stab people and how to get away with things. At the end, I should be good at getting away with stabbing people."

"Nice," Hamlet says.

"Then we'll switch!" you say.

"Super rad!" Hamlet says.

Training montage!! *Turn to 380.*

Don't bother with a montage, just skip to several weeks later when I'm fully trained: *turn to 360*

365 You ask him what's wrong, and...well, there's no other way to put this, so I'll give it to you straight: Hamlet tells you about a spooky ghost and a plan for murdering his stepfather, Claudius, pretender to the throne.

I'll be frank: it sounds crazy. A ghost? MURDER? But he is your friend and lover and you're not going to leave him hanging out to dry. As gently as you can, you tell him you're pretty sure ghosts don't exist, but even if they do, he needs to be certain that the ghost he saw was actually the ghost of his father. What if it was some other ghost trying to mess things up?

That seems to give him pause. Hamlet admits he never actually asked the ghost for information only his dad would know. It's possible the ghost could be an impostor.

"I'll come with you tonight, sweetie," you say. "We'll go together. And if a ghost shows up, we'll figure out what to do."

You're confident no ghost will appear and that this will all just go away. You take his hand and squeeze. Hamlet looks up at you, and you can see his relief.

"Okay," he says, smiling.

Go to see the ghost that evening: *turn to 382*

366 "Case closed!" says Hamlet, closing the book with a flourish.

"Hamlet," you say, "I love you, but that is a book that sucks, which is slang I'm inventing right now to mean 'is not a good thing.' It really took you a week to write that?"

"Ophelia," Hamlet replies, "let's take a moment right now to remember that writing is hard."

You stare at each other during that moment.

"Anyway," Hamlet says, "if you don't like my book, check out this other book I found. It's way better than my book and we can just plagiarize it."

Look book: *turn to 370*

367

The cannons fire in a great explosion of iron and, uh, fire. Aiming cannons is hard though, and while you do kill Claudius, you also kill your mother. In the shocked silence that follows, the crowd looks at their headless bodies, still standing, until both crumple and fall at the same time.

The ghost of your father shimmers into this plane of existence beside you. "I didn't tell you to kill my wife!" he says.

"Um," you say.

"Geez, aw geez," he says. "Now by the Ghostly Emergency Supplemental Act of Revenge on Corporeal Beings for Personally Witnessed Murder Acts of Spouse or Spouses, I have to kill you."

"Oh," you say.

Ghost Dad reaches inside your head and, for just a second, makes his ghostly hand slightly solid, shoving a whole bunch of brains out of the way as he does so. I'm sorry, this is really gross. They come out your nose. I didn't even know that could happen. I'm as surprised as you.

"Bleh," you say, dying, your brains getting all over the place.

You have died and I'm gonna put your score at...apples out of a thousand. Your final choice is to decide how much apples are worth to you, but man, they grow on trees so it's not like they're super rare Pokémon cards or anything.

THE END

P.S. Pokémon cards are a thing I just invented, they're pretty fun.

Turn to 77

368

BAM

That felt good.

Laertes shouts through the door that he's sorry and just wanted to say goodbye before he left for France, but when you open the door a crack, he sticks his head in and says, "I'm just saying: have sex with him and you're damaged goods." You slam the door in his face again, barely missing his nose. You shout through the door that if you're damaged goods, he's an entire shelf of unsellable eggs that went off weeks ago, and also as your brother, he's got an entirely unhealthy interest in your sex life.

MARLO MEEKIN

"Nuh-uh! You're unhealthy!!" Laertes shouts in return, and then you hear him stomp away down the hall. What a jerk! And his retorts don't even make sense.

Return to desk: *turn to 323*

370

You take the book from Hamlet and read the cover out loud: "*The Murder of Gonzago: A 'The Adventure Is Being Chosen by You' Story! Can You Murder Your Brother Gonzago and Then, Playing as Your Dead Brother's Son, Murder Your Usurping Uncle? I Sure Hope So; Choose From Over 300 Different Possible Endings.*"

"That's quite the title," you say.

"Yeah, they used really small type," Hamlet says.

Flipping through the book, you see that it might actually be a really good fit for your purposes! "Hamlet, why do we need to plagiarize this?" you ask. "Can't we just give the king this copy to read?"

"Oh, yeah," says Hamlet. "I guess we don't really have to plagiarize it. But I mean, we still could though."

"Why...why would we want to do that?" you ask.

Hamlet stares at you, then seems to reach a decision. "FINE," he says. Taking the book from you, he opens it up to the front page and rubs out the words "BY ME, HAMLET" as well as the line he'd drawn through the actual author's name.

"What about the cover? You didn't change the name back on the cover," you say.

"Dust jacket," Hamlet says, throwing a crumpled-up piece of paper into the garbage.

"Ah," you say.

Well, what are you waiting for? Let's get the king to read this book! Claudius holds court each morning and they're always looking for new sources of entertainment. Let's do this!

Wait till tomorrow, and give the king the book: *turn to 392*

371

"Sweetie, didn't you already agree to revenge your father's death on the current king?" you ask.

"Yeah," he says, "but the closer I get to it, the more I get to thinking — maybe it doesn't make sense to kill him? I mean we've got a legal system —"

"A legal system that will never believe you talked to a ghost," you interrupt.

"Sure," he says, "but that's not necessary. We don't need to bring that into it. We simply work from within the system to bring him down and bring him to justice. And is capital punishment really the best solution anyway? It's obviously not an effective deterrent."

Hamlet seems to come to an epiphany.

"I think the reason I've been so ineffective at killing Claudius is that I honestly don't believe it's the correct course of action!" he says. "That explains all my actions thus far! Man, I could write a whole ESSAY arguing this!"

Talking's not making much progress here, Ophelia!

Be Hamlet, become convinced by Ophelia's plan, then be Ophelia again and put the plan in motion: *turn to 377*

373

You and Hamlet locate and then follow Rosencrantz and Guildenstern from a distance, never letting them get out of sight or earshot. Eventually they go into a seldom-used castle room. You and Hamlet sneak your way inside.

"But soft, what noise?" says Rosencrantz, and you and Hamlet exchange a glance. They couldn't have heard anything. You're too good.

Guildenstern replies, "What have you done, my lord, with the dead body?" and you and Hamlet both relax. Whatever they heard, it wasn't you.

"Compounded it with dust, whereto 'tis kin," answers Rosencrantz. Guildenstern replies, "Tell us where 'tis, that we may take it thence and bear it to the chapel."

You tap out a message to Hamlet. "WHAT ARE THEY TALKING ABOUT?"

"NO IDEA," Hamlet replies. "THIS IS TURBOWEIRD."

"The body is with the King, but the King is not with the body," Rosencrantz says. He pauses, and then says, "The King is a...thing..."

Guildenstern notices Rosencrantz's hesitation and winces. Then he says, "Dude! The line is 'The body is with the King, but the King is not with the body. The King is a head of state, not an undertaker, duh!'"

"Aw frig, right," says Rosencrantz, relaxing. "Okay, from the top!" He takes a few steps backwards, pauses for a second, then says, "But soft, what noise?"

"THEY ARE REHEARSING A PLAY," taps Hamlet. "HAH HAH, WOW, WHAT ARE THE ODDS."

"THAT MAKES SENSE BECAUSE WE HAVEN'T KILLED ANYONE YET," you reply. "IT MUST BE ENTIRELY UNRELATED TO US AND OUR SWEET QUEST, AND AS SUCH, WE CAN LEAVE NOW."

"YES," taps out Hamlet. "ACT 4 SCENE 2 IS OVER. MISSION ACCOMPLISHED."

You are torn between doing more reconnaissance and just up and killing Claudius now! I feel like you've probably had the skills to kill a single dude for weeks!

Do more reconnaissance! Follow Horatio in a plan that you will call...Act 4 Scene 5: *turn to 332*

Go kill Claudius: *turn to 375*

374

You sneak up behind Claudius as he's praying and are about to snap his neck when Hamlet puts his hand in yours and uses secret awesome spy code to quickly tap out a message: "NO, I'LL DO IT. AND SO HE GOES TO HEAVEN, AND SO AM I REVENGED. THAT WOULD BE SCANNED: A VILLAIN KILLS MY FATHER, AND FOR THAT, I, HIS SOLE SON, DO THIS SAME VILLAIN SEND TO HEAVEN."

"OKAY COOL," you tap in reply.

Hamlet draws his sword and, with one massive blow, cleaves the top of Claudius's head, including most of his brain, from the remainder of his body.

Using your Getting Away With Things skill, you put the sword in Claudius's hand, and the two of you confidently walk out of the chapel. "Oh no!" you shout to some passersby. "I think Claudius just committed suicide in there! Wow, it really looks like he meant it!!"

You get away with it due to your insanely overloaded Getting Away With It stat, and when Hamlet becomes king of Denmark, you become queen. And under your enlightened leadership, every single citizen of Denmark becomes a philosopher scientist karate inventor with a really satisfying personal life.

THE END

P.S. Claudius comes back as a ghost, but he's missing a lot of his brains so it's more pathetic than scary.
P.P.S. It is kinda really awful though.

Turn to 175

375

You and Hamlet leave the room, but Claudius is nowhere to be found. By the time you track him down again, he's in the royal court talking to Laertes. "Okay, so you believe me when I tell you that Ophelia was brainwashed by Hamlet to kill Polonius, right?" Claudius is saying. "And so you are willing to swordfight both of them to the death, right? Ophelia because she killed your father, and Hamlet because he convinced her to do it?"

"Yes," says Laertes. "You have told me a very credible story about how that happened. Plus I never really liked my sister and think she's an inferior person, and not just because she's a woman!"

"THAT JERK! POLONIUS IS DEAD??" you tap to Hamlet. He replies, "POSSIBLY? I GUESS CLAUDIUS WANTS TO FRAME US AND GET YOUR BROTHER TO DO MURDERS TO US??"

"AW MAN, THIS JUST GOT PERSONAL," you reply. "HELLA PERSONAL... TO THE XTREME."

Laertes takes the sword offered to him by Claudius. "Okay, so if they show up, you'll kill them. And just to make sure, I've dipped the blade in poison. Also, I filled this goblet with poison too, so if they comment about being thirsty, be sure to offer them this refreshing beverage."

During this speech, you sneak up behind Claudius, and, without being seen, dip your finger into the goblet. You sniff it. Returning to Hamlet, you quickly tap, "IT'S A BASIC HEBENON POISON: SIMILAR TO HENBANE, BUT ACTS MUCH QUICKER."

"COOL," taps Hamlet. "U READY?"

"Absolutely," you say out loud, removing your hood and stepping from your camouflage. Claudius and Laertes both spin around, gaping at you, totally shocked. "Hey Claudius," you say. "Thanks for killing both our dads."

"Both?" says Laertes, and at this point Hamlet steps forward too.

"She's referring to mine, jerk," he says. Laertes lunges at Hamlet, but you flick your wrist and the next thing Laertes knows your blade is sticking out of his neck. Hamlet glances at you. You bow.

"He's all yours," you say.

Hamlet advances on Claudius. "You killed my father, you killed my girlfriend's father, and you married my mom."

Claudius takes a step backwards, and you grab his arm to hold him in place.

"I really don't think I like you," Hamlet says.

Claudius gulps. "Um," he says, "it was an...accident?"

"Hah!" Hamlet laughs. "An accident? Here, let me show you an accident."

Hamlet mimes stumbling backwards. He knocks over the table Claudius has put the poison goblet on, which sends the goblet and its contents flying towards Claudius. You grab Claudius by the chin and hold his mouth open so the poison falls in, and then allow the goblet itself to hit him, breaking his nose in two places. "That was poisoned," he gasps, shocked. Hamlet picks up Laertes' sword and tosses it to you.

"Why take chances?" you say, stabbing Claudius in the lungs. He dies in incredible pain, and you and Hamlet kiss.

"Mission accomplished, sweetie!" Hamlet says.

"We did it!" you reply.

You kiss some more, killing some assassins who snuck up behind you while I wasn't looking without even breaking your smooch. Nice! You're still making out when the entire royal court walks in the room and sees you there, smooching over Claudius's dead body. These makeouts over a corpse look PRETTY BAD, but you use your Totally Getting Away With It skills to totally get away with it! You get away with it SO WELL, in fact, that you two lovebirds are proclaimed the new queen and king of Denmark!

NICE.

Congratulations, Queen Ophelia! You have earned 670 ultrapoints, you killed a bad guy, you bettered yourself, you became royalty, AND you learned a lot of really awesome skills!

In this book, I mean!!

THE END

Turn to 88

in) for, y…
ything else here!
hy even bother?"

ulia Child's woolly
nammoth taco recipe, F1

Joan of A…

E HEREAFTER HE…

ER HIGH 16º C Actually, surprisingly chilly

arl Hamlet honoured yet again

ormed ghost awarded "Spirit of Spiriting" title for third year in a row

JOSEPH PULITZER

rning an afterlife bent on enge into an afterlife helping ners, King Carl Hamlet has ecome one of the most revered ublic figures in the afterlife, and as such, he's walked away with the Spirit of Spiriting award for the third year in a row.

The award, given to spirits for going above and beyond their civic duty, was judged and presented by God Himself at the Sacred Heights Community Centre Wednesday at a gala event. The award recognized Hamlet's community program, "Scared Straight," which has turned countless wayward souls, seemingly predestined for Hell, into souls ripe for Heaven.

His most famous project, the "Three Ghosts" initiative, which turned selfish money-lender Ebenezer Scrooge into a selfless, God-fearing man, was immortalized in the novel A Christmas Carol by Charles Dickens, who, sadly, resides in Hell.

Speaking at the all-star gala, Scrooge had nothing but kind words to say about Hamlet.

"This guy, now my good, good friend, let me tell you something about him. He scared the hell out of me! Literally! I love Hamlet and what he's done and think that he revolutionized what it means to be a ghost."

Hamlet was no stranger to scaring others. From the very

Hamlet, Page 3

King Carl Hamlet after accepting his award at W…
HA…

Hitchens still refusing to belie… in heaven

"This is clearly a series of ele… …lses within my dying … …lbrated ess…

Accusations of sports team … angels, deities

…ams cite

377

Wow, now you're catching on!

Okay, you're Hamlet! And you decide, as Hamlet, that Ophelia is making a lot of sense. I mean, it is a little weird that she's suddenly so into murdering people, and isn't it also kinda weird how you're going to kill a dude because your Ghost Dad asked you to, even though this ghost can interact with the physical realm and if he can do that, why doesn't he just kill him himself? Wait — this plan doesn't really make a lot of sense, does it? This is crazy! *This whole plan is crazy!!*

Hamlet kicks you out, and you are now Ophelia again.

Hamlet says, "Hey Ophelia, um, I'm not sure we should be killing Claudius after all. Maybe my dad can just do it himself."

"I thought you were down with this revenge thing!" you ask. "Don't you want revenge?"

"Well, um, that's the thing," he says. "Revenge is great and all but I get the impression that maybe there are more productive things for me to be consumed by —" and now you are Hamlet again and you finish his sentence with "— but actually, now that I think about it, hah hah, let's stab that jerk in the brains!" and now you're back to being Ophelia again, and I honestly think you're abusing your reader privileges here, so let's be Ophelia from now on, okay? Besides, you've got Hamlet pretty well set up for a while. He is down to murder a dude.

Hit the books: *turn to 364*

378

The pirate screams at you, livid. He's lost some very important body parts, but he's not going to stop. He's out of control with rage and will fight you right to the end. You can't let your guard down. He'll take you apart with his teeth if you let him.

It's time to finish this, Hamlet.

Deliver the killing blow! *Turn to 163*

379

You eventually find Claudius in a room with Gertrude, and they're just staring at each other and saying nothing. It's — pretty weird? You and Hamlet step forward. "Hi Mom," he says. "Listen, come with me for a bit, will you?"

"Hamlet?" she says, shocked. "Ophelia? What are you doing here?"

"Nevermind that now," Hamlet says, taking her by the wrist and leading her out of the room. "Let's go over here for a bit, okay?"

Claudius moves to leave as well, but you hold on to his arm. "Not so fast, Claudius," you say. "We spent the last few weeks getting really, really good at all the skills needed to kill you."

"Aw nuts," he says.

Anyway, I don't want to get too gory but you kill Claudius with a mace and two knives and a vegetable peeler! Plus you completed the murder alone, so you got all the experience points for yourself. Nice! You then rejoin Hamlet and his mother where you have a very nice picnic down by the river before she even finds out about the murder. It is delightful but also really weird of you to arrange. I don't know. Then I skip ahead in the story some and you and Hamlet become queen and king and have three awesome children, each radder than the last when arranged in order of increasing radditude! Yay!

Oh man, you just read a book that used the word "radditude" sincerely, that's how awesome you / we are! I award us both, let's say, 15 litres of points!

THE END

P.S. Claudius doesn't come back as a ghost to bother you, which is terrific, because he's kind of a jerk in any state of being, and I kinda feel bad for him, who wants to be friends with a jerk, not me that's for sure.

Turn to 226

380

You, reading a book by candlelight, flipping to one page, furrowing your brow, and flipping back.

Hamlet in a lab with a textbook in a recipe stand, pouring a small amount of liquid into a flask, turning the flask's transparent contents a dark, rich purple. The purple liquid exploding, leaving Hamlet blinking and covered in soot.

The pages of a page-a-day calendar, tearing themselves off and fluttering to the ground.

You sneaking around a building at night, stopping to read your book by candlelight, then slapping your forehead and extinguishing the candle.

You sneaking past the armed sentry of Marcellus, Bernardo, and Francisco who never notice a thing.

Hamlet holding a knife in his fist, you touching him gently on the arm, showing him how to let the blade rest in his hand, lightly, gently.

The face of a clock, its hands spinning rapidly.

You and Hamlet in an argument, Hamlet gesturing towards a fresh cut in his coat, you holding scissors in one hand and your *How to Get Away with Stuff* book in the other. You answering his accusations by reading lines from your book, and Hamlet's body language softening until he's holding up the torn fabric, shrugging, smiling. You holding up the book so he can see. The two of you bursting into amazed laughter.

You and Hamlet surreptitiously adding bright green liquid into each other's drink, then passing the mug to each other. The two of you about to drink, then sniffing the drink experimentally, laughing, playfully punching the other, then pouring the mugs out onto the grass. The grass withering and dying instantly.

This image fading into a shot of you and Hamlet, asleep in bed late at night, smiles on your faces and giant stacks of books on each side of your bed.

Congratulations! You have both fully levelled up your skills in sneaking, poisons, stabbing, and getting away with things!!

Proceed with maxed-out skills! *Turn to 360*

381

BAM

That felt great.

Laertes shouts through the door that he's sorry and just wanted to say goodbye before he left for France, and Polonius shouts that Hamlet only wants to get his hands on your body. "He wants to sex it," he shouts.

You open the door and say, "I appreciate your concern but I can take care of myself," which is more than they deserve, and you close the door again.

Through the door you can hear Laertes and Polonius talking.

"Hey, listen: while you're in France, give every man thine ear but few thy voice," Polonius says, then pauses, then says, "That's some primo advice right there, I gotta say."

You roll your eyes and return to your desk.

Return to desk: *turn to 323*

382

Evening comes, and Hamlet leads you to the spot outside where he first saw the ghost. "We have to wait till around midnight," he says. "I think that's when he normally shows up."

To pass the time, you play a storytelling game you enjoy, where you say one word of a story and he says the next word, and neither of you knows where the story will go.

"Once," you begin.

"Upon," he says.

"A," you say.

"Time," he says.

"There," you say.

"Was," he says.

"A," you say.

"Beautiful," he says, looking at you. You smile.

"Prince," you reply, and he smiles back.

"Who," he says.

"Wanted," you say.

"To," he says.

"Kiss," you say.

"His girlfriend," he says.

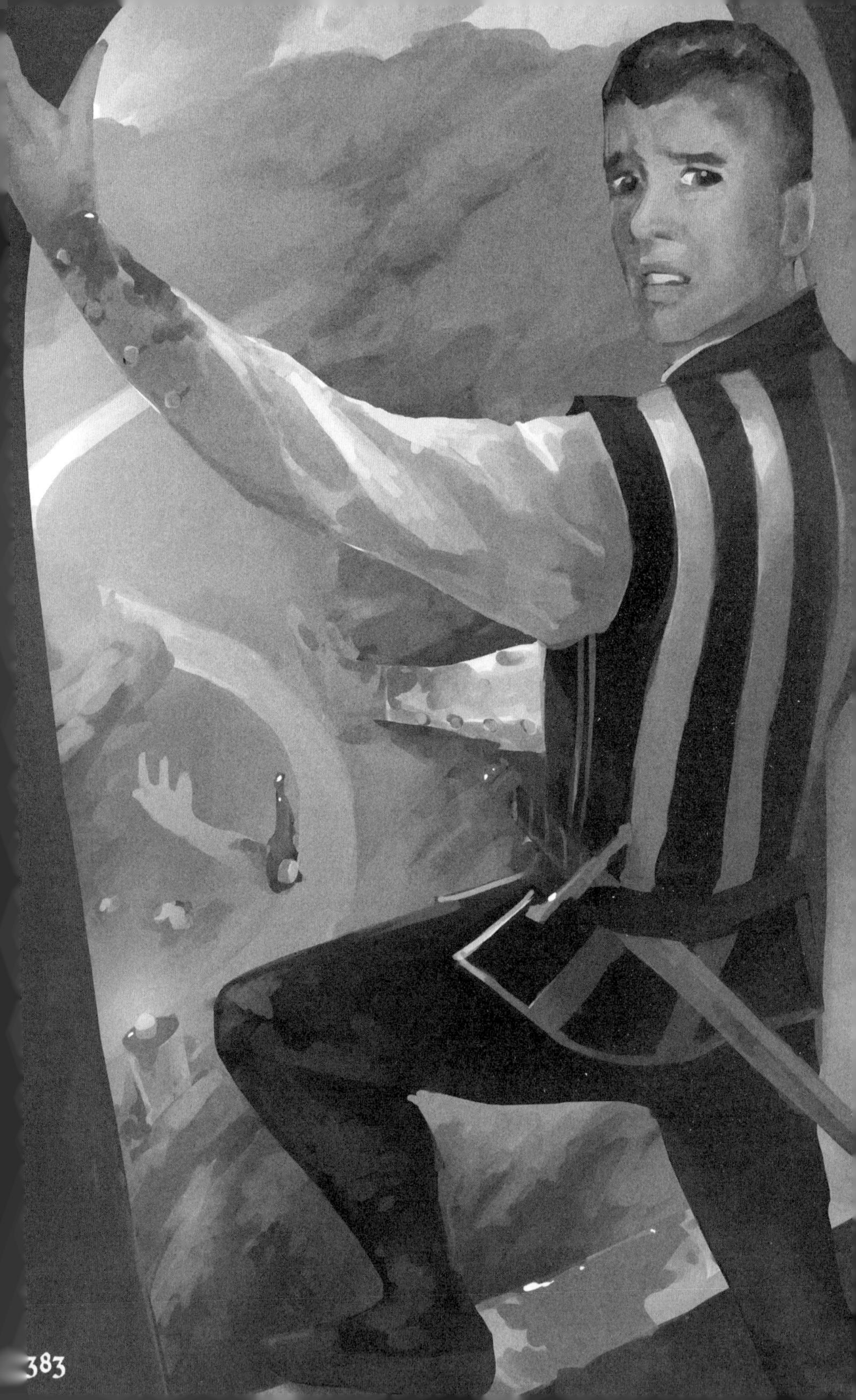

"That's cheating," you say, and then you're kissing.

Make out for a while: *turn to 393*

Don't make out, because, and you can't believe you're thinking this, but what if a ghost catches you making out? *Turn to 398*

384

YES! YES FINALLY YOU ARE KILLING CLAUDIUS. OH MY GOD FINALLY.

OH MY GOD.

Okay let's do this!!

You stab Claudius a few times with the poisoned sword, but man, poison is slow and you've already got it in your system!

So then you pick up the poisoned goblet and force it down his throat, all the while calling him "an incestuous, murderous, Goddamned Dane." Wow. I mean it's a little racist (at least partially self-racist too, so: irony) but still — wow. It's a huge dose of poison and he dies instantly.

What's that? You didn't know poison worked that way? WELL, THAT'S WEIRD BECAUSE I'M PRETTY SURE IT JUST DID.

Meanwhile, as the poison starts to kill you, Laertes forgives you for the deaths you've caused and asks you to forgive him of the same, and you do it. It's actually pretty classy. Then you call Horatio over.

"Horatio," you say, "don't be crazy and chug the poison too. It's your job to tell everyone my story so people know what really happened. You need to tell the people."

"Okay," says Horatio, glancing at the surrounding crowd which has already seen this all go down.

"Oh, and write it down when you do, so future generations will know," you say.

"Okay," says Horatio.

"Oooh! And make it one of those choose-your-own-adventure dealies," you say. "I love those."

"Right," says Horatio.

Suddenly you hear an army marching in! Osric runs in and says that Fortinbras is here and marching on the capital with some English ambassadors. Remember Fortinbras? He's that Norwegian crown prince whose father died and who decided right away to take action! He's almost like a parallel to you, only, you know — better?

Anyway. You're not going to survive long enough to talk to him. You're actually not going to survive long at all. It's time, Hamlet, to choose your last words to Horatio — well, last words EVER really:

"O, I die, Horatio. The potent poison quite o'ercrows my spirit. I cannot live to hear the news from England. But I do prophesy the election lights on Fortinbras. He has my dying voice. So tell him, with th' occurrents, more and

LESS, WHICH HAVE SOLICITED. THE REST IS SILENCE. O, O, O, O." *Turn to 277*

"DON'T LET IT END LIKE THIS. TELL THEM I SAID SOMETHING." *Turn to 247*

"HORATIO, I SHOULD'VE TRUSTED YOU SOONER. LISTEN WELL: THERE'S A SHIP NAMED *CALYPSO'S GALE* OUTSIDE THE HARBOUR THAT CAN HELP YOU DEFEAT FORTINBRAS. HER CREW IS BRAVE AND HER CAPTAINCY SHARED BY ROSENCRANTZ AND GUILDENSTERN. GO AND TELL THEM WHAT HAPPENED. WITH MY LAST BREATH, I ASK YOU DO ME ONE LAST SOLID: SAVE DENMARK." *Turn to 266*

385

"AWESOME," says Hamlet.

"We don't know any writers though," you say.

"Not a problem," replies Hamlet, "for among my princely duties is STUDYING ENGLISH LITERATURE. Also, Danish literature."

"I mean, that's great, but that doesn't make you a writer," you say. "Just like being a history major doesn't make you, I don't know, Julius Caesar."

"Please, Ophelia," Hamlet says, taking your hand. "Give me a week and you'll have your book."

So, you give him his week. In that week you stay mostly in your room and don't hear much from Hamlet. King Claudius seems happy that Hamlet has disappeared from view, so not much happens. Oh! You do figure out a way to measure the specific gravity of alcohol while Hamlet's busy. That's pretty cool. All it requires is a flask that's weighed three times: once empty, once full of water, and once full of the liquid you're measuring, and then you can — but why am I telling you this? You invented the whole technique!

ANYWAY. A week later, Hamlet runs into your room, clutching a manuscript. "I finished the book!" he says.

"Excellent! Can I read it?"

"Let me read it to you! You see, it's one of those amazing READ WHILE AN ADVENTURE IS CHOSEN novels. You choose what happens to the main character! Choose from over three different outcomes."

"Oh no," you say.

"Oh yes," Hamlet says and clears his throat, then holds out one hand in front of him.

"Murder!" he shouts dramatically. "It is what you committed. Is this true??"

Hamlet stares at you expectantly. "Well, is it?"

"You want me to choose here?" you ask.

"Yes please," Hamlet replies. "Your options are yes or no."

SAY YES: *turn to 366*

SAY NO: *turn to 388*

387

Okay! I mean, you ARE already in your room so I guess that kinda makes sense. You decide that it's nap rhyme prime time.

Lying in bed, you clear your throat and hold one hand up above you.

"Time for naps, hooray hooray / Naps are great, that's what I say."

You fall asleep and wake up the next day with the outline of Christina's book pressed into your face. Hey bucko! Looks like you slept through the whole afternoon, evening, AND night!!

Run to the royal court with the book: *turn to 147*

388

"No," you say.

Hamlet raises an eyebrow, then turns to a different page and begins reading.

"Liar!!" he shouts. "You totally killed your brother by poisoning him in the ear! You should admit it right now." He then looks at you. You stare back at him, evenly.

"Your choices are to admit it or not admit it," he finally says.

Admit it: *turn to 366*

Do not admit it: *turn to 389*

389

"No, I do not admit to any murder," you say. "I continue to not admit to any murders."

Hamlet furrows his brow and turns to a different page.

"Liar!!" he reads. "You totally killed your brother by poisoning him in the ear! We all know it. You should admit it right now. You should definitely do that." He looks up from the book. You sigh.

"Your choices are to admit it or not admit it," he explains. "Listen, I'm just throwing this out here, but maybe you should admit it, okay? It would be super great if you did that."

Admit it: *turn to 366*

Do not admit it: *turn to 160*

391

O-okay? You let him into your room. He sits down on the bed and pats the empty space beside him.

You choose to remain standing.

"Listen," he says, "I know you like Hamlet, but he's a prince, so he's going to have to marry someone of his own rank."

"Who said anything about marriage?" you reply. "I'm happy with Hamlet and he's happy with me. We're having fun. Nobody's talking about marriage."

"That's another thing," he says. "Look, if you have sex before marriage, then you'll be ruined for other men and nobody will ever want you. He's only dating you because he wants sex. Don't sex him because I'm your brother and I'm telling you not to."

Throw him out of your room and slam the door in his face: *turn to 368*

Sit down beside him, for some reason, and tell him that he makes a lot of sense (somehow?) and you'll do as he says: *turn to 394*

392

First thing in the morning, you show up to the royal court. Hamlet's got the book, so all you need to do is observe. You look around the room and see that everyone's here: the new king, the old queen, your dad, Hamlet's weird friends Rosencrantz and Guildenstern and Horatio, a bunch of people you've never met — the whole gang! You notice Hamlet talking to Horatio. He's asking him to also keep an eye on Claudius as he reads the story. Couldn't hurt.

Alright. There's nothing left to do. It's go time! Hopefully Hamlet realizes that too!

It turns out he does. "Hey Claudius!" Hamlet says, brandishing his copy of Gonzago. "Why don't you read THIS book today?"

"I certainly don't see why not," Claudius says, and Hamlet passes him the book. Hamlet seems to hesitate on where to go next, but settles on standing behind the king so he can see what he's reading.

As Claudius begins to read, you become really intent on what's happening. In fact, you're staring at Claudius and listening with such insane intensity that you almost feel like you've become the man himself!

In fact, that'd be fun. You are now Claudius!

Be Claudius: *turn to 311*

393

You make out for what turns out to be QUITE a while, as the night is warm and the stars are stunning and there are no bugs here to bite any exposed flesh and before you know it, you've totally made out as much as it's possible to totally make out — NICE — and you fall asleep in each other's arms. If ghosts exist, and if one really did show up, he certainly had the good grace to leave you alone for your makeouts. Also, he was probably embarrassed: you were both way naked!

The two of you return to the same spot the next evening, and the evenings after that, but it becomes more and more a date night and less and less a "a spectre from beyond the grave wants to get some murders done" thing. King Claudius and Polonius are not exactly thrilled with the two of you being together, but on the flip side, any urges to commit regicide that were floating around have begun to fade too. Though you talk about it often, the whole encounter with the ghost, if it really did happen, takes on the quality of a dream.

Rather than do the long-distance thing again, you decide to move in together and get your own place here in Denmark. Together, the two of you work on finalizing the invention of the alcohol thermometer (it works!) and even figure out the other half of it: a way to move heated air throughout a building. Congratulations, you invented central heating! It's an invention that all of Denmark wants, and most are willing to pay for.

While it's not the largest, you do live in the most comfortable estate in the entire country — thanks to the heating money. One bright summer day, as the two of you walk through the castle garden, you get down on one knee and say, "Sweetie, you're the most important person in my life and I can't imagine ever living without you. I want to make you as happy as you make me every single day. Let's get married." You mean every word.

It's not the most traditional proposal in the world, nor is it the most traditional wedding, but it's wonderful and beautiful and perfect. You're very happy. You don't invite Claudius to the wedding.

A few years later, Claudius falls ill with some sort of lung disease, and his doctors are unable to treat it effectively. He passes away only a few months later, having never produced an heir. Shortly after, the two of you become the new king and queen of all of Denmark.

Your first child, Alex, is born five months later, and you all live very happily ever after.

THE END

Turn to 156

394

Really?

Really.

Okay.

You sit down on the bed and tell him you'll do as he says, and that you sincerely appreciate his meddling in your personal life, and THEN you go on to say that if you're going to abstain from sex before marriage, then he should be careful too, because he sleeps around way more than you do, and it's going to be one heck of a sexual double standard if you're "damaged goods" and he's "totally fine."

That's right. I didn't even give you a choice about saying that or not, because you keep choosing the stupid options. Guess you're just gonna have to deal with it, huh?

In any case, there's a knock on your door and before you can answer, your father, Polonius, opens the door. "Normally when you knock, you wait for someone to let you in, Dad," you say.

"You're an idiot if you think Hamlet loves you," he says, then he notices Laertes is in your room too. "Oh, hey Laertes. Have fun on your trip; to thine own self be true."

Laertes nods. "I already told her she's slutty," he says.

KICK THEM BOTH OUT AND SLAM THE DOOR IN THEIR FACES: *turn to 381*

I GUESS...SMILE AND NOD AND PAT THE EMPTY SPOT ON THE BED BESIDE YOU AND LAERTES, INVITING POLONIUS TO SIT DOWN TOO? BECAUSE THAT IS SOMETHING A PERSON WOULD DO? *Turn to 409*

395

SLAP

Holy cow, did that feel good.

Sometimes, you figure, there is a call for physical violence, and probably now was a pretty good time for it. Your dad touches his face and gets up to leave. In the doorway he says, "Was it something I said?"

"YEP!" you shout at him.

He pauses. "Weird," he says and leaves. Laertes shrugs his shoulders, says "Bye, I guess," and leaves as well.

Good riddance. You sit at your desk for a while, calming down and refocusing.

OKAY, LET'S GET DOWN TO WORK: *turn to 323*

396

"Excuse me," you say. The ghost pretends not to hear you. "Excuse me, Mister...Ghost?" you enquire, raising your hand.

"'Sup," says the ghost.

"How do we know you're really Hamlet Sr.?" you ask.

"Oh," says the ghost. "Oh. Um. I guess...ask me some things only Hamlet's dad would know?"

You do so (they're pretty boring questions about family junk, you're not missing out on anything by me not including them here), and the ghost answers them perfectly. Better still, he answers them as only Hamlet Sr. could answer them, and even makes a reference to a running joke you two had a few months ago. "I can't

gobble this!" says the ghost, and then together the two of you shout, "It's tooooo spicy!!" and then you're laughing like what you just said is the funniest thing ever in time.

I don't get it. I guess you had to be there?

Anyway, this is totally the ghost of Hamlet's dad!! IDENTITY: CONFIRMED.

Talk about the murder: *turn to 433*

398

You turn your head away after a few smooches.

"That's enough," you say. "We don't want your dad catching us making out."

Hamlet grins and pulls you close to him. "I think he'd be cool with it," he says. That's a weird thing to say, but you excuse it because you know people can say some really weird things when they're way horny. You kiss some more, but finally push him away for real this time.

"What makes you think he wants to spend the afterlife watching us make out?" you say.

"Well, it's what I'd want to do," he says with a smile. "I mean, if I were me AND I was also the ghost," he explains. You're about to reply when you're interrupted by an awkward cough coming from...above you? Looking up, you see what for all the world looks like Hamlet's dad, Hamlet Sr., only he's transparent and floating and you can see through his bod.

"Hey guys," the ghost says.

You're too shocked to say anything. Ghosts are real, Ophelia! Surprise!

Hamlet looks up at the ghost and waves. "Hi Dad!" he says.

Demand the ghost prove that he's who he claims to be: *turn to 396*

It doesn't matter who he is; the real question is if this ghost is so big into murdering dudes, why doesn't he just murder Claudius himself? Riddle him THAT. *Turn to 412*

399

"On the other hand," you say, meeting the gazes of both Hamlet and the ghost, "the greatest proof that immortal ghosts aren't possible is that we're not overrun with them right now."

The ghost blinks. He hadn't considered that.

"You're the first ghost I've seen, Hamlet Sr., and if ghosts lived forever I expect I'd already have been bothered by caveman ghosts long ago, each of them demanding that I go smash in some other caveman's descendant's head to make up for when THEY got their head smashed in hundreds of generations before I was even born. Old hatreds lasting forever, ancient slights never forgotten, the embarrassing prejudices of our grandparents multiplied a thousand times..." You trail off, imagining how frustrating it'd be to explain to an angry and confused and immortal pre-linguistic caveman who can walk through walls how to better cope with, say, the pangs of despised love, the law's delay, the insolence of office, and the spurns that patient merit of the unworthy takes.

"Right!" says the ghost, considerably cheered. He holds up one finger. "So either immortal ghosts have better things to do with their time, which is good," he says. He then holds up a second finger. "Or I'm the first immortal ghost, which is good because then they're really unlikely and we can't expect that Claudius would be the second one." He pauses, then holds up a third finger. "OR I'm going to ghost-die some day, which is bad."

"Not that bad," you say. "After all, you've died once before and you came through it alright. You can float now."

"True," says the ghost, floating. "Okay. So! Are you guys in or what? Will you murder Claudius and avenge my death??"

Tell the ghost you are in: *turn to 429*

Tell the ghost you are out: *turn to 415*

400

You back your king up, but rather than following with her rook, Gertrude moves her king forward.

"Kg7," she writes. You're not in check for once, so you take this chance to promote your pawn to a queen.

"Yes!!" you say as Gertrude writes down your move as "f1Q."

"How's that taste, Queenie??"

"Oh, it's okay. Shame she can't help you win though," Gertrude says, moving her rook to stand between the two kings. "Rg6+," she writes.

You move your king to the right, and she moves her rook to follow. You move your king back to the left, and she moves her rook to follow you again.

Oh crap. She can keep you in check for as long as she wants. And if you move to the left, she'll take your queen after you move out of check. So your queen IS useless after all. What a waste!

BUT wait, isn't there a rule that if you repeat the same move three times you can call the game a draw? Let me check. Hold on, I've got a rulebook for chess here somewhere. Just a second.

Just a sec.

Okay, yes: there is such a rule!! So that's what you do, sending your king back and forth over again. After three repetitions, you declare a draw!

NICELY DONE, Ophelia!

Stalemate: *turn to 497*

402

Claudius probably thinks you're dead, so he's not going to expect a head-on attack. This plan might actually be perfect!

You reduce your speed so that when you arrive back in Denmark, it's high noon. Your royal castle sits on a hill near the shore, and you sail as close as you can to it, gun ports open.

"Claudius!" you yell. At the top of the hill, you see various servants and members of the royal court looking down towards your ship, murmuring to themselves when they realize none other than Prince Hamlet is the one in charge of this magnificent vessel.

"GET ME CLAUDIUS!" you order, and some of the onlookers disappear inside the castle. While you wait, you whisper to Rosencrantz and Guildenstern to adjust the cannons upwards.

Shortly afterwards, Claudius and Gertrude appear, staring down at your ship.

"Hamlet?!" your mom shouts, shocked.

"Hey Mom," you say. "I'm back from England, and I brought a boat!"

"Could you step to the left about 15 paces?" *Turn to 170*

"Could you ask Claudius why he murdered Dad real quick?" *Turn to 214*

403

WAYS TO MURDER A KING.

by Ophelia and Hamlet

» Poison in the Ear (Done before, we know it works.)

» Stabs (Not always fatal: I saw a dude get stabbed in the leg and then pull out the sword, it was awesome. –Hamlet)

» Stabs in Eye (Always fatal? Probably???)

» Suffocation (Easy if Claudius is sleeping, hard if Claudius is awake and not wanting to suffocate, but easy again if Claudius is in space. –O)

» Drowning (Requires: water.)

» Explosion (Requires: explosions.)

» Implosion (Even harder but might be fun?)

» Bladder Explosion (Requires: water, no bathrooms, social pressure.)

» Old Age (Requires: patience, liberal definition of "murder.")

» Murder Him but Just Make it Look Like Old Age (Requires: makeup???)

» Get Him to Read a Book That's Just Like the Murder He Committed and Then He'll Get Nervous and Confirm His Guilt and Then We Can Stab Him (Requires: book, also seems like "Stabs" would be easier?? –O)

» Make Him Accidentally Pass a Law That Says He Has to Be Murdered Before the Law Can Be Repealed (Note: Hamlet insists we put this here because It's Crazy Enough to Work. –O)

» Blast Him into Space, Which the Ghost Came Back While We Were Writing This to Explain Is a Vast Vacuum Where There's No Air (See: suffocation.)

Looking over the list, you decide to trim it down a little before you make your choice. You come up with a short list of Serious Contenders:

» Stabs, as it's the simplest and there're swords here, like, everywhere.

» Drowning, as you think you can make it look like an accident.

» Blast Him into Space, because Hamlet insists on it.

» and also the stupid book one because, again, Hamlet insists on it.

Hamlet's pretty satisfied with the list. "Your call, Ophelia," he says! What do you choose?

Stabs: *turn to 434*

Drowning: *turn to 511*

Blast Him into Space: *turn to 229*

Get Him to Read a Book That's Just Like the Murder He Committed and Then He'll Get Nervous and Confess and Then We Can Stab Him: *turn to 385*

404

You pick up the skull and hold it out in front of you. You begin to feel...INSPIRED.

"Alas, poor Yorick!" you say. "I knew him, Horatio, a fellow of infinite jest, of most excellent fancy. He hath borne me on his back a thousand times, and now, how abhorred in my imagination it is! My gorge rises at it. Here hung those lips that I have kissed I know not how oft. Where be your gibes now? Your gambols?

Your songs? Your flashes of merriment that were wont to set the table on a roar? Not one now to mock your own grinning? Quite chapfallen? Now get you to my lady's chamber and tell her, let her paint an inch thick, to this favour she must come. Make her laugh at that."

"What my friend means to say," says Horatio, "is that he remembers Yorick and the fun times they shared, but now to look at his gross remains makes him want to drop a barf."

"Ah," says the gravedigger.

"He then asks a dead lifeless skull where its jokes and songs are, and then tells the skull to go to his girlfriend's room and tell her that no matter how much makeup she puts on, she'll end up like him one day," Horatio says.

"Well, not exactly like him," says the gravedigger, "as male and female skulls have several structural differences."

You interrupt them both. "Horatio, do you think Alexander the Great looked like this after he was buried?"

"Yeah, probs," says Horatio.

"This skull is smelly," you say.

"Yeah, probs," says Horatio.

"Do you think it's weird that we can be alive and be kings of the world, but then we die and return to the earth and then someone might use that earth to make mud and use that mud to fix a hole in a barrel?"

"Who uses mud to fix a ho—" Horatio begins, but you interrupt him.

"You can also use mud to patch a wall," you say.

Suddenly, you're startled by noises! It sounds like screaming!

INVESTIGATE NOISES: *turn to 120*

SUDDENLY SIT STRAIGHT UP IN BED, FULLY AWAKE: *turn to 319*

405

You're welcome.

That's very gracious of you.

BACK TO THE FIGHT! *Turn to 431*

406

Gertrude moves her rook to match again, this time noting "Re2" in her book.

"You're in trouble now," she says. "Move away from that pawn, and I'll take him, and you've lost. But stay close and I'll sacrifice my rook to take him anyway, and the best you can hope for is a draw."

"I only understood some of those words!!" you shout, and then you study the board.

Go for the draw: *turn to 427*

Maybe she's lying about taking the pawn? Still play for a win: *turn to 273*

407

Man, that took awhile.

Turn to 438

408

Okay, you do all that stuff. Listen, I'm going to cut our losses here. You're not allowed to be Ophelia for a while.

Be Hamlet: *turn to 71*

409

Polonius sits down on the bed beside you. "So you guys were talking about Hamlet, huh?" he asks. Your brother nods, and Polonius turns to face you. "Hamlet only likes you because you're smokin' hot," he says. "You're an idiot if you believe him when he says you're a great and wonderful and special person. He'll say anything to get in your pants. He's said that you're a wonderful person, right?"

You agree that he has said, and written, some very beautiful things about you and that this means a lot to you.

"That proves it. Listen, you're too dumb to understand what I'm saying, so I'm just going to order you to do the following: stop seeing him, never speak to him again, and put all thoughts of him out of your head."

Slap him across his face and tell him you're not dumb and you can recognize sincere emotion in a sexual partner when you see it: *turn to 395*

Tell him — you'll obey? And then call him your lord. And...follow him meekly out of the room? Agree with everything he and Laertes have said, because all that stuff I wrote earlier about you being an independent woman in charge of her own destiny sounds PRETTY DUMB ACTUALLY, and you'd better do whatever someone else tells you to, because anyone other than you probably knows better about your own life than you do, right? Look, I am now trying to think of the dumbest thing you can do. Please, I beg you, do not choose this option. *Turn to 408*

41

411

"Nice try," Gertrude says, "but you're not promoting that pawn." Gertrude moves her castle to match your king's position. "Check," she says, while writing down "Re3+" in her notes.

You have to get out of check, Ophelia! You need to fix this, lady! Looks like the only way to do that now is by moving your king. You can either move down towards the pawn or up away from it.

PICK ONE; DON'T PICK THE DUD CHOICE THOUGH, OKAY?

Move down towards pawn (Kg2): *turn to 406*

Move up away from pawn (Kg4): *turn to 540*

412

"Excuse me," you say. The ghost pretends not to hear you. "Excuse me, Mister...Ghost?" you enquire, raising your hand.

"'Sup," says the ghost.

"Hamlet tells me you want him to kill King Claudius," you say.

"Yeppers," says the ghost.

"Well, you'll pardon my rudeness, but — why does a ghost need someone else to commit a murder? Ghosts can bang pots around or whatever. Can't you just sneak up behind Claudius and hit him over the head with one?"

Hamlet pulls you aside. "Ophelia, what are you doing?"

"I'm asking a question," you say.

"Who is this creature?" asks the ghost.

"Who am I?" you reply, incredulously. "Don't you know? Aren't you Hamlet Sr.?"

"She has her doubts," Hamlet explains to the ghost. The ghost again addresses you. "YOU DOUBT ME?" he bellows.

"I seek proof," you say, standing your ground. The ghost becomes angrier, redder, almost changing shape. Lightning crackles around him.

"THEN HERE IS THE PROOF YOU SEEK!" he bellows, as a tremendous bolt of lightning flashes out to you.

Rather than electrocuting you, the lightning actually forms itself into a pleasant letter that deposits itself into your hand! In it, Hamlet Sr. explains that while ghosts can bang pots together, it's hard to do, and something like murder is tricky enough to pull off when you're corporeal. Makes sense. The note goes on to mention some of the fun times you've had together in the past and some of your secret shared jokes too. You laugh when you read them. Oh man, this is Hamlet's dad, that's for sure!

You have added the NICE NOTE to your inventory!

But already you know it's like a birthday card, which you'll keep for a while and then wonder when you should throw it out.

The sentiment inside is still sweet, but are you going to keep a giant stack of birthday cards, growing ever larger until you're 80? No. So let's say you drop it now! Less heartbreak that way.

You have dropped the NICE NOTE.

TALK ABOUT THAT MURDER THING WITH THE GHOST! *Turn to 433*

413

Didn't you notice me use the past tense? He's already dead! You and Hamlet were sleeping together (literally: you were literally sleeping together) (that still sounds weird: look, I mean to say you were both asleep and literally not having sex) when Osric, Claudius's favourite courtier, snuck in and slit Hamlet's throat. You only survived because his gurgling woke you up in time to see Osric's blade creeping towards you. You threw yourself out of bed and grabbed the bedside table, knocking Osric over the head with it. He was out cold, but it was too late for your boyfriend. Hamlet's dead.

And you are cheesed.

Right now, Osric is bound to a chair, with a gag in his mouth. You want him to answer a few questions. You undo the gag and he spits at you. In return, you break his nose.

"Who sent you?" you demand.

"Claudius," he says. "He's a ghost now. Says he wants revenge. Says you two killed him. Says he's not going to rest until you're dead." It looks like your worst-case scenario came true, Ophelia.

"What's to stop me from killing you?" you demand.

"Nothing. Claudius said it'd probably end up this way. Didn't think I'd be able to kill either of you. Guess he was only half right," Osric says, and then laughs.

"Then why would you do it?" you ask, incredulous. "Why would you try to kill me, knowing you'd fail and that I'd kill you in return?"

"Because if you kill me now I've got some unfinished business, and that means I get to be a ghost," Osric says. "Claudius says being a ghost is great. Says when I meet him in ghostland he's going to set me up real nice."

He coughs up some blood and then meets your gaze, unblinking.

"Can't wait," he says.

KILL OSRIC: *turn to 158*

LET OSRIC LIVE: *turn to 43*

414

You begin to cannibalistically consume the remains of your ex-girlfriend's father. The flesh has only been in the stew for a few seconds though, so really all you're doing is eating raw human flesh with some stew on it.

Hamlet, you used to be a prince. Now you are a murderous cannibal, covered in blood and gore.

Your hunger has been reduced by 10%. The body has been reduced by 5%.

You have 1 turn(s) remaining.

Continue eating stew: *turn to 337*

Jump out the window to escape: *turn to 232*

Light door on fire: *turn to 254*

415

"Nope! I don't want to murder anyone," you decide. Prince Hamlet agrees with you.

"When I think of punishing a murder with a murder, it makes me feel like — like we're all monkeys, you know?" he says.

"Yeah!" you say. "Like we're all running around, bashing things with our fists when they get in our way." You sigh. "It makes me feel crazy. I think we're better than that."

Hamlet nods, and you pause, thinking.

"That's not even true," you say, finally. "I think even if we're NOT better than that, we should at least aspire to be."

"Oh," says the ghost. "Well, okay."

"We could work within the legal system to convict him of your murder though!" you offer.

"No, that's fine. Save that for some other ending," the ghost says, confusing you both (but I got it because I'm the narrator).

"Anyway I guess I'm gonna go do other fun ghost stuff and not worry about murdering a guy," the ghost says, waving goodbye. "I'll check in later on you two kids though, so think of me before making out, because I just might be in the room!"

"Okay!!" says Prince Hamlet, really enthusiastically, which is weird. Thinking about it later, you still think it's weird.

This whole thing was weird; I'm not gonna lie.

So! I kinda want to say "THE END" here, since you've rejected the adventure promised by this book. But not that much has happened to you, and I feel kinda bad about that, so let's do a REALLY QUICK adventure here for you before the end. Ready?

Okay, you are a horse!! To eat grain, imagine yourself doing that. To eat grass, imagine yourself doing that instead! Eventually a rider takes you as his steed straight into glorious battle. Later on, the sun explodes!!

THE END

Turn to 180

417

You leave Osric there, laughing to himself, and make your way out of the room. You run down the halls, trying to find someone who will help you, but the castle seems empty.

You run into the royal court, where you find Gertrude, surrounded by all of the courtiers. They're holding court at — three in the morning? Then you see the ghost of Claudius, standing there in the middle of them.

"You live forever," he tells them, "and physical pain is forgotten. You get reunited with your family members. Also you can fly. Being a ghost is the best thing that ever happened to me, and I want to share it."

He notices you and waves. "Oh, speak of the devil! Hi Ophelia! Everyone, she's the one who murdered me, and she's the only thing standing between you and eternal ghostly happiness! Everyone will get to be a ghost if they die while trying to kill her!"

You are caught off guard as the entire royal court pounces on you and tears you to shreds. The last thing you hear is Claudius saying, "Oh, she didn't manage to kill any of you? Ah well. You can still become ghosts if you die while trying to kill... that random guy!"

And that is the amazing story of how you died, Ophelia. So! Thanks for playing? You got killed by a bunch of people all at once, and I guess that means you get a final score of...oh, I don't know: a solid B+?

THE END

Turn to 30

418

You respond by copying her move exactly, moving your king's pawn up two squares too. Gertrude quickly jots down something on a piece of paper you hadn't noticed before. "e4 e5," it reads. Beside it she writes, "Copying my moves??" Oh man! Busted!!

"I like to record my games," she says. "For posterity."

"Oh," you say.

Gertrude moves her queen diagonally as far as it'll go, through the hole opened up by her pawn's movement. "Qh5," she writes. She looks up and notices your attention.

"People say you shouldn't use your queen too much in the early game, but what can I say? I love being a queen! Also, I love using them in chess," she adds.

Your move, Ophelia.

Bring out my horsey on my right to protect that little pawn (Nc6): *turn to 310*

Continue copying her moves! I can't lose! (Qh4): *turn to 509*

Bring out a pawn to threaten her queen! She can't boss me around! (g6): *turn to 454*

420 When you are out of turns, the door opens and who should enter but Corambis, Polonius's twin brother! You recognize him from the royal courts.

"I unlocked the door, so you can leave no—" he begins, but then he trips over the twine, stumbling into the body parts you've left in the middle of the room. Incredibly, they do function as intended, and his leg is instantly tangled in your bolas. He trips over the body parts, falling to the ground. On the ground he gets a good look at what's happened in this room and he begins to scream and also vomit everywhere.

This is turning into a difficult day. It turns into a much more difficult day after you get killed for those awful, awful things you did to Polonius!

Nobody even likes your bolas!

THE END

Turn to 60

421 "Not bad," smirks Gertrude. "I thought I'd get you with the Scholar's Mate there."

"That is thematically appropriate as I used to be a scholar's mate," you say, "until the king's brother killed the king and assumed the throne, so we killed him in ghost-mandated revenge, but then HIS ghost came back and convinced everyone else to kill us and they got Hamlet, but I escaped and decided to kill everyone before they could kill me first."

"Yes, I do understand your motivation," Gertrude sighs, bringing out one of her horses and bringing it into play. "Nc6," she writes.

You mirror it, bringing out your horse as well. "Nc3," Gertrude writes and then looks up. "You seem to copy my moves whenever you're not sure what to do," she says. "This isn't actually the first game of chess you've played, is it?"

"Um," you say.

But then in a surprise move, the game proceeds from there pretty well, actually! You exchange pieces of equal value most of the time, until finally you're in this position:

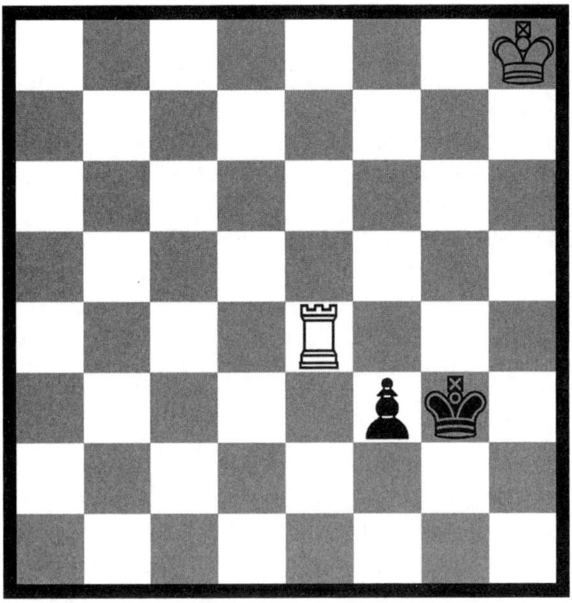

Gertrude has the advantage, but it's your move, Ophelia. You can still win this. But you can still also lose this. You can still lose this really easily, actually.

I guess it's all up to you, huh?

Move the pawn forward (f2): *turn to 411*

Move the king away (Kg4): *turn to 540*

422

You decide to let your father and brother live! The three of you spend all day hanging out in this big empty town with all the corpses in it, but it's kinda tense because you're surrounded by decaying corpses, and also Laertes and Polonius know you killed everyone and could kill them at any time, not to mention that you're always keeping them at swordpoint.

"Aren't we having fun?" you ask, throwing your arms around the shoulders of your family members. "Aren't we one big happy family?"

Polonius and Laertes laugh awkwardly and mumble, "Yeah." You squeeze their shoulders, too hard.

"It's great," squeaks Laertes.

That evening, you don't come across any ghosts. Seems like they're all too freaked out about this whole situation to hang around. Later that night, Laertes tries to sneak out of town to get help, but you catch him, and you and your sword persuade him to go back to bed.

"There's only one way out of this little hamlet," you say.

"I know," Laertes says.

"It's if I murder you," you say.

"I KNOW," Laertes says.

Anyway, this whole thing is weird and messed up, and I'm not really sure how we ended up here. I wanted to tell the story of a young lady who became a queen, but somehow it's turned into *The Story of the Most Successful Serial Killer Ever Who Murdered Everyone in a Town, But Left Her Family Alive for a While, Because Then She'd Have Someone to Picnic With.*

This story has a subtitle: *You Cray, Ophelia.*

THE END

Turn to 513

423

You swerve your king towards Gertrude's castle. Rather than have it captured, Gertrude moves it one square backwards. "Re5," she writes.

This is your opportunity, and you take it. You move your pawn towards the finish line and, AS IF BY MAGIC, it is now a queen. "Write that down in your little book," you say triumphantly.

"Okay," Gertrude says, and she writes down "f1Q" with a little frowny face next to it. I don't think she's happy, Ophelia!

You've got her now. Suddenly, it's like the board opens up to you. You can read it. Possible futures reveal themselves to you. In one brilliant moment, you realize that if Gertrude moves her king, you could move down your new queen and put her king in check, and checkmate won't be far away. And if she doesn't move her king, then you could move your queen over and put her king in check from the edge of the board.

Anticipating your strategy, Gertrude moves her castle to the edge of the board. "Rh5," she writes.

It doesn't matter. Nothing she does can stop you now. You bring your queen up next to your king (Qf6+), putting her in check. Her only option is to move the king down one space (Kh7), and then you move your queen right up to the king (Qg7#), and hey, that's checkmate. Suddenly, those chess symbols Gertrude has been writing down make sense. You're stunned to realize you've actually been using them yourself this entire paragraph!

Ophelia! I think you just levelled up at chess! And you beat Gertrude so badly that now she has to kill herself!

Yeah, I definitely think you just levelled up at chess!

Win chess: *turn to 430*

ANDY

425

You jump out of the window, holding on to your hot-air balloons, and escape to freedom!

So here's the thing: these balloons have enough lift to carry you and then some, which means when you grab hold of all your hot-air balloons and jump out the window, your jump keeps going higher and higher. Before you realize what's happening, you're extremely high above the ground and gaining altitude steadily. You can let go of one balloon in order to reduce your lift, but if you reduce it too much, you'll start falling at an ever-accelerating pace and hit the ground too fast. On the other hand, you can't hold on to these balloons forever. Eventually you'll slip and let go of all of them, in which case you'll be dead for sure. But maybe you'll be over water at that point and survive? Somehow?

Hold on to balloons as long as you can: *turn to 351*

Let go of the smallest balloon and hope for a soft landing: *turn to 349*

426

"I'm assuming command of this vessel!" you say, taking the hat off the captain's head and putting it on your own. The crew acquiesces easily: you're the oldest person on board, and you are also royalty. Lucky for you!

"Report!" you order.

"Mainsail is undamaged; adjunct rigging of the secondary sail has been destroyed by cannonshot but repair crews have been dispatched," replies your first mate. "Hull integrity at 92%. We're sailing in a broad reach."

You recall enough sailor talk to know that means the wind is at your back, but you're sailing at a slight angle to it. It's the safest way to travel, as travelling with the wind exactly at your back makes for a faster but less stable boat. You normally want to minimize your chances of losing control.

On the other hand, with pirates on your tail, maybe now isn't the time to worry about safety.

"What are your orders?" shouts the first mate over the roar of wind and sea.

"We need all the speed we can get. Change course so the wind is directly at our back." *Turn to 225*

"Continue at the controllable speed we're at now." *Turn to 283*

"Turn around and face the pirates head-on." *Turn to 102*

427

You move your king to stay close to the pawn, and Gertrude moves her rook to take it. You take her rook with your king, and yep, that's it — you're both down to a king each. Nobody can win with just a king. It's a tie. You've tied! That's something!

In fact it has a special name!

Stalemate: *turn to 497*

428

You decide to track down these background characters and kill them one by one. You also decide to have a little conversation with each of the people you murderize, because that sounds like a lot of fun.

First up are the gravediggers. You catch them at night, digging a grave. Surprise!

"Whose grave is this?" you ask.

"Why, it's my grave," the first gravedigger responds. "Because I'm the one digging it, see? Tee hee! I use that line all the time and it never gets old! Hah hoo hee."

You raise an eyebrow. "Who is the grave actually for, though?"

"Oh, it's for Ophelia. Ghost of the king says if I try to kill her and fail, then I'll get to be a ghost, and being a ghost is great. Do you know her, this Ophelia?"

"Yeah, pretty well," you answer. "She thinks she'd be pretty good at burying someone alive, but I bet you could do a better job."

"Oh, well, probably not actually!" he replies. "There's not that much to it. You just need to knock someone out so they don't struggle, then bury them, then say a good one-liner as you walk away, like 'Oh look, someone's walking on your grave.'"

"Got it," you say, knocking him and his friend over the head with the flat edge of your sword, sending them into unconsciousness. You bury them together in their fresh grave, filling it up with dirt, patting the last of the dirt down with their shovel. "Nobody likes being buried alive!" you shout over your shoulder as you walk away. You stop in your tracks and turn around.

"But don't worry! In a few minutes, you'll just be buried!" NICE. Okay! Who's next?

Rosencrantz and Guildenstern (Hamlet's friends): *turn to 439*

Marcellus, Bernardo, and Francisco (those sentry dudes!): *turn to 448*

Those courtiers who are always hanging out in the royal court: *turn to 357*

429

Yes! Let's definitely murder someone!!

"We're in," you say. "Aren't we, Hamlet?"

Hamlet nods. "The two of us will avenge you, Father," he says, solemnly.

"Neato," replies the ghost. "Two heads are better than one, right? Okay! Well, I'm gonna go now; be sure to let me know when he's dead!" His transparent body is turning to leave when you realize something.

"Wait!" you shout, and the ghost stops.

"You can become invisible and walk around places, right? Float in the sky whenever you want, all that stuff?"

"Totes," says the ghost.

"Okay, well — can you go do some reconnaissance for us? You know, follow Claudius around, let us know his habits? If we're going to kill him, it'd help to know where he usually hangs out."

"That's easy: he gets drunk in the same tavern every night," the ghost says. "Then he goes home and falls asleep." The ghost looks at you. "If I were you, I'd kill him while he's drunk and asleep," he says and disappears.

You and Hamlet are left staring at each other.

"Okay. Well. Let's make a list of all the ways to kill a dude," you suggest.

You and Hamlet spend the next few days making up just such a list together, and now it's done! It's pretty cool! You should probably look at it!

Examine list: *turn to 403*

430

"Wow," Gertrude says. "You won, fair and square. Though I can't help but feel like we could play that game again 10 more times and you'd lose each time."

"Maybe, but not this time," you say. "Probably because I just levelled up at chess."

"Why are you killing everyone?" Gertrude asks, obviously trying to delay her own death.

"You know why," you say. "The ghost of King Claudius has promised everyone great rewards and powers in the ghost afterlife, but only if they die trying to kill me. As such, he's turned everyone against me."

"Yes, but by killing them, aren't you dooming yourself to be haunted by ghosts for the rest of your life?"

"I don't care. If I'm haunted by ghosts, I'll cut them. I'll bust them up," you say. You glance down at your bloodied sword and fists.

"Bustin' makes me feel good," you add.

"Well, a deal's a deal," Gertrude says. "I promised I'd kill myself." She stands up to do just that. "Be sure to tell everyone that you beat someone at chess so badly that they died!" she adds.

"That was kinda the whole point of that chess game!" you reply.

After Gertrude's dead (and no, I'm not telling you how it happened, you are a SICKO for even wanting to know, what is WRONG with you, also you MURDERED

A WHOLE TOWN and that's weird too, now that I think about it), you're left alone, successful in your mission.

"Who has two thumbs and killed everyone in Hamlet?" you ask, again meaning to say "a hamlet" or "this hamlet," but misspeaking and mis-capitalizing at the same time.

Nobody answers, because they're all dead.

"Me," you tell them.

THE END

P.S. A few days later you move a couple of towns over and start a new life as a professional chess player!
I know!
This is a pretty good ending, all things considered!!

Turn to 249

431

You're still hanging off the edge of the parapet.

"Alright," Marcellus says as he walks slowly towards you, twirling his sword. "Let's see how long you can hang on without hands." He brings down his sword suddenly, aiming for your wrist. You shift your hand quickly to avoid the slice. He tries again, and you dodge again.

"This is how you get your kicks?" you say, a note of desperation in your voice. "By killing innocent women??"

Marcellus ignores you. "Francisco! Help me out!" he shouts over his shoulder, and seconds later Francisco and Marcellus are both raising their swords. At the last second you bring your arms together in the middle of the ledge, just barely dodging their attack. You're not sure you can pull that move off again.

"Again!" Francisco shouts, and they both bring up their swords for the kill. As they do, you simply lift up your hands and fall.

Francisco and Marcellus look at where your hands were, just a second ago, in shock.

"Huh," Marcellus says.

"That was...easy," Francisco says.

Francisco peers over the edge of the parapet, hoping to see your lifeless body lying on the ground below. That's when you stab him in the eye with your sword, pull his body over the edge with a flick of your wrist, flip up from the window ledge you were standing on, stab Marcellus in the chest, put your boot next to the wound, and with one solid kick, you send him sliding off your sword and over the edge to join his friend.

"That's how I get mine," you say.

NICE!!

Okay, who's next? A bunch of courtiers or Rosencrantz and Guildenstern?

Kill all the courtiers: *turn to 357*

Kill Rosencrantz and Guildenstern: *turn to 452*

CROWN Polish!
PRINCE OF DENMARK
FORTINBRAS!

433 You go over the basics of the murder plot with the ghost and Hamlet. And, surprise, you see some flaws in it that Hamlet somehow missed.

"So Hamlet is supposed to murder Claudius," you say.

"Yes," Hamlet and the ghost reply, in unison. Then they notice they replied in unison and fist-bump each other. Well, the ghost's fist goes through Hamlet's fist and stops a little inside it, but you can see what they were going for.

"And then Claudius will be dead and Hamlet will be king," you say.

"Yes," Hamlet and the ghost reply, in unison again. And then they fist-bump each other again and it's even more off this time. They're not even aligned horizontally with each other. Come on, guys.

"So what's to prevent Claudius from becoming a ghost and seeking his own revenge?" you say, raising one eyebrow.

"Um," says the ghost.

"In fact, can ghosts kill each other? Because then the best case for us is that one of you ghost-kills the other and then considers himself revenged. Worst case is that you can't kill each other but instead exist as ghosts forever, which means that the two of you — each with an endless list of sins from long before anyone left alive was born — will continue to meddle in the living world, revenging yourself against each other, back and forth, for millennia to come."

"Oh um, I think —" the ghost begins, then coughs. "No — um, yeah, I think you only become a ghost under certain circumstances."

"Like being murdered when you still have things you want to complete on this mortal plane?" you ask.

"Oh. Right. That'd apply to Claudius too," the ghost says. "Huh."

Continue talking the ghost out of murder: *turn to 116*

Make a counterargument for murder being a good idea: *turn to 399*

434 "Let's kill him with stabs," you say, "as there are indeed swords, like, everywhere."

"I was thinking the same thing," Hamlet says. "Okay! So here's my plan: we wait until he goes to church, ALONE, and then we —"

"— stab him?" you ask.

"No," Hamlet replies. "We don't kill him then because his soul will be pure. Instead, we fake your death, which causes —"

"Wait, what?" you say, interrupting.

"Hold on," Hamlet says, "I'm just at the good part. We fake your death, which causes Laertes to get mad, and then he challenges me to a duel, and then DURING the duel Claudius and Laertes try to poison me — they are secretly on teams — both with the poison-tipped sword Laertes has AND with the poison-filled goblet they keep offering me, but my mom drinks it instead so she's dead, then Laertes and I both end up dead too."

"Um, Claudius didn't end up stabbed in your plan," you point out.

"Oh, well, I stab him just before I die," says Hamlet.

"Sweetie," you say, "I love you but that plan is stupid. It's not even a plan, it's like — it's a series of mistakes that results in everyone being dead. You would really do all that on purpose?"

"I guess," Hamlet shrugs.

"Okay, well, here's my plan," you say. "We go out with Claudius while he's drinking and get seen by everyone, only SECRETLY we're drinking ginger ale instead of booze. Then when Claudius is drunk, we loudly announce we're going back to your place to kiss together in private and also maybe get naked, who knows, because we're young and crazy! But instead, we hide on the path to Claudius's place, and when he stumbles down the road towards us, we stab him and leave. Then we show up at the drinking hall again with kiss marks on us and I say, 'Hamlet, you're the prince...of my heart!' and you say, 'I'm an Opheliac!'"

"Your plan is good," says Hamlet, "though it does lack inaction and needless tragedy."

"Normally those are bad things," you say and Hamlet laughs at you as if you just said that light is both a wave and a particle. (I mean, it is, but how would you know that?? Anyway the point is Hamlet reacts like you said something crazy, that is the take-away here.)

"I'm serious," you say.

"What," Hamlet says, flatly.

"I'm serious, inaction and needless tragedy are typically seen as bad things," you say.

Well, long story short: somehow, since childhood, Hamlet thought the opposite and is REALLY EMBARRASSED to find out he's been wrong all these years. He says, "Why didn't anyone ever tell me?" and you say, "I don't know," and he says, "Aw geez, I must've looked like such an idiot for most of my adult life" and you stay silent because yeah, awkward.

At the end of all this, Hamlet agrees with your plan, and as you walk to the drinking hall where Claudius usually drinks, Hamlet keeps saying things like "Man I always wondered why dictionaries were always so accurate except for their definitions of 'inaction' and 'tragedy'!!"

Arrive at drinking hall: *turn to 442*

435

It does kinda rule, huh? You realize that, WOW, there's a lot of stuff down on the ocean floor that no living human eyes have ever seen! And while your dead ghost eyes won't actually change that fact, there's still lots of cool stuff to explore.

You eventually travel all the way to the Mariana Trench, the very deepest part of the ocean, over 547 fathoms below sea level! Here the water above presses down at over a thousand times standard atmospheric pressure, and the temperature is just above freezing. There are xenophyophores here, which are honest-to-God single-celled organisms so big you can see them with your bare eyes. Why, here's one that's over 10 centimetres long! This is nuts. This whole place is nuts, and you're learning so much!

You give up on your revenge plan and instead devote your (after)life to being a marine biologist and oceanic cartographer. And it turns out Ghost Marine Biology is pretty advanced compared to Alive Human Marine Biology, due in no small part to how you can hang around on the ocean floor for as long as you want and can't die. Nevertheless, you write several seminal ghost books on the subject including *Look at This Weird Bug Thing I Found* and *Gross! Life on the Ocean Floor* and make many hundred thousand ghost dollars.

THE END

Turn to 290

436

This time it's just weird and uncomfortable. There's no other way to put it: it's...well, it's awful.

Your charisma has been reduced by 3 points.

AH WELL, EASY COME, EASY GO. ASK ROSENCRANTZ AND GUILDENSTERN HOW THEY'VE BEEN. *Turn to 13*

437

"I'm sorry, but I still feel like this marriage to Claudius is inappropriate," you say, tenderly wiping away some of his gore off her face. "I am emotionally upset at this."

"Yeah, I mean, I can see that," she replies.

"I'm going off to be a ghost now," you say "and I want you to be as happy as you can be. I'm sorry it didn't work out between us, and I'm sorry I died, but I want you to know that I'm happy and I want you to be happy. Be the best Gertrude you can be, okay? And I'll see you when you die. As a ghost. Because we'll both be ghosts. I think I'll be able to deal with this then."

"Got it," she says.

You float down through the bed and into the ground, where you spend a lot of time learning about rocks. They're really neat! Did you know that there's all these different sorts of rocks?

After a while you realize that if you make yourself corporeal while underground, the same "two chunks of matter can't exist in the same spot at the same time" explosive correction works on the rock too! But instead of exploding, the rock compresses, melts, and then instantly cools around your body, forming a hard, strong, glassy surface. It doesn't take much to go from that to the realization that if you stack this process, you can build tunnels of arbitrary size super easily! So you build a tunnel between Denmark and England, and it's really good for the economy!

THE END

Turn to 500

438

Finally, Claudius walks by drunk, right where you want him to, and you spot him!

You and Hamlet jump out of the bushes, swords at the ready.

"What is the *hic* meaning of *hic* this?" Claudius demands, hiccuping in the way non-stereotypical drunk people usually don't.

"You're a pervy murderer," you say, "and the ghost of the man you murdered has charged us with killing you, so that's what we're going to do."

"Ghosts?! Those exist?" Claudius says, shocked. "Man! I wish I knew that before I murdered my brother!"

"He admits it!" Hamlet says, charging at Claudius with his sword in front of him. You do nothing to stop him. Hamlet seems to need this, and you're happy to let him do it.

"Is he happy being a ghost? It sounds nice," Claudius says.

"WHY DON'T YOU ASK HIM YOURSELF?" Hamlet says, stabbing Claudius right in the body.

"MAYBE I WILL!" Claudius shouts back as blood squirts out of his new holes. "WE WILL HAVE A GHOST-TO-GHOST HEART-TO-HEART AND WORK THIS OUT. IN ANY CASE I AM GLAD TO HAVE CONFIRMATION THAT THE END OF THIS LIFE IS NOT THE END OF CONSCIOUSNESS."

"WELL...GOOD! I HOPE YOU DO HAVE THAT CHAT! YOU NEED TO WORK THINGS OUT; HE IS FAMILY AFTER ALL," Hamlet shouts in reply, stabbing him some more.

"I'M LOOKING FORWARD TO IT, ALONG WITH THIS VOYAGE OF DISCOVERY TO THE NEXT STAGE OF HUMAN EXISTENCE WHICH I NOW EMBARK UPON," Claudius replies and then he's dead.

You and Hamlet walk back to the drinking hall and establish your alibi, then you go to bed. The next morning, Claudius is discovered dead!

GET AWAY WITH MURDER: *turn to 445*

439

You arrive at the house of Rosencrantz and Guildenstern, best buds of Hamlet. They live in Rosencrantz's mom's basement!

"Hello Mrs. Rosencrantz," you say politely as she answers her door. "Are Rosencrantz and Guildenstern home?"

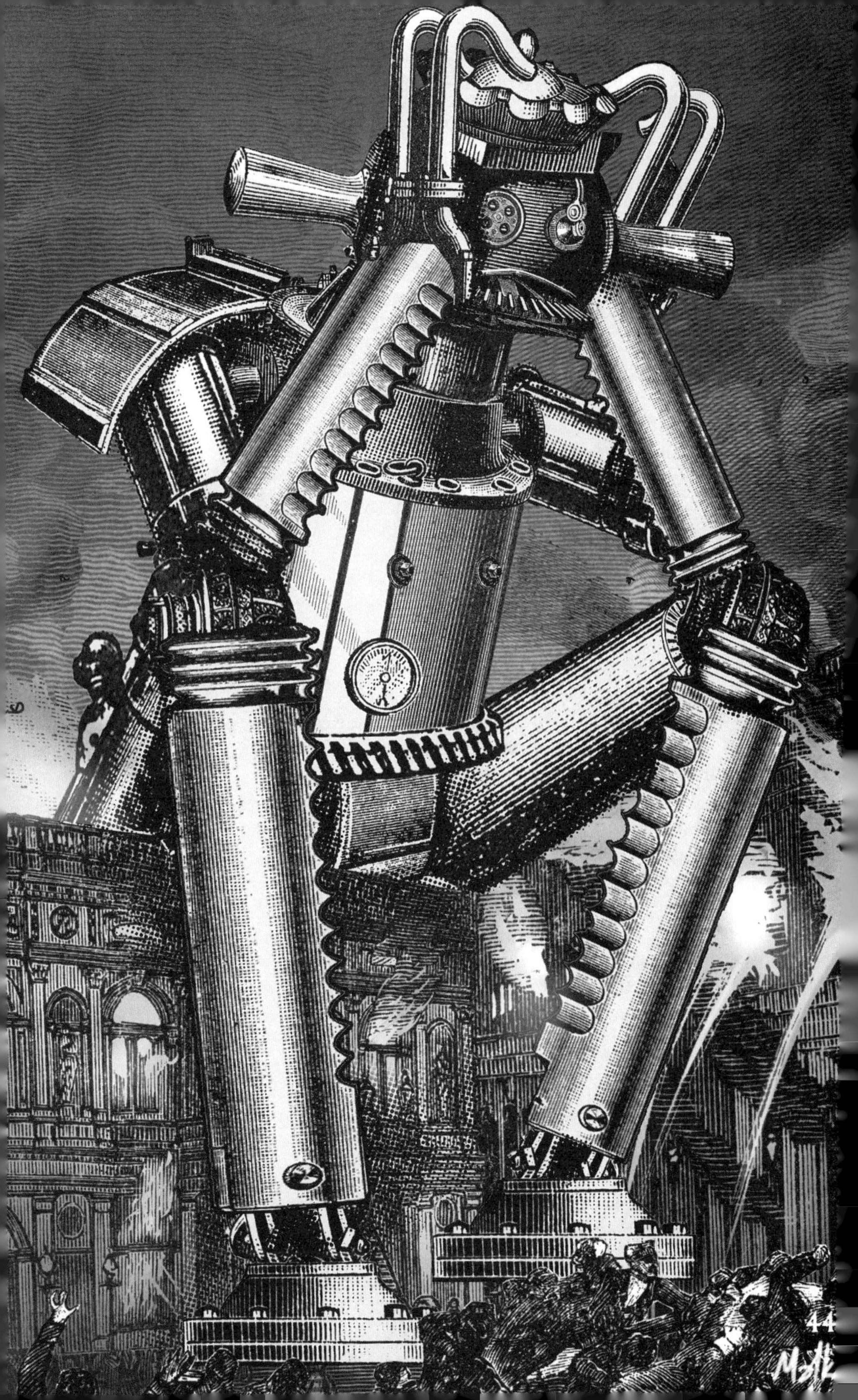
44

"Yeah, they're downstairs," she says. As you walk down the stairs, you become aware of Mrs. Rosencrantz behind you, carrying a large knife.

"Why Mrs. Rosencrantz, you wouldn't be planning to kill me, would you?" you say. She answers by trying to stab you in the back, but you dodge, use her own momentum against her, and send her flying down the stairs. Rosencrantz and Guildenstern look up from the game they're playing to see her body hit the landing.

"That," you say as you descend and step over the mangled Mrs. Rosencrantz, "is going to keep happening."

Ten minutes later, after several trips carrying Rosencrantz and Guildenstern up the stairs and then pushing them down again, all that's left of them are two bruised and broken bodies, their lifeless eyes gazing back at you.

"Hey," you say, "it's not polite...to STARE." TWO IN A ROW!

Who do you want to kill next?

MARCELLUS, BERNARDO, AND FRANCISCO (THOSE SENTRY DUDES!): *turn to 199*

THOSE COURTIERS WHO ARE ALWAYS HANGING OUT IN THE ROYAL COURT: *turn to 357*

441

You put the sword away, and Gertrude continues pressing her attack. You fight back passively, dodging all you can, finally dodging your way out through a window and backflipping to the ground below.

"I'll find you!" Gertrude yells after you. "There was no time limit on our promise! I'll continue trying to kill you until the day I die!"

"Of natural causes!" she adds.

You spend the next several days dodging her attacks and traps. They get progressively more ingenious until one day you break a twig in the forest, which sends a log careening towards a stack of logs, which knocks the logs over like dominoes, which sends a boulder down a hill and off a cliff, which hits a seesaw, which sends another boulder up in the air, which comes down on your head, killing you instantly.

"Nailed it!" Gertrude yells. "Man! I KNEW that had a small chance of working!"

So! Your final score is 66 quadrapoints and one passive-aggressive gift of a book called *Sherlock Holmes Teaches You How to Get Less Stinky at Chess Already.*

Don't worry about that one, Ophelia. It's on me!

THE END

Turn to 280

442

It's not yet booze o'clock, so you and Hamlet set yourselves up in a quiet little corner and start drinking the ginger ale you picked up along the way. While you wait, you talk about your feelings but HAH HAH, THE ADVANTAGE BOOKS HAVE OVER REAL LIFE IS YOU CAN SKIP OVER THE BORING STUFF, SO HERE WE GO.

Suddenly, it's later! Claudius walks in the door! "I'll have some booze," he says, "in celebration of my new wife and kinghood."

It turns out Claudius drinks like a fish, which is an idiom that means he drinks a lot, not that he extracts oxygen from the alcohol he inhales and then expels the remaining alcohol out holes in the side of his head. Soon, Claudius is falling-over drunk, and they're sounding the trumpets that are normally sounded to let all and sundry know that the head of state is wasted.

"Okay!" you say. "Now let's tell everyone we're going home to make out!"

"Already on it," Hamlet says, and he stands up. "Attention, everyone! I am going home to kiss my girlfriend on the lips."

Everyone applauds, except for Claudius, who falls over.

You leave, then double back and run towards the king's chamber, taking pains not to be seen. You find a good hiding spot behind some bushes, where you can see the road clearly but can't be seen yourself. It's actually a really nice spot. It's kind of romantic.

"Let's make out while we wait," Hamlet says. "Oooh, but before we do: what if Claudius takes another route?"

"This is the most reasonable route for him to take," you say, "and even if he does choose another route, we've got OUR ENTIRE LIVES to kill this man, Hamlet. We can try again another night, and we can keep trying until it happens naturally. Now: it's kiss time, but keep one eye on the road."

It was a nice plan, but it turns out that you do miss Claudius tonight. However! All you're trying to do is spot a drunk man who isn't trying to hide, and there's not that many routes back to the castle. Depending on how much attention you pay to the road, you might catch him another night. In fact, I'll work out the odds!

If you pay super close attention: you will catch him in at most 10 nights, nine times out of ten.

If you pay some attention: you will catch him in at most 100 nights, nine times out of ten.

If you pay very little attention: you will catch him in at most 1000 nights, nine times out of ten.

So! How many nights do you want it to take to catch him?

10 NIGHTS: *turn to 438*

100 NIGHTS: *turn to 407*

1000 NIGHTS: *turn to 336*

PAY ATTENTION TO ME, HORATIO THE 20th!
THERE IS NO MORE IN HEAVEN OR EARTH THAN IS DREAMT OF IN REALITY TV.
FOOD

444 You are King Hamlet. All of Denmark is under your command! Everything's going so great for you!

At present, you are in Norway, where just this afternoon you led Denmark's forces to an astounding victory during which you PERSONALLY killed the Norwegian king. Stabbed him right through the head, you did. His eye popped out and rolled on the ground and then you stepped on it. Whoah! Your ass is bad! You are a badass!!

You decide after a day of being good at fighting, you should have a nap. You've earned it! You settle down in an orchard for some nappy times. During your delightful rest, your brother pours some poison in your ear and you die.

Surprise! You didn't know poisons worked that way!

Hah hah, wow! You've barely made one choice so far and you're dead already. Way to go, champ!! You're really good at books, huh? It's just a stellar job you're doing reading here, Chuckles.

THE END

Turn to 542

Okay, FINE, I feel sorry for you. Here's a choice that you can choose.

Become a ghost: *turn to 472*

Do not become a ghost: *turn to 471*

445 Good idea!

The next morning, you and Hamlet get away with murder, and though Claudius's death is suspicious (suicide via multiple stab wounds is...unusual), there's nobody they can pin the case on.

Hamlet is next in line for the throne, but these things do take time, remember? There're ceremonies to plan and coronation foodstuffs to order and such, so you've got some time on your hands. You and Hamlet spend most of the day wandering around trying to be overheard saying things like "Wow, I wonder who the murderer could be, if indeed Claudius was murdered?" and "That information is definitely not within my mind, as I was not involved in this incident." It's weird though because I already told you that you got away with it, so it's not exactly the most productive use of your time, but who cares? Murder! Turns out it's easy! Yep, everything certainly is going great for you, Ophelia! To end this story on a happy note, stop reading right...now. Okay!

So, as I was saying, everything is certainly going great for you, Ophelia! Until that night, anyway, when HAMLET IS MURDERED IN HIS SLEEP BY THE ROYAL COURT COURTIER, OSRIC.

Whoah, what? Save Hamlet! *Turn to 413*

446 You burst into your family's quarters to find your father, Polonius, and your brother, Laertes, sitting there.

"I thought you went to France!" you tell him.

"Cancelled my trip when I learned that HUMAN CONSCIOUSNESS CAN SURVIVE THE DEATH OF A BODY," Laertes says. "That was kind of a big deal."

"Oh, hey Ophelia!" says Polonius. "Speaking of that! You won't believe this, but the ghost of the king wants me to kill you and then I'll get ghost powers!"

"You didn't agree to it though, right?" you ask. "Since I'm your daughter and we're all family?"

"Oh, absolutely, we're family and you're my daughter. But the thing is," Polonius says, drawing his sword, "I always wanted sons."

Laertes draws his sword as well. "And I'm easily manipulated by my father and sexist too!" he says. "Plus, you came here to kill us, right? You don't normally come home with your sword drawn."

"Right," you say. "Oh well. This family was always a little too big for my taste anyway."

You fight. It's two against one, and I hate to say it, Ophelia, but you need more practice. You're just not ready to take these guys on yet. Listen, you get killed and it's awful and I don't even want to talk about it.

THE END

Turn to 57

Okay, so when you try again, remember that there's nothing wrong with getting a few practice murders in first! Beyond the obvious of murder being wrong, I mean. But, hah hah, we're way past that, am I right? Waaaaay past that.

Here's your mulligan.

Go back a move and try it again: *turn to 158*

447 "Abandon ship! All hands, abandon ship!" you yell into the storm. The crew looks at you in shock, but there's not much they can do. "Climb up those ropes, men! Fight them to the last! By God, we'll take their ship from them!"

Your crew screams at the pirates in defiance and surges up the ropes leading to the deck of *Calypso's Gale*. Above them, pirates pour over the deck, climbing down. Your crew will meet them halfway and have to fight their way up. You'd love to join them, but you have to save your friends first.

You race towards the ladder to go below-decks and, sliding down it, find a disastrous scene. When the two ships collided, gunpowder meant for *Vesselmania*'s cannons burst from barrels onto the deck, and oil lanterns were knocked off the walls. The gunpowder is spilling out and the lanterns, still lit, are rolling around the floor as the ship lurches with each wave, caught as she is on *Calypso's* bow. Rosencrantz and Guildenstern are similarly running around, trying to gather up the lanterns before they ignite the gunpowder and kill you all.

You don't think they're going to make it alone.

"Bros!" you yell. They stop and look at you, shocked to see you here.

"Hamlet! Help us pick up these lanterns, bro!" Rosencrantz yells at you.

"There's no time!" you yell. "We've got to abandon ship!"

"If you don't help us, there'll be no ship left to abandon!" yells Guildenstern.

"Yeah dude!!" yells Rosencrantz.

Help them pick up lanterns! *Turn to 155*

Convince them to abandon ship! *Turn to 157*

448

These are soldier-type dudes! I don't think you're ready to take on these guys so soon. And man, if you don't have the narrator on your side, what hope do you have?

LET'S FIND OUT, SHALL WE??

The three of them are up on a castle parapet, looking out over the edge at the ground far below. You walk up behind them. "Hey boys, seen any ghosts lately?" you say.

"Actually, yes, two of them!" replies Bernardo, turning around. "And one said that if I die while trying to kill Ophelia, I'll gain ghost powe—"

The sentence dies on his lips when he sees you.

"Boo," you say.

Bernardo runs, slamming his body into you. You fall off the edge of the parapet, twisting your body in mid-air and catching the edge of the castle at the last second.

Bernardo starts stomping on your fingers. "Ow!" you say. "Ow! That hurts!"

"I don't care! I'm trying to kill you!" says Bernardo.

"Owwwww!" you say, grabbing the ledge with both hands. As Bernardo raises his foot to bring it down hard on you, you thrust yourself up and grab his ankle with one hand. You pull his leg as hard as you can and he goes tumbling over the castle wall. You watch, hanging precariously, as he lands on the ground below in a wet squishy heap.

You turn around and peer up over the edge and see Francisco and Marcellus looking at you in shock.

"Come on, don't be shy!" you shout at them. "I don't bite!"

Wow, Ophelia! You're — you're actually doing a really good job here.

Thank the narrator: *turn to 405*

449

WOW, there are a lot of courtiers. You hide out until nightfall and sneak into their houses, killing each of them in hilarious ways. While you do that, you try to imagine how you'd recount their deaths to a third party, perhaps in prose. You reflect that one of the advantages writing has over, say, real life, is that you can say things quickly without having to go into too much detail. Is it cheating your audience? "I mean, it can be," you reason, "but it isn't necessarily cheating."

"Probably my audience wouldn't want to read about dozens of grisly murders, no matter how good my one-liners are at the end."

"Even if I did cut off the top of someone's head so that their brains fell into their hands while I said, 'Hold that thought,'" you add.

"And then I said, 'Oh wow, that was just off the top of my head!'" you conclude.

Anyway, long story short, all the courtiers are dead and it was awesome!!

All that's left are Polonius and Laertes, Queen Gertrude, and a bunch of people you barely see but who are still technically all up in your hamlet. You decide to kill those people you barely know first, so you'll be levelled up as much as possible for your climactic showdown.

There's a priest who hangs around town ("Say your prayers," you say), a chef ("Try tonight's special: skewers"), a few shopkeepers ("We're having a big sale on stabs this weekend, and EVERYTHING MUST GO"), some ambassadors ("I'm afraid you've been recalled...TO HELL"), and so on until the only people left are people you know.

So!

This is it, Ophelia. There are only three more people left to kill.

Next up: will it be patricide and fratricide with Polonius and Laertes, or a taste of regicide with Queen Gertrude herself?

Kill Polonius and Laertes: *turn to 465*

Kill Gertrude: *turn to 458*

450

You go home, and Hamlet coincidentally shows up a bit later. "Okay," he says, "everything is going perfectly. I am going to go off to England for a while, actually, but it'll be perfect, because while I'm gone you can drown and then I'll have the perfect setup!"

"You mean, I can FAKE drown," you say.

"Yes, perfect. Okay, see you when I see you!" he says, leaving. You know, I don't think Hamlet is that big into this plan.

You've seen less and less of him since this began, and so far you've had to do all the work! He hasn't even done anything, but YOU'VE got everyone thinking you're insane, and also your father got murdered.

You still want to go ahead with the "faking the drowning" thing?

Yes, fake my drowning: *turn to 506*

You know what? This sucks and I have made some bad, boring choices. Can I be Hamlet? I promise I'll make some better choices. *Turn to 503*

Scott C.

452 You arrive at the house of Rosencrantz and Guildenstern, best buds of Hamlet. They live in Rosencrantz's mom's basement!

"Hello Mrs. Rosencrantz," you say politely as she answers her door. "Are Rosencrantz and Guildenstern home?"

"Yeah, they're downstairs," she says. As you walk down the stairs, you become aware of Mrs. Rosencrantz behind you, carrying a large knife.

"Why Mrs. Rosencrantz, you wouldn't be planning to kill me, would you?" you say. She answers by trying to stab you in the back, but you dodge, take the knife from her, and stab her right in the eye.

"Look what you made me do," you say.

I see what you did there.

Anyway, Rosencrantz and Guildenstern hear this noise and run upstairs. You hide at the top landing and they run right past you. You knock on the wall to get their attention. They turn.

"Hey Rosencrantz! Hey Guildenstern! I'm here to kill you now," you say.

They look at each other, and then at you.

"You don't have the guts," Guildenstern finally says with all the bravado he can muster.

"Huh. Let's see if you do," you say and, in a lightning quick strike, slice open his belly. It's gross, but it works pretty good for the joke, so good work.

Guildenstern falls to the ground, dead or pretty much about to be. Rosencrantz backs up away from you, into the kitchen. "You wouldn't stab a man in a kitchen, would you?" he asks.

"I don't...why wouldn't I?" you say.

"Just stalling for time!" Rosencrantz shouts as he picks up a knife from the kitchen counter and lunges at you. You dodge and kick him in the chest, which sends him stumbling back into the kitchen. He hits the wall, which sends the pots and pans stored on top of the cupboards down on top of him. Some of them are cast-iron frying pans. They're really heavy. They're so heavy that they kill him when they hit him on the head.

You pick up one of the cast-iron frying pans off Rosencrantz's body and test its weight in your hand.

"I'd say that's about 10 pounds," you say, and for both our sakes I'm assuming you're not trying to make a "pound as in hit" pun, because wow. Wow. Ophelia, what are you even doing?

Okay! All that's left of these background characters are the courtiers! These murders you've done so far have taken awhile, so it's early morning now and the royal court is not in session anymore (I should tell you that the royal court hours are from midnight to 4 a.m. and noon to 6 p.m.; it's weird but whatever). No worries though! YOU'LL JUST TRACK THEM DOWN AND KILL THEM INDIVIDUALLY.

Kill courtiers: *turn to 449*

453

You walk into your family's quarters.

"Dad," you say, nodding to Polonius. "Bro," you say, nodding to Laertes. "What is up?" As you say that, you notice Polonius and Laertes both have their swords drawn and are advancing on you.

"Now, simmer down, fellas," you say. "We're all family here, right? I'm sure if a ghost told you to murder me you'd come talk to me about it and not attack me outright, right?" Polonius's response is to jab his sword at you. You parry it easily, sending his sword skittering across the room. His hand is attached to it.

"Really, Dad? Well Laertes, brother o' mine, you're certainly not going to try to kill me, right?" Laertes' response is to jab his sword at you too. It works just as well for him as it did for his father, and now both men face you, unarmed. Well, unhanded anyway. Partially unhanded. You cut off their dominant hands is what I'm trying to say.

"Well. Seems I have the advantage, guys. So! Let me ask you a question. What's better, patricide or fratricide?"

They look at each other.

"Give up?" you say. "Me too. Let's find out!"

You slice Polonius and Laertes into tiny chunks.

"Tied for first," you eventually conclude.

They were the last two living people here, besides yourself.

And now they're totally dead!!

Everyone is dead: turn to 466

454

You bring forward your pawn, and in response, Gertrude retreats her queen — right over to the other pawn you moved out earlier, capturing it.

"Qh5xe5+," she writes. "Oh, and check." she says. Darn it, Ophelia! WHAT ARE YOU DOING; THIS GAME IS REALLY IMPORTANT.

There's no place you can move your king to safety, but you can block the queen with a few different pieces. Any piece you offer you're likely to lose though, but you don't really have a choice. Which piece will it be?

Block with my queen (Qd8-e7): *turn to 33*

Block with my bishop (Bf8-e7): *turn to 33*

Block with my horse (Ng8-e7): *turn to 33*

KLANG
RIN
TIN
TIN
CHANG
WANG
CHUNG
KLANG
KLANG
TANG

456 You clear your throat, hold one hand open in the air in front of you, and promise a ghost that you will kill an alive human. This is what you say:

Yea, from the table of my memory
I'll wipe away all trivial fond records,
All saws of books, all forms, all pressures past
That youth and observation copied there;
And thy commandment all alone shall live
Within the book and volume of my brain,
Unmix'd with baser matter: yes, by heaven!

Your Ghost Dad seems pretty cool with that. You have begun quest Kill Claudius! It's worth 3500 experience points.

That's a lot!!

Leave it there and return to Horatio: *turn to 80*

Throw in a li'l sexism for good measure: *turn to 4*

457 You do so, and Gertrude moves her king back a square (Kc6).

The only non-suicidal move open to you is to move your king down a square too, which you do (Ka6). Gertrude counters this by moving her pawn up one tile (b4). Again, you're left with only one option: retreating your king (Ka7) and boy I hope these notations make sense to you, because if not, hah hah, wow we are screwed here.

Gertrude advances her pawn again (b5) and AGAIN there is no option for you but to retreat, which you do. You fall back to Ka8, Gertrude takes your pawn with her king, and um — that's it! You've got no more pieces left to fight with.

You just lost.

Remember when I said you can't win chess with just a king, Ophelia? I wasn't lying, it's a real rule! And I'm sorry, but I don't make the rules. As far as I know the rules were made thousands of years ago by kings or whoever; anyway they're all dead but we're still doing what they told us to do.

Gertrude makes a few more moves to get her pieces in place, and then it's...

Checkmate: *turn to 309*

458 You decide to play this one cool — rather than chopping her head off, you make a poison pill sandwich (that's all it is: pills full of poison between two slices of bread) and give it to Gertrude to eat.

At swordpoint.

She starts to say something to you, but then her mouth is too full of sandwich for you to really make it out. Gertrude dies shortly thereafter! Cause of death? SANDWICH OVERDOSE. It's not a bad way to go, really. If you have to die, you'd like it to be doing something you love, and you do love a good sammich.

You sit down next to the cooling body to collect your thoughts. So far you have killed everyone in the town and gotten away with it. All that's left — the only two living people here besides yourself — are your brother and father. Do you really want to kill them?

If you decide to go for 100%, choose this option: *turn to 453*

If you decide that second place isn't so bad, choose this option: *turn to 422*

459

Good idea, Ophelia! You return to England for your vacation, which lasts longer and longer until it's what you might call a "stay-cation," which is a terrible word, but all I'm trying to say is you live the rest of your days very happily, very far away from Denmark. Here's something you were chuffed to discover: like Denmark, England is full of lots of very interesting, very attractive people, and you make a lot of friends there who are — I'll give it to you straight — stone-cold hunks and smokin'-hot babes.

If you don't want children, then you don't have any. But if you want children, let's say you meet someone amazing (like the person from the hotel!) and have children with them. Or you adopt!

Whatever, man! I'm easy!!

THE END

Turn to 494

460

You are Hamlet! You just saw your stepfather confirm his guilt about killing your father, because he read a book and chose the options that the murderer would've chosen in real life!! He's definitely guilty; this is entirely reasonable; there is absolutely no other conceivable explanation for what you just saw.

After Claudius tore out of the room, your mother followed him, and after she left everyone else left too, leaving the room empty but for you, Ophelia, and Horatio.

"Did you see that? He totally chose the murdery options, and then he freaked out!" you say, really excited.

"There's no denying that!" says Horatio.

"This means the spooky ghost was correct!" you say. Ophelia looks at you for a moment and then opens her mouth to speak.

Wait, hold on, I can't remember — you've made a lot of crazy choices. Did you and Ophelia break up the last time you saw her?

Yeah man, we broke up: *turn to 52*

Actually, before we started reading that book-within-a-book, Ophelia told me we were cool, so we're definitely cool: *turn to 292*

Not only did we not break up, I actually WAS Ophelia before Claudius started reading the book! *Turn to 39*

To tell you the truth, not only did we not break up, but she said she wants to marry me and that I'm the handsomest man she ever did meet. She explained that if you looked up "sexy" in the dictionary, there'd be a picture of me with the caption "We put this here because we knew you wouldn't want to die without ever having seen such a hunky chunk of man." *Turn to 258*

461

Man, it's awesome! And it's SO COOL to be an underwater explorer who doesn't need to breathe. I mean, it's kinda hard to see things without a light source, but your ghostly body glows a little when you want it to, so it's not bad.

The pirate ship itself seems recently sunk. There are bodies trapped below-decks, and yeah, that's unpleasant. The ocean bacteria haven't really started decomposing them yet. Bodies, man. Being corporeal, man. I dunno.

You find the treasure room, and it's empty. It seems like this ship was attacked, raided, and then sunk. Somewhere up above your head, sailing on the surface of the great Ocean Atlantic, is a really tough pirate ship that's just looking for treasure AND/OR trouble. Too bad you're already dead, huh?

But even if you were alive what does a ghost need with money anyway, so I guess this has kinda been a pointless but still awesome endeavour. You explored the ocean bottom and found a sunken ship! Don't let anyone tell you that's not awesome!

Okay! After several more days of very slow travel that we just skipped over because it got boring, you're back on Denmark's shores!

Arrive in Denmark: *turn to 475*

You know what? Go back and explore the ocean some more. The ocean rules. *Turn to 435*

462

Right! Because who better to know how to kill someone than someone who has recently been through that "getting killed to death" process themselves? You wait until Claudius is sleeping (NEXT TO YOUR BELOVED GERTRUDE FOR SOME REASON, HAH HAH, THAT'S WEIRD) then wake him up by tapping him on the forehead a bit.

"Hey, it's me!" you whisper. "Your brother! The one you murdered!!"

"Aw crap," Claudius whispers back. "Ghosts are real?"

"Real pissed at you, anyway," you reply. "Listen, I'll cut to the chase: we are from a time where 'an eye for an eye' is considered to be a good thing to build a justice system around, so I am here to kill you."

"How?" Claudius asks, his eyes wide, terrified.

"Aw geez, so many ways," you say, counting them off on your fingers. "I could startle you and make you have a heart attack, but that takes time. I could throw a pot at your head until you die, but that lacks grace. Instead, check this out."

You move your ghost body so it's floating right above Claudius. He stares at you, his eyes wide.

"I'm sorry," he whispers.

"Way too late for THAT," you reply. You lower yourself to him, face to face, and keep going. His face dominates your field of vision and then you're inside his skull, inside the pink of his brain, his blood darkly obscuring your sight. You sink slowly deeper and deeper into him, lining up your ghost body with his regular body, until you are just about occupying exactly the same space.

Then you make yourself corporeal.

What happens next happens so quickly and with such force that it's hard to describe, but "Claudius explodes everywhere" captures most of it. I mean, you're fine, but man is this disgusting. Literally disgusting. Gertrude wakes up, dripping in gore, screaming.

You, my friend, have achieved revenge.

Still corporeal, you roll over onto your back and apologize to Gertrude. You explain over her screams what happened, and say that you hope she'll be happy being married to a ghost.

Gertrude stops screaming.

"Um, while you were gone I kinda...married Claudius," she admits. "But I never stopped loving you!"

Understand that, just as you can have more than one good friend at a time, the human heart is capable of loving more than one person at a time and be cool about it: *turn to 74*

Get upset that she married your brother: *turn to 437*

463

You jump your pawn ahead two spaces, putting it right in the attacking square of Gertrude's pawn. She takes it (axb5) and you're down to just your king.

I'm sorry, Ophelia. Like I said, there's no way to win at chess with just your king.

But.

But you can TIE with just your king, and that's exactly what you've done! Snatching Gertrude's victory right from her hands, you've tricked her into a position where she's left you no legal move for your only piece: your king. Since it's your turn but you can't move, the game's over. You don't win, but neither does she! This is what they call...

Stalemate: *turn to 497*

464

"I can still defend myself," you say, and with a quick swipe of your blade, you send her short-swords skittering to the ground. She calmly turns from you, picks them up, and begins attacking you with them again.

You knock them to the floor again.

She picks them up and attacks you again.

Days later, you are drinking a cup of coffee with one hand while warding off her strikes with your other hand. It's how you do everything these days. Gertrude attacks you constantly, so while you're doing stuff with your dominant hand, you're constantly defending yourself with your free, non-dominant hand.

As the years go by, you end up with one super muscley arm. And in the end... isn't that the most we all can hope for?

THE END

P.S. The ghosts of everyone you killed think this whole situation is "pretty weird," but whatevs, you live life by your own rules.

Turn to 455

465

You stroll into your family's quarters. Your father is there, and your brother, Laertes, is there too. Looks like his trip to France was postponed when he discovered that ghosts are real, huh?

"Dad," you say, nodding to Polonius. "Bro," you say, nodding to Laertes. "What is up?"

You notice Polonius and Laertes both have their swords drawn and are advancing on you.

"Now, simmer down, fellas," you say. "We're all family here, right? I'm sure if a ghost told you to murder me you'd come talk to me about it and not attack me outright, right?" Polonius's response is to jab his sword at you. You parry it easily, sending his sword skittering across the room.

"Really, Dad? Well Laertes, YOU'RE certainly not going to try to kill me, right?" Laertes' response is to jab his sword at you too. It works just as well for him as it did for his father, and now both men face you, unarmed.

"Well. Seems I have the advantage, guys. So! Let me ask you a question. Do you think I look like you? Because people always said they could see the family resemblance."

"No?" says Laertes, and you cut off his head in three quick strikes. It slides off his neck and onto to the floor.

"Really?" you say to your dead brother. "Because I always thought when it came to me, you were a DEAD RINGER."

You turn to Polonius.

"Imagine he worked as a bell ringer, then it's even better," you say.

"These aren't very good one-liners," he replies, "and I say this as your father. You need, I don't know, an editor or something."

"I suppose I do need to make a few —" you begin, but are interrupted by Polonius.

"Don't say 'cuts,'" he says.

"CUTS!!!" you say, slicing Polonius up and killing him in the process.

"It's been a slice," you say, "but now I must BLADE you adieu."

Polonius comes back to life long enough to say "THAT PUN IS OLDER THAN STALE BREAD. IT IS OLDER THAN THE DUST ON STALE BREAD, ACTUALLY, NOW THAT I THINK ABOUT IT" and then he's dead again.

Ouch. Sick burns on you, Ophelia! But he's dead now, so whatever.

If you're going to kill everyone, there's just one thing left to do, Ophelia!

Kill Gertrude: *turn to 476*

466

You look around. Silence. The sun is coming up, and you can hear the birds chirping, and scattered throughout town are the bodies of the people you used to know. Gertrude. Rosencrantz. Even that guy who was always hanging around at the coffee shop but whose name you forgot. You killed him too, real quick, when you remembered him just now, because best not to take any chances, right?

You go to the royal court and sit on the throne, not because you want to be a regent, but because it is a very comfortable chair. Days turn into weeks, and you tend to spend a lot of time there, thinking. Not much else to do, right?

That's where you are later, lost in thought, when Fortinbras (crown prince of Norway) bursts through the door, along with some ambassadors. "Hey guys, nobody showed up to meet my boat so I thought I'd — oh my gosh, what happened here?" Fortinbras says.

"Hey Fortinbras," you say. "Have you ever met a ghost who promised you great things in the afterlife if you try to kill me?"

"No," he says, and in a lightning-fast motion, you stab him in the throat.

"Let's keep it that way," you say.

TO DO
LIST
·GROCERY SHOPPING

The ambassadors look at you in shock, and then they look at their own bodies in shock, because they are in shock after you cut off their heads from their bodies.

Congratulations, Ophelia! You've killed everyone in this story.

I mean it, I am literally totally out of characters for you to kill. This wasn't where I expected the story to go, but it was extremely badass and it was a lot of fun seeing you take care of business like that.

You live a long (albeit kinda lonely) life, and though you are initially pestered by the ghosts of everyone you totally murdered, there's not much they can do once you start sleeping with the light on.

THE END

Turn to 205

468

You stab her right in the soft parts, and human bodies are pretty much all soft parts!!

"Queen to DEATH SEVEN," you say, thinking it sounds kinda chess-like. I mean — it kinda does? I guess?

Gertrude dies, and that means you will never get to play a game of chess with a head of state, but on the other hand, it DOES mean you killed an entire town. That's something, right? You didn't even use a bomb or anything. You used your HANDS and SWORDS and FLEXIBLE SENSE OF MORALITY.

Look around: *turn to 466*

469

You flip your sword around like a javelin and spear it into the pirate captain's eye. As you pull your sword free, the eyeball comes with it. Eww. You then try to strike his other eye but the captain manages to dodge, and you slice off only a small part of his cornea. But even a small part of your cornea being sliced off is still probably going to hurt pretty bad.

He roars in pain and covers his eyes, blinded. He falls to one knee, showing his back to you.

You tap him with your blade and say the following:

"Did you see that? I cut off part of your cornea! You didn't? Really? Well, I guess you'd better keep your EYES PEELED." *Turn to 162*

"Did you see that? I stabbed out one of your eyes! You didn't? Really? Well, I guess you'd better KEEP AN EYE OUT." *Turn to 378*

"Wow. Looks like you saw...an EYEFUL." *Turn to 253*

470 Yes, well, the bad news is they're not messing around! Rosencrantz and Guildenstern take one look at the bloody corpse of the captain lying at your feet and rush below-decks, tripping over each other on their way down the ladder.

The first mate is staring at the captain's body in shock. A huge burst of lightning flashes across the darkening sky, and rain begins to fall on *Vesselmania*'s deck. *Calypso's Gale* is gaining on you, and her forward cannons are being reloaded. The distance between the two ships is decreasing by the second.

What do you do?

TAKE COMMAND OF THIS VESSEL: *turn to 426*

FOLLOW YOUR FRIENDS BELOW-DECKS, HANG TIGHT UNTIL THIS BLOWS OVER: *turn to 89*

471 You choose nonexistence over being able to float and having spooky powers. It wasn't even a good one, but it is the last decision you ever make.

UNTIL YOU PLAY THIS BOOK AGAIN, THAT IS!!

THE END

P.S. I hope you do play this book again, because there is more to it than dying like an ultrachump in the first two turns, I PROMISE.

Turn to 125

472 Good news! The afterlife exists, and it's full of ghosts! You know this because you're now one of them. You get to spend all your time slamming doors, rattling chains, and telling on the person who killed you!

But here's the thing: I, the author, told you, the reader, that your brother poured poison in your ear while you napped. But you, as Hamlet Sr., have no idea how you died! You slept through the whole thing. So you need to figure out who killed you if you're going to revenge yourself on your murderer, assuming you even WERE murdered. Because remember that for all you know, you could've died of a heart attack!

This is an example of dramatic irony, only since we're in the second person, it's an amazing example of an entirely new species of dramatic irony, something I'm

GROSS.
SUPER GROSS.
SERIOUSLY.

going to call Second Person Pronoun-Paradoxical Auto-Dramatic Irony. You are now aware of information that you're not aware of.

This should be fun!

Accept that you died of a heart attack: *turn to 485*

Listen in on people's conversations and see if any of them talk about how they totally killed you: *turn to 261*

474

"O, WHAT A NOBLE MIND IS HERE O'ERTHROWN!" you shout, glancing at the door.

"THE COURTIER'S, SOLDIER'S, SCHOLAR'S, EYE, TONGUE, SWORD; THE EXPECTANCY AND ROSE OF THE FAIR STATE, THE GLASS OF FASHION AND THE MOULD OF FORM, THE OBSERVED OF ALL OBSERVERS — QUITE, QUITE DOWN!" you scream, wandering around the empty room.

"AND I, OF LADIES MOST DEJECT AND WRETCHED, THAT SUCK'D THE HONEY OF HIS MUSIC VOWS, NOW SEE THAT NOBLE AND MOST SOVEREIGN REASON, LIKE SWEET BELLS JANGLED, OUT OF TUNE AND HARSH; THAT UNMATCH'D FORM AND FEATURE OF BLOWN YOUTH BLASTED WITH ECSTASY!" you holler, fixing your hair in a reflection to make sure it looks as crazy as possible.

"O, WOE IS ME, TO HAVE SEEN WHAT I HAVE SEEN, SEE WHAT I SEE!" you bellow, just as Claudius walks in with your dad.

Nailed it, Ophelia!

Because they're mad sexist, the king and your father discuss your relationship with Hamlet like you're not even there. Near the end, Polonius seems to remember you're there and in a quick aside, he tells you not to say anything because they've already overheard it all anyway.

Nice to be thought of in there somewhere, right?

Anyway, Claudius decides that Hamlet will be sent to England where his insanity can do no harm. They don't seem to notice that you're acting insane, even though I really was being honest when I said you did a great job with your crazy speech. They're jerks. What can I say? They're jerks. I don't care who knows it.

Meet up with Hamlet to discuss what happened: *turn to 515*

475

You make it back to Denmark! The first thing you want to do is track down your brother to take revenge. TURNS OUT that's really easy because he's in the first place you check: the royal court! He's there with your widow, Gertrude!

Weird, they're acting all close and stuff. Oh well. He's probably just trying to comfort her after your untimely death, hah hah; brothers are really great.

Though...maybe not?

Listen in on what they're saying: *turn to 495*

Ignore what they're saying, I'm CERTAIN there's nothing untoward going on: *turn to 477*

476

You find Gertrude in the royal court, alone.

"Ophelia," she says, greeting you cooly. "I see you've had a busy night. It appears I'm the only one left alive, and if I don't miss my guess, you're here to kill me too."

"Right on target," you say.

"Well. Do you care to make it interesting?" she asks. "Should you beat me at a game, then I will allow you to kill me. In fact, I'll even kill myself. But if I win this game, then you will spare me my life."

"What's the game?" you ask.

"The game, dear Ophelia, is the game of kings."

You look at her blankly.

"But queens can play it too. Also, there are horses in it."

You continue to look at her blankly.

"I'm talking about chess," she says.

"Well..." you say, turning over the bloody sword in your hand.

"I mean, I could just kill you with my sword."

"Of course," she replies. "And you could go to your grave having never beaten a HEAD OF STATE at chess. Yeah, better not to have on your resumé that you beat someone at chess SO HARD that they KILLED THEMSELVES."

Gertrude's sarcasm is pretty pointed, I gotta say. But how good are you at chess, Ophelia? You should probably factor that into your decision, as I honestly have no idea how good Gertrude is at it. My bad. I guess somehow I never really thought these ridiculous circumstances would happen?

Just kill Gertrude: *turn to 468*

Play her game: *turn to 521*

477

Using spooky ghost powers, you completely ignore what Gertrude and Claudius say to each other!

That evening, you try to revenge yourself on Claudius by spooking him. The problem is, he never looks in any of the mirrors you're haunting, he assumes wind is knocking over his pots, and he thinks the ghostly wailing from beyond the grave is probably just a sick dog outside who's having a pretty rough go of it lately.

This spooking him isn't going well, man. I don't know what to tell you. You'll have to get your revenge some other way! Maybe by...killing him?

Reflecting on the fact that he did kill you, you decide the only suitable revenge is to kill him as well because why not, you could totally take him, especially since you've already died once and lived to talk about it. But who is best suited to do the killing? You could do it, but you DID have a son partly so you wouldn't have to do every single thing around here!

Kill Claudius yourself: *turn to 462*

Get your son to kill Claudius instead: *turn to 493*

478

Okay, right, but here's the thing: I'm not super cool with having to go through this whole adventure with you in which you induce your only son to commit a murderous act of revenge on your behalf when you're already dead anyway. It's — kinda awful? So if you want to tell Hamlet to go kill his stepfather, you can. In fact, look, you just did. But now you are going to have to live with the consequences, AS THE MAN WHO YOU JUST INDUCED TO MURDER.

You are now your son, Hamlet!

How's that taste, bucko?! Now you have to go do a murder!

Be Hamlet, and promise the ghost of your dead father to kill Claudius: *turn to 456*

But I don't want to be my son! I want to be a ghost!! *Turn to 496*

479

You retreat your king.

"Checkmate in six," Gertrude announces.

You think she's bluffing. She advances her pawn (b4). At this point, you can either move your pawn forward or retreat your king.

Unbeknownst to you, at this exact point in time, the timeline splits! In Timeline Zeta, you retreat your king (Ka7). Gertrude moves her king over (Kb5), and you move your pawn forward (b6). Gertrude brings up her other pawn to threaten yours, and if you use your pawn to take hers, you'll lose it the next turn and be left with nothing. But there's nowhere you can move your king to prevent Gertrude from taking your pawn the next turn, and that's what she does (axb6). You lost.

But wait, because in an alternate timeline, Timeline Zeta Prime, you advance your pawn instead (b6)! Gertrude moves her king forward (Kc6), and since moving your pawn forward would sacrifice it, instead you move your king backwards (Ka7). Gertrude immediately moves her pawn forward (b5), leaving you with only two moves for your king, both of which are retreats, and both of which result in your last pawn being taken. Aw man, you lost in this timeline too!

Geez, timelines, what the heck!

CHECKMATE: *turn to 309*

480

Okay! You become pirates!

It turns out that living on a boat without the support structure of a nation-state behind you is hard and it only gets harder! And it turns out, yeah, that battle you won was insanely lucky for you, and you kinda used up a lot of your luck reserves in it. Dude. You are fresh out of luck.

Two months later your ship is attacked by another pirate ship (*The Mad Cutlass of Atlantis*; it's a pretty cool name, I'm not gonna lie) and you are slaughtered. They even manage to take me hostage! And they're forcing me to say "you are slaughtered" AND to use "you" in the "everyone on board" sense!

Geez. Nice work, Hamlet!!

THE END

Turn to 331

481

You grab a piece of paper and write down the words "HEY I'M NOT HERE TO KILL YOU, I JUST WANT TO KNOW ABOUT THAT MURDER YOU MAYBE WITNESSED?" but in Danish of course, hah hah. You gently shake the woman awake while holding the piece of paper up in front of her.

She's freaked out initially (she was just woken up by a g-g-g-g-ghostly apparition from beyond the grave) but once she reads your note, she looks at you suspiciously and says, "For real?"

You flip over the paper and write "YEAH I'M THE GUY THAT GOT KILLED MAYBE, AND I GUESS I WANT TO REVENGE MY DEATH OR WHATEVER? BUT PLEASE SPEAK SLOWLY AS NORWEGIAN IS NOT MY NATIVE LANGUAGE; I'M FROM DENMARK."

"Oh," the woman says in Danish, "I speak Danish too."

"Kick ass," you reply.

She tells you what she saw and gives you a physical description of the guy. Unfortunately, the man answering to her description could only be one person: your brother, Claudius!!

Congratulations, my king! You now know what you know so that whole Second Person Pronoun-Paradoxical Auto-Dramatic Irony thing has been slain!

OOM! BOOM! BOOM!
Yesss!

You have been awarded 500 experience points, plus you've unlocked a new quest: Revenge Yourself on Claudius.

You're feeling pretty chuffed about this whole situation!

Okay! Let's revenge your death! Your murderer is getting away with it in Denmark.

Swim back to Denmark: *turn to 512*

Wait for the next boat back to Denmark: *turn to 490*

483

"Correct!" Horatio says. "Ophelia, if you get this next question right, you will be my new queen. Fortinbras, if that's who YOU want to be, you've got to get this next one right just to stay in the game."

Horatio looks at you both, then speaks. "Next question: how long is the coastline of Denmark?"

Again you slap in first.

"8735 kilometres!" *Turn to 533*

"7314 kilometres!" *Turn to 90*

"Trick question! No coastline has a precisely defined length, as the length will depend on the method used to measure it. If I use a metre stick, variations in the coast smaller than one metre will be ignored. But if I use a centimetre stick, then I'll include those measurements, but ignore those less than one centimetre! Since coastlines behave like fractals in this regard, there is no single length measurement I can point to without making simplifying assumptions first." *Turn to 256*

484

Your plan is the one you decide to go with! It's too late to try anything today, so you wait a day and go to Claudius's favourite drinking hole that evening.

Soon, Claudius walks in the door! "I'll have some booze," he says, "in celebration of my new wife and kinghood." Claudius then gets SUPER WASTED SUPER QUICKLY, which is really convenient for you.

"Okay, now's our chance," Hamlet whispers to you. "Announce loudly that we're going home to make out, so nobody suspects us. Then we can wait for him on the path back to the castle."

"Why are you publicly reminding me of the plan we've already discussed?"

you hiss, but it was at least convenient because it brought us all up to speed on your plan for avoiding accountability for the murder you're about to facilitate! You do as Hamlet asks, and you both leave. You walk for a few minutes down the path to a dark spot, not too far from the water, and wait. There are no forks in the road up to this point, so you know you'll catch him.

Hamlet wants to make out a bit while you wait, but you point out how it's chilly down by the water and damp too and how this doesn't really get your makeout organs pumping, so he gives up on that little fantasy.

Eventually, Claudius shows up!

Confront him: *turn to 486*

Let him pass: *turn to 489*

485

"PROBABLY," you say out loud to nobody in particular, "PROBABLY I just died of a heart attack. Yes, there's definitely no foul play to investigate here!"

You're not that curious about the circumstances of your own death, but there's certainly room for incurious people in the afterlife. You, for example, spend the rest of your afterlife (which is forever) training little ghost puppies how to be better dogs, and they're so cute and they stay puppies forever and never grow up but just get better and better and cuter and cuter and oh my gosh it's ADORABLE.

THE END

Turn to 38

486

You stop Claudius with a firm hand on his shoulder as Hamlet steps in front of him.

"Hey Claudius, it's me, Hamlet! You wanna go down to the river? Maybe see if there's any frogs?"

"I like frogs," Claudius says drunkenly, "as you can get poison from them and use it to kill people who are in the way of your professional and romantic ambitions."

"Holy smokes!" Hamlet whispers to you.

You bring Claudius down to the river's edge. You and Hamlet bend down on your knees and say things like "Wow, look at that!" and "That frog is CRAZY looking!" and "Whoah, is this one's neck normal?" and before you know it Claudius is pushing you aside, slurring, "I wanna see." Then, completely of his own accord, he trips and falls into the water.

You calmly hold his head down, but then Hamlet stays your hand. "I want to say something to him."

You pull Claudius's head up by the hair.

"We're killing you, Claudius, because you killed my father and turned him into a ghost. Prepare to die."

"Ghosts?! Those exist?" Claudius gurgles, shocked. You push his head back underwater.

"Wait, I've got something else I want to say," Hamlet says. You pull Claudius up again.

"When you turn into a ghost, tell my dad I said hi, and also, make amends with him, okay?"

Claudius coughs and struggles weakly. He whispers something that you can't hear, so Hamlet moves closer to him. Claudius repeats himself, and Hamlet angrily grabs him by the hair and shoves his head underwater, holding it there until he stops struggling. When it's over, you ask Hamlet what he said.

Hamlet looks at you. "He said..."

"Yes?" you say.

"He said, 'If ghosts exist, I'm going to become one. And hell herself won't be able to stop me,'" Hamlet says.

You stare at him for a long moment. "We'd better get back to the drinking hall to establish our alibis," you finally say.

You do that, loudly saying things like "Wow, those were good makeouts! Now I'm back for more drinking!" and eventually go to bed. Claudius is discovered drowned and nobody suspects you.

That night, no ghosts visit you.

No ghosts visit you the next night either. Days and days go by without any ghostly apparitions and you're just about feeling like whatever insanity you may have been witness to over the past several days is finally over. You and Hamlet go to bed, finally relaxing, just a little.

That night, Hamlet is murdered in his sleep by Osric. Surprise!

WHOAH, WHAT? SAVE HAMLET! *Turn to 413*

487

"Ooh, I'm sorry, Ophelia. That's not the correct answer," says Horatio. "Fortinbras, if you can answer correctly, all of Denmark is yours."

Fortinbras looks at you. "Ophelia," he says, "I'm sorry, but you were off in your calculations. The accepted measurement is 1421 kilometres less than the number you supplied."

Horatio does some quick mental arithmetic, then bows before Fortinbras.

"My king," he says.

GRACEFULLY ACCEPT YOUR LOSS AT DENMARK TRIVIA: *turn to 136*

CHALLENGE FORTINBRAS TO A RACE AROUND THE WORLD INSTEAD: *turn to 179*

489

You let Claudius pass you by without comment.

"What the hell is wrong with us?" you say. "We lost our nerve. Maybe we're not up to drowning someone."

"Or maybe we are, but we need to try again tomorrow night, under exactly the same circumstances as tonight," Hamlet replies.

Try again tomorrow night under exactly the same circumstances: *turn to 484*

Look at the list again, maybe there's a better way to kill him: *turn to 403*

490

You go down to the docks and start poking your head into the bridge of every boat you can find, flipping through the captain's logs and itineraries until you find one that's headed for Denmark. And it leaves in just a few minutes! NICE! This is really convenient!

During the voyage, you poke around the boat looking for things to amuse yourself with. You experiment with doing some ghost things like putting your head inside a barrel of wine and then making your head corporeal, but that just causes the barrel to explode with the sudden pressure inside and makes you get wine in your eyes, so you don't do that more than a few times.

It only takes a while before your boat arrives in Denmark!

Arrive in Denmark: *turn to 475*

491

You go home to hide out until Hamlet tells you that his part of this plan is done! You worry that now that you're missing and presumed drowned your room might attract visitors, but you figure you'll be able to see anyone coming and hide.

Days go by. NOBODY COMES. A little concerned that your death didn't take, you put on a disguise and wander around the castle, but yep, everyone thinks you're dead! They're even having a MEMORIAL SERVICE for you. I guess they'll come to clean out your place after that?

You go home to wait.

Days go by.

NOBODY COMES AGAIN. Eventually you get tired of waiting though and wander down to the royal court. As you enter, you're greeted by a gruesome scene so unexpected and bloody that it takes a few seconds to fully comprehend. Gertrude is clearly dead. Claudius is also just as clearly dead. Hamlet's dead too. Aaaaand so's your brother, Laertes. Horatio's alive, but he seems pretty shell-shocked.

"What the hell happened here?" you demand.

Horatio looks at you and opens his mouth to explain. "Um...Hamlet did?" he says, weakly.

"Aw man, aw geez," you say, and then Fortinbras (he's the crown prince of Norway) walks in with some ambassadors! He says Rosencrantz and Guildenstern are dead too, and that he's king now. He settles himself on the throne and looks around his new kingdom.

He seems pretty satisfied at all this, I gotta say!

THE END: *turn to 492*

SCREW THIS!! *Turn to 504*

492

"THE END," you say, and Fortinbras looks at you with one raised eyebrow.

"Um, I mean, I'll just show myself out," you say.

After you leave, Fortinbras takes over Denmark and installs himself as the new head of state. That's kind of baloney, so you move to England because everyone you liked in Denmark is already dead anyway so WHATEVER. While in England, you meet some sexy tourists on vacation!

I'd tell you all about these shenanigans, but you made me swear I'd keep it a secret!

THE END

P.S. It's super hot though, good work there my friend.

Turn to 335

493

Okay. Um, why?

BECAUSE THEN HE'LL HAVE SULLIED HIS HANDS WITH MURDER, AND BETTER FOR SOMEONE NEW TO BE FORCED TO COMMIT THE MURDER ACT THAN FOR ME TO DO IT MYSELF FOR SOME REASON? *Turn to 143*

OH YEAH, WAIT, THIS IS DUMB, I'M ALREADY DEAD AND INVISIBLE AND I CAN FLY; I GUESS I'LL JUST DO IT MYSELF: *turn to 462*

495 "Hey Gertrude," says Claudius. "I sure am happy that WE MARRIED EACH OTHER, even if it was so soon after your first husband died under mysterious circumstances."

Whoah! That certainly was, in terms of exposition, a very efficient sentence!

You decide instantly that your initial revenge plan (haunt a mirror so that instead of Claudius's reflection he sees you, and then you mirror his movements so he's not really sure what's going on, tee hee) is needlessly complex and stupid. Dude killed you AND married your widow! Since you are from olden times, you have an extremely old-fashioned sense of ownership over female sexuality, so this really gets stuck in your craw.

Instead of spooking Claudius, you decide to...

Kill Claudius! COMPLETE THE QUEST! *Turn to 20*

Get your son to kill Claudius instead: *turn to 498*

496 Listen, King Hamlet, you already had your chance to be a ghost and you pretty much wasted it. And now you don't want to do the dirty work of revenge? FINE. You know what? FINE. Go off and have your own adventure; see if I care. Here we go, just fill in the blanks, WHEEEEE WHAT FUN:

You are the ghost of a dead king! You discover a _____ kind of ______ that can be used by ______ to _______ a giant _______. Things are really ______ for a while, but then they _____ into ______.

A side effect of your ______ is that you come back to life again! With a brand-new _____ and everything! But then you die again super quickly. It's very ______. After you die again, your body is ______ into a ______ and then _______ into a terrible _____ so that everyone can ______ until they ______.

THE END

P.S. For that last paragraph, may I suggest you fill it in with "installed," "steel colossus," "magnified," "city-sized monstrosity," "toil at its feet," and "realize they shouldn't have honoured your last wishes"?

Turn to 440

497 Wait a second, you guys didn't figure out what would happen in the event of a tie!

You slice off one of her arms. "You said you wouldn't kill me!" Gertrude exclaims.

"You'll live," you say.

And while it's super awkward to be the only two people in town, especially when that town is full of dead bodies but ESPECIALLY when the only other person alive is the newly one-armed mother of your old boyfriend, you manage.

Fortinbras, the Norwegian crown prince, shows up a while later. He finds all the decaying bodies and pronounces it "super gross," so you cut off his arm too. "Not so strong in the arm now, are you?" you say, but nobody laughs because multilingual puns are like that. People usually don't get them. I don't know what to tell you. This is the world we live in.

Oh, crap! I almost forgot! Later on, you die of old age!!

THE END

Turn to 342

498

Okay. Um, why?

Because then he'll have sullied his hands with murder, and better for someone new to be forced to commit the murder act than for me to do it myself for some reason? *Turn to 143*

Oh yeah, wait, this is dumb, I'm already dead and invisible and I can fly; I guess I'll just do it myself: *turn to 20*

499

You rush back into Gertrude's room.

"Hey guys, me again!" you say. "Crazy ol' Ophelia!"

"I was just thinking, wouldn't it be nice if heat dried up my brains?" says Laertes.

"Because you're so crazy," he clarifies, addressing himself to you. "And that makes me feel bad, so: heat, brains, solution."

"Ah," you say. Ophelia, Laertes is acting crazier than you! You gotta step up your game!

Deciding to do just that, you start handing out some plants we both forgot were in your pocket to everyone in the room. You pass out some rosemary (use the leaves to season a pork chop!), fennel (eat the roasted seeds after a meal to freshen your breath!), rue (feed it to a horse to...induce an abortion? I dunno, that's what it says here, "induces abortion in horses"), columbine (the roots AND seeds are highly poisonous so I dunno how delicious they are; Ophelia, where are you finding these plants), and...a daisy (commonly considered to be a flower representing innocence, nicely done there I guess).

Everyone DEFINITELY thinks you're crazy now, Ophelia. Mission accomplished!

Go home: *turn to 450*

501

You've never been the slappy type, and this is actually your first time attempting this. Rosencrantz and Guildenstern are facing you, so how do you get them to turn around so you can slap their backs? It's not like they'll just turn around on their own mid-conversation, and if you try to manoeuvre around them, they'll obviously keep turning to face you, because that's what polite people do.

Okay, maybe if you tell them to just — no, Rosencrantz, you're moving the wrong way. No, TURN first, Guildenstern — no, you — okay, Rosencrantz, you've turned all the way around: turn back, start over. No, Guildenstern, we're not trying to flip here, we're — okay, sure, we're flipping, but turn-ways. No, okay, Rosen... dude, no, let me show you. Okay. Look, no, you messed it up again. Dude, no, look, it's not that hard. You're obviously both doing this just to pi—

You try to get them turned around so you can slap them on the back, but whatever it was that was going on there keeps happening. Time to cut your losses, and:

Ask them how they've been: *turn to 13*

502

You liked that, huh?

Okay, here's the next song you sing to the king of all of Denmark!

Tomorrow is Saint Valentine's day,
All in the morning betime,
And I a maid at your window,
To be your Valentine.
Then up he rose and donn'd his clothes
And dupp'd the chamber door,
Let in the maid, that out a maid
Never departed more.

(That part is about a woman having sex for the first time!) You continue:

By Gis and by Saint Charity,
Alack, and fie for shame!
Young men will do't if they come to't
By Cock, they are to blame.
Quoth she, 'Before you tumbled me,
You promis'd me to wed.'
He answers:
'So would I 'a' done, by yonder sun,
An thou hadst not come to my bed.'

(This part is about...actually, uh, I'll tell you when you're older.) With that, you make your exit and go back home.

Wait a tick, I just remembered I want to act even crazier!! *Turn to 499*

Wait a tick, I just remembered that I want to continue going home without incident! *Turn to 450*

503

You promise?

I promise. *Turn to 523*

504

"Screw this!!" you shout. "What gives you the right to be king? You don't even know anything about Denmark!"

"Do so!" says Fortinbras.

"Nuh uh!" you shout in reply.

Horatio holds up his hands. "Gentlemen, lady, please! I'm sure we can settle this reasonably," he says. He smiles widely.

A few minutes later, you and Fortinbras are sitting side by side at a table. Sitting at the other end of the table is Horatio.

This is how you will settle your dispute: Horatio will ask you trivia questions about Denmark, and the first person to slap the table and give the correct answer will get a point. It's best two out of three. The winner gets to be ruler of Denmark. It is all quite reasonable.

"Alright!" says Horatio, brushing off his hands. "First question: when...was Denmark first inhabited?!"

You know for a fact that you're unusually fast at slapping tables (what can I say, you had a boring childhood and had to invent your own fun), and as there's no penalty to slapping in first, that's what you do. Then you clear your throat and answer:

"Denmark's earliest archaeological findings date back to the Eemian interglacial period! That's from 130,000 to 110,000 BC." *Turn to 483*

"Denmark's earliest archaeological findings date back to the Devensian glacial period, at the start of the Pleistocene epoch, 2.5 million years ago." *Turn to 294*

"I dunno, but my mom lived here too, so it's got to be at least, like, 30 years." *Turn to 176*

506

You're the boss!

A few days later, you meet up with Gertrude for lunch. "Let's have a picnic down by the river," you say.

"Sure," she says.

Knowing that you'll soon be "dead" has made your madness act a little less intense. You actually feel like you can be yourself, at least for a little while.

At least for lunch.

You and Gertrude talk about many things (your shared interests, your hopes for the future, funny stories from your past) and it's really pleasant. Hamlet and Claudius don't even come up once. It's actually a very meaningful conversation to you both, and you're glad you and Gertrude were able to have it. Later, Gertrude picks some pretty flowers and puts them in your hair, and you do the same for her. Isn't that nice? It's nice. But after that, you both notice that all the little sandwiches are gone and lunch is over. You've got to do it now, Ophelia.

"Hey, I'm crazy!" you say suddenly, standing up and slapping your knees. "You know what crazy people do? Climb dangerous trees!"

"Um," Gertrude says, "maybe — maybe let's not be crazy?"

"Too late!!" you say, climbing up the tree hanging out all aslant over the brook below. You climb out further and further, ignoring Gertrude's protests, until finally the branch you're on breaks and you fall into the river.

"Oh nooooo! I don't know how to swim!" you shout.

"I'll save you!" Gertrude yells, stripping out of the outermost layer of her many-layered fancy royal clothes.

"There's no time, and you might drown too! No, Gertrude, this is how my story ends," you shout.

"Ophelia!" shouts Gertrude.

"Gertrude, tell them what happened to me! Tell them...tell them that I acted crazy and drowned, okay? Maybe work our pretty flowers into it?"

"What?" shouts Gertrude, as you discreetly tread water.

"No, wait, it can be done better," you say. "Here, tell them...tell them..."

You raise up one dripping hand out of the water.

"Tell them there is a willow here that grows aslant from a brook, that shows his hoar leaves in the glassy stream. There with fantastic garlands did I come of crow-flowers, nettles, daisies, and long purples that liberal shepherds give a grosser name, but our cold maids do dead men's fingers call them. There, on the pendent boughs I coronet weeds clambering to hang, an envious sliver broke; when down my weedy trophies and myself fell in the weeping brook. My clothes spread wide; and, mermaid-like, awhile they bore me up: which time I chanted snatches of old tunes; as one incapable of my own distress, or like a creature native and indued unto that element. But long it could not be till that my garments, heavy with their drink, pull'd my poor wretched self from my melodious lay to muddy death."

"Got it," Gertrude says. "Goodbye, Ophelia! I'm sorry I can't rescue you!"

"It's okay! I'm drowning now! Glub glub glub!" you shout.

You take a big breath of air and swim down until you can touch bottom, count to 10, and then swim up to the top. When you surface, Gertrude is gone.

You have successfully faked your own death!! You suddenly feel like you've received 100 experience points and levelled up your Mad Nutty Rhetoric skill.

Go home again, making sure not to be seen: *turn to 491*

507

"Technically correct!" shouts Horatio. "Fortinbras, you and Ophelia are now tied for first. Whoever answers my next question correctly will be the ruler of all of Denmark."

Horatio clears his throat.

"Final question: I am imagining a speculative future country that I will call the United States of America. This country is made out of many smaller states, each with their own name. Which speculative future state am I thinking of when I say that its land area is slightly less than twice the size of Denmark?"

Uh oh.

You slap in and say:

"**Texas.**" *Turn to 533*

"**Alaska.**" *Turn to 508*

"**Massachusetts.**" *Turn to 518*

508

"That, Ophelia, is..."

Horatio pauses, dramatically.

You and Fortinbras glance at each other. It's so tense! Who knows what Horatio will say? Who knows??

"...incorrect," finishes Horatio. "Fortinbras? Any ideas?"

"Um...whichever one was the sixth to enter the Union?" he says.

"CORRECT!" shouts Horatio, leaping up and hugging Fortinbras. "You won, dude! You are totally now the king of Denmark! Whoooahhhh!"

Gracefully accept your loss at Denmark trivia: *turn to 136*

Challenge Fortinbras to a race around the world instead: *turn to 179*

509

You bring out your queen too, mirroring her move perfectly. She moves her queen back one square and takes your queen. You've lost your queen in two moves. This isn't going well for you, Ophelia!

"This isn't going well for you, Ophelia!" Gertrude says, plagiarizing me but come on it's not like she could know!

I'll save you some embarrassment and tell you that the rest of the game doesn't go well for you either, and at the end you are down to your king and a pawn. Gertrude, on the other hand, has been toying with you and has managed to promote ALL of her pawns to queens, giving her a total of nine queens.

Here's how the board is set up:

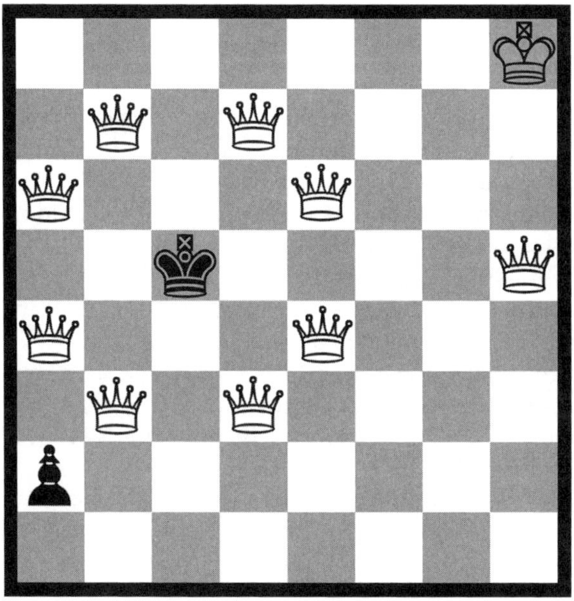

Ophelia, the most impressive thing is that you managed to even GET yourself into this position. It's not easy to end up so screwed in natural play! It is sincerely impressive in its own way. But it is...

CHECKMATE. *Turn to 309*

510

You bring up your horsey's pawn two spaces to form the first step of a zigzag wall.

Gertrude raises her eyebrows. "Congratulations," she says. "You have managed to lose the game in the shortest possible time: two moves. It is impossible to lose at chess any faster. There is no way for you to be worse at this game."

"Not true!" you say. "I could be worse if I didn't know how the pieces moved." Gertrude writes down "Qd5#," then moves her queen diagonally as far as it'll go, putting it beside your pawn.

"The thing is, I'm not convinced you haven't been guessing your way through it so far," she says, "but it doesn't matter anyway." Duuuuude, I'm pretty sure that's...

CHECKMATE. *Turn to 309*

511

You agree that drowning is the way to go. The only problem is that you and Hamlet have different drowning plans.

Your plan is to wait until Claudius is drunk, which won't be long because he drinks every night, and then lure him to the water's edge and hold his head under until he dies. It seems like a pretty good way to drown a dude.

"It'll look like death by misadventure!" you say.

RATHER than doing that, Hamlet's plan is to pretend to be insane, and then the best part is that YOU'LL pretend to be insane too, and then you'll fake your own drowning, which will allow Hamlet to act even crazier, and then he can drown the king when Claudius is not expecting it because who suspects a crazy person to act violently and irrationally, nobody, that's who, because after all the only thing crazy people ever do is speak in riddles and tight, tight rhymes.

"Your plan seems needlessly circuitous and dumb," you say. "And I'm not keen to fake my own drowning. No, I'm afraid I'm going to have to insist that we...

GO WITH MY PLAN INSTEAD." *Turn to 484*

DO YOUR PLAN AFTER ALL, AND I BET MY EARLIER SENTENCE STRUCTURE MADE YOU THINK THIS SENTENCE WAS GOING TO END DIFFERENTLY." *Turn to 514*

512

It's, like, 200 kilometres between the two nations. You know that, right?

APPARENTLY NOT??

So you start to swim back to Denmark, but it's a lot of work to keep your body corporeal so that you can swim, so eventually you get tired and stop. For a while you float above the water, but that gets boring, so for most of the journey you float down to the ocean floor and travel along it.

Hey, there's a sunken pirate ship here. Hey, there might be treasure in it!

EXAMINE PIRATE SHIP: *turn to 461*

IGNORE IT, JUST ARRIVE IN DENMARK: *turn to 475*

514 "I sure did!" Hamlet says. "Okay, perfect. I'm going to go back to the royal court and act crazy-crazy-crazy all the time. You tell your dad about how crazy I am, and then you start acting crazy too, okay? And then this afternoon you can confront me and act crazy in front of everyone, alright?"

"Okay!" you say. "That is, after all, what I just consented to!"

"Perfect," Hamlet says, leaving. "Love you!"

You go meet with your dad and tell him how totally cray Hamlet is, then leave. Back in your room, you start putting together your crazy costume. You shove some flowers in your hair and tangle it up to make it look all messy. Then you put on your nicest dress and get dirt all over it, because only an insane person would ruin such a nice dress!

A little while later, a note is slipped under your door. "MEET ME AT THE ROYAL COURT AT 2 –LOVE HAMMY" it says. "P.S. B CRAY Z."

You show up at council at the appointed time with the appointed crazy, only to find Hamlet there alone. He nods to you and begins a lengthy and very loud soliloquy about the value of life and whether or not he should kill himself. When it's over, he walks up to you. "OH HEY, OPHELIA I DIDN'T SEE YOU THERE," he announces, and then whispers to you, "Act like you're breaking up with me!"

"Why?" you say in a normal speaking voice. "Nobody's here."

"Shh!" Hamlet whispers in return, and then he turns from you. "OH NO, YOU'RE TRYING TO GIVE BACK ALL THE LOVE LETTERS I'VE SENT YOU? BUT WHY??"

You look at your empty hands.

"GET THEE TO A NUNNERY, BECAUSE IF YOU TAKE A HUSBAND YOU'LL TURN HIM INTO A MONSTER. LISTEN, WE'RE ALL JUST PLAIN AWFUL AND THAT'S THAT," he shouts.

"Hamlet," you say, "are you doing this for someone's benefit? Because there's nobody here. Let's do this again in front of Claudius, okay?"

"He's hiding just down the hallway!!" Hamlet whispers to you urgently. "I'm leaving, but I just broke up with you! Talk about your feelings! And do it really loudly so they can overhear!"

"Ohhhhh!" you whisper back. "Why didn't you just say so?" You clear your throat as Hamlet leaves.

Do a nice fancy speech for Claudius's benefit: *turn to 474*

Claudius isn't the shiniest pickle in the shed! Just cover the basics in your speech instead. *Turn to 525*

515 "I think that went well!" Hamlet says.

"I guess it did!" you say. "They think you're crazy for sure, but I don't think they noticed that I was crazy."

"You gotta play it up," Hamlet says. "Sing, talk in riddles, reference sex a li'l. They'll definitely think you're nuts!"

You look at him. "So you're going to England?"

"No, I'm gonna stay here. I'm going to try to trick Claudius into revealing his guilt. In the meantime, you act crazier, okay?"

"Okay, I guess," you say.

You stay in your room and sort of putter around for the rest of the evening and most of the next day. You write down some riddles you can use to sound crazy ("What has two feet and two legs? Give up? BIRDS AND A BUNCH OF OTHER VERTEBRATES ACTUALLY.") but decide you can probably do better.

Things are going pretty well in the writing department when Hamlet shows up again and tells you that he accidentally killed your father!!

"WHAT?" you say, completely shocked.

"It was an accident!!" Hamlet says. "There was talking and then there was stabbing and maybe there was some stew involved and look: I'm sorry."

"He was my father, Hamlet!" you scream at him.

"And because you killed him, I will now kill you!!" *Turn to 526*

"And because he was an emotionally manipulative, sexist pig of a man who did not respect me as a person and raised my brother to do the same, and plus the fact that death comes easily in this time period, I am actually not that upset about his death." *Turn to 516*

516

"Cool," says Hamlet. "That's super convenient."

You nod.

"Okay, well — this'll feed into the whole 'you crazy' thing. Can you go use it?"

You nod again.

"Okay. Terrific. Well, I'm going to go off and be crazy some more. I'll be in touch. Talk soon?"

You nod a final time, and Hamlet's gone.

You spend the next few days wandering around the castle, being as crazy as you can manage. You make up songs about sex and stuff, but I'm not typing them here because I'm not gonna lie, they get a LITTLE bawdy. Oh my.

A few days later, you feel like you're properly prepped for your new, improved crazy act! You decide to try it out on Gertrude. You walk into Gertrude's room and Hamlet's friend Horatio is here too. He's not in on the "just an act" part of your craziness, so lay it on thick, Ophelia!

"How now, Ophelia?" asks Gertrude. Here's what that means: "What's up?" You answer in song, singing about "cockles" (gross).

"Alas, sweet lady, what imports this song?" asks Gertrude. Here's what that means: "Hey wait, how come all the singing?"

You answer in song, singing about a crazy little thing called death. Gertrude tries to interrupt you, but you interrupt her interruption by saying, "Hold on, check this out!" and then you sing a song about showers.

2
3
4
BOSN

Then Claudius walks in! You've got two choices here: you can sing songs to him too, thereby establishing how TOTALLY NUTS you are, or you can break from the plan and just kill him now, because honestly Hamlet's plan isn't exactly the iron-clad gem of brilliance you'd hoped for.

Kill Claudius! *Turn to 527*

Continue singing: that one about "cockles" was pretty good; you wanna sing some craaaaazy songs: *turn to 502*

518

"That, Ophelia, is..."

Horatio pauses, dramatically.

You and Fortinbras look at each other.

"CORRECT!" shouts Horatio, leaping up and hugging you.

"You won! You are now the queen of Denmark! It's so awesome!"

Be the new queen of Denmark: *turn to 534*

519

Evening comes, and you lead Ophelia to the spot outside where you first saw the ghost. "We have to wait till around midnight," you say. "I think that's when he normally shows up."

To pass the time, Ophelia suggests you play a storytelling game, where she says one word of a story and you say the next word, and neither of you knows where the story will go.

"Once," she begins. "Upon," you say. "A," she says. "Time," you say. "There," she says. "Was," you say.

"A," she says.

"Beautiful," you say, looking at her. She smiles.

"Prince," she replies, and you smile back.

"Who," you say.

"Wanted," she says.

"To," you say.

"Kiss," she says.

"His girlfriend," you say.

"That's cheating," she says, but you're already smooching. You begin to really get into making out!

Make out for a while: *turn to 393*

521 "Oh, I'll play your game," you say.

"Excellent," she says, motioning to her throne. "Please, have a seat."

As you sit down and settle in, she quickly sets up a chessboard in front of you, pulling up another throne for the opposite side. She arranges the pieces with the air of someone who actually knows what she's doing when it comes to playing chess, which isn't the greatest sign for you. She's white, you're black. "Since you're the one who barged in here, it's my turn to make the next move," she says, advancing her king's pawn up two squares.

"Ah yes, the Queen's Gambit," you say.

"That's not what that is," she says.

You're — kinda in over your head here, aren't you, Ophelia?

Copy her move on your side — how can she beat an opponent who copies all her moves?? *Turn to 418*

Move your king's bishop's pawn ahead one square. It's the one on your left. *Turn to 81*

522 You bring out your horse's pawn a single square, building a solid wall.

Gertrude writes down your move, which is apparently "g6." After that she writes the note "likes straight lines?"

She notices you reading her notes. "Do you like straight lines?" she asks.

"Maybe I do and maybe I don't," you answer in a way you hope could one day be described by an impartial third party as "coyly."

Gertrude sighs and brings out her bishop's pawn to form a straight line on her side too. "Here's a straight line for you then," she says. "Because straight lines are so unstoppable. You have totally cracked the chess code." On her paper she writes "f4." I think she's making fun of you! And now that I think about it, straight lines aren't super great. DIAGONAL lines are where it's at, because if your opponent takes one of your pawns, that piece is guaranteed to be taken by another pawn! If you move your own guy up, you can make a diagonal line in one move.

More straight lines! (e6): *turn to 535*

Surprise her with a diagonal line (g5): *turn to 524*

523 Well, I mean, that's fair. You haven't exactly been getting the long end of the stick here.

Okay! While we were talking, Hamlet went off to England with Rosencrantz and Guildenstern. They partied, had fun, discovered a note from Claudius ordering them killed, replaced it with a forgery they wrote themselves: the usual hijinks one gets up to on a boat! Only along the way the ship was captured — BY PIRATES. At this moment, Hamlet's boarding the pirate ship, named *Calypso's Gale*. He's literally hanging off the side of the boat from a rope, about to smash through a porthole and take on the captain in one-to-one combat.

Let's see if you can do better than he could. You are now Hamlet!

PUSH OUT FROM THE SHIP, USE YOUR LEGS AS A BATTERING RAM, AND SMASH YOUR WAY INSIDE THROUGH A PORTHOLE: *turn to 106*

524

You bring up your horsey's pawn another space, forming the first steps of a zigzag wall. Gertrude raises her eyebrows.

"Congratulations," she says. "You have managed to invent a new variation of an existing chess move!"

"Oh wow, really?" you say, super excited.

"Yep!" she replies. "It's called the Fool's Mate. You figured out a way to make it even more foolish, because you took just slightly longer to get mated than necessary."

She writes down "Qd1-h5#," then moves her queen diagonally as far as it'll go, putting it beside your pawn, and OH SNAP you just got SCHOOLED at how to win at chess!

By that I mean, Gertrude totally beat you down. You lose, Ophelia!

CHECKMATE: *turn to 309*

525

You clear your throat and hold out one hand in front of you.

He used to be smart, but now he's nuts
The grace of a gentleman, a soldier's guts
He used to be the heir to the throne
But now he's living in the CRAZY ZONE
Lots of women really liked his sexy words
But it made them sad, and I'm one of 'em. Aw turds
He was beautiful and noble but now he's cray-z
And that's all on this subject I've got to say, G.

By the time you finish nobody has shown up, so you run through your speech again, this time in a singsong voice. La la la, that's what you sound like. Toodle doodle doo.

Turns out, that did it! Claudius AND your father walk in the room! They talk about what you've said while generally acting like you're not even there (DISS) and in the end Claudius decides that Hamlet will be sent to England where his insanity can do no harm.

They leave.

They didn't seem to notice that you're supposed to be insane, though, which means you'll have to bring your A-game next time. I guess crazy-tight rhymes don't count?

Meet up with Hamlet to discuss what happened: *turn to 514*

526

You kill Hamlet by twisting his head off like a bottlecap, which are things that I predict will be invented in the future and anyway, bottom line, he's dead now and you are a murderer. With Hamlet gone there's no real need to revenge yourself on Claudius either, so — you don't. You kinda just...wander away? And they never solve the crime because fingerprint identification isn't invented yet either. So wow, I guess that's kinda it for the plot line of this book, huh?

Well!

Hamlet and his dad pal around in the afterlife as ghosts and have a super awesome time of it. Claudius has a long and pretty okay reign, and you have an even longer and even more okay life. It actually turns out that it's pretty easy to live comfortably when you go through life killing people instead of dealing with your feelings, but that's a terrible lesson to learn here, so pretend I didn't say that!!

THE END

Turn to 186

527

Yeah man, let's settle this plot thread once and for all! Who cares who witnesses it??

You pull out two knives and stab Claudius in the eyes, really quickly before anyone can react, and yes, it's one knife per eye. OBVIOUSLY. Claudius runs around blindly and in horrible pain and hits a wall at full speed, which drives the knives into his brain, killing him instantly.

Congratulations! Claudius is now dead! But the bad news is, Gertrude and Horatio kinda (and by "kinda" I mean "literally") witnessed the whole thing.

Kill the witnesses: *turn to 530*

Try to explain it away: *turn to 544*

529

"Hey dudes, can you help me with these knives? Osric kinda walked into them and I think he's...hurt?" you say.

"...to death?" you add.

Rosencrantz and Guildenstern bend over the body and I think you've been consistent enough in your choices that we can both see where this is going. In the interests of saving time, here's what happens next:

» you kill Rosencrantz and Guildenstern, look up, and see Marcellus and Bernardo looking down at you,
» you kill Marcellus and Bernardo and then see Francisco waltzing into the room,
» you kill Francisco and look up and who should be staring at you horrified but Reynaldo (he is another dude you know),
» you kill Reynaldo and are moving his body out of the way to make room for another when you bump into Voltimand and Cornelius, two dudes home from Norway,
» you kill Voltimand and Cornelius and are stacking their bodies like logs when a gravedigger and a priest wander in the room,
» it proceeds in this fashion until the room is filled floor to ceiling with dead bodies and the only person you haven't seen all day is Hamlet. And then guess who walks in the door?

Greet Hamlet with "Hey sweetie! How's your day been going? Mine's been going just great!!" *Turn to 345*

Try to explain it away: *turn to 541*

530

Pulling the knives out of Claudius's eyeball holes, you throw them, stabbing Horatio through his tongue and the bottom of his mouth and piercing a hole right into his jugular, while at the same time nailing Gertrude through the ears. "Speak no evil," you say to Horatio. "Hear no evil," you say to Gertrude. "That's a good line to say because I got them in the ears and tongue," you say to nobody in particular. Is it to me? You don't have to explain it to me, Ophelia, I do totally know what's going on. Both Gertrude and Horatio are dead within the next five seconds. So that means they're dead right about...NOW.

You look around, taking in the king's body, the queen's body, as well as the body of your boyfriend's best friend. H-hooray? You're busy congratulating yourself on so efficiently eliminating all the witnesses when your brother, Laertes, enters the room, sees what's happened, and freezes in shock.

Kill Laertes: *turn to 301*

Try to reason with him: *turn to 544*

DAVID
HELLMAN

532

"Ooh, I'm sorry, Ophelia. That's not the correct answer," says Horatio. "Fortinbras, if you can answer correctly, you're back in the game."

Fortinbras doesn't even look at you. "Ophelia was over in her calculation by 1421 kilometres."

Horatio does some quick mental arithmetic, then nods. "Correct," he says. "You are tied for first. The person who answers my next question correctly will be ruler of all of Denmark," he says.

Horatio pauses.

"Final question," he says. "I am imagining a speculative future country that I will call the United States of America. This country is made out of many smaller states, each with their own name. Which speculative future state am I thinking of when I say that its land area is slightly less than twice the size of Denmark?"

Uh oh.

You slap in and say:

"Massachusetts." *Turn to 518*

"Texas." *Turn to 508*

"Alaska." *Turn to 533*

533

"That, Ophelia, is..."

Horatio pauses, dramatically.

You and Fortinbras glance at each other. It's so tense! Who knows what Horatio will say? Who knows??

"...incorrect," finishes Horatio. "Fortinbras? Any ideas?"

"Um...whichever one was the sixth to enter the Union?" he says.

"CORRECT!" shouts Horatio, leaping up and hugging Fortinbras. "You won, dude! You are totally now the king of Denmark! Whoooahhhh!"

Gracefully accept your loss at Denmark trivia: *turn to 136*

Challenge Fortinbras to a race around the world instead: *turn to 179*

534

"Thank you, Horatio," you say. "My first act as queen is to order the removal of the usurper Fortinbras from our land and shores. Back to Norway, bro!" Fortinbras asks if he has to, and you insist that he really does. He complains but leaves. Hooray!

After he's gone, Horatio says he's just got to tell you everything that happened, but he needs to write it down first. You assume it's so that he can get his thoughts straight, but then he shows up with a document where you have to make choices to see what happens. "You play as me," he says. He turns the book over in his hands, clearly proud of it. "Choose from one of 15 possible endings!" he says.

On your first run-through, you finish the story after only a few pages and nothing close to what actually happened happens. Unless, while you were hanging out in your room, Horatio somehow won the lottery, found a magic sword, and married every woman and a few of the dudes?

"No, no, you're making the wrong choices!" Horatio says, clearly frustrated with you. This is stupid, so you make him show you the run he wanted you to play, and since you're the absolute head of state he totally has to! And while Horatio reads his own book, he explains all about Hamlet's final duel (good gosh but it sounds like a pretty silly time) and how everyone ended up dying except for Horatio and I guess Osric and some ambassadors.

"Wow," you say. "Um, maybe Hamlet wasn't as noble in reason and infinite in faculty as I always thought he was."

"Evidently not," Horatio says, looking up from his book and out at all the dead bodies that surround you in the royal court. You walk up to examine one of them and, after a long silence, you speak again.

"He wanted Claudius dead for weeks, Horatio. He had weeks to take him out and this is how he finally does it. I guess he wasn't exactly a god of apprehension, huh? I mean, like, in the 'apprehending a criminal' sense of the word?"

"Nopers," Horatio says.

You agree that Hamlet sure was a real piece of work, and then you order Horatio to clean up the room and bury the bodies. After they're moved out and all that blood washed away, the royal court is pristine again.

You sit on your throne and consider your next move.

All of Denmark is yours to control. You can act for social justice; you can expand her borders; you can take over the entire world. Heck, you could do all three if you want to. You're Queen Ophelia.

It's time to rule Denmark as the most effective monarch ever in time and not be distracted by your boyfriend's antics, and you're all out of boyfriends.

THE END

P.S. Your final score is 996 out of 1000 because, wow, you sure knew a lot about Denmark and that always counts for something!

Turn to 536

535

Gertrude humours you and allows you to move each of your pawns forward one square, so you can form your little straight line.

In the meantime, she solidifies her pawn structure into what you want to call a Modified Sicilian Formation — but come on, what do you know about chess — advances her other pieces, takes control of the centre board, and generally dominates the rest of it too.

Miss U

You lose in 10 moves, and on the second-last move, Gertrude admits to being a little embarrassed it took her that long.

"I guess I felt sorry for you," she says. "I was like, no way she's this bad. No way. I cannot conceive of a world where even an amateur is this terrible at a game with rules this simple."

"Oh well," she says.

CHECKMATE: *turn to 309*

537

Cleo laughs. "I'm sure there's something that two people like us could get up to," she says. "What do you feel like?"

Before you can reply, a huge explosion rocks the hotel! Debris showers into the room, knocking Cleo unconscious. Looks like that takes care of the boredom thing: you're under attack!

BY TERRORISTS!!

Hah hah, screw this dating thing: you have three terrorists to kill!!

RUN DOWN TO THE SITE OF THE EXPLOSION: *turn to 68*

538

Tricked into deciding that maybe revenge isn't the best thing to obsess about once you're already dead and have fun ghost powers anyway, you instead do that job you just picked, and it's amazing. It's more than amazing: you turn what could've been a simple thing to do in the afterlife into an actual social movement that accomplishes tons of good. Everyone rad in the afterlife sees your work and thinks you're great, and man, this place is CHOCK FULL of awesome people, so that's really something. Your work has inspired an entire world.

Thank you.

And good work, King Hamlet! You managed to overcome your stupid thirst for revenge AND made the afterlife awesome AND didn't mess up your only son's life either! This is really awesome! You did a great job! I'm gonna give you like 50 billion decapoints!!

THE END

Turn to 376

540

You move your king up a square, and Gertrude moves her rook to match. "Check again," she says, marking down "Re4+." You keep this up, moving your king up to get out of check, as Gertrude moves her rook to keep pace, putting you back in check. But you've run out of road: any more moves forward and Gertrude's king will put you in check.

At this point, Gertrude's written down "Kg5 Re5+" and "Kg6 Re6+."

What do you do? Chess is hard, man! I wish I could help you, I really do. But while all the cool kids were outside playing chess, I was cooped up inside, studying how to make imaginary people say things! They called it "creative writing," but they never warned me it would end up like this!!

Reverse course (Kg5): *turn to 400*

Cut to the left instead (Kf7): *turn to 423*

541

You gesture at the room, soaked in the blood of an entire town. There's so much death in this room. Geez.

"Obviously," you begin, and then pause, unsure of how to continue. "Obviously, what happened here is that…everyone…suicided?"

"In stacks?" Hamlet asks, unconvinced.

"No, those ones died of…old age," you say.

You look at the bodies for a second.

"Those who died of old age did so while lying down on top of the people who were already dead," you explain.

"This whole thing is cray!" Hamlet screams, his eyes wide. "It's more than cray!" He grabs you by the shoulders. "It's cray cray! It's cray cray cray! It's cray cray cray cray! It's craaaaaaaaaa—"

You knock Hamlet over the head with the flat of your palm, intending to knock him out, but your Killing People skill has gotten so pumped over the past hour that you do insane damage and your boyfriend dies.

Daaaaamn!

You add him to the stacks and then wander around town for a while, looking inside all the empty houses, staring at those empty beds, your gaze lingering on dining rooms with tables still set for dinner, waiting for families that will never again return home.

You begin to feel "guilt," a human emotion!

But nobody wants to read a book where they feel bad about their choices, so let's skip over to the point where some foreign diplomats visit and you don't want to get arrested so you have to hilariously convince the diplomats that everyone's still alive by running around and moving the dead corpses like puppets!!

THE END
…FOR NOW

Turn to 416

543

Hamlet is at the door!

That's right, turns out that simply wishing for someone to be at your door doesn't change who's actually there. You don't control reality with your THOUGHTS, Ophelia. Sheesh.

Anyway, Hamlet opens the door and steps into your room. "It's me," he says. You haven't seen each other for a while; it's so great to see him. You run up and throw your arms around him and you smooch. It's just like old times.

But the moment passes, and when you look at his face you can see concern written all over it. He's troubled by something.

Ask him what's troubling him: *Turn to 365*

Wait for him to tell you: *turn to 334*

544

You gesture at the freshly bloodied room.

"Obviously," you begin, "a horrible accident happened here. As you know, magnetic fields can pull ferrous metals towards them, and while nobody is more shocked at what happened here than I am, I think we can agree that an important first step here is to figure out exactly how a superconducting magnet managed to interact with these incredibly dangerous knives that I was carrying for some reason." Your audience is unconvinced, and the next thing you know, you're brought before a court of your peers and sentenced to death for murder. Hamlet doesn't even speak up on your behalf! What a jerk.

"When you die and you're a ghost, we're not getting together," you tell him.

"Maaaaan," he says. "We might though."

"Not happening," you say, and then the executioner brings down his axe and separates your head from your body and your self from your life.

So!

You killed Claudius, which WAS the goal you set for yourself, but you didn't exactly do it in the most non-stupid way. I guess I'm going to award you…88 decapoints?

SCIENCE CORNER: Decapoints are not legal tender and cannot be traded for anything!!

THE END

Turn to 111

545

You stay silent, but King Claudius addresses you anyway. He says he's king now and it's time for you to stop mourning, as your father is dead and everyone has to die sometime, right? Man up, he says. Walk it off, he says. Drop me a letter about it at "Not My Problem, #1 Cheer Up Already Lane, Dopesville, Denmark," he

says. Your mom agrees with him, and then when they're done insulting you they leave.

You kinda wish you'd insulted him when you had the chance?

In the meantime, you're alone in an empty council room and feeling pretty sad! An empty room offers a ton of possibilities, WHICH INCLUDES THINGS YOU CAN DO INSIDE THIS EMPTY ROOM, SUCH AS:

TALK TO YOURSELF ABOUT HOW YOUR LIFE IS IN RUINS AND HOW EVERYTHING JUST SUUUUUCKS: *turn to 128*

LEAVE THE ROOM: *turn to 69*

YOU'RE FINALLY HOME, AND IT'S BEEN WEEKS SINCE YOU EMBARKED. SIT ON THE THRONE AS THE PRINCE OF DENMARK. *Turn to 34*

547

You take down the torches from the wall and tie a few beneath each bag. The bags are light but sturdy, and quickly fill with hot air from the torches. You now have a collection of hot-air balloons, each capable of carrying some load up, up, and away into the sky. They will continue rising until the torches extinguish themselves, which could take hours. By that time, they could've floated anywhere!

You have 1 turn(s) remaining.

There are several hot-air balloons here.

JUMP OUT THE WINDOW TO ESCAPE, USING HOT-AIR BALLOONS TO PREVENT YOUR FALL: *turn to 425*

TIE BODY PARTS TO HOT-AIR BALLOONS AND PUSH THEM OUT THE WINDOW: *turn to 40*

WAIT HOLD ON, I'M SUDDENLY HUNGRY: EAT STEW: *turn to 339*

Well
DANG

ARTIST BIOGRAPHIES

John Allison is a writer and artist based in Manchester, UK. You can see his comics at scarygoround.com. (Nodes 63, 467)

Kate Beaton draws pictures of historical people making silly faces for a living. Ryan North has taught her how to be a true friend, a true hero, and the importance of blasting her quads in a mega workout. The last one is the most important. harkavagrant.com (Title page, Node 1, Final page)

Brandon Bird has been making weird art and putting it on the Internet for a number of years. Accolades include a Webby Award for having the weirdest site on the Internet (brandonbird.com), as well as a hug from Eric Roberts. He is the author of *Brandon Bird's Astonishing World of Art* from Chronicle Books. (Page iii)

Sam Bosma is a sentient orb discovered in an abandoned mine, of average height and build for an orb. (Node 517)

Vera Brosgol lives in Portland, Oregon, where she makes picture books and comics. More of her work can be seen at verabee.com. (Node 494)

Scott C is the creator of the online series *GREAT SHOWDOWNS* (greatshowdowns.com) and *Double Fine Action Comics* (doublefine.com) and the picture books *Zombie In Love* and *East Dragon West Dragon*. He was Art Director at Double Fine Productions for such games as *Psychonauts* and *Brutal Legend*. (Node 451)

Emily Carroll is a cartoonist living in Stratford, Ontario. Some of her comics can be found over here: emcarroll.com. (Node 211)

Alex Culang and **Ray Castro** are the artists behind *Buttersafe* and *King Death*. They're like a living buddy cop movie, if both guys drew comics and neither were cops. Alex is the one with the glasses, and so is Ray. (Nodes 125, 390)

Anthony Clark is a cartoonist and illustrator from Indiana. He was last seen exactly 20 years ago on a night just like tonight. You can find more of his work at nedroid.com on your computerbox. (Nodes 144, 386)

Rebecca Clements does way too many comics at KinokoFry.com, usually pretty fun, silly, and colourful. Also lots of illustration at rebeccaclements.kinokofry.com which is much the same. She's Australian and often lives in Japan. (Node 271)

Tony Cliff is the author of the critically acclaimed, *New York Times*–bestselling *Delilah Dirk* series of adventure-type graphic novels, available online at delilahdirk.com and anywhere books are sold. His fondest Shakespeare memories involve unintentionally adopting a passable-but-evidently-amusing Sean Connery accent to read the role of Duncan during a grade 10 English class. Ah, youth. (Node 520)

My name is **Becky Cloonan** and I am bard to the bone. (Node 539)

Danielle Corsetto is the creator of *Girls With Slingshots*, a webcomic about two girls, a bar, and a talking cactus. Other works include *The New Adventures of Bat Boy* for the Weekly World News, three *Adventure Time* OGNs for BOOM!, and a pretty, pretty picture for this book. She lives in Shepherdstown, West Virginia, with two cats and a lot of tea. (Node 410)

Evan Dahm lives in Brooklyn and is from Asheville, North Carolina. Since 2006 he has been making overambitious fantasy comics and putting them online at rice-boy.com, including *Rice Boy, Order of Tales*, and *Vattu*. He is left-handed. (Node 57)

Lar deSouza hails from the Great White North where he plies his trade drawing online comics and the occasional commission. He lives in a small town in Ontario, Canada, with his lovely wife, two beautiful daughters, and four tolerant cats. You can find him online at: leasticoulddo.com, lfgcomic.com, and lartist.com. (Node 326)

Aaron Diaz is the creator of the comic series *Dresden Codak* (dresdencodak.com). He is based out of Portland, Oregon, and is the world's foremost expert on pretending to know about dinosaurs. (Node 35)

Becky Dreistadt is a painter who makes the comic *Tiny Kitten Teeth*. She is known for painting cats and not ghosts or people being murdered, but those are very fun things to draw too! beckydreistadt.com, tinykittenteeth.com (Nodes 85, 397)

Ray Fawkes is the creator and illustrator of the graphic novel *One Soul* and the Possessions series, as well as writer of *Constantine, Justice*

League Dark, and other books for DC Comics. rayfawkes.com (Nodes 60, 205)

Eric Feurstein is an artist and game developer living on the moon. You may have heard of him! He's the guy living on the moon! His ongoing comic series *Rutabaga: Adventure Chef* can be read here: RutabagaComic.com. (Node 202)

Jess Fink is an illustrator and cartoonist. Her graphic novel *We Can Fix It! A Time Travel Memoir* is published by TopShelf. Her erotic Victorian comic *Chester 5000* is also published by TopShelf and can be read at jessfink.com /Chester5000XYV. Her illustration work can be seen at JessFink.com. She lives in New York, but she is originally from outer space. (Node 335, 356)

Gillian Goerz (Gillian G) is a Canadian artist, illustrator, and cartoonist. See more of her work at GillianG.com. Her webcomic jerkfaceahole .com can be read wherever Internet connections are found. (Node 473)

Dara Gold is an artist and illustrator from Toronto. During the day she creates artwork for cartoons and video games. At night she draws and paints with tea. facebook.com/daragoldart, daragold.ca, @dara_gold (Node 488)

Zac Gorman draws comics about video games, monsters, and growing up, which is something he still hopes to do someday. He draws the webcomic *Magical Game Time*, and you can find more of his comics and drawings at zacgorman .com. (Nodes 26, 119)

Meredith Gran is the author of octopuspie .com and the *Marceline and the Scream Queens* Adventure Time comic. (Nodes 401, 416)

KC Green draws and writes in that order. He writes the comic *BACK* (backcomic.com) and writes and draws the other comic *He Is a Good Boy* (hiagb.com). He also does freelance from time to time, like the illustration(s) in this book(s). He's ready to go to sleep. (Nodes 135, 546)

Dustin Harbin is a cartoonist and illustrator from North Carolina who will eat an egg any way you prepare it. More info at dharbin.com. (Node 130)

Christopher Hastings is a graduate of the School of Visual Arts. He's the creator of the *Adventures of Dr. McNinja*, which can be read at drmcninja.com. He lives in Brooklyn with his wife, Carly, and their dog, Commissioner Gordon. (Node 175)

David Hellman draws the webcomic *A Lesson Is Learned But The Damage Is Irreversible* and created the graphics for the acclaimed video game *Braid*. In 2015 he released a graphic novel called *Second Quest*. He continues to work on projects across comics, animation, and games. But he wishes to be remembered for his philanthropic efforts. davidhellman.net (Nodes 290, 531)

Tyson Hesse has a college degree in who cares from the school of whatever. He's animated characters on video games like *Skullgirls* and illustrated on comic books like *Bravest Warriors*. He has two comics of his own: *Boxer Hockey* and *Diesel*. (Nodes 95, 513)

Faith Erin Hicks is the writer and artist of *Friends with Boys* and the Eisner Award–winning *The Adventures of Superhero Girl*. She is currently writing and drawing a graphic novel trilogy called The Nameless City. She lives in Vancouver, British Columbia. (Node 432)

Mike Holmes is an illustrator who has drawn for *Adventure Time*, *Bravest Warriors*, *Munchkin*, and the Secret Coders books series. He lives in Brooklyn, New York, with his wife, Meredith, and their pets. (Nodes 115, 372)

Andrew Hussie once traded credit cards with the author. He burned through so much of Shakespeare's dough before the clueless bard could figure out what a credit card even WAS. The dude never recovered financially. Inks on his illustration were by Rachel Rocklin and shading by Shad Andrews. (*The Murder of Gonzago*)

Matthew Inman is the best-selling author and artist behind the one-man comedy operation known as *The Oatmeal*. theoatmeal .com (Node 98)

Jeph Jacques does the Internet comic strip *Questionable Content* (questionablecontent.net). When he isn't drawing that, he is playing guitar or petting a dog. (Nodes 342, 547)

Chris Jones is a Canadian-based illustrator. He enjoys telling stories visually, and his colorful style focuses on humor and expressiveness. His illustrations appear in books, graphic novels, magazines, and educational materials. Portfolio: mrjonesey.com (Nodes 161, 482)

Dave Kellett is the cartoonist behind *Sheldon* (sheldoncomics.com) and *Drive* (drivecomic .com), and is the filmmaker behind the comic strip documentary *Stripped* (strippedfilm.com). He's about 5'8", and loves hugs. (Nodes 77, 536)

John Keogh is a weirdo from the edge of society. He cannot be contacted in any way. (Nodes 70, 353)

Kazu Kibuishi is a graphic novel author and illustrator. He is best known for being the creator and editor of the comic anthology *Flight*, for creating Daisy Kutter, Copper, and for his ongoing series *Amulet*. boltcity.com (Node 192)

Mike Krahulik (aka Gabriel, aka the Storm Wizard) draws the comic strip *Penny Arcade*. penny-arcade.com (Node 221)

Braden Lamb grew up in Seattle, studied film in upstate New York, learned about Vikings in Iceland and Norway, and established an art career in Boston. Now he draws and colours comics, and wouldn't have it any other way. bradenlamb.com (Node 528)

Kate Leth is a writer and crystal witch. She makes comics about superheroes, feelings, and kisses, primarily. She cannot be killed. (Node 331)

Joe List is a cartoonist and designer from the North of England. He is the creator of the webcomic *Freak Leap* and the defacement blog *The Annotated Weekender*. To read some comics, simply type FreakLeap.co.uk into a computer, blink twice, then hit return. (Node 241)

Vancouver-based artist **Sam Logan** chose the cartoonist path. As the author of *Sam and Fuzzy* and co-author of *Skull Panda*, he has the market cornered on bear-based online comics. samandfuzzy.com, skullpanda.com (Nodes 141, 256)

Mike Maihack is an illustrator and comic creator living out of the far too hot and humid southern climate that is Lutz, Florida. He draws all sorts of stuff although most of his time is spent working on his all-ages sci-fi series *Cleopatra in Space*, published by Scholastic/Graphix. When he's not doing that, however, Mike enjoys hanging out with his loving wife, his two boys, and a Siamese cat who tolerates their existence inside of her home. mikemaihack.com (Node 307)

David Malki ! is the author of the comic strip *Wondermark*, co-editor of the *Machine of Death* fiction anthology series, and creator of *Machine of Death: The Game of Creative Assassination*. His work appears regularly in periodicals nationwide and at wondermark.com. He lives with his wife in Los Angeles and he likes to fly airplanes. His King of England illustration in this book was shaded by Sarah Barczyk: sarah-barczyk.de. (Nodes 269, 446, *The Murder of Gonzago* (cover design))

John Martz is a Toronto cartoonist. His books include *Destination X* from Nobrow Press, *A Cat Named Tim and Other Stories* from Koyama Press, and the picture book adaptation of Abbott and Costello's *Who's on First?* from Quirk Books. His website is johnmartz.com. (Nodes 226, 346)

Choose your own **Brian McLachlan** bio: (a) His book, *Draw Out the Story: Ten Secrets to Creating Your Own Comics* is awesome; (b) Made the hilarious laugh-out-loud webcomic *The Princess Planet*; (c) Was born at the age of five and can eat raw fire; (d) Your adventure ends here. (Nodes 169, 249)

Dylan Meconis read *Hamlet* for kicks at age 13, reciting the "best parts" aloud to her parents at breakfast. She would then set aside Shakespeare's profound commentary on mortality to read all the newspaper funny strips. You may learn the tragic results of this early choice by turning to dylanmeconis.com. (Node 7)

Very new to the comics scene, **Marlo Meekins**'s webcomics went viral immediately. Meekins's comics are salty-sweet, raw, never superficial but always fun. She's arrived into the comic world with a new style of soft palettes, a nostalgic wink to old cartoons with a dash of Spumco (she's a former Spumco artist). marlomeekins.tumblr.com and @marlomeekins on Twitter (Nodes 30, 369)

Carly Monardo is an artist and comedian living in Brooklyn, New York. Her art has been featured in games, television, and framed on the walls of friends! carlymonardo.com (Nodes 88, 303)

Rosemary Mosco is a field naturalist with a passion for science communication. Her cartoons, which find humour in the natural world, have appeared in print publications, games, and video podcasts. You can make her day by showing her a new kind of fern. (Node 149)

Randall Munroe is the author of xkcd.com. (Node 363)

Ethan Nicolle makes the comic and TV show *Axe Cop* with his nine-year-old brother Malachai. He also writes and draws another webcomic called *Bearmageddon* and is a writer for Dreamworks Animation. He does other stuff too but it's not really worth getting into all that right now. (Nodes 49, 455)

Shelli Paroline escaped early on into the world of comics and science fiction. She has now returned to the Boston area, where she works as an unassuming cartoonist and designer. She and her husband, Braden Lamb, illustrated the expertly written *Adventure Time* comics and *The Midas Flesh*. shelliparoline.com (Node 22)

Em Partridge is a writer/drawer/thing maker/dog petter from Vancouver Island. (Nodes 180, 286)

Ryan Pequin is a tiny man who lives in Vancouver, British Columbia. He draws things for a living and that's sorta neat, right? He makes comics at threewordphrase.com. (Nodes 107, 419)

Jonathan Rosenberg is the creator of online comics *Goats* and *Scenes From A Multiverse*. Most of his childhood memories were erased in a freakish blimp accident. Rosenberg's interests include sleep, sarcasm, and cheesesteaks. (Node 500)

Jeffrey Rowland was born in Oklahoma and started making comics when he was seven years old. After three years of not being published, he went on hiatus until 1999 when he decided to start again, this time on the Internet. In 2004 he almost got killed by a spider and now he owns and operates TopatoCo.com, a company with lawyers and a forklift. Sometimes he still draws comics too. (Node 246)

Andy Runton is the creator of the breakout all-ages series of graphic novels, *Owly*, featuring a kindhearted little owl who's always searching for new friends and adventure. Relying on a mixture of symbols and expressions to tell his silent stories, Andy's heartwarming style has made him a favourite of both fans and critics alike. Visit him online at AndyRunton.com. (Node 424, Yorick skulls)

Kean Soo is the creator of the graphic novel series *March Grand Prix* and *Jellaby*, and was an assistant editor and regular contributor to the award-winning *FLIGHT* anthology series. Born in England and raised in Hong Kong, he currently resides in Toronto. His online home is at keaner .net. (Nodes 104, 186)

Noelle Stevenson is a cartoonist and writer. Her debut graphic novel, *Nimona,* won the Slate Cartoonist's Studio Prize, was nominated for a Harvey Award, was a *New York Times* Notable Book, and was a finalist for the National Book Award. She is also the cowriter of the multiple Eisner Award–winning comic series *Lumberjanes* and has written for Disney's *Wander Over Yonder*, Marvel, and DC Comics, among others. She is a graduate of the Maryland Institute College of Art. She lives and works in Los Angeles. (Nodes 166, 257, cover)

Kris Straub, humour scientist, is the man behind *Broodhollow* (broodhollow.com), *chainsawsuit* (chainsawsuit.com), *Starslip* (starslip.com), and *F Chords* (fchords.com). (Node 505)

Alex Thomas is the writer and designer of the video games *The Banner Saga* and *Killers and Thieves*, but also gets to do art sometimes, which is a nice change of pace. (Node 383)

David Troupes draws the online comic *Buttercup Festival* (buttercupfestival.com), and has published two books of poetry with Two Ravens Press (tworavenspress.com). He was born and raised in Massachusetts, and currently lives in England with his wife and daughter. When he's not writing, drawing, or working, he's walking. (Node 38)

Zach Weinersmith is the creator of *Saturday Morning Breakfast Cereal*. He recently wrote a gamebook called *Trial of the Clone*. In his spare time, he enjoys writing short biographies of himself to appear in Ryan North's books. (Nodes 287, 443)

Tony Wilson draws and co-writes the webcomic AmazingSuperPowers.com, and does art and animation for the mobile game company So Choice Softworks. He lives in a tall tower with his 15 daughters, each more beautiful than the last. (Node 111)

Steve Wolfhard is a Canadian living in Los Angeles with his American wife where he's into boardgames, curling, and storyboarding on *Adventure Time*. He is the former creator of *Cat Rackham* and *Turtie*. (Nodes 44, 542)

Once he murders "Jim Zub," **Chip Zdarsky** shall claim his rightful place at the end of the contributor bio pages. (Nodes 54, 376)

Jim Zub is an artist, writer, and art instructor based in Toronto, Canada. He's worked on comics for a slew of publishers including Marvel, DC, Image, Dark Horse, IDW, Dynamite and Udon. Find out what he's up to lately at jimzub .com. (Node 318)

Hah hah, nice try champ! Opening the book to the last page to see how the story ends isn't gonna help you out with this little volume of non-linear branching narrative structure!!